One Hundred Horses

ONE HUNDRED HORSES

Drama as Novel, Memoir as Drama

Barney Nelson

Published by
Barbara J. "Barney" Nelson

www.barneynelsonauthor.com
Post Office Box 787
Alpine, Texas 79831

Parts of this book are heavily based on memoir and journalism. However, stories, names, dates, characters, places, and incidents portrayed have all been heavily blended, fictionalized and/or changed. No identification with actual persons (living or deceased), places, buildings, or products is intended or should be inferred.

All photos were taken by and are the sole property of Barbara J. "Barney" Nelson and her daughter Carla G. (Nelson) Spencer.

ISBN: 979-8-218-45287-2

Library of Congress Control Number: 2024912097

Cover and interior design by Letitia Wetteraeuer

DEDICATION

Don and Linda Coleman

Contents

Introduction

"This study aims to provoke . . . paying particular attention to the dialogue novel as a subgenre that has been largely overlooked by both literary critics and narratologists." –Bronwen Thomas (from Fictional Dialogue: Speech and Conversation in the Modern and Postmodern Novel*)*

"The time has indeed arrived, beyond question, for great screenplays to be read, admired, and considered as literature." Frank Capra (from the 1986 Anthology of Best American Screen-Plays *edited by Sam Thomas)*

"I thought about the act of putting together a collection that could be larger than its parts." –Meghan O'Rourke (from a tribute to Louise Glück in The Yale Review*)*

I'm a small-town country girl who became a writing and literature teacher at a small border university in Texas. That doesn't sound very impressive, but Shakespeare himself didn't write for academic high-brows. Still, it would be a stretch to hope that this collection of unproduced and previously unpublished autobiographical fiction in dialog might someday be considered literature. Authors don't make that determination, readers and audiences do.

I do call my stuff "cowboy" and claim my characters are "speaking the lingo." That is not a stretch. I have been a cowboy journalist for most of my adult life—still am—and have been listening to cowboys talk for over 67 years. I lived the cowboy life from a childhood of riding ponies and raising cattle on an Iowa farm to eventually living for thirteen wonderful years on the famous 06 Ranch in West Texas, during the years when it still ran a chuckwagon and carried a 100-head remuda. I also ran my own small cattle herd for a while. (For more about my life and work see my book: *Making Circles: The Memoir of a Cowboy Journalist*, University of Oklahoma, 2021).

After I divorced, I returned to college, eventually becoming a college professor, and concentrated on ranching, cowboys, horses, and cattle in literature. My master's thesis was on Shakespeare's use of horsemanship for character development. My PhD dissertation was on how wild and domestic animals had been stereotyped (*The Wild and the Domestic: Animal Representation, Ecocriticism, and Western American Literature*, University of Nevada, 2000). Every magazine article, book, newspaper column, or academic paper that I've written has had connections to the cowboy/ranching world, as did most of the classes I taught.

Those of us who lived the cowboy life have always been disappointed in the way our culture has been represented in movies and television. Maybe we need a demise of the "western" and birth of more authentic material. But I'm not the first with that idea. After watching a burlesque in 1898 called "The Texas Steer," Andy Adams was so shocked that he started writing. His first project was a script for an authentic portrayal of cowboy trail drivers in a play he called "The Corporal Segundo," and based on the years he had spent trail herding. It is still the best thing I've read about trail herding. I hereby give him credit for the first authentic cowboy drama.

After I retired, I taught myself script writing. I've read all the "How to Write a Script" books, so I'm quite familiar with protagonists and antagonists, beats, cats, plot points, holes, over-writing, loglines, treatments and dramatic arcs. But, life doesn't really happen that way.

I taught world literature at the college level for many years. So instead of "block busters" I have been influenced by the nuances of Nō drama and haiku, the practical lessons in Masaai folktales, the underdogs in Australian outback poetry, and South American gaucho ballads. I prefer a desert breeze to the WHAM! BAM! cartoon action of modern movies. I've tried to use subtle motivation, small doses of action, and characters who don't really change. Hamlet doesn't change, his world does. That's part of the tragedy.

I do believe characters should learn lessons, gradually discover and reveal their true hearts. It's the audience who should be changed —becoming more understanding and less judgmental of rebellious or troubled youth and developing sympathy and empathy toward unwed mothers, chauvinistic men, those who are just "doing their job," angry women and illegal immigrants. My characters learn to recognize and embrace their own qualities and situations, find romantic partners who appreciate them as they are, and vice-versa. My action and dialog resemble real life more closely than novels. In real life we don't recognize a dramatic moment until 20 years later. My goal is to leave readers with a peaceful "feeling" that they just realized something they've always known, but they're not quite sure what that was.

Unfortunately, I also received a painful initiation and education into the closed world of writing for the American cinema. To be brief, I can't sell (or even give away) a script without an agent and can't get an agent until one of my scripts is produced. I must also join a writers' union, with similar closed criteria plus a few thousand dollars in union dues. As long as Hollywood is ruled by unions, an independent writer like me can't even persuade anyone to read what I have written. Meanwhile, the movie business castles are surrounded by moats full of crocodiles ready to "help" by milking money from naïve newbies (which I explain in more depth in the Acknowledgements).

By the time a script reaches the big screen, it's also been "improved" by other writers, directors, producers, actors . . . an endless list. The original script has usually been changed so much that union arbitrators often have to settle high stakes financial battles over who gets credit, not simply for the number of words, but for story, craft, content, structure, style, characterization, chemistry, dialog, point of view, and all the other additions beyond words, like music and lighting. I believe that without the story and dialog, as a foundation, all those bells and whistles are reduced to distractions, which Shakespeare proves every time someone produces one of his plays on a bare stage without costumes. Yet dialog-heavy movie scripts are supposed to be difficult to make into "moving" pictures. Personally, I believe that by trading visual extravaganza for depth of dialog, cinema has suffered. Shakespeare's plays are almost completely dialog, concentrating on the strengths and foibles of human nature. Murders, suicides, and battles appear mostly as exotic details, mostly off stage. As poet Amit Majmundar says in a beautiful tribute to Shakespeare, "We are well on our way to forgetting the cultural background that made these plays watchable. They will remain readable, though, for some time yet." However, he warns, "The cultural shift away from long-form reading, the screen's preference for spectacle over dialog" may cause Shakespeare to become "even less intelligible." Without Shakespeare's dialog, what would Hamlet be or not be about?

Development of character through action, setting, and plot are born in the dialog. So this collection by no means represents "final" scripts, ready for production. I offer them as they come from my pen, not after those who have never lived this life, never knew people like these characters, and never had these feelings get their hands on it. We read stage plays as literature, so why not screen plays? Why not analyze and discuss them in literature classes? Why not read them for pleasure?

Every writer has their own unique view of the world and their own goals and values. I provide realistic, everyday people—not heroes or superheroes. I don't create larger than life characters but simply normal people making small mistakes while trying to find a life purpose and a suitable partner. My grandmother used to say we are all as happy as we make up our minds to be. So I don't create utopias or hopeless dystopias because the real world is neither. It's a pretty good, often beautiful, place that's misunderstood, unappreciated, and complicated. What makes one person happy often makes another miserable. My plots are not about winners and losers, triumphs and destruction, or good and evil. There is no pursuit of power or wealth. Lives are not glamorous. Nobody is murdered or seduced. Instead my characters look for compromise and alternative perspectives.

Most of my plots are love stories (no violence or sex scenes) but not very funny, so I call them romantic dramas. Although, they're not very dramatic either, maybe more Chekhovian than high concept, just quiet dramas about realistic cowboys in believable situations, looking for someone who appreciates their unique qualities. My characters might actually find each other in the real world (no marriage between royalty and blue collar, no city slickers saving the ranch). I hope this book will be useful for creative writing or literature teachers, especially those located in small, rural, ranching or farming communities, Indian reservations, and along the Mexico border.

Although these romances are completely fiction and the characters are all blends, almost every word and detail is "true": someone said it and it actually happened, just not exactly in the combination presented here. Some names may correspond to real people who inspired the character, but none of these should be mistaken for the real person. I also fully realize that if any of these scripts are ever produced as actual movies or stage plays, all the dialog and details I've so carefully woven together may all be changed by everyone involved from the actors who speak the lines to those who bring them coffee.

A friend who provides livestock for movies warned me that this business will break my heart. He said at first he tried to help directors and producers "get things right" but he finally had to stop caring and just do his job. Well I still care. With this book and my choice to self-publish it, I am trying to prevent my heart from being broken. I want readers to have a chance to meet and get to know my characters before they are changed, maybe ruined by Hollywood. So, what you have in your hand is raw story telling from one pen—mine—that might not ever "work" as a motion picture or stage production, but might work on the page.

In proper movie script format, each scene begins with a brief heading that indicates shifts from inside (Int.) to outside (Ext.), location (Red Barn, Tom's Pick-up, Crow Fair), and time of day or time passing (Early Next Morning, Night, Immediately After). I've omitted (or never created) distracting instructions for film crews like camera angles or lighting. I provide a brief description of the scene, action and actors before they begin to speak. When they do speak, I sometimes indicate how a character might say the words (sarcastically, embarrassed, teasing). I've described music and costume changes only when important. Missing are all the pieces added to the puzzle that don't rely on words or pieces added and juxtaposed strategically in the editing room by directors and producers: actors, cameras, music, art, technology, expressions, pauses, symbolic close-ups, etc.

Four chapter scripts are designed for full-length movies, one for a stage play, and one for a monologue. As a journalist, my strengths are photography and dialog. I introduce each with a little background on where my inspiration came from: family history, my cowboy photography, journalism, or just my life, family and friends. I also illustrate each with a few of my photographs that will, I hope, help readers visualize what might be an unfamiliar world. I hope these photographs will fill in for the missing "pictures" that help make cinema so compelling, yet leave enough room for readers to enjoy using their own imaginations.

Fiction has become a broken mirror of avant-garde styles that blend and overlap what were once clear boundaries. Today the Internet offers 144 genres and subgenres of fiction writing. We have speculative fiction, auto-fiction, non-fiction novels, fictionalized journalism, high fantasy, cyberpunk, science fiction, magical realism, and historical-dramatic musicals . . . a growing list. I am offering my personal mix as "drama as novel, memoir as drama" to be read and imagined instead of passively watched. I also hope, of course, that movie producers looking for fresh material might stumble upon my work. I hope it's obvious that I didn't just make up this cowboy world that I write about, but I actually lived in and understood it.

Here, on the pages of a self-published book, I take full responsibility and am willing to live or die on my ink-filled sword.

Horsehair Bracelet

Inspiration for Horsehair Bracelet

"For so many centuries, the exchange of gifts has held us together. It has made it possible to bridge the abyss where language struggles."
—Barry Lopez

Horsehair Bracelet is loosely based on a true story that I witnessed during the 1970/80s while living on the 06 Ranch. As I remember it, the cattle roundup crew was camped at Willow Springs Camp (where I lived at the time) when the Border Patrol picked up our cook's three assistants, who also cowboyed. Someone had reported them. After they were taken away, our boss and several cowboys pitched in to help the cook. I photographed the cowboys washing dishes at the wagon. Border Patrol deported and dropped the three illegals back across the border. But they walked across the desert and returned to the ranch faster than anyone thought possible—a distance of at least 100 miles—within 24 or 48 hours. Their feet were so swollen and scratched that they couldn't wear anything except their tire-tread sandals for several days. My character Efren is a composite of those three illegals.

When I heard that our boss intended to help them obtain citizenship because of this heroic effort, I wanted to help them learn English and brought them children's books from the Sul Ross library. I also asked someone (maybe our cook?) to explain that I wasn't insulting their intelligence with children's books, but that reading books with simple sentences and lots of pictures was the way we native speakers all learned English. Later roundup crews included one illegal cowboy from Canada (who never got caught), and one legal cowboy from Australia. So my goal was to tell a cowboy version of immigration as accurately and honestly as possible.

Although we are Anglos, my Latina character Sarah is a composite of me, my daughter, and granddaughter, three generations of real cowgirls who worked for the 06 and ate at the wagon, plus a few traits from other female cowboys I admired. Readers and critics suggested I give Sarah more backstory to explain why she loves the cowboy life so much and why she is attracted to Efren. I have tried to do that, but I doubt my daughter, granddaughter, and I could ever explain our own feelings to someone who doesn't feel them too.

My character, the old chuckwagon cook Ramón, is loosely based on a legendary local cook, Ramón Hartnett. I often served as his grocery fetcher because he butchered both English and Spanish and his temper flared when he was misunderstood. Nobody wanted to get on the wrong side of the cook, so I was the sacrificial lamb. Eventually I loved him like my own grandfather and called him "Tio" (meaning uncle in Spanish). He cooked for the ranch's end-of-roundup dance parties, and I made Ramón polka with me to "El Rancho Grande" one year. I took a million photos of him cooking and his camp. I learned by watching how to make several of his dishes (especially his camp bread) and published several articles about him. He could not read or write, yet he was paid more and given more respect than any of the cowboys and by anyone who visited his wagon, from millionaires and singing stars to New York City film crews. He tolerated guests graciously, but his main concern was always reserved for the hardworking cowboys, and he watched over them like a mother hen, mixed with fighting rooster. I borrow many events, a few quotations, personality traits and habits from our real cook, but my character of Ramón is fiction.

Although the 06 did occasionally host visitors like Charlie Daniels or Waylon Jennings, who sang around the evening campfires, more often it was one of the Mexican cowboys who sang. Their norteño folk songs were traditional favorites of border cowboys, especially "El Rancho Grande." It is also a rural Latino tradition throughout the Americas for singers to "duel" with each other, and coyotes will sometimes "answer" human voices. In his book, *The Coyote*, folklorist J. Frank Dobie writes of listening to a singing vaquero in South Texas challenge coyotes to a duel, inspiring my character's singing duel with coyotes.

Little habits like whether a cowboy kept track of and reused one coffee cup (to save the cooks from unnecessary dishwashing) seemed to hint at their character and how respectful they were toward others. Although the immature and inconsiderate character (Billy) is purely fiction, we did have cowboys who exhibited some of those traits until they were retrained. Our real cook held shovels full of glowing coals under cowboy pockets if they got between him and his fire. Cowboys living around a chuckwagon observe more rules of etiquette than Emily

Post. The cooks always ate last (to make sure they cooked enough food) and tolerated extra or fewer mouths to feed as long as they were kept informed. All the activities around the chuckwagon from etiquette to where everyone sat or stories told are based on typical behavior that I observed, heard, personally experienced, or absorbed through the years. Cowboy rules are seldom spoken, instead should be learned by observation, and become even more numerous and serious once livestock is involved. Good intentions count for nothing. Anyone who wants the privilege of joining a cowboy crew must earn it, so my character's father does not comfort Sarah when she makes mistakes. Silence is the usual form of punishment for infractions. Teasing is usually a sign of friendship.

My character, The Boss, is based on our real boss at the time, Chris Lacy, an excellent cowboy and one of the crew, working just as hard every day as any of his employees. He spoke fluent Spanish. The setting is based on the o6 ranch, which still ran a chuckwagon during the 13 years I lived there. Lacy's great-grandfather, Herbert L. Kokernot, Sr., founded the o6 Ranch, so my fictitious Ko brand (pronounced Kay-oh) is a nod to both the Kokernot family and the o6 brand. The o6 is pronounced "oh six." It represents a Navy "officer six," or captain, as one of the Kokernot ancestors served under Sam Houston as a ship captain in the Texas navy during the fight for independence from Mexico. Many indigenous mixed-race (Indian/Spanish) ranchers also fought for their homeland on the side of Texas.

Details about immigration, Mexican history, and Efren's character, backstory and motivation were inspired by several interviews I did in Mexico for *Western Horseman* magazine from 1984 to 1986.

In Cuidad Chihuahua, I interviewed Carlos Ochoa. To find him I had asked Mexican cowboys from Chihuahua, gringos from Texas, and people living along the Rio Grande to suggest someone who would be an ideal representative. "If you want the best cowboy in Chihuahua, you need Carlos Ochoa," said my Mexico contacts. "One of the Ochoas," said Texans, and along the border, "Ah, yes, Carlos Ochoa." He seemed to be a legend on both sides of the river, exactly what I was looking for.

When I tracked him down, one of the first things he said to me was, "We have a lot of poor people in Mexico, but the cowboys are the only ones who are proud of what they are." He said his family on his dad's side "were always ranchers since they came from Spain." But his family lost their ranches in the ejido land grab. Carlos then crossed the border to rodeo for and graduate from college at New Mexico

State, married an American girl, and began working for some of the large New Mexico ranches. When he wanted to return to Mexico, she didn't, and they divorced. He returned alone, remarried, and managed a large ranch in Northern Mexico for seven years. When it too was broken up into ejidos, Carlos was out of a job. But soon the Cattle Growers Association of Chihuahua scooped him up to design and run a modern livestock auction. With his good salary, he began gradually buying ejidos when the city owners gave up. By the time I met him he had already put together a small ranch of his own. "That sounds like I'm a rich son-of-a-gun," he laughed, "but I'm really working for the bank." A lot of information about ranching in Mexico and especially the ejido situation came from Carlos.

Fourth-generation Mexican rancher, don Alberto "Beto" Musquiz flew his private plane to Alpine, picked up and flew me and my family (illegally!) to his Rancho la Rosita in Coahuila for an interview. So I was a "wetback" working in a foreign country without a work permit. I met his proud cook and cowboys and photographed them working both cattle and horses. Beto raised and sold horses from US bloodlines all over Mexico, including to charros. He ranched with traditional skills, like teaching horses to line-up side-by-side to be caught and bridled. In Mexico horses are taught to face the cowboys, and in the US to face the fence. He said, "I've never met a rich man who didn't want to be a cowboy or a rancher." A true caballero, he was completely opposite of the stereotypical macho Hispanic man. He held dual citizenship and did business on both sides of the border. Beto spoke only English to his children, and his beautiful wife Cornelia, spoke only Spanish to them (although both were fluently bilingual). They wanted to make sure that Little Beto and Maria would grow up fluent in both languages too. I stayed in their home for several days and remained friends for years. After Beto's death, I invited the grown-up Maria to appear on an academic conference panel that I organized in Reno, Nevada to talk about her experiences while ranching as a female in Mexico.

Another important interview happened in Guadalajara. I think Beto recommended my subject Ricardo Zermeño, who at the time was the president of the Asociacion Hacienda Sta Cruz del Valle, Mexico's 1981-82 national charro champions. Richardo was also the national champion of coleadero (tailing bulls) and competed in fancy reining and trick roping. I had contacted the Zermeño family to request a translator during my visit because, although my Spanish can get me fed and to a bathroom, it's not even close to interview quality. They promised to provide a good one, but her English turned out to be about equal to my Spanish. However, what I was able to observe and photograph was so beautiful that I was still able to publish two articles in *Western Horseman*: "Born a Charro" (about Ricardo) and "Victoria: A Charra of Mexico" (about his sister).

Part of the charro tradition is the exhibition of maleness (machismo) through bravery and bravado. For the women, the emphasis is on genteel femininity as they perform fine horsemanship maneuvers (escaramusa) riding side-saddle in yards and yards of long, traditional dresses and petticoats. The Zermeño family, headed at the time by Ricardo's father, don Ricardo, lived in a walled fortress encompassing four city blocks of Guadalajara. Don Ricardo's home was in the center and each of his four sons lived in homes on corners of the property. The main house was like a charro museum with huge collections of saddles, trophies, and memorabilia. Over the fireplace hung paintings of his sons' charro weddings. Horse stables were nestled among the homes, rose gardens, manicured lawns, and flowering trees. A uniformed groom saddled horses for Ricardo and his sister for my camera. Nearby, we visited their private (also walled) charro arena and bar for entertaining. Because of the proudly displayed corozon (heart) cattle brand on everything and paintings of ancestors, I assumed Ricardo's roots originated in ranching, probably lost during the ejido reform, although language prevented a proper interview. I also found Guadalajara such a beautiful city that even the slums were covered with blooming vines and small gardens. Although we communicated mostly through smiles and demonstrations, the Zermeños inspired the charro details for Efren's family. My own feelings inspired preferring the wide open spaces to the confines of the charro ring, no matter how elegant. I once heard a friend describe a property he had purchased along the border as an ideal place that was big enough he could walk around in it, but that would be too small for Sarah, Efren, and me.

Probably my most important inspiration for Efren was Nicasio Ramirez (1897-1987), a legendary cowboy who worked for the 06 Ranch for most of his later life. By the time I met and photographed him, Nick was in his 90s. H. L. Kokernot, Jr. had wisely chosen Nick as the cowboy instructor for his six-year-old grandson, Chris Lacy, who would someday run the ranch. Nick was most famous for being able to rope and dally with either hand, but he could do anything: ride bucking horses, drive a fresno team, skin and quarter a beef by himself, build the perfect branding fire, and make his own gear from jackets to mecates and cinches. Out of necessity, most cowboys on both sides of the border make a lot of their own horse gear out of rawhide, leather, or horsehair, and some become artists. Although Nick was born into a wealthy land-owning family in Chihuahua, he loved cowboying on the big ranches, some so vast he said the men couldn't see all the way across the herd once it was thrown together. During the revolution in Mexico, some of Pancho Villa's raiders struck a ranch where Nick was attending a party, and Nick killed one of the raiders. Instead of hanging him, they kidnapped the young ganadero. One night, as they rode close to the Rio Grande, Nick slipped away, crossed the river, and rode all the way to Nevada before he felt safe enough to stop. Years later in 1921, he returned to Mexico long enough to marry his sweetheart who was still waiting. Quickly returning to the US, Nick found work on ranches in California and Arizona before finally landing at the 06 in Texas.

Nick could tail a steer or forefoot a horse like a charro, used his chaps like a matator when sorting cattle, roped deer when the cowboys were hungry for venison, and tied down roped calves with their own tails. Although his fellow cowboys once matched him against another good West Texas roper (which he won), Nick normally never used his skills to show off—only for work. Humble, polite, and a master of everything he touched, his one fault was gambling. He said it began when the boss invited him to play poker one night, but he declined. So the boss sent him to chop wood. After several hours of chopping wood, he said he never made that mistake again. Efren's statement that he only showed off "when the stakes were high" is a nod to Nick's gambling. Except for the murder, Nick's story is almost a mirror for Efren's. Although a composite of many, Efren carries the name for one cowboy from Mexico who worked for the 06 for most of his life as both a cook's helper and cowboy, Efren Pulido.

I've been living 100 miles north of the US/Mexico border since 1968. I've hired illegals, fed them as they traveled through and eaten food they cooked. I've cowboyed beside them and photographed them. Nearly all are very hard workers, the highest compliment I know how to give. I've been a guest in their homes and taught their children in my college classes. I've watched the typical illegals change from poor but good people looking for a job to tattooed gang members looking for easy money. When illegals began passing through in groups of 50, I could no longer afford to feed or trust them and always kept myself armed when living on remote ranch camps.

I've also had cowboys, cooks, ranchers, Border Patrol agents, and several friends who (or whose ancestors) crossed the border read my script for accuracy, including several members of the Ramón Hartnett family. Some are descended from early Texas settlers who had never crossed a border, but as the border moved and the flags over Texas changed, their citizenship changed. Some are fluently bilingual; some speak little or no Spanish. Most of us speak a little Tex/Mex and often joke that we speak neither language well. Immigrants of both genders sometimes came with spouses, married gringos, or every payday sent money back to Mexico for spouses, sweethearts, or family left behind. Perhaps I was naïve, but I never knew an illegal who cheated on a wife left behind. Some regularly returned to Mexico and returned, some never came back, and some never returned to Mexico. Some claimed they could stay closer to their families through letters than in person. Maybe they weren't all saints, but neither are gringos. I tried to incorporate as many of the various versions of US-born native Hispanic, Mexican-American, and immigrant that I knew about.

In academia, I've worked for and beside Hispanics from numerous backgrounds, and spent some time in teacher's lounges. Each semester, at least half of my students had roots in Mexico. I've helped many, who for various reasons spoke mostly Spanish at home, struggle through college English, always reassuring them that knowing two languages was a strength, never a handicap, no matter what their test scores said. I often told them of my own frustrations while struggling to learn Spanish. Like Sarah, the Spanish words I picked up from border cowboys were not always useful in "polite" society. The Spanish word for egg, for example, does not mean the same thing in a restaurant as it does in a branding corral. I smile to myself every time I hear someone order "huevos rancheros." So I would usually warn my students that although my Spanish pronunciation was pretty good, I couldn't actually speak it . . . but I knew most curse words and insults, like fea and gorda, so be careful.

My scenes in a summer religious encampment are based on the real Bloys Camp Meeting that began in 1890 and still happens in the Davis Mountains every August. I have attended a few times and eaten at a couple of the cooksheds sponsored by the original founding families. I've also been inside a tiny but beautiful adobe church in Lajitas that would be a perfect setting for an intimate wedding.

The inspiration for the scene of Efren's bath comes from one of my favorite personal indulgences: taking a late evening bath in a cement water trough out in a pasture somewhere near a windmill. There is nothing as soothing or relaxing as sun-warmed water, a windmill fan turning, and the night birds calling with no sign of civilization within ten miles in any direction. Being a female, I didn't witness or photograph any cowboy baths, but I did photograph them cleaning up for a meal sometimes.

The story of the cowboy "assholed" out of the tree by a bull actually happened to Bill Fowler. When the cowboy telling it noticed my five-year-old daughter and apologized, she actually said, "Oh, that's ok, Mama calls Daddy that all the time." The rest of the details about how many bones the cowboy had broken and how tough his horses were to ride actually pay tribute to a different local cowboy, Apache Adams. The story about Consuelo teasing Ramón about cooking in her kitchen like he was cooking outside, I heard the real Consuelo tell at the wagon almost the way my character tells it. Many cowboys, myself and family included, have outdoor kitchens like the one Efren uses behind his café that are complete with small chuck boxes, and we use their lids like kitchen counters. The story Sarah tells about overhearing her father and Ramón discussing the raising of self-sufficient children happened to me. I was telling a cowboy friend that I tried to let my daughter make her own decisions unless it was life threatening, and then I stepped in. He said, "When it really is life threatening, you ain't gonna be there." Raising children around livestock is serious.

A couple years ago, I submitted an earlier version of this script to the Austin Film Festival. It didn't win any awards, but I did get some very helpful feedback:

> **Concept:** *The writer has such a clear and powerful grasp on the world of this script. The detail of cowboy life in Western Texas is very interesting to read and the world seems to come alive off of the page for the reader. The intricacy and nuance of the immigration debate is also a very important concept in this script and the writer has a clear perspective.*

> **Plot:** *The love story of Sarah and Efren is strong throughout and the writer does a good job at weaving Efren's struggle for citizenship through the lens of a love story. The script focusses so much on the two of them alone that, as the script goes on, we lose the complexity and depth of the other characters and their journeys.*

Structure: *The opening is incredibly strong in this script and the reader is brought into the story very quickly. The pacing and visual description of the opening is also especially strong. The story loses steam in Act 3. Sarah's journey seems to take over as the main story as Efren disappears and reappears. Because we do not know what drives Sarah like we do with Efren, the story is weakened. Staying with Efren in Act 3 and/or giving us more of Sarah's hopes and drives could greatly improve the last 30 pages.*

Characters: *Because the opening is so strong it sets up Efren and Ramon in such a deep and interesting way. Efren's character stays strong throughout but the rest of the characters don't get the same amount of attention and the script could be improved by adding depth, especially to Sarah. We find out a lot about Efren's backstory and history and how he sees the world through Sarah's conversations with her father and Ramon but we don't get let in on Sarah's history and what drives her. This would help improve act 3 when the story solely relies on those two characters to carry the end of the script*

Dialogue: *The dialogue and action lines of this script have incredible detail which helps to elevate this script. The characters speak in a straight forward way and it reads like a literary choice that the writer has made to show who these characters are. The action lines sometimes tell the audience how to feel and the writer could trust their dialogue a little bit more. Some of the action lines also are written in a way that makes sense to a reader but would not make sense if you were just seeing them visually, for example "Some who stayed in camp or came early enough may have already had one or two cups of coffee and set or hung their cups on something (a nearby rock, somewhere on the wagon, or on the woodpile) so they can refill it after eating without taking another clean cup. (No one 'right' way.) Sarah arrived via pickup with her father, and has not had coffee yet." Instead of explaining, the action would be elevated if the writer focused on what the audience will exactly see on screen.*

Overall: *Overall the writer has created a rich and interesting world in this script. The love story of Efren and Sarah is strong throughout but could be deepened by knowing more about*

*what drives Sarah and what is in her past that draws her to
Efren and encourages her to wait so long to be with him. This is
especially important in Act 3 as the focus changes from the two
of them to mainly on Sarah to hold the audience. Sometimes
the action lines are written in a way that would be unclear
visually and sometimes go a little too far in describing exactly
how the audience should feel, like for example: Sarah's father
is a little taken aback at hearing his daughter call Efren one of
"those people" so when he repeats her words, they have an edge to
them. "FATHER Well, by wearing those sandals, 'those people'
can step in the Border Patrol's own tire tracks and leave no
trace..." The dialogue is written strongly and the writer can trust
the reader more. Oppositely, when it comes to the detail of the
cowboy lingo, the writer could explain the intricate world more,
for example phrases like "remuda" and to "jingle horses" could
be briefly described so that the reader is let even further into the
world of the script.*

I tried to weave most of these suggestions into the version included here.

The love story between Sarah and Efren is totally fiction. My plan was for their relationship to begin and grow as an allegory for the struggle toward citizenship. In both cases, trust is the foundation and should not be freely given but earned, tested, and proven over and over and over – even when it seems unfair. Choices for both love and country are often made for all the wrong reasons and with disastrous results. In the cowboy world especially, motivation for both must be based on something besides economics and surface attraction. In the end, both Sarah and Efren represent the old-fashioned "American Dream" and to keep it, they will need to "prove and prove and prove."

The following collection of my cowboy photographs, mostly taken in the 1980s, will hopefully give readers a glimpse into the world of big ranches, chuckwagon cooks, Mexican cowboys and ranchers, and big, loose, remudas of horses in order to imagine that life.

    INSPIRATION FOR HORSEHAIR BRACELET

   INSPIRATION FOR HORSEHAIR BRACELET

Horsehair Bracelet

EXT. DESERT LANDSCAPE, NIGHT

It is a dark but moonlit night in the Northern Mexico and Far West Texas Chihuahua desert. Silhouetted by moonlight, a lone male figure, wearing a cowboy hat splashes across a shallow river (Rio Grande) and hurries across the desert grassland, hiding from passing vehicles, then moving on. He wears an old black felt cowboy hat, wetback tire-tread sandals, small backpack, and carries a plastic gallon milk jug filled with water that glows in the moonlight. He stops to refill the jug at a silhouetted windmill, hears coyotes yipping and smiles, then hurries on. Periodically he looks up at the sky to spot the Big Dipper to keep headed north.

EXT. CHUCKWAGON, MID-MORNING

Time passes to morning with a fly-over of West Texas grassland showing great distances between towns, few roads. We zero in on a ranch house and barn. A shed roof covers an open-sided, outdoor cooking area. Nearby sits an outhouse. A pickup with chuckwagon trailer attached is backed up under one edge of the shed with the chuckbox lid open. A cook fire burns under the shed. Over the fire two fire-blackened metal buckets hang from S-hooks in the middle of a pot rack. At one end of the pot rack over coals hangs a huge also blackened enamel-ware coffee pot with no lid. The location (Willow Springs, o6 Ranch, Alpine, TX?) is difficult to escape from or see an unexpected visitor arriving. No trees or bushes nearby for hiding. Two Hispanic cooks are working comfortably with each other, both very clean except for their boots and bottoms of pant legs. Both wear white cooks' aprons over long-sleeved blue or gray chambray work shirts and baseball caps. Both clean shaven. Ramón is a 70ish, Mexican-American, short barber-shop haircut, wears gray work pants and leather pull-on work boots. Efren, his assistant, is 25ish, a Mexican citizen with a short ponytail, wears loose-fitting Levi 501 denim jeans and well-worn cowboy boots. Ramón is telling stories while teaching Efren to make camp bread. Efren listens and watches closely, occasionally moving off to tend to his other chores: peeling potatoes, cutting them into French fries, frying them over the fire, stirring beans, adding fresh coals. Both are speaking Spanish (displayed in bold). In a film English subtitles should be provided across the screen. Their Spanish should be almost inaudible, causing Spanish speakers to strain to hear the words and non-Spanish speakers to quietly concentrate on reading subtitles. No scary music. (The quiet is designed to lull the audience almost into boredom.)Efren should speak grammatically correct Spanish while Ramón speaks a border dialect sprinkled with Tex-Mex slang and mispronounces a few words in both languages. Both cooks concentrate on the cooking.

In the middle of a big dishpan of flour, Ramón brushes out a little low place and pours a tin coffee cup of canned milk into it (no modern cooking or measuring utensils).

RAMÓN *(In Spanish)* Buttermilk is better, but we seldom have that.

With a silverware teaspoon, he dips salt from a large labeled container and dumps it in, does the same with one spoon of baking soda from a large labeled container. He does not read the labels but works through feel, smell, and touch. He digs the ends of his fingers full of lard from a large labeled lard bucket.

RAMÓN *(In Spanish)* Old Gavino, the cook who taught me, started feeding bites of this bread to one of the horses. That old horse came right up to the fire to beg for bread.

Ramón stirs the ingredients in the low place together with his hand, gradually flipping flour into it until he forms a soft ball on top of the rest of the flour.

RAMÓN *(In Spanish)* One time it rained so hard water ran through camp an inch deep. We shoveled a ditch around the fire, but no dry ground for coals. So I set my biggest skillet under the chuck box lid, put coals inside and set my oven on top. Hot cast-iron will crack in cold rain.

He lifts out the ball of soft dough and slaps it into the hot, cast-iron, footed Dutch oven that has been sitting over some coals nearby. With his knuckles curled like a gorilla hand, he taps the dough out to the edges of the oven like a fat tortilla. The dough looks like one big biscuit.

RAMÓN *(In Spanish)* I don't roll it into balls. This is faster. The cowboys will break off how much they want.

The cast-iron oven lid rests on a rock to keep the inside of the lid clean. It has a few coals on top to keep it hot. He lifts the lid with his gonch hook (a 5' metal rod with a small hook at one end), places the lid carefully on the oven, and tamps the lid tight with his gonch hook. He adds a few more coals under the oven and on the lid as they burn to ash. While the bread bakes, he sits/leans on a nearby tall stool, his hand resting on the gonch hook. Efren tends other chores but listens and watches.

RAMÓN *(In Spanish)* How long depends . . . hot or cold weather, wind. Don't peek. Just <u>know</u> when the bread is golden. Even I burn some now and then *(laughs)*. Some cowboys like it burnt.

Ramón props the lid back on the rock, tips the circle of golden bread onto a clean rag in his hand and tosses it into a metal bread keeper on the open chuck box lid (which is being used like a kitchen counter). The bread breaks at least into two pieces. Immediately he starts a new batch. Efren circles back to watch often, always listening to both instructions and stories. He doesn't talk.

RAMÓN *(In Spanish)* Make it thin and they'll eat a lot. Make it thick and they won't eat so much *(laughs)*. Sprinkle sugar and cinnamon on top for a dessert.

EXT. FULL CAMP VIEW, CONTINUING

While our attention is on the cooks, gradually the black edges of the film image take on the silhouetted shape of two uniformed, cowboy-hatted, 40 to 50ish Hispanic Border Patrol Agents, one on each side of the frame (as though we walked up between them). Neither the cooks nor the audience should notice the agents until suddenly one of them speaks.

BORDER PATROL AGENT 1 *(loud, in Spanish and then English)* **Buenos días.** Good morning, Ramón.

Both cooks (hopefully also the audience) jump at the sound of his voice. Efren looks around quickly for a place to hide or run. His face looks like a trapped animal.

RAMÓN No!

Ramón steps between the agents and Efren, threatening them with his gonch hook.

EFREN *(In Spanish to Ramón)* **Ramón, it's OK. I have nowhere to hide.**

Resigned, Efren removes his apron, hangs it up, and fishes his backpack from the wagon. He quickly swaps his cap for his old cowboy hat and hangs the cap with his apron. Ramón quickly hands him an empty gallon-sized plastic milk jug, two cans of peaches, and offers folded money from his own pocket. Efren refuses the money, stuffs the peaches into the backpack, and fills the jug with the water hose. Meanwhile, one agent retrieves their 4-wheeled drive, crew-cab pickup from where they parked it.

RAMÓN *(Switching to English)*Why are you bothering us? He is not hurting anyone. This is a good man.

BORDER PATROL AGENT 2 Someone complained, so we had to come.

RAMÓN I'm seventy years old.

BORDER PATROL AGENT 1 Sorry, Ramón, we know you need him. We are just doing our jobs.

RAMÓN There's not enough money in the world to pay a lazy US citizen to do

this work. Plus it would take me 10 years to train a gringo.

BORDER PATROL AGENT 1 We know. We're sorry, Ramón. We just enforce laws. We don't make them.

BORDER PATROL AGENT 2 Do you vote?

RAMÓN No.

BORDER PATROL AGENT 2 Well maybe you should. . . .

BORDER PATROL AGENT 1 *(interrupting)* . . . although it never seems to help no matter who wins.

Efren climbs into the crew seat of the BP pickup. He is devastated, head hanging. Agents look sad as they drive away with Efren, their dust transitioning into smoke from the cook fire.

EXT. CHUCKWAGON, MID-DAY

*Time has passed and the cook fire is now smoking (not being tended properly). Ramón is running late, rushing around, struggling to do everything himself. The cowboys (a mix of ethnicities and ages, all wearing chaps and spurs) come in for lunch. A few slip off their chaps and hang them somewhere out of the way, most retrieve a tin cup from the same hook and use it to get water or coffee. The boss (Mr. K) 40-50ish, Anglo, is dressed just like the rest of the cowboys. The only difference is that his shirt pocket is monogrammed with the ranch brand: **Ko Ranch.** He is semi-bilingual and walks quickly to Ramón. The boss's concerned expression shows he knows something is wrong. One cowboy, Frank (father) stands nearby, listening. He is a*

Mexican-American man with greying hair, 55ish. Ramón speaks quietly to the boss as he keeps working, trying to finish lunch for the hungry men.

RAMÓN I'm not ready, Mister K. The damn chotas snuck up on us when they knew we'd be the busiest and took Efren.

BOSS Don't worry. We can wait.

RAMÓN This is too much for me alone.

BOSS Will Efren come back?

RAMÓN Yes. He wants this job. He took only his traveling pack with his sandals and two cans of peaches.

BOSS How long?

RAMÓN If they drop him across border, three days.

BOSS And if they fly him to Mexico City?

RAMÓN Two weeks. He left the guitar and saddle he shipped to me. He'll be back, but roundup might be over.

The Boss now speaks loud enough for the crew to hear.

BOSS Don't worry. We know how to help you. We'll pitch in.

Boss looks around at the crew, they all look concerned and nod yes.

BOSS If Efren is not back in three days, I'll find a replacement.

The boss grabs a spoon to stir the beans. One cowboy takes over French fry duties, another takes a fresh round of bread from

Ramón and drops it in the bread container to save Ramón steps. A 20ish young cowboy grabs the water hose and fills the two blackened water buckets that hang over the fire and fills the coffee pot. We notice a long braid of black hair and realize the young cowboy is a girl, Sarah, Frank's Latina daughter.

Time passes, they eat. Sarah sits off to one side a little, beside her father (Frank).

SARAH You never hire wetbacks, Father.

FATHER Our small ranch needs the same skills, but not this many men. A ranch this big has to find and hire many extras, too many for your mama to feed. It's also easier to find cowboys than cooks.

SARAH I feel so lucky Mr. K lets me come.

FATHER He wouldn't if you weren't a good hand.

SARAH I like working with just our family on our own place, but coming here is like stepping back in time. It's paradise.

FATHER I feel the same way. It's like a vacation.

SARAH Except for mama.

FATHER: *(Laughs)* Well, someone has to stay home and do our work so we can play. She used to ride with us here too, before you and your brother were born.

SARAH I never knew that!

FATHER She was a good hand, like you. Then she enjoyed you kids more, or she said she did.

SARAH I've never even seen her horseback.

FATHER I think she likes the challenge of looking after our ranch while we do this.

SARAH Maybe she even thinks getting rid of us is a vacation?

FATHER *(laughs)* Maybe.

SARAH I miss my brother since he got married and moved to New Mexico, but I also consider getting rid of him a relief.

FATHER *(laughs)* To be honest, so do I. Some fathers and sons work well together, some don't.

SARAH While he was young, you were a god to him. As he got older, you got dumber and dumber.

FATHER *(laughs)* Yup. By the time he was 21, I couldn't even close a gate properly. He was ready to be his own boss.

SARAH You are still a god to me, Father.

FATHER Thank you, Mija. But as soon as you fall in love, my pedestal will topple.

SARAH I'm going to be a teacher, not a wife.

FATHER *(smiling knowingly)* We'll see.

After eating, the cowboys scrape their plates and stack them on the dishwashing table as usual. The boss grabs one of the buckets of water hanging over the fire that are now steaming and carries it to the dishwashing table. Immediately, two other cowboys and Sarah, jump up to help. One of the cowboys grabs the other bucket of hot water. Sarah walks to the wagon, grabs the bottle of dishwashing soap and tucks it under her

arm. Then she grabs the two big galvanized dishpans off the side of the wagon. She sets the dishpans side by side on a long folding table and squirts dish soap into one. The Boss pours one bucket of hot water into each dishpan. One cowboy rolls up his sleeves and starts washing, one rinses and stacks. Sarah hangs the two now empty water buckets back over the fire, refills them with the water hose, grabs a clean dish towel from the wagon and returns to the washing table to dry dishes. The boss and another cowboy help Ramón scrape and carry heavy cast-iron ovens and skillets to the washing table and as Sarah's stack of dried dishes accumulates, carry those to the chuck box and put them away. All laugh and tell stories while working.

EXT. DESERT LANDSCAPE, NIGHT

Time passes to night. Similar to the opening scene, Efren hurries across the desert landscape. Silhouetted against the night sky, he refills his water jug at a windmill, opens and closes gates, hides from passing vehicles, shades up and naps under a bush at high-noon. One day and two nights pass as Efren hurries on foot. His appearance deteriorates.

EXT. CHUCKWAGON, MID-MORNING

Across the screen appear the words "Two days later." Ramón is struggling and hurrying to cook lunch, looks very tired, removes his cap to wipe his brow with a red bandana he pulls from his back pocket. Sarah obviously stayed behind to help Ramón and wears a clean white apron. She fries potatoes over the fire. Efren, dirty, exhausted, and unshaven limps into camp wearing his backpack, no water jug. No one speaks. Efren looks fierce, like a soldier after a battle. A few pieces of grass hang from his dirty, uncombed hair. He does not look at

*either Ramón or Sarah. He wears home-
made tire-tread wetback sandals and old
double-knit brown pants. The bottom of his
pant legs are frayed and torn from catching
on brush and cacti, a few thorns and burs
are embedded in the fabric. Sarah steps
back, obviously afraid of him. She quickly
removes and carefully lays the white apron
she has been wearing on the chuck box lid
and hurries around to the cowboy side of
the fire and out of the way. Efren quickly
grabs a tin cup from the wooden cup box,
ladles water into it from a white water
bucket hanging on the side of the wagon,
and gulps down two cups of water. He sets
the cup nearby. Efren grabs the washbasin
off the nearby wash stand, takes it to the
fire where he ladles hot water from a bucket
into it and goes back to the washbasin stand
to wash his face and hands with the bar of
soap. When finished, he drinks another cup
of water, always using the same cup and
setting it in the same place. Efren puts on
Sarah's discarded white apron and gets to
work immediately, periodically sipping more
water. Ramón has not stopped working
but nods at Efren gratefully and looks with
admiration at Efren's feet. Efren's feet are
terribly swollen, very dirty, very cracked and
bloody.*

EXT. CHUCKWAGON, NOON

*Cowboys arrive for lunch. As soon as her
father arrives, Sarah steps to his side.*

BOSS *(in Spanish)* **Efren! I'm so glad to
see you!**

*The Boss shakes Efren's hand while Efren
keeps working with his other hand.*

BOSS *(in Spanish)* **We move camp today
into the mountains. You'll be safer there. I
appreciate how quickly you returned.**

Efren continues working, hurrying.

EFREN *(in Spanish)* **De nada.**

BOSS *(in Spanish)* **I will do what I can to
get you a green card, maybe citizenship.**

*Efren nods but his expression says he doesn't
believe. Sarah stares at Efren's feet and then
looks at him with pity. He sees the pity in
her face and his face deepens into anger.*

EFREN *(to Ramón in Spanish)* **I don't
want pity.**

FATHER *(quickly to Sarah)* Sarah, don't
show sympathy. He won't like that.

SARAH But, Father, his feet . . . how can
he even walk?

FATHER He has just proven how strong
he is, not how weak. Show respect, not
pity.

SARAH Why did the boss call him "a
friend"?

FATHER He didn't. His name is Efren . . .
E-F-R-E-N. It's an old-fashioned Mexican
name, not very common today.

SARAH Maybe he was named after a
grandfather.

FATHER It could be a Tarahumara name.
Most brown-eyed Mexicans like us are
part Indian. The Spaniards usually had
blue eyes.

SARAH I didn't know that.

*She continues to watch Efren with a mix of
pity and fear.*

FATHER Mexican is a nationality, not a
race.

SARAH I do know that.

FATHER Good. Today, while the cooks move camp, we can go home early and eat supper with Mama. We'll have to rise early to get up on the mountain in time for breakfast.

Sarah keeps watching Efren.

SARAH Do ranchers get in trouble for hiring wetbacks?

FATHER Wetbacks?

SARAH You know what I mean. Do ranchers get in trouble for hiring non-citizens?

FATHER They are starting to, maybe sometimes pay a fine.

SARAH Why? They work so hard and humbly, and we seem to need them desperately.

FATHER Well, a few years ago ninety-nine percent were good people looking for work, like your grandfather. Today we get too many bad ones: gang members and criminals coming to sell drugs, steal . . . or kidnap someone's daughter.

Sarah looks at her father and then back at Efren.

SARAH He looks like one of the bad ones.

FATHER Maybe. But we don't know him yet.

SARAH Are you saying we should trust him?

FATHER No, especially not you, but Ramón does. I say we watch and wait.

INT. PICKUP CAB, AFTERNOON

Time passes. Later that afternoon Sarah and her father are driving home, away from camp as shadows lengthen. Inside the pickup cab they talk.

SARAH Why do those people wear sandals made from old tires?

Sarah's father frowns at his daughter. He repeats her "those people" words with an edge.

FATHER Well, by wearing <u>those</u> sandals, <u>those people</u> can step in the Border Patrol's own tire tracks and leave no trace, or at least only to good trackers. Tracks are hard to see, especially on dry, rocky ground from a moving vehicle. The sandals help <u>those people</u> cross the dirt roads and scraped barriers where the agents look for tracks.

Sarah glances sideways at her father, sensing that she hit a sore spot.

SARAH Did grandpa wear sandals like that?

FATHER *(laughs)* No. He came horseback. Border Patrol agents were scarce then and not as many roads. His wife, your grandma, never wore them either because she didn't cross any border.

SARAH What do you mean?

FATHER Your great-great-grandfather fought with Sam Houston, just as the boss's family did. When Texas eventually joined the United States, your grandma's family became U. S. citizens. They didn't move; the flags just changed.

SARAH I never knew that.

FATHER I'm sorry. I should have told you long ago.

SARAH It sounds like our Mexico border used to be more like a fence between ranches.

FATHER Many miles of it still is . . . just an old barbed wire fence with a ranch on either side.

SARAH Why don't our schools teach that?

FATHER History is complicated, full of wars and alliances with and between British, French, Spanish, Native American, and many others. Friends and enemies are still switching sides.

SARAH Is the trouble caused by language?

FATHER Maybe. It is easy to misunderstand when you can't communicate. You already sound like a new and improved school teacher.

SARAH Thank you. That's my plan. I'd rather be a cowboy forever, but I know that's not realistic.

FATHER Unless you marry a cowboy.

SARAH So . . . , my second choice is to teach some of our border history. Kids here need to know about windmills, fences, ranching, and candellia wax. History is more than wars and U. S. presidents.

FATHER I know how much you love to cowboy. So why did you volunteer to give that up to help Ramón today?

SARAH I knew the boss couldn't, and none of the cowboys wanted to. If Mr. K would have asked one of them to get off his horse while I rode, the whole crew would have been mad at him and especially at me.

FATHER You're very sensitive to cowboy feelings.

SARAH So I volunteered. I know what a privilege it is for me to ride here.

FATHER You work as hard as any man, you're a better hand than some, and you don't even get paid.

SARAH That's why I'm planning to teach school—to get paid.

Sarah's father smiles and looks at her with pride and a little sadness.

EXT. CHUCKWAGON, DAY

Meanwhile back at the chuckwagon, Ramón and Efren pack up camp. Ramón drives a dirt road up into the mountains. Two cowboys follow behind Ramón's pickup and chuckwagon trailer while driving 50 to 100 loose horses. They follow behind to avoid getting dust from the horses into the chuckwagon. One cowboy rides in front so the horses will follow him, and one keeps stragglers caught up from behind. After a few miles, the remuda veers off onto a trail. (Note: Difficult to film or expensive to film scenes from this kind of actual work and scenery might be available from a 1984 documentary "My Heroes Have Always Been Cowboys" with Waylon Jennings, and directed/filmed by Leo Eaton, both now deceased.)

EXT. MOUNTAIN CAMP, EVENING

That evening, we find ourselves in a mountain camp. The chuckwagon is now set up near a small galvanized tin building (o6 Ranch #9 Camp?). Several cowboy teepee tents stand on the other side of the building. Nearby is a large woodpile of "found" live oak (meaning not cut with a chainsaw). In the opposite direction about 30 yards from the camp sits a wooden outhouse. In the near distance is a windmill with a water trough. Beside the chuckwagon, a pipe, obviously attached underground to the windmill, sticks conspicuously out of the ground with a water faucet at the top. A long water hose is attached to the faucet. About two hours before sunset, Efren grabs the wash pan, a bar of soap, and one bucket of hot water from the fire. He starts limping out toward the windmill, carrying it all.

EXT. WINDMILL, EVENING

At the windmill, Efren strips off all his clothes (nice discrete shots of a sexy, muscular man) and pours hot water into the wash pan to scrub his clothes one at a time with the bar of soap. Periodically he throws the soapy water on the ground and dips out clean water from the trough to rinse the clothes, being careful not to get soap in the livestock water. He hangs his wet clothes on the windmill or a nearby bush to dry. When finished with his clothes, he pours fresh hot water into the wash pan to wash his hair and dips out cold water from the trough to rinse it. He repeats the process to soap his body and rinse. Once clean, he climbs into the water trough to soak. While waiting for his clothes to dry, he relaxes and enjoys the cool breeze. He (and we) listens to the windmill creaking, night birds cooing, and coyotes singing.

EXT. OPEN COUNTRY. BEFORE DAWN

The next morning, we follow a pickup's lights across the wide open country.

EXT. CHUCKWAGON. BEFORE DAWN

The camp is lit only by the fire and a lantern hanging on the chuck box. Efren looks rested from a good night's sleep, freshly clean-shaven, and wearing his now clean but ragged clothing. He is still wearing sandals with feet still too swollen for boots. Father and Sarah exit the pickup and walk to the fire. Ramón is in an especially jovial humor this morning. Ramón scoops a shovel full of coals from the fire as he always does, but instead of using the coals to cook, he steps around behind Billy, a young too-fancy-dressed cowboy. Billy is standing in the cooks' space between the fire and chuck box and Ramón holds the shovel of coals under Billy's back pockets. The other cowboys watch silently until the heat soaks through and Billy jumps and howls, rubbing his butt. Now everybody laughs. Billy quickly moves around to the cowboy side of the fire and out of the cooks' way.

COWBOY *(to Billy)* I've never known anyone dumb enough to need that treatment twice.

Billy scowls. Ramón "innocently" walks on to place the shovel full of coals under his pancake griddle (a bent circular piece of steel). As soon as a few drops of oil dripped off his spatula sizzles on the griddle, he pours on pancake batter in small circles. Once the food is ready, Ramón hollers and he and Efren take their seats in metal folding chairs on the outside of the line of ovens and pans resting on coals: beans in a white enamel pot, crisp bacon in a warm

Dutch oven with no feet or lid. All food is served from the ground. Ramón sits behind the griddle. Efren sits behind a skillet half full of hot oil.

RAMÓN Aaiiiee. Comida!

EXT. CHUCKWAGON FOOD LINE, CONTINUING

The cowboys are now free to enter the sacred cooking space to grab a plate and a fork from the chuck box and line up for pancakes. They don't stand in line . . . more like follow. As they walk, we hear the jingle of their spurs. When near and especially inside the cooking area, everyone moves carefully to avoid getting dirt into the food. No clowning around. As each cowboy stops in front of the griddle, Ramón asks how many pancakes they want. He speaks English to some and Spanish to some. Efren tries to follow his lead.

RAMÓN How many pancakes?

COWBOY Three.

Ramón gives him four. No matter how many each cowboy requests, Ramón gives him one more pancake than requested. Then the cowboy moves down the line to Efren.

EFREN *(in halting English)* How . . . many . . . eggs?

COWBOY Two.

Efren cracks exactly the number of eggs asked for into the hot oil and then places the perfectly fried eggs on each plate with a spatula.

RAMÓN *(to Sarah)* How many pancakes, cowboy?

SARAH One.

Ramón gives her two. When Sarah reaches Efren, he assumes she speaks Spanish because she looks Latina.

EFREN *(in Spanish)* **How many eggs?**

SARAH *(afraid)* I don't speak Spanish.

Ramón leans over to explain quietly to Efren.

RAMÓN *(in Spanish)* **Sarah looks Mexican but was born and went to school here and speaks only English. Her father speaks both.**

EFREN *(nodding, in halting English)* How . . . many . . . eggs?

SARAH *(smiles gratefully at Ramón)* One.

Efren carefully places one egg on her plate and she hurries to her father's side. When the boss goes through the line, he hands Efren a stack containing new jeans, shirt, socks, whitey-tighties, and a towel.

EFREN *(in Spanish to boss)* **I don't want charity. Please, take these out of my paycheck.**

The boss smiles and nods yes. Efren places the stack on the ground behind his chair. Sarah's father, obviously pleased at how Efren responded, translates for her.

FATHER He said he didn't want charity and wants Mr. K to take the cost of the new clothes out of his paycheck.

SARAH He looks so fierce, but maybe he's one of the good guys?

FATHER Maybe. It's too early to decide. Be careful, Mija.

Sarah's father looks at her protectively.

EXT. CHUCKWAGON PERIMITER, CONTINUING

Sarah eats her breakfast quietly off to one side, close to her father, both sit on old metal folding chairs. Most of the cowboys stand up to eat or squat on their heels. They can't hold a plate, eat, and hold a cup of coffee all at the same time. Those squatting place their coffee cups nearby on the ground. Those standing, scrape and place their plates in the dishpan, then walk to wherever they stashed their personal cup. Billy gets a clean cup out of the wooden cup box on the chuckbox lid and notices one of the cowboys retrieving a cup hanging from a piece of wire under the shed roof.

BILLY How come you don't just get a clean cup?

COWBOY *(frowning)* I don't like to wash dishes.

BILLY But we have a dishwasher.

Billy points to Efren with his chin. Nobody answers. Two cowboys look at each other. After Sarah eats her food, she takes her plate to the dishwashing table. She comes back to the chuck box and digs her favorite tin cup out of the wooden box containing cups. Her favorite is a vintage "Revolutionary tin mug" (the rim and handle stay cooler than the more modern enamelware or stainless steel cups). It is probably the oldest cup in the wooden box, a little rusty, dented and bent.

BILLY Sarah just got a clean cup.

Billy nods toward Sarah. Efren notices, knows he is talking about Sarah, but can't understand. Frowns.

COWBOY She just got here with her father.

Carrying her cup, Sarah steps to the coffee pot hanging over the fire and pulls a red bandana out of her back pocket to use as a hot pad for the coffeepot's hot handle. Before she touches the handle, Efren grabs it with his bare hand and pours her coffee. Their hands almost touch. Sarah jerks back, still afraid of him.

SARAH Thank you.

EFREN *(in Spanish)* **De nada.**

Sarah walks quickly to the chuck box to add canned milk (no sugar). She picks cinnamon from one of several matching tin boxes of spices, adds two shakes to her coffee, and stirs it with the mutual spoon left on the chuck box lid for that purpose. Efren has carefully watches how she prepares her coffee. Sarah heads back to her chair to drink it.

FATHER *(to Billy)* C'mon Billy. Our turn to jingle horses.

Billy puts his cup in the dishpan. Father hangs his on something.

BILLY *(following him into the dark)* Why do we call it "jingle horses" instead of gather horses?

FATHER *(impatiently)* Because it's dark.

Billy looks confused.

We can't see beyond the circle of light from the campfire and lantern. But as Billy and Frank head into the darkness, we can <u>hear</u> *their spurs jingle.*

EXT. HORSES ARRIVE, CONTINUING

A few minutes later, still too dark to see, but we <u>hear</u> the thunder of shod horses running on rocks past the camp and then the jingle of Frank and Billy's spurs. The rest of the cowboys quickly finish their coffee and or plates, take plates to the dishpans, and find a spot to set or hang their cups, Sarah included. All then vanish into the darkness to catch and saddle horses for the day's work. Only Ramón and Efren remain at the chuckwagon.

EFREN *(in Spanish)* Who's the girl?

RAMÓN *(in Spanish)* Frank's daughter. She's a good hand and a lady.

EFREN *(in Spanish)* Is the rooster her boyfriend?

RAMÓN *(laughs, in Spanish)* She's smarter than that.

Ramón looks at Efren out of the corner of his eye.

EXT. PASTURE, DAY

Time passes. We watch a montage of the cowboys at work: gathering cattle, sorting, branding, supper, sundown, darkness. We see pickup lights drive away in the darkness.

EXT. CHUCKWAGON FOOD LINE, EARLY MORNING

The next morning, again before dawn, pickup lights return to camp. It's breakfast again, same scene as the previous morning.

RAMÓN *(to Sarah)* How many pancakes, cowboy?

SARAH Just one, please.

Ramón gives her two, she shakes her head and smiles.

EFREN How . . . many . . . eggs?

SARAH Just one, please.

Efren gives her two. Sarah shakes her head and smiles slightly.

SARAH I see Ramón is teaching you his ornery tricks.

Efren turns to Ramón for a translation.

RAMÓN *(translates quietly in Spanish)* She says you are very handsome.

Efren's face shows that he knows Ramón is lying. Sarah's father laughs at Ramón's translation.

EXT. CHUCKBOX, CONTINUING

While the cowboys eat, Efren pours coffee into Sarah's favorite cup and adds canned milk at the chuck box. Then he pulls out one spice can, reads the label and puts it back. Pulls out another, reads "cinnamon" and shakes it twice over the cup. The moment Sarah finishes her food, Efren's hands offer to trade her empty plate for the cup of coffee he has prepared for her.

EFREN *(mixing English with Spanish)* Coffee con milk y cinnamon no azucar?

Sarah is shocked and looks quickly at her father who nods yes. She takes the cup and tastes it.

SARAH *(to Efren)* Thank you. It's perfect!

The cowboys are all laughing and talking, staring at the fire, or eating, nobody notices Efren's small gesture except Ramón and Sarah's father, who catch each other's eye. After depositing Sarah's plate in the dishpan, Efren whispers to Ramón.

EFREN *(in Spanish)* What does "perfect" mean?

RAMÓN *(in Spanish)* Good, no defects, has everything desired. Be careful, my son. There are more things to fear in this country than chotas.

EFREN *(in Spanish)* That is true everywhere. I am not afraid.

EXT. VIEWS OF ROUNDUP, DAY

As the sun comes up, we watch a montage of catching horses before sunrise, gathering a pasture, branding, and afternoon chores (shoeing horses, counting pieces of ears from "ear marking," cleaning "oysters," getting branding tools ready for the next day), and eating supper.

EXT. CHUCKWAGON, JUST BEFORE SUNDOWN

Efren and Ramón are finishing the supper dishes. Efren is now wearing the new jeans, cuffed to stay out of the dirt, and the new shirt, but still the sandals. After Ramón and Efren button up camp for the night, they sit side by side near the chuck box. The only light left in camp is the chuck box lantern and the campfire burning down to coals. One cowboy gets up to put a little more wood on the fire.

COWBOY Did you hear about the bull that ass-holed Bronc Williams? *(he notices Sarah)* Sorry, Sarah. I forgot you were

here. You're such a good hand, I forget there is a lady under that hat.

SARAH Oh, don't worry. Mama calls daddy that all the time.

Everybody laughs, especially Sarah's father. In the background Ramón leans over to translate for Efren. We don't hear them, but Efren frowns.

COWBOY So Bronc roped this sharp-horned bull in Pinto Canyon. The bull turned out to be a little stouter than expected. Pretty soon the bull was teaching Bronc's bronc to lead.

The cowboys laugh.

COWBOY Bronc had to bail and climb a mesquite, which was a little too short, so the bull stuck a horn in his back pocket. Jerked him down and started smearing blood on the rocks.

The cowboys laugh.

COWBOY Tommy Valenzuela happened along about then, so Bronc only broke a couple of ribs.

The cowboys laugh.

FATHER Bronc can turn a bronc into a roping horse faster than anybody.

COWBOY Yeah, if it survives.

ANOTHER COWBOY And nobody else can ride it.

Cowboys all laugh and nod agreement.

COWBOY How many bones has Bronc broken now?

FATHER All of them, I think, at least once.

BILLY Hey, Cookie, how many bones have you broke?

RAMÓN Broke lots of horses, oooha! Broke horses for the Gatocito Ranch when I was sixteen. Broke three every year for Jesse Morris for twenty-one years. Broke ribs seven times, broke knee, broke ankle, broke both wrists, broke shoulder. So I said, "No more!" and I quit.

While talking, Ramón walks back and reaches into the wagon for an old Spanish guitar and hands it to Efren. Efren looks around at the cowboys to see if they want him to play.

BOSS *(in Spanish)* Let's hear some music, Efren.

Efren tunes the guitar a moment, then magically his fingers begin to dance across the strings, playing a few bars of Malagueña to demonstrate his skill.

SARAH *(to her father)* Wow!

Efren hears and stifles a smile. Then in a beautiful voice, he begins to sing an old Norteño folk song, "El Rancho Grande."

EFREN *(Singing)*

> Allá en el rancho grande,
> Allá donde vivía,
> Había una rancherita,
> Que alegre me decía;
> Que alegre me decía:
> Te voy a hacer tus calzones
> Como los que usa el ranchero
> Te los comienzo de lana
> Te los acabo de cuero.

> Allá en el rancho grande
> Allá donde vivía,
> Había una rancherita,
> Que alegre me decía;
> Que alegre me decía:
> Cuando se muera mi suegra
> Que la entieren boca abajo
> Que si quiere salirse
> Que se vaya mas abajo

This is obviously a cowboy favorite. Several try to sing along whether they speak Spanish or not. They get louder on familiar lines. Efren never looks at Sarah, but she watches him intently.

EXT. CHUCKWAGON CAMPFIRE, NIGHT

When Efren stops singing, night has arrived and we hear coyotes yipping. Efren smiles broadly and yells at the coyotes to sing.

EFREN *(in Spanish)* Cantar, Amigos!

Then Efren breaks into "Celito Lindo" stopping after each stanza to wait until the coyotes answer. This song has many versions, and we probably don't need all verses. Efren changes "Sierra Morena" in the opening stanza to Sierra Madre because Sierra Madre is the mountain range that he came from.

EFREN *(singing)*

> De la Sierra Madre,
> Cielito lindo, vienen bajando,
> Un par de ojitos negros,
> Cielito lindo, de contrabando.

> *(Chorus)* Ay, ay, ay, ay,
> Canta y no llores,
> Porque cantando se alegran,
> Cielito lindo, los corazones.

Efren waits for the coyotes to answer.

> Pájaro que abandona,
> Cielito lindo, su primer nido,
> Si lo encuentra ocupado,
> Cielito lindo, bien merecido.

Efren sings the chorus and waits for the coyotes to answer.

> Ese lunar que tienes,
> Cielito lindo, junto a la boca,
> No se lo des a nadie,
> Cielito lindo, que a mí me toca.

After he sings the chorus at the end of each stanza, he waits for the coyotes to respond.

> Si tu boquita morena,
> Fuera de azúcar, fuera de azúcar,
> Yo me lo pasaría,
> Cielito lindo, chupa que chupa.
> (Chorus)
> De tu casa a la mía,
> Cielito lindo, no hay más que un paso,
> Antes que venga tu madre,
> Cielito lindo, dame un abrazo.
> (Chorus)
> Una flecha en el aire,
> Cielito lindo, lanzó Cupido,
> Una flecha en el aire,
> Cielito lindo, que a mí me ha herido.
> (Chorus)

After the final chorus, he stops singing and waits for the coyotes, then shouts at them.

EFREN *(in Spanish)* You win, mangy little dogs of song. I surrender.

Efren walks back to the wagon and puts the guitar away.

COWBOY *(to Ramón)* What did he say?

RAMÓN He said, "You win, mangy little song dogs. I surrender." He was singing a traditional duel with them.

SARAH That was amazingly beautiful. *(turns to her father)* How can he possibly have learned to play and sing like that?

Sarah's father shrugs. Ramón translates what she said to Efren.

RAMÓN *(in Spanish)* She said you sounded like a sick rooster crowing.

Efren isn't fooled. Sarah's father laughs at Ramón's translation and rises.

FATHER We better head back down the mountain, Sarita, you have classes tomorrow and it won't take me long to spend the night.

Sarah dutifully gets up, retrieves her coffee cup from its "spot," places it on the dishwashing table, and follows her father toward their pickup. Her father turns to Ramón to let him know he will have one less mouth to feed for a week.

FATHER I'll be back for breakfast.

RAMÓN No Sarah?

FATHER No Sarah. You and Efren will have one less mouth to feed next week. Her Spring Break is over, so it's back to college. She'll want to come back next week-end though.

Efren looks up when he hears his name. Ramón translates.

RAMÓN *(in Spanish)* We'll have one less mouth to feed for a few days. Sarah won't be back until next week-end. She has college.

EFREN College?

RAMÓN To be a high school history teacher.

EFREN *(in Spanish, mostly to himself)* **The clock ticks.**

EXT. CHUCKBOX CLOSE-UP, DAY/NIGHT

The camera zooms in on an old fashioned alarm clock in the chuck box, the hands of the clock speed around to pass a week. Then across a starlit sky, the words "The next week-end" appear.

EXT. DESERT LANDSCAPE, NIGHT

We fly over a huge expanse of moonlit country with no electric lights visible in any direction, except one tiny speck of light and the lights of one pickup headed toward it.

EXT. CHUCKWAGON CAMP, NIGHT

The speck of light turns out to be Ramon's lantern. By its light he pours gasoline out of a red metal container into an empty food can and tosses the gasoline on wood already laid in the fire ditch. He strikes a match and throws it at the wood. Woosh! Fire explodes and camp lights up.

Efren is now dressed like a cowboy, worn boots and old black felt hat. He is also wearing a clean white apron and busy cooking breakfast, as usual.

Cowboys gradually appear out of the darkness, retrieving their cups and pouring themselves a cup of coffee. After drinking, they hang or set their cup where they can find it again. Sarah and her dad step out of the pickup. Sarah walks to Ramón and hands him four children's books.

SARAH *(to Ramón)* please give these to Efren and explain for me. Father says Mr. K wants to help him get a green card, maybe even citizenship.

RAMÓN Yes.

SARAH To pass the tests he must learn English. These are library books, not a gift, not charity. I will need to take them back next week-end, and I will bring new books to trade for these.

RAMÓN OK.

SARAH Please tell him that I'm not insulting his intelligence with children's books. Reading books with lots of pictures and easy words is how we all learned English in school. This Spanish to English and English to Spanish dictionary is mine. He can return it when he has a chance to buy his own.

RAMÓN How do you know he can read?

SARAH *(smiling)* Because he doesn't smell the spice cans like you do. He reads the labels.

RAMÓN *(nods)* You are very observant.

SARAH I've been to cowboy school. It's much harder than college.

RAMÓN *(nods)* He will take good care of the books, and he will study.

SARAH Tell him to learn English songs and sing in English. That will help too.

Efren hurries through clean-up. When the horses thunder past, Ramón waves him away. Efren hangs up his apron and follows the cowboys. Ramón turns to finish the dishes alone.

EXT. CORRALS, ALMOST DAY LIGHT

At the corrals, just before sunrise, we see a few brief vignettes of roping and saddling horses. Sarah catches her own horse with a hoolihan, like all the other cowboys, and saddles her own horse. She watches Efren but he does not look at Sarah.

EXT. LEAVING CORRALS, DAWN

As the sun rises, the crew rides out behind the boss (who always rides in front) to gather the pasture. Sarah rides beside her father.

EXT. HORSEBACK, MORNING

Just after sunrise, Sarah rides up beside Efren.

SARAH So, you're a cowboy too?

Efren doesn't understand, but seems embarrassed and irritated. Ignores her. Sarah tries to speak to him in Spanish.

SARAH *(in poor Spanish)* **Savvy vaquero?**

Efren flashes anger and rides away from her, she looks hurt and confused.

EXT. LANDSCAPE, EARLY MORNING

The camera pulls back and scene widens to show the crew gathering a huge pasture. Montage of the day's work: gathering, penning, sorting, branding. Sarah is often watching Efren, but he is all business, never looks at her.

Once most of the work has been done, Efren hurries to unsaddle and turn his horse loose so he can return to the wagon to cook. After the noon dishes are washed, while the other cowboys take naps and rest, Efren walks out to the corrals to shoe a horse. Sarah watches him walk to the corrals but does not follow.

EXT. CHUCKWAGON, EVENING

Later that day, when the afternoon work is finished, Efren helps Ramón cook supper. When they finish dishes and buttoning up camp for the night, Efren removes his apron and walks over to join the cowboys. Ramón sits alone at his place by the wagon and Sarah joins him.

SARAH What is Efren's problem?

RAMÓN Problem?

SARAH I tried to be friendly this morning and rode up beside him. I asked if he was also a cowboy. He just rode off like I made him mad.

Ramón hesitates. His face shows he's not sure how he should answer.

RAMÓN Efren grew up horseback. His grandfather managed a big ranch in Chihuahua, but the government took it and cut it up into ejidos.

SARAH What do you mean?

RAMÓN Well, the city people thought the ranchers lived luxurious lives, so they persuaded the politicians to take the land from the rich and give it to the poor. The cut-up ranches were called ejidos.

SARAH How could they do that?

RAMÓN Votes. The hacienda owners, cowboys, and small towns couldn't out vote the cities.

SARAH So what happened?

RAMÓN The city people were not farmers or cowboys. They couldn't make a living on small pieces of desert, nobody could. The grass turned to dust. It wasn't long before they wanted their city lives back.

SARAH What happened to Efren's family?

RAMÓN When the big ranches split up, all the cowboys lost their jobs. A lot of our good cowboys, like your grandfather Nicasio, came from Northern Mexico. Efren ranks right up there with the best.

SARAH If he's such a good cowboy, why does he work as a cook's helper?

RAMÓN *(grinning broadly, proudly)* Because cooks get paid twice as much as cowboys.

SARAH Money isn't everything.

RAMÓN No, it is not.

SARAH Tell him he did a good job today. He is a real good hand.

RAMÓN *(frowns and folds his arms across his chest)* He knows.

Sarah's face shows she feels rebuffed even by Ramón, looks hurt. Her father motions for her to come and they head to their pickup.

INT. PICKUP CAB, NIGHT

As Sarah's father drives through the darkness, their faces are barely visible.

FATHER Something wrong, Mija?

SARAH This morning I tried to be friendly and asked Efren if he was also a cowboy. I even tried Spanish. It just seemed to make him mad.

FATHER What did you say?

SARAH I said "Savvy vaquero?"

FATHER So how would you feel if one of the cowboys rode up and asked you if you understood "cowboy"?

SARAH Oh . . . I see. I insulted him and made myself sound dumb. Ramón was also disappointed in me.

FATHER What did you say?

SARAH I asked him to tell Efren that I thought he was a real good hand.

FATHER: Would you ever ask Ramón to tell one of the other cowboys that you thought he was a real good hand?

SARAH No. That would be silly.

FATHER Treat Efren with the same respect you would give any other member of this crew. Don't sound condescending. Treat him like you want to be treated.

SARAH *(pouting)* I am always saying or doing the wrong thing.

Her father doesn't comfort her.

FATHER And "vaquero" might not be the right word for him as it means average cowboy. He's not average. One Spanish word for a really good hand is "jinete." Some jinetes are good men and some beat or cheat on their wives. The word "caballero" sort of means a gentleman jinete. You decide.

SARAH I appreciate your willingness to give up sleeping in camp to drive us back and forth so I can come . . . and your patience with me.

FATHER I know how much you love it.

The camera follows their pickup lights away from the fire and into the darkness until it disappears.

EXT. CHUCKWAGON, BY LANTERN AND FIRELIGHT

Meanwhile, back in camp, the dishes have been washed and camp tidied up, everyone is relaxing for the night. Ramón and Efren sit beside the chuckbox. Ramón is just finishing a cigarette, gets up and retrieves the books Sarah brought and hands them to Efren.

RAMÓN *(their exchange in Spanish)* Sarah left these for you to help you learn English.

EFREN *(frowning)* No . . .

RAMÓN *(interrupting)* She borrowed them from a library. They are not a gift, not charity, and she will need to return them next week-end.

EFREN *(looks at the books, hands them back disgustedly)* These are for children!

RAMÓN *(impatiently)* She said to tell you she's not insulting your intelligence . . . although maybe someone should, or at least your arrogance . . . she's a teacher. She said reading books like this with lots of pictures makes learning English easier.

Efren opens one book and begins to study. Ramón smiles to himself and puts his feet up on a small stool, soon falling asleep. The scene fades into the night sky and the words "A week later" appear.

EXT. CHUCKWAGON, EARLY MORNING DARKNESS

Sarah and her father arrive for breakfast. Sarah hands more books to Ramón who is sitting on his stool beside the wagon. He has the previous week's books ready to hand back to her.

SARAH This time the children's books are about United States history and government. Efren will need to learn that too.

RAMÓN You will be a great teacher someday.

SARAH I hope so.

She takes the returned books to her father's pickup before approaching the food line. As in previous scenes, cowboys are going through the line for breakfast. Sarah arrives at Efren's station to order her egg.

EFREN *(heavy accent)* Thank you. Books. Perfect. How many eggs, Señorita?

SARAH *(smiling)* One, please.

EFREN You hungry later.

Sarah smiles broadly, pleased with his English.

SARAH Good English! OK, Jinete, two please.

Efren looks at her intently when she calls him a jinete, places two perfectly cooked eggs on her plate, and smiles slightly.

EFREN Good Spanish.

EXT. BORDER PATROL SURVEILANCE CAMERA FOOTAGE, NIGHT

Footage in black and white (or green) from heat sensing scenes of large groups of illegals, crossing Rio Grande, getting into and out of semi-trucks, railroad cars, and shattering a window to rob a liquor store. (Camera angle looking down, not heroic.) A passing car illuminates one man's face that is full of gang-style face tattoos. A few guns are seen silhouetted in headlights.

EXT. CORRALS. DAY.

Then we return to the ranch and some corrals. The branding work is almost finished. Sarah walks over next to the boss to eat.

SARAH Round-up ends tomorrow, right?

BOSS Right.

SARAH Are we having a little party as usual?

BOSS Yup. Ramón will cook supper next to the barn at Antelope Flat. After supper we will do a little dancing and drink a beer or two. Bring a date if you want.

SARAH No date. Plenty of cowboys here to dance with.

BOSS *(smiles)* Yup. The best of the best too.

The Boss looks proudly around the circle of eating cowboys.

EXT. PARTY AREA, LATE EVENING

The circle of cowboys fades into a new scene at the party. The cowboys are now cleaner but still wearing plain work clothes and drinking beer. Hay is stacked unevenly around the edge of the barn floor, like a space to dance had been cleared rather than hay bales set around the edge of a dance floor to sit on. The big barn doors are open. A few wives and children are scattered on the hay, mostly talking, some couples dancing, and youngest children sleeping. Kids all dressed like miniature cowboys. Some wives wearing long skirts with boots and some in jeans. Cowboys and kids wear hats, women don't. Sarah's mother (greying black hair) dances with Frank. She is wearing jeans, a long tunic t-shirt, and boots. The chuckwagon is parked nearby but the meal is over. Ramón and Efren are finishing the dishes. When the band starts playing "El Rancho Grande," Sarah wearing a long denim skirt, nice blouse tucked in, with boots, no hat and her hair loose, walks out of the barn to the chuckwagon and up to Ramón.

EXT. CHUCKWAGON, NIGHT

SARAH Come on, Ramón, polka with me.

RAMÓN I'm all sweaty and dirty.

SARAH That's just cowboy cologne. Come on. . . . Pleeeaaase.

He takes off his apron and follows her to the dance floor. Ramón is a great Norteño polka dancer and so is Sarah. Efren watches them longingly while he finishes packing up camp and closes the chuck box. He takes off his apron and waits for Ramón to return. Sarah walks Ramón back to the chuckwagon. Just as Sarah and Ramón return to the wagon, a slow dance starts to play. Sarah walks up to Efren and holds out her hand.

SARAH Señor Caballero, will you dance with me? Por favor?

Efren looks at Ramón, who nods yes, then Efren "lets" Sarah drag him "reluctantly" to the dance floor.

EXT. DANCE FLOOR, NIGHT

Efren dances very well but very formally with Sarah, not too close. Her father is watching. He and Efren exchange a glance.

EXT. CHUCKWAGON, NIGHT

After they dance, Sarah walks Efren back to the chuckwagon. Ramón has disappeared (on purpose). Efren reaches in his pocket for a hitched horsehair bracelet that he has made with all natural colors. He hands it to Sarah.

EFREN Gift for books. Hair from your horses' tails. To remember.

SARAH Oh, Efren, it's beautiful! Did you make it? Of course you did.

Efren's expression says he doesn't quite understand, but can see that she likes it.

EFREN *(in Spanish)* De nada.

Sarah offers her wrist, he ties on the bracelet, spending a little time fastening the knot-clasp. She looks at it admiringly and smiles at Efren.

SARAH Will I see you in the fall? Speak English!

EFREN *(searching her eyes)* Good night, Señorita. English yes.

Sarah heads back to the barn. Soon a cowboy is leading her to the dance floor, but she turns back and watches the cooks drive away.

INT. RAMÓN'S PICKUP CAB, NIGHT

Inside the pickup Ramón is driving. Efren sits in the shot-gun seat.

RAMÓN *(in Spanish)* Be careful, my son.

EFREN I am.

RAMÓN *(in Spanish)* American girls are spoiled and need constant attention. They are not faithful. They don't respect a man's work.

EFREN *(in Spanish)* This one does.

RAMÓN *(in Spanish)* She will break your heart.

EFREN *(in Spanish)* Maybe.

In the side mirror, Efren sees Sarah look back to watch them drive away and smiles to himself.

INT. CAMP MEETING OPEN SHED, AFTERNOON

In the next scene, we are inside a large open-sided cook shed with a dozen large picnic tables and a cooking area at one end (location Bloys Camp Meeting near Fort Davis in August?). Sarah is sitting at one of the long tables talking to another young girl, 20ish, any ethnicity. They are almost alone in the huge space.

GIRL Interesting bracelet. Horse hair?

SARAH Yes. From the tails of horses I used to ride. Brings back good memories.

GIRL Did you make it?

SARAH I'm not that talented.

GIRL Then who?

SARAH A very talented guy.

GIRL Good memories?

SARAH I'm not sure. I haven't seen him in months. He came from Mexico and has probably returned.

She touches the bracelet fondly.

GIRL But you're hoping he didn't?

SARAH *(laughs)* How can you tell?

GIRL By the way you look at and touch that bracelet.

SARAH He is probably the poorest man I've ever known, yet he made me feel like a queen with nothing but coffee, horsehair, and a song.

GIRL I hear ya. The ones driving fancy cars, buying expensive dinners and jewelry make me feel cheap.

SARAH Love is complicated.

GIRL Unexpected.

SARAH And can disappear so quickly.

GIRL And usually does.

They both stare at cracks in the table. Then change the subject.

GIRL This is my first Camp Meeting. Thank you for guiding me through the food line.

SARAH I've been coming since before I was born. My mom is a great-granddaughter of one of the founders.

GIRL How did this get started?

SARAH Well, in 1890 churches were non-existent and ranches were miles apart. So a traveling preacher invited several ranch families to meet him in this grove of oak trees for worship on a certain day in August.

GIRL He just believed they'd show up?

SARAH Maybe hoped is a better word. But they did. The ranchers brought chuckwagons and camped five days. Lots of visiting, marriages, and baptisms.

GIRL Sounds fun.

SARAH It was. They came back every August, and now their descendants and friends come. The original families still try to feed everyone cowboy-style. All denominations were and are still welcome.

GIRL So nothing has changed?

SARAH Well, they built a roof over the tabernacle seating in 1912 because our prayers always bring rain.

GIRL Doesn't it usually rain here in August?

SARAH *(laughs)* Yes, but we like to take the credit. Anyway, it is just a wonderful, relaxing time to count our blessings and visit.

GIRL It seems the tourists have found it too.

SARAH It's getting too big . . . like a small town now with all these cabins. I don't recognize half of these people.

Suddenly someone comes up behind them and reaches around Sarah's shoulder to offer a cup of coffee in a tin cup like her favorite – with milk and cinnamon. Sarah knows who holds the cup before she even turns around.

SARAH Efren! What are you doing here?

EFREN I cook.

He notices she's still wearing his bracelet.

SARAH (*taking a sip of the coffee*) Perfect! You remembered.

The girl realizes this must be "the guy" and fades away. Sarah is so intent on Efren, she doesn't even notice the girl leaving.

EFREN No forget. First time I make coffee, you say perfect. Ramón say what perfect mean. He say truth!

SARAH (*laughs*) I am about to walk over for evening worship. Can you come with me?

He reaches in his shirt pocket and pulls out a green card and shows it to her.

EFREN Yes. No more hide. Green card! Boss said he get papers. Now believe!

SARAH Wonderful!

Sarah jumps up, hugs Efren, then both awkwardly back away.

SARAH My father says Mr. K always keeps his word.

EFREN Boss say to immigration ranch cook skilled and no find ranch cooks here.

SARAH Well, that's true! If you played baseball, it would be so much easier.

EFREN What?

SARAH (*laughs*) Nothing.

EXT. ON ROCKY ROAD TO TABERNACLE, CONTINUING

They walk down a path to the pavilion, talking as they walk.

SARAH How is English?

EFREN Difficult.

SARAH You seem to understand me.

EFREN Yes. More difficult to speak.

SARAH I am happy to see you.

EFREN (*smiles*) I am happy to see you.

He points to her bracelet and smiles. She smiles back.

SARAH I wish you had your guitar.

EFREN I wish I had my guitar.

SARAH Very good English! If you had your guitar, what would you sing?

EFREN Celito Lindo. After song, Ramón say you say I sound like rooster.

SARAH (*laughs*) No! I said your music was beautiful! Ramón was teasing.

EFREN Yes. Ramón is Ramón. I knew.

SARAH And your guitar playing . . .
Wow! You are so talented.

INT. OUTDOOR TABERNACLE, CONTINUING

They arrive at the tabernacle. Like the cookshed, it is roofed but open on all sides. They sit together near the back and to one side, away from most of the crowd. Muted in the background, we hear a preacher begin the evening sermon.

PREACHER In Mark 5, verse 36, Jesus said, "Don't be afraid, just trust me." What does Christ mean by trust? . . . *(fades out)*

Impulsively Sarah reaches for Efren's hand with the hand wearing the bracelet, pulls his hand into her lap, and holds it between both of hers. He freezes and stiffens, she laughs.

SARAH Don't be afraid. I won't hurt you.

EFREN Not afraid.

He gives her a smoldering look, more like a warning that instead of fear he is struggling to stifle his desire. He removes their hands from her lap and holds her hand between them. Sarah gives him a bit of a smoldering look right back.

SARAH Nor am I.

Sarah brings their hands back into her lap where she holds his hand with both of hers again. They exchange long eye-contact. Efren swallows hard.

EXT. ALONG ROCKY ROAD FROM TABERNACLE, LATE EVENING

After the service, Sarah lets go of his hand as they walk along the rocky gravel road back to her family's cabin.

EFREN One breakfast, I asked Ramón what you said. He said you said I handsome.

SARAH *(laughs)* No! I didn't <u>say</u> it, but I did <u>think</u> you were handsome.

EFREN *(mischievously)* I knew. I want English to understand <u>you</u>. No Ramón.

SARAH Yes. He likes to play tricks. You are learning so fast.

EFREN For you. Do you like me?

She hesitates, a little shocked, not sure what to say.

SARAH I know nothing about you . . . except that you work very hard. You're dependable, considerate, humble but proud. You don't want pity or charity. You are a master cook, cowboy, guitar player, and singer. You are indestructible, determined, empathetic . . .

EFREN *(interrupting)* Stop. No understand words.

SARAH *(laughs)* I'm not finished. You make sacrifices for your future. You like coyotes. You tell the truth . . .

EFREN *(interrupting)* And bad?

SARAH Oh, yes. *(mischievously)* You have a temper. You brag. You are a show off. You are stubborn. You have old-fashioned ideas about how women should behave.

EFREN *(frowning)* Stop!

SARAH *(teasing)* But I'm not finished. You have many more terrible faults . . . *(laughs)* . . . Do I have any faults?

It is almost dark. Along the road, they meet Billy.

BILLY Sarah . . . the cook's helper? Really? Is a wetback the best you can do?

Billy keeps walking toward them. Sarah glares at him and takes hold of Efren's hand again.

SARAH Yes. He's the best I can do.

Billy walks on past them. Efren looks confused and takes his hand away from hers.

EFREN No need help. What he say?

SARAH Ignore him.

Efren turns around and starts to follow Billy.

EFREN I teach respect.

Sarah quickly grabs Efren by the arm.

SARAH No! Don't lose your green card over some pendejo.

Efren is shocked and turns quickly to face her.

EFREN How you know word?

SARAH The cowboys. They say it all the time. They said it means stupid person. I am trying to learn more Spanish.

EFREN Happy for Spanish, but not cowboy Spanish. Look up words.

SARAH OK. . . *(confused, pause)* Now, where were we? . . . Oh, yeah, do I have any faults?

EFREN *(resuming a good mood)* No. Sarah es perfect.

SARAH Perfect answer!

EFREN So . . . do you like me?

SARAH I don't know you.

EFREN Name a man you know better.

Sarah's expression changes as she realizes how well she has gotten to know him.

SARAH Only my own father.

EFREN Do you know me from what someone said?

SARAH No, from what you <u>do</u>. You learn so fast, mostly on your own. You treat me like a lady or even a queen . . .

EFREN *(interrupting)* Words are words. Deeds are deeds. Efren is Efren.

SARAH Yes, he is.

EFREN And Sarah es Sarah.

Sarah's mood changes to very serious. She hesitates . . . looks sideways at him.

SARAH Ramón told me you had a wife and five kids in Mexico.

Efren laughs, then notices Sarah is not laughing. He flashes anger, struggles to find words.

EFREN Ramón is Ramón. Efren is Efren.

SARAH <u>Do</u> you have a wife and children in Mexico?

EFREN No! Do you have husband and children?

Insulted, he walks away into the darkness and doesn't look back.

SARAH Efren . . . wait . . . Efren . . . I'm sorry.

EXT. CAMP MEETING, DAY

We watch a montage of Sarah looking for Efren for four days. She goes to the shed where he cooks. Every evening, she sits where they sat during evening service, but she doesn't find him and he doesn't return. We spot him once sadly watching her from the shadows, but she doesn't see him.

INT. TABERNACLE, EVENING

Then finally, while Sarah is at evening service, Efren slips into the folding metal chair beside her and checks to see if his bracelet is still around her wrist. It is. Sarah is a little angry and not sure how to react or what to say.

SARAH Why did you disappear? Now we have run out of time. We always run out of time.

EFREN You don't trust me. You believe lies.

SARAH I will never trust you if you keep disappearing.

EFREN *(with frustration)* Patience es importante. In Mexico mañana no joke. In USA the clock ticks, ticks, ticks.

SARAH Yes, and now Camp Meeting is over. Why didn't you come back?

EFREN I have nothing. Someday, I will. I no ask you wait.

SARAH Maybe I want to?

EFREN If you don't trust me, you will not. *(struggling for words)* If I said I rope with either hand?

SARAH I would know you are teasing me.

EFREN *(frustrated)* My ride home . . .

Efren gestures helplessly for words, rises and turns to leave.

SARAH See you at fall roundup?

Efren does not answer. Walks away.

SARAH *(to herself)* I hope so.

EXT. CORRALS, EARLY MORNING

Words across the screen say "Fall roundup, two months later." It is almost daylight and cowboys are in the corral catching horses. One by one each cowboy ropes a horse and leads it out of the corral to saddle. Soon only Efren and Sarah are left in the corral. Their relationship is strained. They haven't spoken to or looked at each other.

EFREN *(stiffly)* May I catch your horse?

Sarah hands him her rope, his bracelet still on her wrist.

SARAH *(stiffly)* Little Red, please.

Efren hangs his own rope on a nearby post and faces her.

EFREN Now watch . . . <u>right</u> hand.

Very obviously he builds a loop in Sarah's rope with his right hand, throws a hoolihan right handed, catches Little Red, and hands her the coils and rope.

EFREN Now watch . . . <u>left</u> hand.

He grabs his own rope off the post and turns to face her. He very obviously switches hands with his rope, builds a loop left-handed, turns, throws a left-handed hoolihan, and catches his horse.

SARAH *(amazed)* You <u>can</u> rope with either hand! You were <u>not</u> teasing. I'm so sorry I didn't believe you. . . Again.

Sarah's father had also been watching, and his face shows that he is also amazed.

EFREN Yes. Again! Ramón is Ramón and Efren is Efren. Words are words. Deeds are deeds. I trust you. You think I lie. I must prove and prove and prove.

Efren turns away sharply, leaving Sarah standing with the coils of her rope in her hand. . . (which transitions to later that evening after supper as). . .

EXT. CHUCKWAGON AREA, LATE EVENING

Sarah's father stands with the coils of a rope in his hand. The cowboys have up-ended one of Ramón's big white water buckets and are throwing left-handed hoolihans at it, laughing and doing a horrible, awkward job. Efren is the star of the evening, giving lessons on switching hands. He easily ropes the bucket using either hand. Great admiration all around, especially from Sarah's father.

EXT. CHUCKWAGON, CONTINUING

Sarah does not participate. Instead she fixes herself a cup of coffee and then sits beside Ramón where Efren usually sits. They watch the roping.

SARAH Efren told me he could rope with either hand, and I thought he was teasing me. I practically called him a liar. He will never forgive me.

RAMÓN Never is a very long time.

SARAH Yes, it is.

RAMÓN Did Efren make that bracelet?

SARAH Yes, I never take it off.

RAMÓN I know that and so does he. *(laughs)* He put a knot on it that no one else can untie. You would have to cut it off.

SARAH *(laughs)* I should have known.

RAMÓN People are tricky. Knowing the difference between truth and lies is a skill that's hard to master.

SARAH Yes. And you sure don't make that any easier with your tricks.

RAMÓN *(laughs)* Everyone can be fooled.

SARAH Why do you do that?

RAMÓN *(overly innocent)* Well, as you say, cowboy school is more difficult than college school. . . and cooking school is more difficult than cowboy school.

Sarah shakes her head in mock frustration.

SARAH Cooking school is certainly the most aggravating.

RAMÓN Trust should be earned, not given easily.

EXT. SARAH'S FATHER'S HOUSE, EARLY EVENING

Time has passed to a few months later. Efren drives up to Sarah's father's house in an old but freshly washed pickup and knocks. He now has a short barber-shop haircut and wears a new black cowboy hat. Sarah answers the door, obviously very happy to see him.

SARAH Efren! You have a pickup!

He steps aside and makes a sweeping gesture toward the pickup.

EFREN Now I can take you on a date. I have somethings to show you.

SARAH OK!

She starts walking toward his pickup.

EFREN Don't you need permission?

SARAH *(laughs)* This isn't Mexico.

He frowns, but follows her to the pickup, opens her door, she gets in, and he drives.

EXT. CAFÉ, EARLY EVENING

They pull up to a tiny, square, very old adobe building: stucco has peeled off the mud bricks in several places. On the street side it has one windowed door and one small window, both covered from the inside by vintage Saltillo serapes (subdued colors, not garish like modern serapes). Above the window hangs a weathered grey board with used horseshoes bent into letters that say

"Café Rancho." On the door between the window and the serape is a hand-lettered cardboard sign that says "Closed." No hours are posted. Efren unlocks the door and holds it open for Sarah.

INT. CAFÉ, CONTINUING

Inside we see clean hardwood floors, two old tables. One table could seat six, the other could seat four, but only two chairs exist, both at the table for four. Two doors on the back wall. Above each door hangs a weathered grey board with bent horseshoe letters. One says "El Baño" and the other "La Cocina." Everything is spotlessly clean but otherwise completely unadorned. Both tables are covered with white table cloths made of clean bedsheets. In the center of each burns a kerosene lamp with sparkling clean chimneys and well-trimmed wicks so they do not smoke. The table that could seat four is set with two metal chuckwagon-style plates and two glasses of water with no ice. Two Sarah-style tin cups sit beside a bottle of red wine, already opened. A fork and red bandana "napkin" lay beside each plate. Efren's guitar leans against one chair at the table. Efren formally seats Sarah and pours them each a cup of wine.

EFREN A toast! Bad wine served in a crystal glass, you must believe is good. But bad wine served in an old tin cup, just throw it away.

They laugh and click cups.

SARAH *(sips)* The wine is very good. *(looking around, confused)* So . . . are we going to eat here?

EFREN Maybe. The food is very good, cooked on a fire beyond that door.

He points to the door labeled "La Cocina."

EFREN The music is also very good. But the owner is the only employee and he is busy impressing a lady right now *(he sits)*.

 SARAH *(suddenly realizing)* You <u>own</u> this place?

Efren pulls three small cards from his shirt pocket.

EFREN Yes. Here is my bank account card, my Social Security card, and my driver's license. We are celebrating.

SARAH Oh, Efren, congratulations! A toast: To your future!

EFREN To <u>the</u> future! *(click and sip)* Do you want a song as an appetizer?

SARAH Yes. Please.

He picks up his guitar, sits, and sings in English "Everyone Knows Juanita." (This is a very bawdy Mexican folksong. I have substituted the worst words.)

EFREN *(singing)*

Well, everyone knows Juanita
Her eyes each a different color
Her teeth stick out, her chin goes in
Her knuckles, they drag on the floor.

Her hair is like a briar
She stands in a bow-legged stance
And if I weren't so ugly,
She'd possibly give me a chance.

SARAH *(in mock anger)* That was terrible! What a waste of your beautiful talent. What have you done with my perfect caballero?

EFREN *(laughing)* I wanted to show you that Efren can have fun. I'm not always serious. But maybe you will like this song better.

His expression changes to serious, gradually changing to passionate while he sings in English "Have You Ever Really Loved a Woman."

EFREN *(singing)*

To really love a woman
To understand her
You gotta know her deep inside
Hear every thought

See every dream
And give her wings
When she wants to fly
Then when you find
Yourself layin' helpless in her arms
You know you really love a woman

When you love a woman you tell her
That she's really wanted
When you love a woman
You tell her that she's the one

'Cause she needs somebody to tell her
That it's gonna last forever
So tell me have you ever really
Really, really ever loved a woman?

He rises, leans his guitar against his chair, continues singing acapella, and holds out his hand to invite Sarah to dance. They dance very close, barely moving.

EFREN *(singing)*

To really love a woman
Let her hold you
'Til ya know how she needs to be touched
You've gotta breathe her, really taste her

'Til you can feel her in your blood
And when you can see your
Unborn children in her eyes

He looks into her eyes.

EFREN *(singing)*

You know you really love a woman

When you love a woman
You tell her that she's really wanted
When you love a woman
You tell her that she's the one

'Cause she needs somebody to tell her
That you'll always be together
So tell me have you ever really
Really, really ever loved a woman?

You got to give her some faith, hold her
    tight
A little tenderness, you gotta treat her
    right
She will be there for you, takin' good
    care of you
You really gotta love your woman, yeah

And when when you find
Yourself layin' helpless in her arms
You know you really love a woman

When you love a woman
You tell her that she's really wanted
When you love a woman
You tell her that she's the one

'Cause she needs somebody to tell her
That it's gonna last forever
So tell me have you ever really
Really, really ever loved a woman?

Just tell me have you ever really
Really, really ever loved a woman?

Just tell me have you ever really
Really, really ever loved a woman?

He sings the last two repetitions with his eyes closed and with deep emotion. They kiss and stand embracing for a moment.

Both start to get nervous, and Sarah breaks the spell.

SARAH I'm hungry.

EFREN *(laughs)* OK.

SARAH Your music is enchanting. Do you know what that word means?

EFREN No. *(he bows like a waiter)* One moment.

He disappears out the La Cocina door.

INT. CAFÉ, CONTINUING

Efren returns with another metal plate, carrying it like a polished waiter. On it is a "pizza" already cut into four slices.

EFREN One specialty of this house is pizza pastar . . . Pasture Pizza.

With a flourish he places the food on the table.

SARAH *(laughing)* I'm glad you didn't name it Pasture Pie. It looks like Ramón's bread, thin and crisp, with cheese . . . *(takes a bite)* asadero?

EFREN Yes, Ramón's wife makes it fresh from her goats.

SARAH . . . and crumbled bacon, spinach, and pineapple . . . all of my favorites!

EFREN All of your favorites.

SARAH You are so observant, so thoughtful. *(taking another bite)* Delicious. Thank you.

EFREN What are my favorite foods?

SARAH *(a little embarrassed)* I have no idea. Probably whatever is left after the cowboys go back to work.

EFREN *(laughs)* Yes. I have never tasted Ramón's cherry cobbler.

SARAH *(laughs)* . . . or probably his donuts.

EFREN How do I take my coffee? Do I even drink coffee?

SARAH I don't know.

She makes a face like asking if she's in trouble.

EFREN *(laughs)* Do you want to see my kitchen?

SARAH Yes, please.

He walks toward the La Cocina door and opens it for her.

EXT. LA COCINA, CONTINUING

Efren's "kitchen" is just an outdoor cooking area, similar but on a smaller scale than Ramón's chuckwagon camp. The fire is similar with only one bucket hanging from the pot rack for heating water. The chuck box is half as big. A lantern hangs from it. Four oak stumps with short boards nailed across the top sit near the fire as chairs. Efren points to a tall wire "fence" with a thick trumpet vine covering it and a handwashing area set up in front.

EFREN Beyond that arbor is an outhouse, El Baño.

SARAH *(looking around admiring)* I love it! This whole place feels like a cowboy camp. So traditional. So classy.

EFREN I came here wearing wetback sandals. Today I own a pickup and a small building. Someday, I will have more . . . maybe even indoor plumbing . . . for you. Hopefully, citizenship.

SARAH And so fast . . . and as a cook.

EFREN Cooking pays better than cowboying.

SARAH Ramón always says that. But you need to be happy too. Money isn't everything.

EFREN I am happy you say that. I did not come here to seek my fortune but to enjoy the cowboy life.

SARAH You are an excellent cowboy. And so many other things. I have no words to tell you how wonderful your music is. No words. You are an artist with horsehair. *(she touches her bracelet fondly)* Are you sure you <u>want</u> to cook?

EFREN For now, maybe always. I have always liked it. The more I learn the more I like it. Cooking is also insurance in case of injury and when I get too old to cowboy.

SARAH I guess cooking also helps guarantee citizenship.

EFREN Yes. Ranchers can still find and hire good cowboys. But camp cooks are rare on both sides of the border.

SARAH So, will this be your restaurant?

EFREN No. This is actually my home. I sleep upstairs in a loft. I have no furniture up there, just my bedroll. Ramón and Mr. K. loaned me these tables and chairs. This place is not for customers, just to

entertain . . . a place for a poor man to
take a date.

INT./EXT. CAFÉ, VARIOUS TIMES

The scene with Efren and Sarah fades out, followed by a montage of scenes in Café Rancho to show time passing: Christmas with a few simple decorations, Ramón and his wife eating with Efren; some of the other cowboys with dates and Efren as their singing waiter/cook; sometimes alone with Sarah, on Valentine's Day giving her a small heart-shaped box of candy and one red rose. Sometimes Efren and Sarah's dad drink beer in La Cocina; sometimes Efren sits alone and plays his guitar; sometimes he dances with Sarah while he sings acapella, fun and laughter and romance.

INT. CAFÉ, NIGHT

Another night at Café Ranchero just Sarah and Efren, sipping wine in tin cups and eating flat red enchiladas, chopped onions on top and one fried egg, with a side of refried pinto beans.

SARAH Ramón said your grandfather once managed a large ranch in Chihuahua until it was broken up into ejidos. Then he lost his job . . .

EFREN *(interrupting)* That is Ramón's story, but not mine. My grandfather did manage a big ranch, but his father owned it.

SARAH So that explains your music?

EFREN Yes. Young Mexican dons learn many useless things: manners, grammar, music, how to bow to a lady. *(he bows)*

SARAH Not useless.

Sarah's expression shows confusion (is he joking or trying to impress her)? She is fighting the urge to doubt him again. Efren interprets her confusion as wondering if he would be spoiled.

EFREN Don't worry. I'm not a spoiled rich boy in disguise. My situation is genuine. I had to teach myself how to survive with a gallon jug for water and two cans of peaches. My ancestors' wealth was mostly taken by revolution and the rest split between nine children and countless grandchildren.

SARAH What happened to your parents?

EFREN Grandfather had enough inheritance to buy three city blocks in Guadalajara. He built a charro arena, several houses, horse stalls and gardens, with walls around it all. My father and his three brothers are famous charros, my sister rides escaramuza. They enjoy it, but the charro ring was not for me.

SARAH Why not?

EFREN Would <u>you</u> be content to ride inside a small circle all day, around and around?

SARAH *(smiles)* No.

EFREN Would <u>you</u> prefer to dress up fancy and pretend to be a cowboy or work alongside real ones?

SARAH I understand. But I've never been able to explain to anyone why I love to cowboy so much.

EFREN The only people who understand us are those who feel the same way.

SARAH That's true of music too.

Sarah's mention of music here is a foreshadowing that Efren does not pick up on. Her expression shows her disappointment. His shows he didn't actually connect her love of his music to the possibility that she might also be a musician or singer. He goes on with his own story.

EFREN My parents are still young, not ready to pass on any inheritance. Even when they do, it will all be split yet again among five children. I did not want to wait. Mostly, though, I was enchanted by grandfather's big ranch stories from Chihuahua and Coahuila.

SARAH I see you learned what enchanted means.

EFREN Yes. *(smiles)* I hoped to live that life. That was not possible in Guadalajara, so at fourteen I struck out on my own for Northern Mexico.

SARAH Ramón said the ranches there had all been split up.

EFREN Yes. But when the disillusioned city people wanted to sell their dusty little ejidos, a few wise families started buying and put a few big ranches back together, piece by piece.

SARAH How did you find jobs?

EFREN *(smiles)* The same as here. I enjoyed learning from the old cooks, enjoyed cooking, and especially enjoyed being around the cowboys who ate my food. As they got to know me, they would take me horseback. Pretty soon I was riding every day and seeking out the best for advice.

SARAH Who taught you to rope with either hand?

EFREN The best roper I knew was left handed. When I asked him to teach me, he said he would have to teach me left-handed. He said learning to rope would feel awkward no matter which hand I used, so I could later teach myself to rope right handed. He said being able to rope with both hands might help me someday.

SARAH *(teasing)* To show off.

EFREN *(laughing)* Sometimes, but I try not to show off too often . . . only when the stakes are high.

He gives her a smoldering look.

SARAH And use your fancy roping skills to impress pretty girls.

EFREN Only if a girl is observant and also loves this life. Girls like that are very rare and very precious.

SARAH *(smiles)* Thank you.

EFREN And you? What are your hopes and dreams?

SARAH I love to cowboy, but I know that's not possible. So I am studying to be a high school history teacher. But I hope to have children someday and cowboy with them. So I'm not sure which to choose.

EFREN Why not all?

SARAH Teaching, cowboying, and children don't seem compatible, especially for a girl.

EFREN They could be if you pick the right man.

Sarah stares at him for a beat and changes the subject back to him.

SARAH So why did you cross the border?

EFREN Bigger ranches. I heard West Texas still had some big ones like my great-grandfather's used to be.

SARAH And your future?

EFREN Like most cowboys, my dream is to someday own my own ranch. Today that is only possible in Mexico, and maybe not even there. My green card allows me to legally own cattle and land in both countries, so I can follow opportunities that might arise. But mostly I want to live the cowboy life. I can work for bigger ranches than I will ever afford to own.

SARAH Yes. My family leases a small ranch but my father and I prefer to work for the big ones too . . . *(pause)* . . . Do you miss your parents?

EFREN We write. I think we say more and stay closer through letters than we would in person. You have a lot of questions.

SARAH Do you want to go back to Mexico someday?

EFREN Mexico is beautiful once you get past the border. Even the slums of Guadalajara are covered in gardens and flowers. My family thinks the whole United States looks like Juarez. If I decide to go back or if I have to, will you go with me?

Sarah hesitates, looks at him, not sure what he is asking.

SARAH I don't speak much Spanish.

EFREN *(laughs)* Good. If you get mad at me, you can't run away.

SARAH Are you asking me to marry you?

EFREN *(smiling sadly)* Not yet. I want citizenship first. I don't want you to wonder about my motives. Plus a green card is as easily revoked as given. We non-citizens are ping pong balls for your politicians. I want your father to know I can take care of you.

SARAH *(flashes to anger)* I don't need to be taken care of. Half the responsibility in a marriage should be mine. Like you, I don't want pity or charity.

EFREN Taking care of you is not pity or charity. It is a sacred responsibility. You will take care of me too, like helping me to learn English.

SARAH I overheard my father and Ramón talking about raising self-sufficient children. My father said he lets me make my own decisions and mistakes, unless it becomes life threatening. Ramón said that if it was truly life threatening, then my father wouldn't be there. Neither will you.

EFREN *(firmly)* I need your father's blessing.

SARAH This isn't Mexico. I am a grown woman about to graduate from college. I don't need my father's blessing for anything.

EFREN I do. I want your father's trust, respect, and permission.

SARAH Then you won't have mine.

EFREN Then I will take you back to your father's house.

EXT. CAFÉ, NIGHT

They leave the café. Sarah opens her own door to climb into the pickup and slams the door.

INT. PICKUP CAB, NIGHT

Inside the pickup, we zoom in on Efren's face while he drives: unsmiling, jaw set, determined. The scene fades out.

EXT. CHUCKWAGON AND RANCH, DAY

Time passes. We see a montage of Efren cooking and cowboying, reading books by lantern light, becoming friends with Sarah's father. We see Sarah walking across the stage to receive her college diploma, embracing her parents after. Her father is holding his hat in his hand throughout.

MOTHER: Well, Sarita, you are also about to graduate from cowboy to school teacher. Does that make you happy?

SARAH To be honest, no. But Father told me you were also a cowgirl when he met you. Did it make you happy to become a wife and mom instead?

MOTHER Most of the time. I do still miss the big wide open country but I can still ride horses once in a while on our own place.

SARAH Growing up is painful.

FATHER Just don't grow up.

Father puts his hat on jauntily. All three laugh. Mom and Sarah look at each other knowingly, shake their heads at him, then all three join arms and walk away together.

EXT. CHUCKWAGON, EVENING

Time passes to another roundup. Efren has finished his chores, removes his apron, and joins the cowboys. He doesn't look at Sarah who stands alone off to one side of the fire. Efren and Sarah's father carry on an animated conversation in Spanish. Ramón sits alone near the chuck box, smoking a cigarette, and enjoying the peaceful evening. Sarah fixes herself a coffee and joins Ramón.

EXT. CHUCKWAGON CLOSE-UP, EVENING

Sarah and Ramón sit in silence for a while.

SARAH Ramón, does your wife take orders from you?

RAMÓN Of course. *(pause)* But please don't tell her I said that.

SARAH *(laughs)* What is she like?

RAMÓN Aieee. She's the meanest woman I ever met. She won't let me cook in her kitchen because she says I think I'm cooking outside . . .

As he answers, he motions like he is throwing salt at a skillet and brushing flour and dough off his hands and clapping them together like he does in camp. Obviously he'd make a mess if done inside a house.

RAMON . . . throwing salt at the skillets and brushing flour and bread dough off my hands, making messes all over her floor and stove.

SARAH *(laughs)* Has Efren met her?

Ramón looks suspiciously at Sarah sideways and glances toward Efren. He notices the horsehair bracelet still on her wrist.

RAMÓN Oh, yes. He is afraid of her too.

SARAH I thought the men in our culture were supposed to be macho.

RAMÓN *(laughs)* Only when our women give us permission. Does your mother obey your father?

SARAH *(laughs)* Only when she wants to.

RAMÓN Yes. And women seldom want to. We have some bad men, of course, just as any culture does, but you are too smart to get mixed up with one like that.

SARAH *(nods)* Did you ask your wife's father for permission to marry her?

RAMÓN Of course! He and I get along great.

SARAH Did you ask her mother's permission?

RAMÓN No, and I probably don't have it yet.

SARAH *(laughs)* How long have you been married?

RAMÓN Fifty-two years . . . five children, ten grandchildren, two great-grandchildren, so far. Every day I think it might not work out, but I still have hope.

SARAH *(laughs)* Well, good luck.

RAMÓN *(more seriously)* I came north to find a job. My sweetheart stayed in Mexico with her parents. I promised to come back. She waited three years, with not even a letter because I never learned school. Her family had no telephone. But she waited. Her mother thought I was going to make a bitter old maid out of her beautiful daughter. Her mother had her heart set on at least the governor of Chihuahua for a son-in-law.

SARAH Why did she wait?

RAMÓN She knew she would never find a better man.

SARAH How did she know you'd come back? How did you know she'd be waiting?

Sarah looks toward Efren and watches him for a moment. Ramon notices.

RAMÓN We both had hope.

SARAH How could you trust each other that much?

RAMÓN Trust is for children, Mija. You can't put anyone in a cage. The best we ever have is hope.

SARAH So was it easier after you married?

RAMÓN Marriage is never easy. Nothing is easy if you want to be good at it.

SARAH You're a very wise man, Tío. How did you get so wise?

RAMÓN Making mistakes.

SARAH I have made so many. But I don't feel any wiser, even though I just graduated from college.

They stare at the fire for a moment.

SARAH I have accepted a job teaching English in Marfa next fall, and have rented a little house there.

We see a flash of reflected light in Ramón's glasses. He watches it intently. The light blinks twice. We follow his gaze but see only distance and mountains with a lone buzzard drifting in the thermals. He rises to dig something out of the wagon and bring it to Sarah. It looks like a wad of white cloth.

RAMÓN Efren asked me to give this to you.

SARAH A used dish towel?

The cloth is heavy when she takes it. She unwraps it to find a small pistol completely enclosed in an old but well-oiled leather holster.

RAMÓN It belonged to his grandfather. He does not want to get caught with it. The chotas will confiscate it.

SARAH But this is Texas. Guns are OK.

RAMÓN Only for citizens.

SARAH But Efren and I . . . we are not friends . . . anymore. You keep it.

Ramón looks away, off into the distance. She waits, staring hard at him.

RAMÓN Efren does not want to say goodbye. He said he will come to get it someday.

Sarah's face changes from frown to hope.

SARAH OK. I will take it.

RAMÓN Has your father taught you to handle guns?

SARAH My mother has, mostly rifles and shotguns for hunting, but I have handled a pistol some. Mom gets nervous when Father is away at a roundup like this. Especially since so many bad men are coming across the border now.

Sarah carefully removes the pistol to look it over. We see bullets. It's loaded. She replaces it in the holster, wraps it again in the white dish cloth, and cradles it carefully in her lap with both hands (like she did Efren's hand at Camp Meeting). She starts to choke up and struggles to fight back tears.

SARAH This will probably be my last round-up. I will miss all of this so much . . . my horses, you, and . . .

She can't finish, begins sobbing quietly, tears streaming.

EXT. CAMP AREA, CONTNUING

Suddenly the laughter and roping sounds stop. Sarah and Ramón look up quickly toward the cowboys. Out of nowhere, a Border Patrol agent in green uniform has appeared among them.

RAMÓN *(spits)* Chotas.

In a few seconds, another BP agent drives up in a BP van with a drug dog. The van driver runs the dog around through the cowboy teepees, the shed, and along the chuckwagon . . . finding nothing.

SARAH A drug dog? Here?

RAMÓN You are naïve, Sarah. Not all cowboys are innocent. We have had a few who use drugs . . . only marijuana as far as I know . . . so far.

Finding nothing, the BP agent re-loads the dog and begins searching teepees and warbags. Meanwhile the other agent has been checking papers. Sarah has choked off her tears, but is still emotional, her eyes red, cheeks tear stained.

SARAH Efren has a green card. He'll be OK, right?

RAMÓN For now. But more and more keep coming, and many are bad.

SARAH Immigration used to be about freedom. Freedom to practice your religion, freedom to speak, to make choices. Now it's all about economics.

RAMÓN I came because there were no ranch jobs in Mexico. I wanted a place to raise a family. Now it's all about drugs.

SARAH Yes. Teachers are being warned. The schools are more dangerous.

RAMÓN Our Mexican cowboys are all legal, but we have a Canadian.

SARAH *(draws a sharp breath)* Jeremiah!

RAMÓN The laws keep changing. Now the chotas must check everyone they don't personally know, even the white boys.

SARAH And Peter? He's from Australia.

RAMÓN Peter has some kind of work permission. Each country is different. Too many laws, all different.

One of the cowboys is properly "wearing" an Aussie stock whip across his back and one shoulder like a rifle. He goes to his warbag in the shed and brings back a handful of papers. The agent looks them over, hands them back, and they shake hands. But it

is not going as well for the Canadian. He has animatedly engaged the BP agent in an argument. Mr. K steps between them and puts an arm around Jeremiah. Mr. K pulls his tally book and a pen from his shirt pocket and hands them to Jeremiah who writes in it and hands it back.

RAMÓN Jeremiah must be giving Mr. K an address to ship saddle and bedroll.

SARAH But he has a pickup too?

RAMÓN Mr. K will find a way. The good ones get caught. The bad ones slip through.

Jeremiah shakes hands all around, waves at Ramón, who waves back, and blows a kiss to Sarah, who blows a kiss back. He climbs into the BP van like Efren did and looks just as dejected. Both agents now head toward Ramón and Sarah. Sarah carefully adjusts the dish towel in her lap and covers it with both hands. Agent 1 notices that Sarah has been crying (explaining the dish towel in her lap). Both touch the brims of their hats to her.

BORDER PATROL #1 You OK, Sarah?

She nods, sniffles, and looks down at her lap.

BORDER PATROL #2 Sorry, Ramón, we are going to have to search your wagon for weapons.

Ramón nods permission. Sarah looks sideways at Ramón.

RAMÓN So . . . what are you going to do, Mija?

She looks at Ramón, more tears well up and fall.

SARAH Wait.

Ramón nods approval. Sarah's father motions for her to come. She carefully hugs Ramón goodbye, holding the dishtowel-wrapped pistol carefully to one side.

INT. PICKUP CAB, EVENING

Inside the pickup as they head away from camp, Sarah's father waits patiently for her tears to stop before trying to talk. Sarah notices him eyeing the crumpled white cloth she cradles in her lap.

SARAH A going away gift from Ramón for my new house in Marfa.

FATHER A used dish towel?

SARAH Ramón humor. And to soak up my tears.

Her father nods understanding and the scene fades out.

INT./EXT. VARIOUS LOCATIONS, VARIOUS TIMES

Time again passes and we see a montage of Sarah loading boxes into a small older model car, hugging both parents, driving away with tears, then moving boxes into her little house, teaching, cooking, grading papers, attending meetings, occasionally driving by Café Rancho (never open), searching at Camp Meeting but never finding Efren. Christmas, Valentine's Day, and Easter all come and go. At night she hugs a pillow and cries.

INT./EXT. VARIOUS LOCATIONS, VARIOUS TIMES

Meanwhile, we see a montage of Efren cooking, cowboying, studying. He is so tired that he falls asleep in his folding chair after supper. Ramón picks up the book he's dropped and wakes him gently. He speaks English to him now.

RAMÓN You need some rest, my son. You can't keep up this pace.

Efren opens the book again.

EFREN I must hurry.

INT. TEACHERS' LOUNGE, DAY

The scene shifts to Sarah sitting in the teacher's lounge at a small round table sipping coffee out of a Styrofoam cup. She stares at the cup while it morphs . . .

EXT. CHUCKWAGON, EARLY MORNING

. . . into a dream of her favorite tin cup back at the wagon with Efren offering her that first cup of coffee. When her awareness returns to the lounge, . . .

INT. TEACHERS' LOUNGE, DAY

. . . a fellow teacher is sitting at the table with Sarah.

TEACHER 1 Sarah? . . . Earth to Sarah . . .

SARAH Oh! Sorry.

TEACHER 1 You were a million miles away.

SARAH Actually only about forty.

TEACHER 1 Huh?

SARAH *(laughs)* Nothing. How's it going?

TEACHER 1 I need a distraction. How's your love life?

SARAH Seriously?

TEACHER 1 Seriously.

SARAH Well . . . it's non-existent as usual.

A second teacher walks into the lounge. She overhears a little of their conversation and joins them at the table.

TEACHER 2 That can't be true. You're smart, pretty, and employed.

Sarah looks affectionately at both teachers.

SARAH Well . . . there was a guy once *(twists the bracelet)* but I haven't seen him in over a year.

TEACHER 1 What was he like?

SARAH *(laughs)* Handsome, talented, hard-working, but quick to anger and disappear. You, know . . . the usual.

TEACHER 2 Dump him.

TEACHER 1 Agreed. Plus I happen to know that Coach Thompson has his eye on you: handsome, talented, hard-working, easy going and sticks around.

SARAH *(laughs)* Not interested.

TEACHER 1 So how long are you going to wait for your crabby Prince Charming to reappear?

SARAH I don't know. I guess until I find a better man.

TEACHER 2 The clock is ticking.

SARAH Yes, it is.

Teacher 1 and Teacher 2 look at each other.

TEACHER 1 Why do you wear that old string of horsehair around your wrist?

TEACHER 2 Because <u>he</u> made it for you, right?

SARAH Not exactly.

TEACHER 1 Come on, Sarah, we know he made it. You told us.

SARAH Yes, but it represents more than the maker.

TEACHER 1 The horses you used to ride?

SARAH Yes, but even more. I'm not sure I can explain.

TEACHER 2 Try. We've got time.

SARAH The horses were my best friends. They gave me wings. Horses are part of my heritage and . . . the history of my family. Horses gave me my values. They represent the life I want. They represent the best part of my life. Maybe the maker understood all that.

TEACHER 2 So are you saying you want to go back to ranch life instead of teaching?

TEACHER 1 Isn't being a teacher what you went to college to do?

SARAH *(looks at them fondly)* Horses have always been my first choice. But I'm a female. With the right man, maybe I could have both?

TEACHER 1 So Coach Thompson represents giving up horses?

SARAH Maybe. But maybe also my identity, my life, . . . maybe my future. I don't know. I just know I'm not ready to cut off the horsehair bracelet yet.

Sarah fondles her bracelet tenderly. The two teachers give each other a look.

TEACHER 1 So what if he never comes back? Are you willing to just wait forever?

SARAH I don't know. Maybe I'm not even waiting for him.

TEACHER 1 A bird in the hand is worth two in a bush, you know.

SARAH That's a cliché. Maybe a bird in the bush is worth more than one in a cage.

TEACHER 1 Oh, Sarah, come and have a drink with us after school today. We'll have you home by dark.

SARAH Sweet of you to ask, but I have papers to grade.

TEACHER 2 It's Friday! Come on. You're gonna burn out if you don't mix in a little fun.

SARAH Thanks, but no. A very wise man told me his future wife waited three years for him without a single letter or phone call. I've still got two years to go before I give up.

TEACHER 1 What's so special about this non-existent, slow-moving frog prince?

SARAH We want the same life and the way he makes me feel.

TEACHER 2 Abandoned?

TEACHER 1 Forgotten?

SARAH *(laughs)* Sometimes. But when he is around, he makes me feel like a queen . . . or actually a cowboy, maybe even a ranch wife. Besides, I know he will be back someday. I have his grandfather's pistol.

TEACHER 2 What?!

SARAH I also know he is working long hours and studying to get citizenship.

TEACHER 1 Citizenship!

Both teachers look at each other in shock.

TEACHER 2 Then he's just after somebody . . . <u>anybody</u> to marry.

SARAH Maybe. But if so, he's sure going about it all wrong. It's more like he wants to make sure I trust him. And I want him to trust me.

TEACHER 1 Sarah, Sarah, come drink with us! You <u>really</u> need a drink if you're pining your life away over an illegal.

TEACHER 2 How many tattoos does he have? Do you give him money?

SARAH I know you're just trying to help, but he's not like that. I'm OK.

TEACHER 1 OK is not good enough.

SARAH See you guys Monday.

Sarah rises and tosses her Styrofoam cup in the full trash can, stares at it a moment, retrieves it, rinses it at the sink, writes her name on it, and sets it near the coffee maker. Then she gathers up her stuff, looks sadly at the clock hanging on the wall, and leaves. Her two teacher friends watch her and look worried.

TEACHER 2 I don't want to sound like a racist . . . but citizenship? Oh . . . my . . . God!

TEACHER 1 We gotta fix this.

INT. SARAH'S HOUSE/ BEDROOM, NIGHT

Time passes to a night with Sarah in bed asleep, awakens to hear men whispering in Spanish just outside her open but screened bedroom window. The digital alarm clock beside her bed displays 12:05 AM in large red light. Sarah's face shows panic. Silently and moving slowly, she slips her hand between the mattress and box spring. She carefully pulls out Efren's pistol and removes the holster. Through the window she can see silhouettes of men in her yard. Finally, she musters her calm but stern "teacher voice."

SARAH *(in Spanish)* Get out of here!

VOICE *(in Spanish)* Is your husband home, Señora?

SARAH *(in Spanish)* Get out of here!

VOICE *(in Spanish)* We want to speak to your husband.

SARAH *(in Spanish)* Last warning. Get out of here!

Sarah hears muffled laughter, so she points Efren's pistol at the window screen and pulls the trigger. BAM! Then complete silence. The men have disappeared without a sound. Sarah grabs her phone from the night-stand beside her bed and punches in a number.

SARAH Hello, Dispatch? Please send the sheriff quickly to 1109 East Siesta Road? I just fired my pistol into a crowd of men who were whispering in Spanish outside my bedroom window. I may have hit someone. I am not sure they are gone. I am alone. Please hurry. . . *(listening to a reply)* . . . Thank you.

Sarah waits in the darkness clutching Efren's pistol. The red lights on the digital clock beside her bed shows 12:15, then 12:30, then she hears a siren and sees flashing lights. Sarah hasn't moved and still doesn't.

SHERIFF'S VOICE *(outside)* *(shouting)* Sarah, it's Sheriff Johnson and Deputy Martinez. Please don't shoot us.

She sees two men with flashlights outside her window. She does not move or speak. When her alarm clock reads 1:10, she hears a knock on her front door.

SARAH *(shouting)* Just a minute!

She gets out of bed, lays the pistol on her bed, throws on a bathrobe, and quickly picks up the pistol, obviously still frightened.

EXT. SARAH'S FRONT DOOR, NIGHT

When Sarah opens her front door, two uniformed men stand waiting. Both are dressed in jeans, cowboy hats and boots, and long-sleeved khaki Sheriff shirts with pistols and cop stuff strapped to their belts and shirts. Sarah opens the door slowly, peeking out, visibly afraid, pistol in hand but pointed toward the ground. Sheriff Johnson's eyes are glued on her pistol. He is smiling and speaking calmly.

SHERIFF Sarah. It's OK. You're OK now. Everything's OK. They're gone. When we notified the Border Patrol, they were already looking for about twenty illegals who had tripped a sensor. They radioed capture before we even finished searching around your house.

Sarah lets out a deep breath and visibly relaxes.

SHERIFF Now . . . can I have your pistol, please?

SARAH *(resisting)* Oh, please, Jim, no! It's not mine. It belonged to the grandfather of a dear friend who loaned it to me. Please don't take it. Please.

SHERIFF *(laughing)* I'm not going to take it. I won't leave you unarmed. We can't get here fast enough. I just need the brass and to make sure only one round was fired. Deputy Martinez and I didn't find any blood, so we don't think you hit anyone. I promise to give your pistol right back.

She reluctantly hands it over. He removes the spent casing, puts it in his pocket, and hands the pistol back to Sarah.

SHERIFF Nice old pistol. Looks well-cared for. Be sure to clean it since you fired it. You might need it again tomorrow or even later tonight.

SARAH *(fighting to calm down, talking fast)* I'm so thankful I had it. I never dreamed I'd actually aim a gun at and pull the trigger on a human being.

SHERIFF You did exactly the right thing.

DEPUTY These guys are not like the ones who used to come from Mexico one at a time, looking for work.

SARAH I told them three times to go away and heard two of them laugh after my third warning.

DEPUTY Most are not even from Mexico. They're gang members and drug runners from Venezuela, Guatemala, and Nicaragua.

SARAH They kept asking to talk to my husband. I was afraid they were making sure there was no man around.

DEPUTY They're not looking for jobs; they're looking for easy money.

SARAH All I could think to do was pull that trigger.

SHERIFF Some of them are armed, sometimes well-armed. But if you are inside a dark house and don't turn on a light, you'll have the advantage. Even when there is no moon, you can see them in the starlight, but they can't see you.

DEPUTY Immigration used to be about hope. Now it's about drugs, human trafficking for sex, recruiting new gang members. They're not like our grandparents, Sarah.

Dispatcher voice crackles on the radio and says in police jargon that none of the 20 illegals in custody with the Border Patrol had been wounded.

SARAH What did she say?

SHERIFF She said none of the 20 illegals had a gunshot wound. *(laughing)* So we won't have to hang you on the courthouse lawn.

SARAH That's not funny, Jim.

SHERIFF Sure it is. Don't worry. I'd get hung first if I tried to throw everyone's favorite school teacher in jail for protecting herself. Deputy Martinez will circle through your neighborhood every 15 minutes until morning.

SARAH Thank you, Jim. And you too, Manny.

SHERIFF Maybe that will help you relax and get some sleep.

SARAH I'm not expecting to sleep any more tonight . . . maybe never again.

DEPUTY Don't let the bad guys get in your head, Sarah. You handled the situation perfectly. We are very proud of you. And here, take this.

He hands her a small package labeled "Screen Patches."

SARAH What?

DEPUTY To repair the hole in your window sceen. One mosquito <u>will</u> keep you awake.

SARAH *(laughs and then sobers)* Are the bad guys going to make it more difficult for the good guys to get citizenship?

DEPUTY Maybe, but we hope not. Anyone working toward citizenship right now needs to hurry though. We never know when the political winds will shift.

Sarah looks very worried as the scene fades out.

EXT. SARAH'S HOUSE, LATE AFTERNOON

In daylight, one week later Efren, driving a shiny new blue Ford F-350 pickup with **TL** *painted in white on the door, pulls up in front of Sarah's little house. He has a bouquet of yellow bells wildflowers (Esperanza) in his hand. She runs out the door before he is halfway up the sidewalk.*

SARAH Efren!

She catches herself just before throwing her arms around him. Choking back tears, she takes a step backward and switches quickly to mad.

SARAH How did you find me?

EFREN *(shrugs)* A man always knows where his woman is.

SARAH *(irritated)* What makes you think I'm your woman?

Efren points to the bracelet on her wrist. Sarah quickly hides the bracelet behind her back.

SARAH I looked for you at Camp Meeting. Your café is never open. You just vanished . . . again!

EFREN I've been busy.

SARAH You keep breaking my heart over and over.

One tear escapes and rolls down Sarah's cheek. He reaches up and brushes it away with his thumb.

SARAH Your pistol probably saved my life.

EFREN I know. Deputy Martinez told me. I treasured it because of my grandfather. Now I treasure it even more.

SARAH I was so afraid.

EFREN I know. But you were also very brave, just the kind of woman who would make a perfect ranch wife.

Sarah's emotions are riding a roller coaster and keep shifting.

SARAH You lied. You didn't want me to hide it; you gave it to me for protection.

EFREN No Ramón lied. He knew the chotas were coming and wanted to make sure they didn't confiscate it. He also wanted to make sure you and I would see each other at least once more. He knew we'd had a fight.

SARAH I actually wondered if Ramón couldn't keep it because maybe he wasn't a citizen or maybe even a felon.

EFREN It's OK, Sarah. Mistrust can be a good trait. It keeps you safe.

SARAH But not even trusting Ramón?

Efren doesn't answer. They just look at each other for a beat.

SARAH So why didn't you come to get it immediately?

EFREN After I thought about it, I was worried for your safety. I knew if I told you that I was worried about you living alone, you wouldn't have accepted it. You're a stubborn woman, you know. I stayed away partly to make sure you kept the pistol.

SARAH So in a way you <u>did</u> lie? You <u>do</u> lie.

EFREN Only when the stakes are high. And I'm so glad I did.

SARAH I even hid it from my own father. He still doesn't know I have it.

Efren hands her the flowers. She takes them.

SARAH Yellow bells. My favorite wildflower.

EFREN In Mexico we call them **esperanza**.

SARAH Hope.

EFREN Yes.

Efren takes her in his arms and then holds her out by her shoulders to face him.

EFREN I have a new job managing the **TL** Ranch about 20 miles from here. They furnish beef, utilities, a ranch pickup, gasoline, and a nice, three-bedroom, adobe house. Indoor plumbing, like I promised. The road to town is good, all-weather caliche. Let's go see it? She pushes him away.

SARAH I haven't seen or heard from you in a year. A year!

EFREN Did you find a better man?

SARAH What made you think you could just reappear and I would be waiting? And, yes, I have a boyfriend.

EFREN *(looks doubtful)* Can he rope with either hand?

SARAH *(hesitates)* Yes. . . No.

EFREN Then come with me.

SARAH How long before you disappear again?

EFREN Never.

He pulls a card out of his pocket.

EFREN Voter registration. I pledged my allegiance to the United States three days ago.

Sarah covers her mouth in astonishment. Her eyes fill with tears. He pulls her close again. She keeps her arms crossed across her chest, holding the flowers between them, but doesn't pull away.

SARAH Do you still own the café?

EFREN Yes.

SARAH Will you still cook at Camp Meeting?

EFREN It only lasts a week. My new boss is one of the partners in the camp where I cook.

SARAH Will you still help Ramón?

EFREN He plans to retire after spring branding, so cooking for the ranches that have always depended on him will become my responsibility. I have already found a good apprentice, one of Ramón's grandsons.

SARAH How can you do all of that and manage a ranch?

EFREN *(shrugs)* You said I am indestructible. Mr. K said he would get papers for me and he did. He made this all possible . . .

SARAH No. <u>You</u> made it possible. He just recognized your worth.

EFREN Still, I can't let him down. The **TL** owner knows how much his neighbors depend on a cook. He said I can adjust putting out our bulls so that our calves hit the ground either earlier or later than everyone else's.

SARAH *(pulling away again)* But if you work that hard, I will never see you.

EFREN I would not see much of a school teacher wife either, except on week-ends and summers. If you want to teach, you can. If you want to quit and cowboy with me, you can. If you want children, to cook with me, to start a business, become a writer, lay on the couch and eat candy . . . whatever you want. I'm ready.

SARAH But I will be alone so often.

EFREN Three cowboys will be working for me at the **TL**. They will be around when I'm away.

SARAH Can you handle all of that?

EFREN If I choose a wife wisely: one who has the skills and understanding to help me, and *(mischievously)* if I don't spend too much time dancing and playing a guitar.

SARAH *(softening)* But you will sometimes play for me, sing to me, and dance with me?

EFREN Whatever you want. Whenever you want.

He frees her from his embrace, takes a sep back, and holds out his hand like asking her to dance.

EFREN I offer you space. The shimmering blue distances beyond roads and highways, breath-taking timelessness. I offer you places best seen on horseback, too vast to walk around in. We both love places like that. Someday perhaps we will lose it, but today I can give you horses and miles and miles of desert grass. Let's go look.

SARAH Your English is too good now. You will talk me into anything.

EFREN *(laughing)* Without English, you would have won every argument.

SARAH As a teacher, I learn new words every day.

EFREN I will keep up.

SARAH Do you use tobacco?

EFREN No.

SARAH Does a wife sometimes need a beating?

EFREN Never.

SARAH Do you ever get drunk?

EFREN No. I practice moderation . . . except in one thing.

SARAH And what is that?

EFREN *(suggestively)* I will show you on our wedding night.

SARAH Show off!

EFREN Only when the stakes are high.

SARAH Are you asking me to marry you?

EFREN Yes.

SARAH Did you ask my father for permission?

EFREN Yes . . . and Ramón. We are officially blessed.

SARAH Did you ask my mother?

EFREN No. *(looking guilty)*

Sarah looks at him for a long minute and finally shakes her head no.

EFREN *(shocked)* No? Is your answer no?

SARAH You have broken my heart too many times. You have disappeared too many times . . .

EFREN *(interrupting)* I don't believe you.

SARAH . . . and most importantly, you never once asked if I could sing.

EFREN Sing?

SARAH Yes. I sing in the community choir and sang the lead in two summer theater musicals. I love to sing, but you never asked.

EFFREN This can't be happening!

He believes her now. He's terrified and searches her face for some sign of forgiveness. But she averts her eyes and shows no emotion. After a long pause, he turns to walk away, looking defeated and broken, like he did when the Border Patrol captured him. When he almost reaches the end of her sidewalk, Sarah's teacher voice rings out.

SARAH Stop!

Efren freezes in his tracks.

SARAH My only boyfriend made this bracelet. I just wanted you to know what a broken heart feels like so you won't ever break mine again. Of course I will marry you.

Efren does not respond. He stands frozen, his back to her. Now it is Sarah's turn to get nervous.

SARAH Efren? . . . I think you are supposed to kiss me now.

EFREN A moment ago my heart was shattered. Now I am so happy, I'm afraid my heart will stop.

SARAH *(laughing)* No it won't.

She walks to him and turns him around.

SARAH I love you, Efren. Yes, I want to marry you, but I don't expect perfection. Your love of music and cowboy life made me realize that in spite of all your many faults, you are the perfect man for me.

Efren's eyes are closed tightly, his lips tremble with emotion. She kisses him . . . and he <u>really</u> kisses her back. The scene fades.

EXT. LA COCINA, NIGHT

Time passes to the backyard of Efren's café. He sits on one of the stumps by the fire, the only light. Sarah hands him his guitar, sitting close on another stump. They both stare into the fire. Efren begins playing. As a duet they sing "We've Only Just Begun" (lyrics by The Carpenters). Efren and Sarah are singing:

> We've only just begun to live . . .

EXT./INT. VARIOUS LOCATIONS, TIMES

They continue to sing as scenes from their lives and future are shown. The montage bounces between the singers and the scenes.

We see an intimate Catholic wedding with priest, in a small adobe church (the one in Lajitas?). Sarah radiant in white bridal dress and veil, Efren in black tux, three charros (his brothers) in full black

regalia as groomsmen; one bridesmaid (his sister) dressed in pink escaramuza regalia, the other two bridesmaids' (Sarah's two teacher friends) wear the same pink color but in modern dresses. All girls carry bouquets of native grasses. Sarah's also has a few esperanza blooms sprinkled in. The men wear a loop of braided horsehair as boutonnieres. In the pews sit Efren's elegant parents, Sarah's parents and brother, the rest of the cast, a few wives and children, including uniformed sheriffs and Border Patrol agents.

(singing)

> . . . White lace and promises
> A kiss for luck and we're on our way
> We've only just begun
>
> Before the risin' sun, we fly
> So many roads to choose
> We'll start out walkin' and learn to run
> And yes, we've just begun
>
> Sharing horizons that are new to us

Time passes, Efren and Sarah sit in a hand-made swing on the porch of their small adobe ranch house watching it rain.

(singing)

> Watching the signs along the way
> Talkin' it over, just the two of us
> Workin' together day to day

Night scene with Efren cooking, Sarah grading papers at their kitchen table. He hands her a cinnamon latte in her favorite kind of tin cup.

(singing)

> Together . . .
> And when the evening comes, we smile

They toast each other with tin cups of wine in Efren's café.

(singing)

> So much of life ahead
> We'll find a place where there's room to
> grow

Sarah now pregnant, Efren's hands cradling her belly, and feeling the baby move.

(singing)

> And yes, we've just begun
> Sharing horizons that are new to us

Next scene, both are horseback, riding out into open country with a child riding a pony between them.

(singing)

> Watching the signs along the way
> Talkin' it over, just the two of us
> Workin' together day by day

Washing dishes together, arguing, but eventually smiling and kissing.

(singing)

> Together
> Together

> And when the evening comes, we smile

We fly over wide-open ranching country at the golden hour of sunset, ending back at Efren's outdoor kitchen and campfire where the montage began.

EXT. LA COCINA, NIGHT

(singing)

> So much of life ahead
> We'll find a place where there's room to
> grow

> And yes, we've just begun . . .

As the music and light fades, coyotes howl and yip.

THE END

Fire Water

Inspiration for Fire Water

Like cowboys, Native American characters are usually portrayed in one of two ways: either demonized as murdering savages or romanticized as noble savages who live innocently in harmony with nature. Cowboys and Indians are either victims or live in a utopia that never existed. I wanted to portray truth, although as a trained academic, I realize that "truth" is illusive.

A major source for this chapter was a two-part article I wrote for *Western Horseman* magazine (April and March 1993) called "Ranching on the Reservation." For it I interviewed several Indian ranchers who also served on their tribal livestock boards. I knew it would be easy for a white reporter to make cross-cultural mistakes, so my first nervous question to the first rancher was what he preferred to be called—First Nation, Native American, Indian, or by tribal affiliation? He said, "When people ask my nationality, I say cowboy." When he took me to the family grave site that included a son who had been killed in a car accident, the only headstone said "Cowboy."

My two articles concentrated on Northern Cheyenne rancher Butch Small one month, and on Crow ranchers Elias and Tobias Huggs, and Kenneth and Wailes Yellowtail the next. The full-blood Huggs were descendants of Chief Pretty Eagle, and I photographed them at a scenic spot named after that ancestor. When I asked to photograph college graduate Wailes, who was running the family ranch, he insisted that I include his father Kenneth, and saddled an extra horse. I also talked to Theo Huggs, Chris Small, Gordon Small, John Small, and Dennis and Ethelene Shoulderblade.

Both cowboys and ranching Indians are physically and mentally embedded in place, in the land, weather and animals. My introduction reads:

I'm not sure what I expected when I set out to interview Native American ranchers. What I found was that the reservations are just miniatures of the rest of the American West. They have personality clashes, "public" land conflicts, political manipulation, jealousy, and the most beautiful cow country I've ever seen. Indians leasing "public" tribal lands complain about tribe members camping near livestock water, leaving gates open, and recreation. Non-ranching Indians complain that the Indian ranchers have too many restrictive rights on 'their' (reservation) land.

I never changed my mind and the parallels only deepened. Like writers of "westerns" most—if not all—Native writers come from urban situations. They're not cowboys. Most see themselves as victims, neighbors no longer help neighbors, empathy is a lost art, and cooperation seems to be a sign of weakness. We can't fix what's wrong with our world unless we can fix our own country, our own region, our own tribe, and our own family. Answers can only be found in places where something is already working. So by spot lighting a few working solutions, I've tried to create believable situations where warring individuals learn to work together toward a common cause in order to give their kids a better life. Can world peace begin with one small group, working separately and then together to improve the future for one runaway boy? Maybe. My characters champion Indians as cowboys, helping themselves and writing their own stories. But my work can't make it past today's cancel culture. When my work is labeled "cultural appropriation," my rural voice is silenced.

Bits of personality, actual dialog, competitive feelings between Cheyenne (Custer's menace) and Crow (Custer's scouts), and mixed feelings about the Custer reenactment (where Crows pretend to be Cheyenne) all come from those interviews and experiences. I was invited to a sweat lodge (which I declined) and saw the multicolored plat-book maps at Crow Agency. Blue squares (land that had been sold to non-Indians) far outnumbered yellow (Indian owners) and white (tribal owned) squares, my notes say 90% of the Crow reservation was owned by non-Indians. Two ranchers mentioned getting their start in ranching with nothing but a cast iron skillet.

My notes include words from Crow Chief Plenty Coups who advised his people to become farmers and ranchers. Although I didn't use the quote in the final article, he said, "Education is your most powerful weapon. With education you are the white man's equal; without education you are his victim." But I don't think he meant "education" the way we mean it today. Plenty Coups was born in 1848 when "school" usually meant "graduation" at eighth grade if not sooner. According to Yale professor, Walter Russell Mead, "Benjamin Franklin's formal education ended when he was 10 years old." At Plenty Coups death in 1932, only five-percent of Americans even owned an automobile, which would mean fewer than 5,000 since the USA population was under 200 thousand at the time. I believe what Chief Plenty Coups meant by "education" was to learn something—anything—and learn it well. Become a master at hunting, beading, cooking, farming, or ranching. Or as Northern Cheyenne rancher, Butch Small, said, "Everybody must produce. Some people were hunters, some were arrowhead makers, some were storytellers. It's the same today. If they weren't so busy fighting, they'd have done real well raising horses."

My ancestors were pioneer trail blazers, often living with Indians as their closest neighbors. A few were killed by Indians and some were famous for killing Indians. We trace one line back to Mayflower pilgrim William Bradford and almost all lines back to the American Revolution. Although to my knowledge, I carry no Native American genes—I might. My seventh-great grandfather Peter Pence was born in Lancaster, Pennsylvania in 1732, his occupation listed as basket maker. He was also famous as a hunter and scout and rose to lieutenant as a Revolutionary War soldier. He returned from one battle to find his remote cabin burned, his wife and most children killed by Indians. His twelve-year-old daughter Rachel, my sixth-great grandmother, had escaped by hiding under a log and defending her position with scissors. Revenge caused Peter to become a famous Indian fighter. Rachel married Michael Sisler, Sr. whose family first bought land in Iowa in 1851. Most of my ancestors arrived in Iowa before statehood.

On my father's side, his grandmother traces back to James Taylor, but we don't know who James' father was, so his back trail vanishes in 1814 when he married Margaret (Locke) Davis. Of course James and Margaret named their first son and my third-great grandfather James Locke Taylor. Margaret was the widow of Samuel Davis, who might have been killed in the war of 1812. We assume fourth-great grandpa James was a soldier too, as each generation since bred sons who donned US military uniforms. However, because a man named James Taylor was also one of the first settlers of the Virginia Colonies, there were and still are zillions of James Taylors scattered through the generations, impossible to trace. Many James Taylors were frontiersmen, their children seldom christened, and the far flung Taylor families seldom found by census takers. James Locke Taylor first bought land in Iowa in 1845.

I give my character, Wolf, a white Indian fighter's last name of Taylor. Wolf is ashamed of that white blood. I never met a white person who was not proud of their native blood if they had any, and I never met a native who was proud of white blood if they had any. Maybe that wasn't always true because we live in a complicated world and one generation's shame is another generation's pride. I have also met pure-blood Indians who never lived on a reservation and met "whites" and Hispanics who grew up and spent their entire lives on one. A large number of enrolled Seminole, Cherokee, and Creek are also black. The reservations have been diverse for generations.

In 1906, my second-great grandfather Isaac Taylor, Sr. and his wife Della struck out for South Dakota. They left their Iowa farms with some of their married children and took along the younger children, plus their eldest son (of course named James Taylor). I found several homesteads filed on by a James Taylor, but can't be sure it's my uncle. We do know that Isaac Taylor, Sr. homesteaded on the Crow Creek (Lakota) Reservation in Convent Township. Great-great-grandpa Isaac was famous for two things: hunting wolves and raising both riding and pulling horses. We assume the Taylors kept moving with the frontier in order to sell horses to Indians as well as to incoming soldiers and settlers. When they weren't busy fighting, the Taylors did real well raising horses.

I have a collection of old photograph postcards sent to Iowa from South Dakota and handed down to me by a Taylor uncle. My South Dakota Taylor uncles were cowboys at a time when most of the entire Lakota nation's grass was leased out to Texas ranchers for grazing. One uncle became a famous bronc rider and one served as sheriff of Hyde County from 1917 to 1920. Several postcards depict native people. On the back of one, Sheriff Grover Cleveland Taylor says he had learned to speak Lakota: "This country all know me. I can talk the language fairly well now." We think the postcards were made by Frank Cundill, an Iowa neighbor who may have followed the Taylors to South Dakota in 1911. Cundill homesteaded at Firesteel, in the middle of the

Cheyenne River Sioux Reservation, and turned his camera on history as it happened.

Isaac and Della's daughter Emma, my great-grandmother, married John DeGear before her parents moved on to South Dakota. Their son, my grandfather Bill, appears on one postcard wearing woolies. His horse is very clean and shiny, so the postcard was probably used to advertise Taylor horses. When I was very young, we made at least one trip to visit the South Dakota Taylors. Old family photos show my brother and I with an adult male Indian in a chief's headdress and me with three young fancy dancers. Were they friends, relatives, or just exotic entertainers?

My grandfather and father were master hunters and fishermen. We trace the DeGear (numerous spellings) line back along rivers, always making a living with hook and bullet, selling fish to markets or door to door, along with nuts, berries, and watercress, often illiterate. Their provable DeGear back trail grows cold at Peter DeGear a War of 1812 soldier, but may lead back to French Canadian, perhaps French Basque, and perhaps to Corne Degar found in a 1682 Virginia patent book. About 1958, my parents left Iowa for Arizona where I spent my teen years. Like Dad, my mom was also an avid hunter and fisherman, so nearly every week-end our family of four camped out somewhere on the White Mountain Apache reservation to hunt and fish. These experiences inspired action for my characters, like Tom fishing to relax and Wolf living off the land, camped beside a creek.

I attended junior high and high school in Mesa, where I became familiar with the Mormon (Church of Jesus Christ of Latter-Day Saints or LDS) religion. Their "Book of Mormon" was basically a history of native tribes in the Americas. Because one LDS goal was to treat one's own body like a temple, most Mormons did not drink alcohol. Many Native Americans who converted to that religion did not drink either.

I worked two summers (1964, 1965) as a curio shop girl at the Grand Canyon, becoming especially skilled at selling Indian jewelry. I could explain not only the different styles of sandcast, inlay, overlay, naja and squash blossom, or petit point and needle point, but was usually able to determine where many of the turquoise stones had been mined. My boss took me along on a few buying trips to meet the makers and pawn shop owners, so Indian jewelry plays a few bit parts in the script.

Many Grand Canyon employees at the time were Hopi, and I especially enjoyed a friendship with Milton Honanie at the Bright Angel Curio Shop. Milton was a jolly grandfather-figure who watched out for teen workers like me. Among the curios, we sold "Apache Kisses," a taffy that came in a cardboard teepee. We thought that was pretty silly since Apaches used brush wickiups, not teepees, and asked Milton one day where to find Hopi kisses. He said, "Tusayan," which at the time was a bar at the south entrance of the park. Today Tusayan seems to be a town. We curio girls liked to pull pranks on the tourists and Milton always had good ideas. He taught me several Hopi words and a little Hopi song. One day I proudly sang the song for one of the Hopi chiefs. The song was evidently bawdy, and the chief was not amused. Milton's Hopi words also turned out to mean something other than what he said they meant. From then on, the chief insisted that the Hopi language would no longer be taught to the curio shop girls. My character of Uncle Clint has a little streak of Milton in him: good hearted but a bit of a trickster.

After high school, I spent my freshman college year at Eastern Arizona Junior College in Thatcher where Hansen Ahasteen (Navajo) and I became great friends in art class. My roommate was Hispanic, and we were the only white girls in our dorm. The rest were either Apache or Navajo. We girls often had deep discussions about the agonizing process of growing up while dealing with alcoholic parents and trouble. Most were polite kids who cared deeply about their parents and about tribal traditions. Some were unwed mothers, divorced, or abused.

Our dorm was usually quite peaceful although I did need a sense of humor when the Apache girls decided to throw me in the shower in my pajamas or tumble their empty soda cans in the clothes dryers after hours to upset our dorm mother. My characters Tychee (Apache) and Joy (Navajo) both draw personality traits from girls I met at EAJC, including 1965 Miss Navajo Nation and Princess of the Flagstaff Pow Wow, Kathy Dahozy; Princess Runner-up, Ernestine Scott; and Miss Apache, Verna Patton. Joy is named in honor of Joy Harjo, but also has a bit of Luci Tapahonso, Leslie Marmon Silko, and Louise Erdrich mixed in, Native writers that I admire. Joy also has a bit of my mom, who worked for the Arizona Bank, first as a cashier, then loan officer, then vice-president. A few character traits for Joy's boss come from my favorite Texas bank president, David A. Moore, who for years loaned me travel money on only my signature as I chased stories.

The character of the white reporter is sort of based on me. I was editor of the EAJC newspaper and the elected reporter for the rodeo club. My boyfriend at the time was a half-Apache cowboy who had quit high school. His pickup had no windshield and the door on the passenger side did not open. I remember one incident at a drive-in movie when we were on a double date. The boys were interested in the movie, but we girls wanted to talk. So the boys made us get out and sit on top of the pickup cab, where we swung our legs like windshield wipers to continue aggravating them. Next they tied us back-to-back to a speaker pole with their nylon catch ropes, gathered up some empty popcorn boxes, placed them around us, and lit them on fire to burn us "witches" at the stake. Like, I said, I needed a sense of humor.

But college life was not always funny. My reporter character's memory of the drunk Indian beating up his pregnant wife happened to me, recreated as accurately as I can remember. The Sheriff's name was James "Skeet" Bowman. I don't think I ever knew the names of the couple. They didn't live in my dorm. I don't think the pregnant wife sought me out for help; she was just desperate. I never saw her again but the husband came into the student center a few days later while I was working. He was dressed nicely, shined boots and new black cowboy hat. He didn't look at me or speak, just purchased a canned soft drink from the vending machine. I imagined maybe it was his way of showing me he didn't always behave the way I had seen him, but it may have just been a coincidence. He may not have even recognized me. I never saw him again either. Maybe they both left school.

I also really did have a crush on the legendary Sonny Jim. I "passed" as Apache and ran barrels at a San Carlos All-Indian rodeo in 1965 or 66 when he was competing at that same rodeo. I watched him quiet a bull that was fighting a chute and re-train a borrowed bulldogging horse. He was amazing, but probably best that I never actually met him. He had a "reputation" with the ladies.

After marriage, I lived and worked on Texas ranches for 20 years. While living on the Nail Ranch in Albany, Texas I sponsored high school students who created a magazine (*The Old Timer*) similar to the one described in the script. Through the years, I had two fairly close Indian cowboy friends and worked cattle with them. One drank himself to death as a young man. The other called his drunk alter-ego Virgil, but somehow stopped. I never knew what made Virgil go away and leave him alone or even if he knew himself. Watching from the outside, it seemed like he just got very busy cooking, working, building saddles, training dogs and horses, serving as pickup man for rodeos, and filling up every spare minute of his time. All of his friends drank, but he stopped. He liked the movie "Stay Away, Joe." I didn't. My character of Joe Champlain is a mix of Virgil, Elvis's character in that movie, and problems with alcohol that I witnessed in college, on the streets of Flagstaff and Show Low and in cowboy bars. I thought Elvis was a very poor role model, especially in that movie.

Although I haven't seen him in years, I consider Hank Realbird (Crow) a personal friend from Cowboy Poetry Gatherings and brought him to Alpine one year to participate in the Texas gathering that I was directing at the time. As a cowboy journalist, I got to know, photographed, and interviewed several more Indian cowboys and ranchers. I attended a small branding at the Duck Valley Reservation in Nevada. During a brief interview one night in Nevada, Mike Thomas, a Shoshone/Paiute buckaroo, maybe explained best my script's underlying theme—the need for a purpose. He said, "See, all the rest of these reservations, they got a lot of mines and they go to work in the mines or the highway department or something. Around here, all there is is just cows. Either you be a cowboy or you be a drunk or a bookkeeper and type eighty words a minute, big deal."

I've always been fascinated by the idea of a Zen "practice"—or at least my flawed understanding of what that means. To me finding a purpose is finding a practice. It doesn't have to be fancy. Evidently people can spend a lifetime trying to "master" making and serving tea or raking sand. My practice is writing—something I will never "master" but the journey gets more and more interesting. I've known people who felt that way about their jobs, crafts, hobbies, or recreation. Since horsemanship and ranching are skills that can never be finished or mastered, they make good choices for a life practice. Finding a purpose and trying to master it seems to keep some people from developing or with curing addictions—although, I suppose a good practice is just a positive form of addiction.

I also interviewed Jeff Gray, a Miniconjou Cheyenne River Sioux who was maybe the most highly skilled buckaroo I ever met. One of my best photographs is of Jeff moving one hundred loose horses across country. That photograph appears on the cover of this book and inspired the title. The horses belonged to the o6 Ranch where Jeff was working at the time. He wasn't trying to buy a wife with them, but the way he handled them would have convinced any horseman of his worth as a prospective son-in-law. Grandfather, Wolf, Tom, and Eagle all share some of Jeff's personality traits. For another article, I watched, contacted, and wrote about a San Carlos Apache lawyer, Steve Titla, who was trying to help Apache, Hispanic, and white ranchers stop wolf reintroduction on reservation land in Arizona. Titla and every

Indian cowboy or rancher I talked to inspired my characters' attitudes toward wolves.

Following a divorce, for a while I ran my own small herd of cattle on leased grass, getting started much like my characters describe. I could never make a living at it, so I began college teaching. To keep that job, I needed a PhD. So I sold my cattle and headed to the University of Nevada, Reno. Although I didn't gamble, I did often eat in Reno casinos, especially John Ascuaga's Nugget. Casinos keep their gamblers happy with great but low-priced food that even a poor college student or cowboy could afford. I never knew when Ascuaga himself might saunter by and sit down for a quick visit. He made the Nugget feel like a home away from home. We graduate students and professors had many deep discussions about the pros and cons of gambling during my two years in Nevada. UNR offered classes in both gaming management and treating gambling addictions. Those experiences inspired the casino scenes.

For many years I also wrote for RANGE magazine, a publication that attempted to find common ground between environmentalists and ranchers. Several of my articles compared bison and cattle: breeding, grazing, diseases, facilities, and history. My inspiration for Wolf's naïve questions about fire and his gradual disenchantment with bison, as well as Grandfather's answers and Tom's partnership proposal comes from research done for that magazine, as well as from interviews with Indian ranchers who shared fences with bison.

I've personally fought lots of grass fires (11 in one year on the 06 Ranch where I lived) and have friends who are professional grass firefighters, including one local female who ran a crew of hotshots. Her crew lived in Northern Mexico. They were dropped into rough country all over the west with her as their boss and translator. I've researched controlled burning, and my granddaughter has done some of it. I have been to the Paraguayan Chaco and the town of Filadelfia, founded by Mennonites, where I was told about Guarani Indians living off the frugal Mennonites' dump. Although I couldn't speak their language, I photographed native Guarani cowboys drinking traditional mate from a cow's horn mug, saddling horses, and working cattle in log corrals.

I have a rancher friend in northern California who bought old Indian cars (Pierce Arrows), and learned to restore them. They are now worth a fortune. Another 30-year friend was maybe the best tracker, lion hunter, and wolf trapper ever known, Roy McBride, part Cherokee. During the last half of his life he practiced his tracking and "dark magic" (scents and 1080 poison) for the benefit of the animals he spent the first half of his life almost eradicating. I often typed his reports and science papers. Those friends inspired my details about tracking and old cars.

I learned to weave mohair saddle cinches on a board for extra cash and made jewelry for horses out of my grandmother's silver spoons. Living on the edge of poverty in the cowboy world, I developed deep respect for recycling and making beauty out of junk. I still sleep in an old iron bed that I found in a dump and restored 50 years ago. So the inspiration for the kids' Crow Fair "art" comes from those experiences.

I believe real cowboys and ranchers from all races and creeds have suffered cultural appropriation. So, yes, I'm a white girl writing a script with Indian characters, but I'm not sure anyone else of any tribe or race could have written **THIS** script.

Fire Water

EXT. DRIVE-IN MOVIE, NIGHT

In black and white, sepia-toned to indicate the past, set in 1970-80s with four young Indians (two boys, two girls, all dressed like cowboys) on a double date at a drive-in movie. They are sitting on top of the cab of their 1950/60ish pickup, watching "Stay Away, Joe" kissing and laughing. Music is Elvis singing first stanza of "Stay Away, Joe," which gradually fades to drumming. The teens are sharing gallon jugs of sweet red wine (Ripple?) and leave the movie very drunk. Scene ends with a terrible car accident. Upside-down pickup with totally smashed cab, wheels spinning. The bottle of wine on its side near one of the wheels symbolically drips its red contents onto the ground where it is absorbed, like blood. Drum beats begin to sound like heart beats, then follow the rhythm of the drips, then stop, symbolizing no survivors.

EXT. GRAVE SITE, SUNDOWN

Music of a single flute. In sepia-toned black and white, still indicating the past, at sundown a young adult man (the father of one victim) holds his saddled horse by one rein and his hat in his other hand while he kneels on one knee at a gravesite.

The grave is marked with a cross made of welded together horseshoes. The sun is setting, his head bowed in defeat.

EXT. GRAVE SITE, SUNDOWN

In color, sundown at the same recognizable grave, an old man, Grandfather, is dressed like a modern rancher/ cowboy, well groomed, short hair, strong Indian facial features. He holds a cowboy hat with the same hat crease and kneeling at the same grave, strikes the same despondent pose. He's an older version of the young father. A soldier's dog tags now also hang from the cross and catch the sun. After a silent prayer, the old man stands, turns, and begins talking to a white female Reporter, blonde hair in ponytail.

GRANDFATHER I had three sons, no daughters. At twenty-two my eldest son drove away from a drive-in movie very drunk. Killed himself and three friends. I'm not sure if this gravesite is where our story ends, begins, or stays stuck.

REPORTER *(holding a notebook and pen, pulling a small tape recorder out of her pocket)* I'm so sorry. Do you mind if I record this?

GRANDFATHER This is not for publication. In my culture, a story should provide guidance. This one does not.

REPORTER I understand. *(puts away recorder and notebook)*

GRANDFATHER It was his first date with a new girlfriend. She left behind a

daughter from a previous relationship.
The other couple also left a daughter.
They had been watching "Stay Away, Joe,"
a movie starring Elvis Presley who played
a drunken, womanizing, crazy thief of an
Indian. The girls all loved Elvis and our
young men wanted desperately to impress
those girls.

REPORTER I remember that movie
and the book, but I always heard that
Native people loved it and thought it was
hilarious.

GRANDFATHER I'm sure you have also
heard that Native people love wolves. But
the Cheyenne, Lakota, Arapaho, all tribes
that were part of the great Indian horse
culture didn't love wolves because wolves
crippled and killed our horses. Those who
lost children to drinking didn't love that
movie either. Elvis inspired behavior that
crippled and killed our children.

REPORTER I see.

GRANDFATHER My surviving son,
Clint, does not drink, and neither does
his wife. The dog tags belong to my
youngest son who was killed in Iraq. His
body was never recovered, so this became
his grave too. I raised his only child, Tom,
and he does not drink.

REPORTER That's admirable.

GRANDFATHER We are serious
ranchers, not clowns like Elvis.

*In sepia, clips of Elvis chasing cattle in a
convertible from the movie.*

GRANDFATHER We still struggle against
stereotypes implanted by movies. We are
not the larger-than-life gods of history
who lived in harmony with nature and
each other. But we are not thieves or
savages either. We are simply people with
human flaws and problems, just like you.

INT./EXT. BIA OFFICE, DAY

*Fly over a small reservation town showing
stark contrast between rez poverty and
the glitzy BIA office. Inside, two men
study a large map of the reservation. Tom
Greyhorse, 25ish, is dressed like a modern
rancher, clean shaven, short hair, not
outstandingly handsome, maybe acne scars.
His Uncle Clint, 50ish, is overweight,
jovial, and also dressed like a modern
rancher.*

TOM It makes me sad, Uncle Clint, to
see so many blue squares representing
reservation land now owned by non-
Indians.

UNCLE Every reservation map looks
like this today, Tom, or worse. The last
I heard over ninety percent of the Crow
Reservation is now owned by non-
Indians. We Cheyenne have hung on to,
or bought back, more land than most
tribes.

*Close-up of the map with colored blocks
indicating ownership As they talk, the
camera closes in on particular squares.*

TOM I know it has something to do
with the 1920 Allotment Act, but I never
completely understood.

UNCLE When no one owns the land,
everyone fights over it and no one takes
care of it. So the US government decided
to <u>help</u> us.

TOM *(groaning)* Yeah, "We're from the
government. We're here to help."

UNCLE *(laughs)* Yes. They divided
reservations into tribal owned *(points*

to white squares) and individual owned *(points to yellow squares)* allotments. Individual Indians were usually awarded 1000 acres of dry range land or 40 acres of farm land.

TOM Some got more than others?

UNCLE Yes, Tom. It was similar to homesteading. Farm land *(points to some)* or land located near water *(points)* was worth more than dry grazing land *(points)*.

Camera zooms back out to show them standing at the map.

UNCLE The idea was to be *(air quotes)* "fair." As usual, it was a disaster, and maybe even intentional.

TOM What do you mean?

UNCLE Individual owners could sell their allotments to the highest bidder.

TOM And the highest bidders were always white.

UNCLE Unfortunately, yes, or from more wealthy tribes. Those who sold, quickly bought new pickups *(a short scene of pickups lined up along the street)* or drank it up and were right back where they started, fighting and complaining. Gradually the tribe owned less and less of the reservation.

TOM And once that deeded land was gone, those who sold had nothing to mortgage and no way to borrow from a bank.

UNCLE Right. Those who did not sell are still ranching today. Some inherited ranches built by their grandfathers and

fathers, like me. Others, like you, built their own ranches piece by piece by leasing grass from the tribe.

TOM If you get single-minded enough, you can still do it.

UNCLE I admire you, Tom, but I couldn't have done it the way you have, not with a wife and three kids.

TOM Few people want to live frugally.

UNCLE In bad drouths or hard winters, ranchers sometimes had to give away their calves to save their cows.

TOM I know one Crow rancher who started out with three of those orphaned calves, raised them on a milk cow, and owned a nice ranch when he died.

UNCLE Today our tribe raises money from grass leases like yours so that when private land comes up for sale, the tribe can buy it back. We are gradually regaining some of that lost land, the blue squares.

Return to a close-up of the map as he points out the blue squares.

TOM The old Yellowtail lease that joins my current lease is coming up for renewal.

Tom points out the property he wants on the map.

TOM So, Uncle Clint, I want to bid on it. I want to expand from 500 to 1000 cows.

UNCLE Can you handle that many?

TOM I plan to train and hire our kids to help me. They need to learn how to work.

They walk outside the building and lean on the sides of Tom's older-model pickup bed, one on each side, to continue talking.

UNCLE You are kin to half the members on our tribal livestock board, and most of them support you, Tom.

TOM Except those who still blame our family for that fatal car wreck.

UNCLE You are the only one who remembers and can't forgive us. Hundreds of wrecks just like it have happened since. Anyway, as you know we give first preference on grass leases to Cheyenne who want to ranch but don't already have a lease. Since you do, you'll have to wait until the second round.

TOM I know.

UNCLE But I don't know of any Cheyenne who can raise enough money to pay the lease <u>and</u> buy livestock, so you will still have a good chance.

TOM I know. But, white or Crow ranchers will also be circling that lease like buzzards.

UNCLE Some Cheyenne might even accept a bribe to front for one of them.

TOM You serve on that livestock board, Uncle Clint, so are you with me?

UNCLE Of course, Tom. But we all serve at the whim of the tribe, so it gets political fast. If the tribe smells the possibility for a higher bid, they will be slashing at the heels of the livestock board like a pack of wolves.

Tom begins to walk toward the driver's door of his pickup, opens it and sits in the driver's seat. They continue talking through his open window.

TOM My hope is that no new Cheyenne comes forward and no one cheats. I hope to sign before open bidding on the third round. Once white or Crow ranchers are allowed to bid against me, I will lose.

UNCLE Do you have enough money?

TOM Of course not, I'm a rancher. I never have enough money. But the bank does. I've never even been late on a payment.

UNCLE That won't matter to those white bankers.

TOM Are you saying they're racists? The loan officer I deal with is black.

UNCLE Because of that damn Elvis movie, money lenders think Indians are impossible to collect from.

TOM No, Uncle Clint, they don't loan money to us because of jurisdiction, not race. If an Indian decides not to pay back a loan, there's not much the bank can do.

UNCLE You'll see.

TOM But they trust <u>me</u>.

UNCLE They might trust you to pay back a loan to buy a horse or even a pickup because they can repossess those.

TOM I have never had anything repossessed. I've built good credit.

UNCLE When you ask for enough to go from five-hundred-cows to a thousand, they won't risk that much money on an Indian.

TOM My father was killed in Iraq fighting for this country. I will get the money.

Tom starts his pickup and drives away. Uncle Clint shouts after him.

UNCLE You'll see.

EXT/INT. BANK, DAY

Fly over to contrast rez poverty with the glitzy bank building.

Show small town reservation scenes, people sitting, walking, riding horseback or driving pickups. Tom is sitting in his pickup outside the bank watching people enter and leave, trying to muster his courage. He sees a white man enter with a bouquet of flowers.

INT. BANK. DAY

Tart Wilson, 35ish, white, wears a "used car salesman" suit and tie, overly charming businessman-type. Tart hands the flowers to Joy Begay, 25ish, pretty, slightly overweight, secretary-type. Joy is soft-spoken, shy, wears her hair in a traditional Navajo bun and wears a few pieces of Navajo jewelry. She sits behind a typical bank assistant's desk.

TART Good morning, Princess Joy. These should brighten up your day.

He sits uninvited, and Joy shows a little irritation.

JOY Thank you, Tart. You are always so thoughtful, but please don't call me a princess.

TART *(ignoring her)* I will leave if a customer walks in. Let's talk.

JOY I need to keep working.

TART How is your mother?

JOY Fine.

TART She made a very wise decision. This is no place for women.

JOY The bank?

TART The reservation. You should follow her example and move to Billings.

Tom comes in and approaches Joy's desk with his hat in hand, notices the flowers, frowns, and waits patiently at a respectful distance. Joy sees Tom and tries to get rid of Tart again.

JOY I have a customer, so you must go.

TART *(seeing Tom)* He probably just needs to cover a bounced check. He can wait. I'll pick you up at six for dinner. Oh, and wear that little black dress I like so well. It makes you look slimmer.

JOY *(more irritated)* Fine, but I must get back to work. I don't want to lose my job.

TART They won't fire a beautiful Indian girl like you.

Joy half-heartedly smiles at the condescending compliment. Tart finally rises and walks past Tom without looking at him. Tom walks up to Joy's desk, looks at the flowers, and then at her. Tom is <u>not</u> smiling.

TOM Good morning, Ms. Begay. I'm here to see the loan officer.

JOY He's expecting you, Mr. Greyhorse. Follow me.

Joy picks up a folder off her desk, walks into an adjoining office, and hands the folder to the Banker, an African-American man wearing a nice business suit, sitting behind a big desk. While the banker stands to shake hands with Tom, Joy walks back out and closes the door behind her. A few moments later, she's on the phone when Tom walks out, jaw set, angry, does not look at her, and strides out the door. Joy hangs up the phone and the banker comes out of his office to hand the folder back to her.

BANKER Sometimes I hate my job. If I had enough of my own money, I'd loan it to that man. Nobody is more hard working and trustworthy.

JOY But the bank has loaned Mr. Greyhorse money several times in the past? Why not now?

BANKER Not this much, Joy. My hands are tied by jurisdiction. I hope God forgives our government because they know not what they do. The more they try to help, the more they hurt good men like that one.

JOY What do you mean?

BANKER Off the reservation, I could loan the sorriest human twice what that man needs. On the reservation, if he defaults on the loan, the bank would have to fight through tribal court, state court, and federal court—and probably lose. Over protection has been a terrible burden for Indian businesses and ranchers.

JOY I see.

BANKER The tribe owns the land, so Tom can't use it as collateral. All he has to guarantee the loan is his already mortgaged cattle and his reputation, which is bullet proof, but our bank directors can't approve a loan that big on anyone's signature, not even his. I had to say no.

JOY I see.

EXT. ON A TROUT STREAM, DAY

Tom is fishing. Uncle Clint drives up in his older model pickup and parks near Tom's pickup.

UNCLE The bank turned you down, didn't they?

TOM Yes, Uncle Clint, they turned me down. That's why I'm fishing.

UNCLE I told you they're racists.

TOM The banker is not a racist, but his Indian assistant might be.

UNCLE How so?

TOM She's dating a white man.

UNCLE How can she be a racist if she loves someone from another race?

TOM Maybe she doesn't like her own race.

UNCLE Or maybe nobody from her own race has had the courage to ask her out.

TOM Me?

UNCLE *(shakes his head at Tom's density)* So what are you gonna do?

TOM I don't know.

UNCLE What about this year's calves?

TOM Selling my steer calves will pay my current lease and my winter feed bill with about twenty bucks left over for next year's groceries and gasoline. I planned to keep my heifers to stock the new lease.

If I sell them all, they'll only bring about half of what I need.

UNCLE You could buy cows and the bank would mortgage them, but that still wouldn't pay for the lease.

TOM Right.

UNCLE If you put all the energy you burn trying to ranch into a real business, you'd be a rich man.

TOM Ranching is a real business, just not usually a profitable one, as you know. Maybe it's just in our blood to chase cows on horseback. I'd die if imprisoned in an office. The Cheyenne have always been horse-loving people.

UNCLE But those horses don't love you back.

TOM Sure they do. Mine do.

UNCLE Right. See how much they love you if you run out of oats. You're just like the BIA to them.

TOM *(laughs)* Hadn't thought about it that way. And my cows are even worse. At least the horses have to do a little work for their oats.

UNCLE Your cows don't even know you exist.

TOM They don't know we plan to eat their children either. Maybe gratitude is overrated?

EXT. WOLF'S TEEPEE, DAY

Wolf Taylor: handsome, long straight hair, traditionalist, looks very Indian, no shirt. He is sitting on the ground in front of his traditional-style green canvas teepee. He is talking to the same white female reporter who was interviewing Tom's Grandfather. A small campfire burns between them. As they talk, Wolf is weaving a mohair saddle cinch on a board that he holds on his lap. Joe Champlain, a realistic alcoholic (fat, dirty, ugly, stinky and dressed similar to Elvis in "Stay Away, Joe,) stumbles up, drunk and speaks to the white reporter.

JOE *(Slurring)* Hey, pretty lady, would you like to join me later in the sweat lodge?

REPORTER No. *(Joe shrugs and stumbles off)*

WOLF I assume that you are not interested in Indian men?

REPORTER Not that one. But I have been—in the past—a couple of times.

WOLF But it didn't work out?

As they tell their stories in voice-over, flash back to show the action in sepia to indicate past.

REPORTER No. The first time was just a crush. I was 17 and he never knew I existed. I had a half-Apache friend who taught me to barrel race. I wore my then dark brown hair in two long braids, so she helped me pass as Apache to enter an All-Indian rodeo at San Carlos and ride her horse.

Historic Indian rodeo scenes in sepia.

WOLF And you had to pay her to ride her horse.

REPORTER *(laughs)* Of course. I'm sure nobody was fooled. They all knew I wouldn't win any of their money, but they definitely got some of mine.

WOLF *(laughs)* Right. No white girl is going to beat an Apache in a horse race.

REPORTER My crush was on Sonny Jim. I saw him crawl into a chute with an upset bull and calm it right down. He retrained someone's box-fighting bulldoggin' horse in one run.

WOLF I heard of him but never met him. He was sort of a legend. Lots of women had a crush on him, especially white women. And the second time?

REPORTER The second time was more real, and we knew each other.

WOLF So what happened?

REPORTER He was perfect when sober but he drank at the time, sort of like that guy *(nods toward the direction Joe went).* Since I grew up in Arizona, I had seen the streets of Flagstaff on a Saturday night. I knew I couldn't live like that. I had also seen the results of a lot of domestic violence—always caused by drinking.

WOLF Like what?

REPORTER I started college at Eastern Arizona Junior College. I was the only white girl in my dorm, mostly Apache and Navajo. Many of them had joined the Mormon church and so didn't drink at all. They'd also seen what drinking had done to their parents. But if they did get drunk, it got ugly.

WOLF For example?

Scenes of the following fight in sepia with voice over.

REPORTER Maybe the worst was one time when I was working my shift in the student recreation center. One of the

married—and pregnant—Apache girls came running in for help. She was beat up, bleeding, clothes torn, patches of hair jerked out. I pointed to the phone, told her to call the sheriff, tell him to hurry, and I'd try to stop her husband.

WOLF That doesn't sound very smart.

REPORTER Right. I ran into the street where he was swaying, trying to stay on his feet, shirt off, bloody fingernail scratches across his chest. He held a rock in each hand, hissing through his teeth. I was terrified, but when I told him to stop, he stopped. We stood there facing each other. He kept threatening to kill me, but never took another step.

WOLF You were lucky.

REPORTER After what seemed like hours, but probably only 15 minutes, the sheriff screeched up in his car, scattering gravel and jumped out yelling at <u>me</u>: "Don't you ever pull a crazy stunt like this again!" Then he calmly turned around to cuff the husband and haul him to jail. The sheriff never said a word to either the husband or the wife.

WOLF The sheriff was probably more concerned about the safety of a white woman than a couple of drunk Apaches.

REPORTER She was beautiful, her husband very handsome and on our rodeo team. Both were good students. I often wondered what happened to them and if the baby survived the beating.

Wolf adds a stick of wood to his small fire to keep it burning.

WOLF Sadly, abuse does happen, especially when passion gets mixed with alcohol.

REPORTER Too many writers write about the violence and the drinking. So I'm looking for better stories. But I seem to be searching for answers that don't exist.

WOLF Not everyone behaves that way. So how did your second love story end?

REPORTER He somehow got himself sober. But I kept watching and waiting for a relapse. By the time enough years had passed to convince me he would stay sober, my chance had passed. He'd found another girl.

WOLF Did he know how you felt?

REPORTER Nope. *(pause)* But I'm supposed to be the reporter here. What's <u>your</u> story?

WOLF Off the record?

REPORTER *(frustrated)* As you wish. That seems to be all I'm getting from anyone.

WOLF My grandmother was killed in a one-car rollover. Drunk driver, her date. She left a baby daughter, my mother.

REPORTER I think I've heard this story?

WOLF It's common. My mother was then raised by two alcoholic aunts, and none of them ever had much luck with love. Mother married several times. When she and my father divorced, Dad raised me and my older brother. My brother started drinking very young. When his drinking killed him in a car wreck at 17, my dad started drinking. Two years ago, Dad stood over my brother's grave, put a pistol to his head, and pulled the trigger. So I stay away from alcohol and love.

REPORTER Wow. I'm so sorry.

Wolf shrugs, gets up and grabs a metal one-pound coffee can with a home-made twisted wire handle that's been sitting beside the small fire and walks to the nearby creek to dip it full of water. Returns, puts another stick of wood on the fire, and sets the water can on the fire to boil.

WOLF I have a half-sister from a different father who lives here on the reservation, but we live in two different worlds. She has an office job at the bank and you see how I live. She stays in touch with our mother who now lives in an apartment in Billings. I seldom see my sister and haven't seen my mother since she divorced my dad.

REPORTER You have such an interesting lifestyle, but I'm searching for happier stories. I think we've heard too many of the sad ones. I want my writing to give your people hope.

WOLF No offense, but my people need to give ourselves hope, find our own answers, and write our own stories. Like your government, your people have already helped my people to death.

REPORTER I understand. Thank you for your time.

We watch the reporter drive away, turn toward the main highway and off the reservation.

INT. CASINO COFFEESHOP, DAY

Tom is ordering breakfast, sitting in a booth alone. We see and hear all the signs and sounds of an active casino. Tychee, 35ish, beautiful, long straight black hair, looks Apache, sophisticated, city Indian, casino boss, dressed like a New York businesswoman but wearing a few tasteful pieces of Indian jewelry.

TYCHEE Hello, Tom, may I join you?

TOM Hello, Tychee. I guess you can sit anywhere you want since you are the boss lady here. Are you sure you want to sit with someone from the family who killed your parents?

TYCHEE *(sitting)* We all might forget that story if you didn't carry such a burden of guilt and keep reminding us. I have a business proposition for you.

TOM I'm just here for breakfast.

TYCHEE You really don't like this casino, do you?

TOM I don't like gambling.

As they talk insert historic scenes of Indians gambling and gaming.

TYCHEE But gambling is part of our heritage. Our people have always loved games: horse racing, stick games, hoop games, hand games, lacrosse, . . .

Insert a black and white, sepia clip from "Stay Away, Joe" of Elvis shooting craps and betting on horse racing.

TOM *(interrupting)* We had two kinds of games: games of skill and games of luck. The games of skill increased physical fitness, dexterity, and taught perseverance and hard work. The games of luck taught nothing. Our people sit and wait for good luck and blame all their problems on bad luck.

TYCHEE Yes. Even this casino gets too much credit and too much blame. But one thing we can provide is capital, and I've heard you can't get that from the bank.

TOM How do you know so much about my business?

TYCHEE You are surrounded by people who either love you or hate you. Both come here after easy money and gossip.

TOM I'm not here for either, just breakfast, and I will pay for that.

A server arrives with Tom's food.

TYCHEE Poverty is the root cause of our people's trouble.

Tom prepares his food to his own liking as they talk.

TOM No, addiction is. Someone may have convinced you of the importance of wealth in college, but this casino simply trades one addiction for another. Gambling is just as addictive as alcohol or drugs, sex, sugar, digital games, thrill seeking, even *(he uses air quotes)* "helping" others can become addictive. There's an endless list of what people can become addicted to if they get a little shot of happy juice from it. The more sips you take, the more you want. Casinos have made a science out of just how often to dole out drinks. Carpet patterns, ringing bells, even lack of windows and clocks— all play into your false sense of timeless happiness.

TYCHEE *(aloof)* We provide counseling for those who become addicts.

TOM Sure you do. It eases your conscience, just like welfare eases the white conscience, but it doesn't help one single person.

TYCHEE Yes it does. We help hundreds, maybe thousands. This casino provides jobs to hundreds of our people. We provide scholarships, elder care, and police. We are building new reservation schools, a hospital, a modern fire hall. Our tribe needs money and as the manager, I can provide it. It is the most lucrative business we have ever found. You ranchers can hardly pay your winter feed bill. Can you build a school?

As Tom talks show scenes of buffalo skinning, an Indian kid handing meat to his mom, a scene at an Indian hospital.

TOM Maybe. I'm building a log barn right now where I plan to teach kids the skills needed for ranch jobs. Idleness and boredom are causing their troubles, not poverty. The federal government, tribe, and casino provide everything, so there's no accountability, no incentive, no pride. Everyone needs a purpose. Our kids need a purpose. Some friends and I took a few kids to learn to harvest and skin bison at Yellowstone Park. They were so proud to bring meat back to their families. You should have seen their faces.

TYCHEE I heard one of the adult men came down with Undulant fever after skinning a bison that was carrying brucellosis.

TOM He may still recover—how many lives has this casino ruined?

TYCHEE Not as many as we've saved.

TOM Who does your counting? The same person who figures the gambling odds?

TYCHEE Ranching is a form of gambling too, you know.

TOM I'm probably addicted to hard work and improving my cowboy skills. The key is to be careful what you become addicted to, and I'd rather gamble on Nature.

TYCHEE Do you want the capital I'm offering or not?

TOM I started my ranching business with nothing but a frying pan. I don't need your free money. Maybe it's safe now, but you know as well as I do that this casino will attract the Mafia, prostitution, all kinds of shit—if it hasn't already.

TYCHEE I think this conversation is over.

As she rises and walks away, Tom returns to his meal.

TOM Have a nice morning, Tychee, or whatever time it might be in here.

EXT. WOLF'S TEEPEE, DAY

Wolf is squatting on his heels near a fire, eating from a small cast-iron frying pan. A metal can with wire handle sits on the side of the fire, keeping water hot. Tychee walks up wearing a very urban, sophisticated black pin-striped suit with cropped pants, silk blouse, black stiletto heels, and Indian jewelry.

TYCHEE Good morning, Wolf. May I join you?

He pours a little loose tea into a tin cup and adds hot water, handing it to her.

WOLF I just finished breakfast, but I can offer you some wild rose hip tea and a willow backrest.

She slips off her high heels, lowers herself cross legged, settles comfortably against the backrest, and sips.

TYCHEE Perfect. Thank you. This is very good.

WOLF Thank you. But you didn't come here to drink tea with me.

He picks up a saddle cinch he's been weaving, now almost finished; he's adding a colorful design and cattle brand.

TYCHEE I may have an opportunity for you.

WOLF I'm listening.

TYCHEE That's a very nice saddle cinch, by the way, but I have never seen you ride with a saddle?

WOLF I prefer the old way—bareback. I make these to sell to cowboys.

TYCHEE I know you object to cattle grazing, want to preserve rather than exploit nature, and want to start a school to teach the old ways to our youth.

WOLF Sounds like you have done some homework on me.

TYCHEE Easy homework. Just a quick look at you and your lifestyle gives away most of it. The rest was a guess mixed with gossip.

WOLF I'm still listening.

TYCHEE I hope you might agree that the casino is not so different from our traditional games and gambling. But a growing faction thinks we are a bad influence and want the casinos shut down. I'm here to expand our public relations outreach.

WOLF I'm still listening.

TYCHEE The old Yellowtail Ranch lease is up for renewal and no Cheyenne has been able to raise enough money. I don't want to see it fall into the hands of a white rancher or another tribe.

WOLF I'm still listening.

TYCHEE The casino would like to offer you financing. You can change the ranch into a cattle-free nature preserve. Are you interested?

WOLF Very.

He sets aside his weaving and concentrates on her.

TYCHEE As you know, I sometimes hide troubled youth at the casino. I can provide strong muscles to help you.

WOLF Sounds good. We've been partners before. I also want to build a summer school for Indian youth.

TYCHEE We can finance that too, and I would like to stay personally involved with it and teach jewelry making. I have traditional skills in quills, beads, feathers, teeth, and shells. Will you accept me?

WOLF Sure. Your jewelry has always shown me that you still have an Indian heart even though your clothes come from the city.

TYCHEE To provide money for worthwhile projects like this, I must walk between two worlds. But you are right, my heart has not changed. Thank you for seeing beneath the pinstripes.

He interprets her words as sexual innuendo and decides to test it.

WOLF Would you like to join me in the sweat lodge sometime?

TYCHEE *(not backing down)* I would like that very much.

They look at each other for a beat. Maybe a spark? Wolf blinks first (or takes control)?

WOLF Good. Someday I might invite you.

EXT. BANK OF A TROUT STREAM, EVENING

Tom is dry-fly fishing, wading in the cold water wearing old tennis shoes that have replaced his boots. No fancy equipment but a decent fly rod that he uses expertly, a hand net hangs from a belt loop.

UNCLE Bad news, Tom. Today Wolf Taylor was granted the old Yellowtail lease you wanted.

TOM I heard. That's why I'm fishing. At least the grass will stay in Cheyenne hands. And maybe losing that lease is best for now.

UNCLE How best?

TOM The bank has asked me to serve as a native voice on their board of directors. I don't know how much of my time that will take.

UNCLE Interesting. Are you just a token Indian or can you make a real difference?

TOM I'm hopeful. Where did Wolf get the money?

UNCLE Casino.

TOM I see. Wolf is no rancher, what does he plan to do with the grass?

UNCLE Nothing. He plans to make it a nature preserve, no cattle, just as he has always wanted. He also plans to build a summer school to teach traditional skills to kids.

Tom catches a nice trophy-sized trout, dips and releases it.

TOM That solves another problem. I probably won't have time to start my cowboy school for a while. So it all sounds good, except for the ungrazed grass.

UNCLE Grass looks beautiful waving in the wind—until lightning strikes. Fire is good unless there is too much fuel.

TOM Then it takes everything: trees, buildings, fences, wild and domestic animals, birds, scenery, even seeds in the soil if hot enough.

UNCLE Education is expensive. Especially <u>real</u> education and I think Wolf is about to begin school.

TOM Yes. And since we share a fence line, I will unfortunately be forced to pay for some of his lessons.

As they walk back to their pickups, they run into Joe Champlain, drunk, trying to fish. Joe has his line tangled up in a bush. He's trying to untangle it with not much success. Tom and Uncle watch him for a minute, then look at each other and shake their heads.

UNCLE That guy is going to drink himself to death.

TOM If he doesn't drown first or jerk a hook in his eye. I'm sure he left all my gates open getting here. I better back track him and close them, although I suppose he will just leave them all open again on his way back to town.

UNCLE We Native ranchers have the same trouble with our fellow tribe members that white ranchers have with tourists on their federal BLM and Forest Service leases.

TOM Hunting, fishing, and camping near water so our livestock can't drink.

UNCLE Gates left open, trash strewn around.

TOM And people who live 3,000 miles away think we all need their help. They can't solve their own problems, but they think they can solve ours.

UNCLE Non-ranching Cheyenne complain that ranchers place too many restrictions on them even though our deeded land doesn't belong to the tribe.

TOM Yes, water always belongs to someone.

UNCLE And we own our hay fields.

TOM Just like tourists on federal land, non-ranching Indians don't know when they are on private or reservation property. Our people practice the same politics, jealousy, dishonesty, and manipulation as white people. Nobody has answers.

UNCLE Including me. I can't even get along with my wife, who I love dearly.

TOM *(laughs)* So, I assume you are moving back in with me and Grandfather <u>again</u>?

UNCLE If you'll have me.

TOM Of course. Home is where you go when no one else will put up with you. Just like the reservation.

INT. CASINO RESTAURANT, DAY

Tychee is sitting in a booth in the casino restaurant waiting for someone. Joy walks up to her.

JOY You wanted to see me?

TYCHEE Yes. I've always considered you a little sister because of our shared tragedy. Sit.

JOY *(Sitting)* You mean the car wreck that killed your parents and my grandmother?

TYCHEE Yes. Your mother grew up an orphan, just like me. She was a good woman who always chose bad men. I don't want to see you make the same mistakes.

JOY How do you know about my dating life?

TYCHEE The reservation whispers and this casino has eyes and ears. I see and hear too much.

JOY Are you saying that Tart Wilson is a bad man?

TYCHEE I'm saying he follows a pattern. He picks gentle women, like you, then showers them with bouquets, nice dinners and sweet talk. He monopolizes their time while their friends drift away. His sweet talk will gradually change to small criticisms, requests for you to dress a certain way, lose weight, and suggestions for your further improvement.

JOY I have noticed some of those things already. He knows I was an unwed teen mother and has voiced his disapproval. He also wonders what I did to cause my son to run away.

TCHEE *(exasperated)* For the ten-thousandth time, Joy, you did <u>nothing</u> wrong. I'm sure your son thought he was keeping you from finding love. Kids tend to blame themselves when they sense a parent's unhappiness.

JOY But I wasn't unhappy, not until he ran away.

TYCHEE He was almost grown. I think he also wanted to find a male role model. But I've said all this many times before, so back to Tart. And stop trying to change the subject. Gradually he will convince you that no one else would want you and that you are lucky to have him.

JOY I don't need a man. I can take care of myself.

TYCHEE I know you can. I'm just warning you how abuse begins. It isn't always physical, sometimes mental abuse is worse and you will begin to believe you deserve less.

JOY How did you get so wise?

TYCHEE Casinos operate on psychology.

JOY Lately I have been feeling uncomfortable around him.

TYCHEE Good. Keep your eyes open and follow your instincts. Tart has gone through a dozen women, leaving them crying, convinced they were not good enough.

JOY So what do you suggest?

TYCHEE Back off. You will see his true colors. As he gets more aggressive, stay strong. Get rid of him and then pick your own man. Don't wait for someone to pick you.

JOY How would I know who to pick?

TYCHEE You will know.

JOY But you are also still single?

TYCHEE *(laughing)* I didn't say it would be easy or guarantee that if you pick one he will pick you back. But living single is better than trying to create a good life with a bad man.

JOY Seriously, what should I look for?

TYCHEE Someone who admires you and what you do, encourages you, and helps you chase your dreams. Someone who gives you wings instead of clips them.

JOY You're right. I seldom look for that.

TYCHEE In the white culture, fathers paid men to take daughters off their hands before they became old maids. When our men wanted wives, they risked life and limb to steal enough horses to impress our fathers. You are worth 100 horses, Joy. Never forget that.

JOY *(laughs)* Thank you, Sister. Now I have some advice for you. Get out of this casino before it's too late.

TYCHEE *(nods sadly)* It may already be too late for me.

EXT. WOLF'S SCHOOL SITE, DAY

Stacked peeled logs, two logs high, the beginning of Wolf's log school house, appear in the back ground. Wolf is very sweaty, no shirt, busy peeling bark off a log. Joe Champlain is asleep in the shade of the two stacked logs. A young teenaged Indian boy is helping Wolf by picking up the bark. He wears baggy basketball shorts, old high topped athletic shoes with no socks, and a black t-shirt with the sleeves cut off. His long hair is tied in a Navajo-style bun. He slips out of sight just before Grandfather Greyhorse rides horseback into the scene.

GRANDFATHER Good evening, Wolf.

Startled and surprised, Wolf looks quickly around for the boy, but he is gone.

WOLF Good evening, Mr. Greyhorse. You surprised me, and I'm not easily surprised.

GRANDFATHER I heard you hope to teach our old ways to our youth. That's good. I think I am our oldest living Cheyenne. One regret is that my eldest son once caused your family great pain. So I have come to see if I can be of any service to you, to see if you have any questions that perhaps I could answer.

Wolf sits on the log, Grandfather does not dismount. They stay silent for a while. We hear only the wind in the pine tree needles.

WOLF I have had several grass fires lately. How did our people live with fire?

As they talk show authentic historic scenes of Indian life.

GRANDFATHER Fire was a great gift, a great necessity for cooking and warmth in winter. But it was very difficult to control or out run.

WOLF I am discovering that.

GRANDFATHER The taller the grass grew, the more dangerous fire became. Grass fires are more dangerous than forest fires.

WOLF So what did we do?

GRANDFATHER For one thing, we set small fires constantly. We did not just fight wars, sit around and tell stories, or play drums and dance as the movies show. We worked hard managing this land. We cleaned out springs, planted wild rice and willows, raised corn and squash, placed rocks in streams to slow erosion, built dams, irrigated.

WOLF I'm listening.

GRANDFATHER Using the wind, we set fire to the tall dry grass so it would burn in a direction away from our encampments. When grass is burned regularly, fire will crawl helplessly on the ground, around the big trees and leave them unharmed, also keeping down brush. Even children could easily step over those small fires. Old diaries written by white settlers describe our forests as so park-like they could drive their wagons between the trees.

WOLF We can't set fires today because of homes and towns in all directions, and the fires are fierce.

GRANDFATHER To some degree that was true back in the old days as well. If our fires burned a neighboring tribe's village or hunting territory, they went to war with us. So we used another tool along with fire.

WOLF I'm listening.

GRANDFATHER We followed the buffalo, and not just for meat and hides. Their grazing kept the grasses short.

WOLF I will look into grazing so I can set small fires again.

Grandfather has made his point, so he changes the subject by nodding toward the sleeping drunk.

GRANDFATHER Is that Joe Champlain?

WOLF Yes. He comes out here every few days, asking for a job. I've been trying to trade his labor for clothes or groceries because I know he will just buy alcohol if I pay him with money.

GRANDFATHER How does he help you?

As Wolf talks, we see flashbacks of Joe trying to help Wolf but he's too drunk.

WOLF He doesn't. His drinking has made him helpless and worthless. I've tried several things. I can't trust him with an axe or he will cut his toes off. He can't run errands because he will run my pickup into a tree. I can't even have him pick up bark or wood chips because he will drop and scatter them everywhere.

GRANDFATHER I could smell him before I saw him.

WOLF Yes. He doesn't keep himself clean. He has that alcoholic odor. I think he comes here because he is lonely.

GRANDFATHER Perhaps it was a blessing that my son and your grandmother died young. I would not want to see them like this.

WOLF Maybe I allow Joe to hang around to remind me of what I don't ever want to become.

GRANDFATHER We all need a purpose. Maybe this is Joe's purpose, to be a reminder.

WOLF I don't know how to help him.

GRANDFATHER Nor do I. We must respect both fire and firewater. We named them well.

They look sadly at Joe in silence until grandfather rides away.

EXT. OUTSIDE BANK FRONT DOOR, DAY'S END

Joy places a "closed" sign on the bank's front door, locks it, and heads to the parking lot. Tart is waiting near her car.

TART Good evening my beautiful Indian princess.

JOY Please don't call me that.

TART Indian or princess?

JOY Neither, Tart. I have told you several times that I am not interested in seeing you anymore.

TART Sure you are. You're just playing hard to get.

He grabs her arm and pulls her in for a kiss.

JOY Stop it! Let me go! Don't even talk to me.

A board of directors meeting has also just broken up and the directors come out the back door of the bank into the parking lot. Tom hears distress in a woman's voice, his head snaps around to see Joy struggling with Tart. He rushes silently to her aid and places one hand ominously on Tart's shoulder, gripping it hard enough that Tart winces in pain.

TOM You heard the lady. Let her go.

TART This is none of your business, just a lover's quarrel.

The black banker and two other directors (one Hispanic) arrive to stand behind Tom, watching and listening. Tom's hand remains locked on Tart's shoulder.

BANKER Are you OK, Joy?

TOM This gentleman is about to leave.

Tart releases Joy. Embarrassed, she quickly gets in her car and drives away. Tom releases Tart.

BANKER *(sternly to Tart)* I've noticed you in the bank several times, Mr. Wilson, bothering my assistant. She has made it clear that she does not return your interest. It's time to ask you to take your banking business elsewhere or we will file a restraining order.

Tart glares at them, gets in his car and drives away.

Tom and the other board members turn toward their various vehicles.

INT. BANK LOBBY, DAY

Tom removes his hat when he enters the bank and passes Joy's desk on his way to a meeting.

TOM Good morning, Ms. Begay.

JOY Good morning, and thank you for the other night. You turned up in exactly the right place at exactly the right time.

TOM *(laughs)* That is what a cowboy is always supposed to do.

JOY Well, I was very happy to see you, and please call me Joy.

TOM I will call you Joy everywhere except inside this bank. Here I should probably continue to call you Ms. Begay.

JOY As you wish. And one more thing, my boss asked me to invite you to what he calls an "inner circle" dinner party for the board and their wives at his home this Saturday at 7:00. He wants us both to come and to bring dates.

TOM I will come, but alone. I don't have anyone to ask.

JOY I have no one to ask either, so would you . . . *(pause)* . . . would you want to pick me up about 6:30? The dinner begins at 7:00.

TOM *(astounded)* Really? I'd be honored.

JOY Yes, really. And the honor is mine.

They look at each other for a beat.

INT. TOM'S PICKUP, NIGHT

Tom drives up in front of Joy's house to drop her off after the banker's dinner.

TOM That was an interesting evening. Those white people and their wives were very welcoming to what was probably their first time to break bread with native people.

JOY Why do you call them white people? I think my African-American boss and the Garcias would find it quite amusing that you consider them white.

TOM *(laughs)* Old habit, I guess. My grandfather's generation always considered anyone *(uses air quotes)* "white" who was not Native American. White didn't mean a race to them, but a culture, a way to live.

JOY I've also been invited to many of these dinners and have sometimes taken a date.

TOM *(looks at her questioning)* Then their first time to share a meal with a Native man?

JOY *(hesitant, guilty)* Maybe. My dates have always been white, meaning Caucasian.

They both laugh.

JOY My mother was abused by men from different tribes. She was Navajo and thought only Navajo men abused, so she married a Lakota the first time. Her second was white but he abused too. She said men were sometimes gentle when sober, but not when drunk. She never found an exception. My father was Navajo.

TOM Although some tribes supposedly revered their women, historically men from all cultures have not treated women very well.

JOY I have seen that first hand.

TOM Abuse comes in many forms— physical, mental, spiritual—and has not only been practiced by all races, but all genders, sexual preferences, and religions.

Parents sometimes abuse their spouses, especially Indian women.

JOY Yes, I've seen examples.

TOM We must all train ourselves to control anger and resist violence.

JOY Like you did by just placing your hand on Tart's shoulder?

TOM *(laughs)* I guess a traditionalist would say I was counting coup. It was once considered more brave and honorable for Native men to touch an enemy than kill one.

JOY You are representing more than yourself on that bank board.

TOM I know. I did not want those other directors to see me beat that guy into a puddle, which is what I wanted to do.

JOY The way you handled it was much better.

TOM Thank you. *(noticing)* Uh, oh. Looks like you have a flat tire.

JOY Oh, no!

TOM C'mon, *(gets out)* I'll help you change it. I've had lots of practice.

JOY *(getting out)* I can change a tire.

TOM I'm sure you can, but you look very pretty tonight. So let me help.

EXT. JOY'S HOUSE, CONTINUING

Tom walks to the tire, looks at the ground, walks all the way around the car, checking each tire, then walks off a ways and back. He is reading sign. Joy watches and wonders silently what he is doing. When he returns to the flat tire, he looks intently into the distance, then seems to remember that he was about to change a tire and gets to work. Time passes to after the tire is changed.

TOM Your spare should get you to the shop in the morning but your tires are very bald and need replacing.

JOY Oh, gosh. I don't pay close enough attention. I will buy new tires tomorrow. Thank you for telling me.

EXT. TOM'S RANCH PORCH, NIGHT

Tom and grandfather are drinking coffee waiting for daylight.

TOM A curious thing happened last night, Grandfather. As you know, I gave Joy Begay a ride to a bank dinner party and then home.

GRANDFATHER It's called a date.

TOM It was just a ride. A woman like her would never go on a date with me. I'm not in her league.

GRANDFATHER *(displeased)* You are a Greyhorse.

TOM Anyway, when I dropped her off at her house, her car had a flat. Someone had let the air out.

GRANDFATHER Friend or enemy?

TOM I'm not sure. It would seem enemy, but her tires were dangerously bald, so it was almost lucky that she had the flat when she did, that I was there to change it, and to tell her it was time to buy new tires.

GRANDFATHER Ever since your run-in with Tart Wilson, I have been watching your back. I sometimes find tracks that seem to be following you, but not his.

TOM So I either have a harmless shadow or a very patient enemy?

GRANDFATHER Yes, and by the way, since Uncle Clint and his wife seem to have trouble living together, we should build a dog-trot bunkhouse/cookshack.

As grandfather explains the dog-trot, from his shirt pocket he retrieves his drawing for the new building and shows Tom.

GRANDFATHER At one end, we could have a bunk-room for a couple of cowboys. I could live in the cookshack at the other end and cook for them. . .

TOM *(interrupting)* And with a dog-trot style you'd have a shady breeze way between the two buildings for resting. . .

GRANDFATHER . . . perfect bachelor quarters, just in case you might want this house to start a family of your own.

TOM And just where do you suggest I find a woman to start a family with?

Grandfather sips his coffee.

INT. INSIDE TOM'S KITCHEN, BREAKFAST

Tom, Grandfather, and Uncle Clint are cooking on a woodstove, setting the table, and sit down to eat together. The room is unadorned but clean, no electric gadgets.

GRANDFATHER Someone is definitely watching us, a young boy.

UNCLE How do you know it's a boy?

Grandfather and Tom exchange a glance, as though saying Uncle Clint should already know how Grandfather would know it is a boy.

GRANDFATHER *(patiently)* The tracks are too small and shallow for a grown man, and the stride is not long enough. Women urinate between their feet, boys do not.

UNCLE *(laughing)* And I thought I was a tracker because I can tell pig and deer tracks apart.

TOM Usually.

Tom is teasing, doubting his Uncle's tracking ability.

Grandfather adds some teasing also.

GRANDFATHER Sometimes.

UNCLE OK. Sometimes.

TOM Is he friend or enemy, Grandfather?

GRANDFATHER He doesn't seem to be a thief. He has never approached a building looking for something to steal. He simply watches us work, usually after he has climbed a tree.

UNCLE He must know you'd find his tracks?

GRANDFATHER People who have never been taught to read sign, or don't practice . . .

He and Tom exchange another glance and look at Uncle Clint.

GRANDFATHER . . . don't think about sign, don't realize how careful they need to be. He's smart though and knows his

bike leaves tire tracks. He rides it mostly on asphalt, so it took me a while to figure out he was coming from the casino.

TOM The casino?

GRANDFATHER Yes. He takes different routes and keeps his bike off dirt until he has no other choice. He hides the bike in different places. He comes just before daylight and leaves when we eat at noon.

TOM He might be an orphan, a boy with no father, or the son of a father with poor tracking skills.

Tom and Grandfather exchange a glance again and look at Uncle Clint who pretends not to understand what they are getting at.

UNCLE CLINT What?

TOM I will saddle up early tomorrow and try to catch him.

EXT. TOM'S PORCH, SUNRISE

The next morning, about sunrise, Tom rides up to the porch where Grandfather and Uncle are drinking coffee. A boy rides behind Tom's saddle. The boy is the same one who disappeared at Wolf's camp and is dressed in the same baggy basketball shorts, old high topped athletic shoes with no socks, and a black t-shirt with the sleeves cut off. His long hair is tied in a Navajo-style bun.

TOM I caught our evil spirit. He says his name is Eagle and he's an orphan, probably both by choice.

Eagle does not speak.

TOM He says he's been washing dishes for his meals and a place to sleep at the casino but wants to be a cowboy. Maybe we could let him sleep in the barn and be our chore boy until he earns enough money to buy some boots and a used saddle. What do you think?

UNCLE Sounds good to me. Washing dishes is making my hands soft.

GRANDFATHER Let's take it one day at a time. Going from no father to three might be more than he will want. Come on, Son, let's go get your bike.

Eagle slides off the horse and follows grandfather to the pickup.

EXT. TOM'S PORCH AT RANCH, SUNRISE

Tom walks out with a coffee cup in hand, sees smoke rising. Uncle Clint and Eagle roar up in a pickup, scattering gravel.

UNCLE Tom, there's another fire on Wolf's lease. This looks like a bad one and coming our way. They've already called in hotshot crews and dozers.

Tom drops his coffee cup and races around gathering up a jacket and equipment.

TOM Help me load shovels, Uncle Clint. Eagle, grab the wire cutter in case we need to cut fences to release cattle or horses ahead of the fire.

UNCLE Where is Grandfather?

TOM I don't know, but I'm sure he saw the smoke.

EXT. WOLF'S SCHOOL SITE, SUNRISE

The logs at Wolf's school site are now stacked four high.

Grandfather races up horseback. Wolf appears from behind the logs as soon as he hears his name.

GRANDFATHER Wolf! Wolf! Are you here?

WOLF What's wrong?

GRANDFATHER Fire headed this way fast. Hidden by the trees. The road is closing. Save yourself. I have our horses and yours.

Grandfather gallops away, Wolf jumps in his pickup and speeds away. We see Grandfather driving a large herd of horses across the country, away from the fire. Wolf's pickup barely makes it through while burning trees fall behind him, closing the road.

EXT. FIRE, DAY/NIGHT

Heroic scenes of Native American hotshot crews fighting the fire. Close ups of their Insignia on helmets and jackets, maybe a few of their faces (give them a tribute!).

EXT. FIRE LINE, DAY

Tom, Eagle, and Uncle Clint are sooty, exhausted, and following on foot behind a dozer that is plowing a fire line. They shovel up and toss smoking wood and cow patties farther into the blackened burned area.

EXT. BURNED FENCE, DAY

After the fire, Tom, Eagle and Uncle Clint, now cleaned up, survey the burned area from horseback. Eagle now wears jeans, boots, sleeveless t-shirt, and no hat. He rides bareback.

Tom stops near a burned section of fence with shreds of burned fence posts dangling from sagging burned wire.

TOM We lost at least two miles of fence here. There goes my winter feed money.

UNCLE It would have been much worse without those hotshot crews who dropped out of the sky like angels, almost before we could get to the fire ourselves.

TOM Those guys are amazing. But Wolf is a bad neighbor and becoming a liability to the tribe.

UNCLE Yes. The livestock board and tribal council are not going to like this. Those hotshots don't come cheap—not to mention how upset the Crows will be if sooty run-off clouds the water in their precious Blue Ribbon trout streams. Fishermen always win the wars around here.

TOM There was no lightning. Have you heard any rumors about a cause?

UNCLE Casino gossip says it was Joe Champlain. The hotshots found his burned body and burned pickup near a campfire, plus two empty wine bottles. They think he was drunk, as usual, built a fire—maybe to cook—and it got away from him in the tall grass. Signs looked like he tried to stomp it out and caught his clothes on fire. He has always been a problem to the tribe and his family, but nobody should die like that.

TOM *(sadly)* And Wolf and his descendants will always feel responsible.

UNCLE To some degree it is Wolf's fault. All of that ungrazed grass is just a fire waiting for a spark or stupidity, especially both. Wolf's school was also

a total loss. I feel bad for him, but he ignores advice.

TOM His ideas are great in theory, but not in practice.

EXT. CHARRED RUINS OF WOLF'S SCHOOL, DAY

Wolf is sitting cross-legged in the soot, his hands, moccasins, and clothes sooty and black. Smoke from the burned logs of his school and the forest beyond rise behind him. He looks dejected, not sure what to do. Grandfather and Eagle ride up horseback.

GRANDFATHER Hello, Wolf. I'm very sorry for your loss.

WOLF I am glad to see you, Mr. Greyhorse. Thank you so much for warning me and gathering my horses. I owe you my life.

As they talk, Wolf gets up and starts picking through the rubble to see what's salvageable. He finds his small cast iron skillet, smiles, and bushes off the ashes almost lovingly.

WOLF And Eagle, I'm surprised to see you. I've been wondering where you went.

Grandfather waits for Eagle to explain, but he does not.

GRANDFATHER We caught him sneaking around watching us and put him to work. He said you taught him to ride, and he wanted to be a cowboy.

WOLF Well, he's in good hands now, wiser hands than mine. I tried to follow your advice, but I couldn't afford bison fences and corrals.

While they talk, show scenes of bison ranches with very stout corrals, aerials of the Crow bison herd and the deep canyons surrounding them. Scenes of cowboys working bison, their belligerence, maybe tearing up a gate or two.

GRANDFATHER Yes. Bison are more expensive than cattle, both to buy and manage. They do not respect fences. They just put their heads down and push through, sometimes laying a fence down for miles. They need much stouter posts, wire, corrals, everything—and all of that costs money.

WOLF I talked to several Crow ranchers. Anyone who shared a fence with bison cursed them. Even while using Bighorn Canyon to isolate the bison, the Crows still can't build corrals strong enough to test and vaccinate them against brucellosis. Every time there is an outbreak, they have to destroy the entire herd, wait a few years, and start over.

Eagle dismounts, hands grandfather the reins to his horse, and begins to help Wolf by dragging burnt wood and stacking it neatly off to one side.

GRANDFATHER Brucellosis, usually called Bangs, is very dangerous. Most ranchers have been able to free their cattle of it through testing and vaccinating. But to do that with bison, you must build corrals that will hold them. It's also more difficult to hire cowboys who want to handle buffalo. Even horses prefer Herefords. Did you plan to harvest them from horseback with bows and arrows?

Eagle listens intently to the conversation but does not speak, keeps working. He finds an axe head and hands it to Wolf.

WOLF No. I know our traditional hunting style would result in lots of

broken bones if not deaths, both to horses and humans, and probably always did.

GRANDFATHER Yes, again the movies make it look fun and easy. More often we drove thousands off cliffs and wasted tons of meat. You could never afford to do that today. So you'd need to shoot and butcher them in the pasture and risk causing undulant fever in any one who touched infected carcasses.

WOLF Buffalo always carry brucellosis?

GRANDFATHER Today, yes. It causes all grazing animals, wild or domestic, to abort their young and causes a chronic fever in humans. You would not want to expose tribal members or children. Although seldom fatal, the fever and weakness ruins their lives.

WOLF But I don't want to raise white man's cattle.

GRANDFATHER Why?

WOLF Cattle graze differently.

GRANDFATHER So say white environmentalists. Grazing is grazing, Wolf. Nature intended grass to be grazed not protected.

WOLF Bison don't destroy the land like cattle do.

As they talk, we see old black and white actual photos of barren land studded with buffalo chips after the passing of a buffalo herd. We also see scenes of bison grazing and cattle grazing as they talk.

GRANDFATHER Buffalo herds completely destroyed everything in their path as they grazed, much worse than cattle. That's why our people followed and camped in their tracks where we were safe from fire. Bison stomped the soil into powder with their hooves and left the ground littered with buffalo chips. Buffalo wallows, places where they rolled to shed wool or fight insects, are still visible after a rain as small shining lakes, scattered across the prairies like silver coins *(show aerials)*. Fresh, short green grass that sprang up after a rain made safe playgrounds for our children. Their chips provided fertilizer for the new grass and fuel for cooking fires.

WOLF Buffalo were here first.

GRANDFATHER Those who read sign in the oldest rocks and bones say shrub cattle and horses were here thousands of years before the buffalo.

Show rock art with cattle and horses.

WOLF But bison meat is healthier than beef.

GRANDFATHER Lean, grass-fed beef is just as healthy. The extra fat feedlots add causes the problems. Those who lead active lives need fat. Those who lead sedentary lives need leaner meat. Plus bison carry all their meat in the hump and shoulder. Skinny butts don't produce many steaks. Don't let advertisers fool you, Wolf. You can read sign. Look, compare, experiment, test, and control your ideas like small fires.

WOLF Right now, I'm terrified of any fire. Mine are getting worse and I can't stop them. I'm also losing confidence in my ideas.

GRANDFATHER Graze off the tall grass and then set small fires. Perhaps one of the hotshot crews would come to your school to teach you and your students how to fight and control fire. You will need help from many young muscles and those young muscles need lots of work to stay out of trouble. Don't be too proud to ask for help. *(to Eagle)* Let's go, Eagle, we've got fences to rebuild.

WOLF I'm sorry about your fences too. Thank you, Mr. Greyhorse. Thank you, Eagle. I have been so stupid.

Wolf finds a tin cup, brushes off the ashes, and sets it beside the frying pan and axe head.

GRANDFATHER You are not stupid, Wolf, just learning. Learning is good. Real education never ends and is usually painful. I'm sure my own last words will be, "Dammit, that didn't work either."

All laugh. Grandfather and Eagle ride away together.

EXT. TOM'S CORRALS— EVENING

Tom and Eagle feed four loose horses in the corral by hanging homemade gunnysack morals on their heads that contain oats. Eagle hears a car coming and disappears. Tom notices him leave. Then Tom sees a car pull up to the corrals. Joy steps out wearing boots and jeans and walks up to the fence to talk, so Tom can continue his evening chores. Tom is stunned to see Joy at his ranch, not sure what to do.

JOY Tom, I'm sorry to bother you. Do you have time to talk?

TOM Of course. *(he starts nervously working again)*

JOY I have a personal favor to ask.

TOM I'd be honored.

JOY Will you help my brother?

TOM Your brother? I didn't know you had a brother. Does he live closeby?

He steps inside the nearby barn to get a flake of hay in each hand and as he talks, he walks around the corral and drops the flakes about 15 feet apart.

JOY Wolf Taylor. We share a mother, but different fathers, so we have different last names. Wolf's father was a Lakota who carried a white ancestor's name. Wolf says the Taylors were Indian fighters. He is ashamed of that and maybe the reason he became such a traditionalist.

TOM Most Indians were also Indian fighters and many still are. If that is something to be ashamed of, then we should all be ashamed.

JOY *(laughs)* True. I think Wolf is also ashamed of his white blood because of how his father treated our mother. Anyway, he needs to graze his lease to stop the fires. I know you tried to get that grass for your cattle, but because of my job, I can't tell Wolf. You will need to talk to him. Maybe you could suggest something that might help you both?

TOM Wolf and I have never been friends because of his desire to stop cattle grazing on reservation lands. He will be against anything I suggest. Grandfather has already talked to him and he said Wolf wanted to graze buffalo.

JOY I seldom see him. But he did come in and talk to my boss about bison. Of course the bank advised against it and wouldn't fund him. Even the casino refused to finance bison. According to gossip, he has since talked to some Crow ranchers and your grandfather again. I think he is now ready to consider cattle.

Tom grabs two more flakes of hay and drops them for the other two horses.

TOM Wolf also blames my family because one of my uncles was driving the night his grandmother was killed in a car wreck. If he is your half-brother, she must have been your grandmother too?

JOY Yes.

TOM I'm so sorry. Your grandmother and my dad's older brother were on their first date. I knew she was survived by a baby daughter from a former relationship and that daughter later had two sons, one of them Wolf. I never knew she also had a daughter.

JOY Even before the wreck, our mother was already being raised by our grandmother's two sisters, both alcoholics. Mom did not have a good life. After she grew up, she married several times and had three children: Wolf and a brother from her first marriage, me from a third.

TOM The shame for my family keeps increasing. I am so sorry.

JOY I feel shame too. My family tree resembles a tumbleweed. The wreck was no one's fault. They were all drunk. Any one of them could have been driving.

TOM Thank you for saying that, but I don't think Wolf sees it that way. I don't think he will want to talk to me.

Tom starts to remove the morals from the horses so they can each go find a flake of hay.

JOY The fires have humbled him, especially when the hotshots found Joe Champlain burned to death. Wolf knows his ideas have caused harm, but he is too proud to ask for help.

TOM Why are you giving me this opportunity?

JOY My boss says you are an honorable man. My brother wants to be an honorable man too but he is idealistic and naïve. He needs your family's practical knowledge. I'm asking more for his benefit than yours.

TOM And I assume this conversation is confidential?

JOY Yes. Now that you are on the bank's board of directors, you know how important that is.

TOM I am honored you asked and that you trust me. I will make Wolf an offer and keep our conversation sacred.

JOY *(laughs)* Sacred! Wow. No one has ever said that before, but yes, I supposed that's what confidentiality should mean.

TOM They say it takes a village to raise a child. It seems to take several villages to raise a man.

JOY Or a woman. I look forward to seeing you at the bank.

She drives away. Tom looks after her puzzled. Eagle reappears.

TOM What happened to you? Are you afraid of girls?

Eagle nods yes.

TOM Me too.

EXT. TOM'S BURNED FENCE, MORNING

Wolf rides up bareback, native style. He approaches the fence where Tom and Eagle work to rebuild it. They are taking turns driving steel posts into the ground with a two-handed post driver.

WOLF *(to Eagle)* Hello, Eagle. *(to Tom)* You want to talk to me?

TOM Yes. Thanks for coming. How did you find us?

Tom glances at Eagle so Wolf knows Tom is asking for Eagle's benefit. Wolf glances at Eagle and nods to let Tom know that he answers for Eagle's benefit. They are silently showing mutual respect for each other's ability to read sign as well as communicating to each other that much of what they will ask and explain today will be for Eagle's benefit. They will show respect, even when their conversation is not "friendly," meaning each will fiercely defend his own beliefs.

WOLF I just followed the burned grass. It's only two miles across country from my camp—or what's left of it.

TOM I want to show you around, explain my methods, and maybe make you an offer to help you stop the fires.

WOLF I'm listening.

TOM Pickup or horseback?

WOLF We are horse people.

TOM Good choice. I've seen you ride at the Custer reenactments. I envy your horsemanship.

WOLF Thank you.

TOM You did a good job teaching Eagle. He is already a better horseman than I am.

Eagle catches the compliment, flashes pride, then hides it.

TOM We will meet you at my corrals in a few minutes.

Tom points with his chin in the direction of the corrals.

EXT. TOM'S BARN, A FEW MINUTES LATER.

Wolf rides up and dismounts to wait as Tom and Eagle saddle up and swing into their saddles as cowboys. Eagle is now wearing spurs on his boots and rides an old saddle well repaired and oiled, still no hat. Wolf leaps up bareback, like a native rider. They ride and talk.

TOM That's a young man's way to mount. My grandfather still rides, but he couldn't if he had to get on by leaping and maintaining his balance without stirrups.

WOLF Our great-grandfathers did.

TOM Our great-grandfathers seldom lived past 40. Those who didn't die in battles with other tribes starved to death in winter. Roping something out in the pasture to doctor it or pull a calf struggling to be born would also be impossible without a saddle. In theory our old ways sound wonderful, but not in practice. Today they must be supported by casino money or as entertainment for ticket-buying tourists.

WOLF Your cowboy ways are also reenactments.

TOM Most are still practical and sustainable. Horseback is still the cheapest and most humane way to take care of livestock. I use the best of the old ways and the best of the modern. I market my cattle through video sales and use vaccines, but I keep my tallies on a stick . . .

Tom pulls a stick with notches out of his shirt pocket.

TOM . . . with a knife. Almost all cow work must still be done with horses and old skills. But I also carry a calculator, computer, and checkbook in a briefcase in my pickup. Eventually we load the cattle onto diesel 18-wheelers, but maybe middle-man processing could be done the old way.

WOLF Like killing, skinning, and butchering? No brucellosis?

TOM Yes, and maybe even cooking. Families are small today, often only one, like you, and many cook only in microwaves. The only place you can find a slice of prime rib is in a casino. Maybe our people would eat more meals together if cooked old style? Maybe we could wean our people from sugar and junk food. And, no brucellosis unless our cattle get too close to some buffalo.

Eagle intently listens to the conversation, but does not speak or ask questions. They stop at a gate. Eagle steps off to open it. Tom and Wolf ride through and wait for Eagle to close the gate and get back on before they continue on or continue their conversation.

WOLF But who are "our people"? Do you mean only full blood Cheyenne? Only those raised on this reservation? Those with no non-Indian blood?

Half? Quarter? One drop? Today most reservations are a mix of tribes, races, and religions, some more mixed than others. Today at Crow Fair it's impossible to tell enrolled tribal members from tourists just by looking.

TOM Yes. When people ask my nationality, I usually say "cowboy." Even though I'm a full-blood Cheyenne.

WOLF For many generations we have had opportunities to meet and marry spouses who are not from our tribe.

TOM That is true worldwide.

WOLF We know who our mothers were, but not always our fathers.

TOM Yes. A family name means your mother was married to that man when you were born. No other guarantees. The Virgin Mary gets a lot of credit for raising God's son, but Joseph had to have been a saint too.

Eagle smiles, the first sign of emotion to appear on his face.

WOLF *(laughing)* Your thinking blazes its own trails.

EXT. PASTURE COLLAGE, CONTINUING·

Show the three men riding across the country, looking at fences, gates, streams, cattle, wildlife, an unfinished new log building. Sometimes Wolf and Tom dismount to look at soil and plants, or burned areas while Eagle holds their horses. Tom sometimes hands something to Eagle for his close inspection too, always giving him a chance to follow the conversation even though Eagle doesn't speak.

EXT. RIDGE TOP, CONTINUING

The three riders stop on a ridge overlooking a valley below with a creek running through it.

TOM I'm sure you know bituminous coal lies under this valley and that some tribal members want to sell the mineral rights. I think we are both against tearing up this valley for coal.

WOLF Yes. I'm very much against that.

TOM And do we agree that we don't want the tribe to sell our water rights along Rosebud Creek?

WOLF Yes. I keep telling them it doesn't matter how much money we're offered, how can we live without our water? It's the same deal as selling Long Island for colored beads.

TOM Agreed. Someday a barrel of unpolluted drinking water will be worth more than a barrel of oil, a load of coal, or even gold.

WOLF Since we've been riding I've seen sign of deer, antelope, elk, bear, wild turkey, grouse, prairie chicken, coyotes, bobcats, and mountain lion.

TOM But no wolves.

Tom and Wolf eye each other. Tom wants to know where Wolf stands.

WOLF I think one wolf on this reservation is enough.

TOM *(relieved, laughing)* Hah! In spite of your white man's last name, you have a Cheyenne heart.

WOLF I don't want to ride crippled horses. People who call themselves nature lovers have never seen the destruction wolves cause to all animals. They claim wolves only kill crippled animals.

TOM But they never explain how all those animals become crippled.

WOLF Yes. Wolves nip and slash sometimes 10 or 20 before weakening one enough for a kill.

TOM Meanwhile the others limp off to live a few more days.

WOLF And horses are ruined for life.

TOM I have heard White Mountain Apaches describe heifers that are still alive but wolves have eaten their calves while still inside the womb, along with nearby reproductive organs.

WOLF It's hard to love a wolf.

TOM Unless you're a hungry wolf pup.

WOLF *(smiling and shaking his head)* Your thinking trail is hard to follow.

TOM You and I live closer to nature than most.

 WOLF You have helped me see this with my own eyes after your grandfather reminded me to open them.

TOM Ranchers are the true environmentalists. The best stewards of a resource are those who make their living from it. If you're a deer hunter, you protect deer. Fishermen protect fish and water. Loggers protect forests. Farmers protect soil. If you're in a business that depends on grazing, you must take care of grass.

WOLF Yes. I was wrong about cattle grazing.

More scenes of Wolf and Tom taking turns pointing to something and the other nods. Eagle listens to every word. The sun and shadows should show the passing of a day.

EXT. TOM'S CORRAL, EVENING

Back at Tom's corrals, Tom and Eagle unsaddle and brush their horses. Eagle follows Tom's every move like a shadow. Wolf remains horseback.

WOLF Thank you for this day. You have given me much to think about.

TOM As have you given me.

WOLF Maybe we are not so opposite.

TOM Maybe. We've never tried working together as cowboys <u>and</u> Indians.

Both laugh, Eagle smiles again, Wolf rides away.

INT. BANK LOBBY, DAY

Tom walks into the bank for a meeting and passes Joy's desk.

JOY Mr. Greyhorse, may I have a word?

TOM Of course.

JOY Thank you for talking to Wolf. He came in and told my boss how you showed him around your ranch and explained similarities between cows and bison, and that they can even interbreed. You convinced him that grazers came in all shapes, colors, and personalities, just like people and to classify them as different species is similar to dividing humans into separate species. He said you knew every plant, track, and bird call. He said he had never met anyone who felt as strongly about Cheyenne land as he did—until he rode with you. Thank you so much.

TOM It was my honor. We have made a deal, not only on the grass as you suggested, but maybe on his dream as well. We traded this year's grazing for logs from the old school building I had never completed. My logs will be easy to move and quickly replace the ones he lost in the fire. We also plan to work together on teaching practical skills to native youth. I need ranch hands but few of our young people have those skills, so I want to help them learn.

JOY That is such great news! Thank you so much.

TOM No, thank _you_. It was your vision.

JOY I'm so happy for my brother.

TOM What about you? Do you have any dreams?

JOY No one has ever asked me that before.

TOM Are you happy with this job? What do you see in your future?

JOY I will need to think about it.

TOM I guess I will be passing your desk quite often, so I will ask again after you've had time to think.

Joy smiles.

TOM And please call me Tom, Mr. Greyhorse is my grandfather.

JOY Tom it is. But I should probably continue to call you Mr. Greyhorse here inside the bank.

TOM _(smiles)_ As you wish, Ms. Begay.

EXT. TOM'S PASTURES AND WOLF'S CAMP MONTAGE, DAY

Tom drives a fork lift, loading his logs onto a logging truck and unloading them at Wolf's. Wolf is rebuilding, erecting new teepee poles. Then Grandfather, Uncle Clint, Tom, Eagle, and Wolf are all horseback, driving a large herd of cattle through an open gate into tall grass. Then a scene of the cattle grazing the tall grass. Tom rides up alongside Wolf.

TOM We can move all of my cattle onto your grass until we get it knocked back to a safer level.

WOLF Won't we need more cattle to eat both your grass and mine?

TOM Yes. But winter is coming and snow will reduce fire hazards, so we should wait until early spring, after snow melt. We can buy more cattle then with a loan from the bank because we can mortgage cattle.

WOLF I couldn't get a loan on buffalo because I didn't have the fences. Even the casino wouldn't finance buffalo.

TOM I couldn't get a mortgage for your lease because the land belongs to the tribe.

WOLF How soon will we be able to cut ties with the casino?

TOM Next fall . . . _if_ we have no fires, don't lose any fences, our vehicles keep running, it rains regularly, nothing gets sick, horses don't get lame, cattle prices remain high, . . . *(teasing)* oh there's a very long list of if's.

Wolf looks worried. Tom laughs.

INT. BANK LOBBY, DAY

Tom arrives at the bank, nods and smiles at Joy.

JOY You are early for today's meeting. Have a seat.

TOM Are you sure?

JOY *(laughs)* I'm allowed to talk to customers, especially bank directors. I have an idea that I want your thoughts on.

TOM Is it about your dreams?

JOY You are a mind reader. Yes it is. I want to be a writer.

TOM Wow! That's great! My grandfather talks constantly about how our people need better stories because that's how values are traditionally passed from generation to generation. We have turned that responsibility over to reporters, song writers, tv, and Hollywood—who make us into either larger-than-life saintly nature nuts, drunks, victims, murdering savages, or cartoons.

JOY Yes. And most native writers—or those who at least claim native blood— spend too much time creating utopias and blaming or excusing. Our female writers make Indian men sound like monsters.

TOM Some are.

JOY But we don't need to hear that. Too many of us have lived or still live those stories. We need role models. We need to learn how to make wiser choices. We need the kind of stories your grandfather tells.

TOM Sadly the only people I have ever seen listen to my grandfather are white, female reporters. No native men, women or children. We treat our elders like old fools, like the Grandfather in "Stay Away, Joe."

Show a black and white, sepia, clip of the grandfather looking stupid in the Elvis movie.

JOY Yes. I hate that book and movie. I want to change almost every story it tells.

TOM That sounds like an excellent goal. What's stopping you?

JOY I don't know how to write.

TOM Sure you do. I've watched you write all day, every day here at the bank.

JOY That's different. Storytelling is a much deeper and more symbolic kind of writing. I'd be a hummingbird pretending to be an eagle if I tried to write like that. For example, I don't know how to use metaphors.

TOM *(smiling)* Like you just did with hummingbirds and eagles?

JOY *(a surprised smile)* Hmmmm.

TOM The same brain that moves your tongue moves your pen, and the fastest way to learn is to do and maybe teach storytelling through writing at Wolf's school?

JOY *(searching his face)* But I must keep my job at the bank.

TOM Of course. I don't ever intend to stop ranching, just add on. Ranching keeps me so busy I don't have time to eat, but when I find something else I really want to do, like this bank board, then extra time magically appears. When you love what you do, no burden is too great.

JOY You keep finding ways to make me excited about the future.

TOM You are finding your own path. This is your vision.

JOY Then you are helping to open my eyes.

EXT. WOLF'S SWEAT LODGE, NIGHT WITH FULL MOON

Wolf and Tychee sit watching a bonfire burn outside the sweat lodge. Each is wrapped in a wool Pendleton blanket.

WOLF My long ride with Tom Greyhorse the other day gave me much to think about.

TYCHEE Like what?

WOLF Like, how to find real and rewarding work for reservation kids instead of reenactments of the past or utopian dreams of a future that isn't possible.

TYCHEE What part of the future isn't possible?

WOLF Living like I do. If everyone killed their own wild meat and harvested wild rice and berries, this whole reservation couldn't support ten people for a month. Tom's cow herd can feed 60 people every day indefinitely. By letting him graze my lease to stop the fires, together we can feed 120 people every day.

He stands to give Tychee a hand up.

WOLF Ready?

She nods, rises, and they walk into the sweat lodge where a smaller fire burns.

INT. WOLF'S SWEAT LODGE, NIGHT

They both sit down cross-legged on opposite sides of the fire and both drop their blankets. Tychee is wearing a bikini and Wolf a traditional breech cloth. They begin to tell each other stories, matter-of-factly, while slyly looking each other over.

TYCHEE So, are you saying you want to modernize? Stop bathing in the creek and cooking on a fire?

WOLF I'm not sure. For now, I agree with the Greyhorses that we need to be more realistic and protect our resources.

TYCHEE Are you suggesting that I shouldn't make jewelry out of natural bits, like seeds and animal teeth? Isn't that better than using mined metals and plastic beads?

WOLF Our people have always been good at recycling and finding a use for everything. Maybe beads from recycled plastic would be even better than collecting from nature.

TYCHEE Hmmm. I like the challenge of creating beauty from junk. I met a rancher from California once who was eating in the casino. He said when he was a kid, he went to the reservations to buy junk cars and taught himself to restore them. Now he has a whole barn full of Pierce Arrows. Every now and then, he sells one or two and buys more land. He said his neighbors and family thought he was crazy for dragging home all those old *(air quotes)* "Indian cars."

WOLF *(laughs)* Like selling Long Island for colored beads, we have let so much of value slip through our fingers. I met a hunter once who radio-collared jaguars in Paraguay. He told me about some persecuted German farmers who settled in the Chaco jungle. No one could make a living there, not even Indians. But, he said, those Germans figured out a way to collect and store rain, planted farms and fed their people, started ranching. They built a town, a grocery store, schools, a hospital, everything they needed. They were so frugal that they hardly produced any trash. Yet, he said, several members of a Guarani tribe eventually settled near the German dump and were able to live off what little those frugal Germans threw away.

TYCHEE Good stories. You have given me much to think about.

WOLF Maybe "Beauty from Junk" could be the theme of our school?

TYCHEE I like that, especially since so many of our people consider themselves junk.

WOLF We are going to make a good team.

TYCHEE I hope so.

As sweat begins to glisten on their skin in the firelight, we discreetly leave them talking in the sweat lodge where things will probably get steamy.

EXT. INDIAN SCHOOL MONTAGE, DAY

Wolf helping kids learn to ride, leaping on and off without a saddle. Tom moves cattle through a gate onto tall grass with several kids riding bareback. Wolf shows kids how to find and harvest wild honey. Tychee shows kids how to make candles from beeswax. Tom teaches kids to shoe horses and weld the used horseshoes together for tables. Native hotshots show kids and Wolf how to do a controlled burn. Tychee and kids look in junk piles and pawn shops for items to rob for jewelry.

Tom works with a colt and a kid in a round pen. Grandfather teaches kids to read sign and set snares. Wolf teaches them to skin animals, make rawhide, tan leather, and cut strips for braiding. Tom shows them how to pull and wash horsehair.

Tychee and/or Wolf show them how to braid or hitch or twist the clean hair and rawhide to make ropes and belts and other decorative but practical items. Tom shows kids how to wash, oil, and repair old junked saddles.

EXT/INT. SMALL CAFÉ, NOON

Tom and Joy are served food.

JOY Thank you for inviting me to lunch today. I usually eat alone, so this is nice.

TOM For me too. I usually eat at home with three homeless men: Grandfather, Uncle Clint, and a young cowboy who works for us.

JOY I heard that your Uncle Clint had moved in with you and your grandfather again.

TOM I suppose everyone knows that he and his wife struggle to get along. She asked him to leave again. He did. But they have three young kids, and she can't handle the ranch alone. So they keep trying to patch up their problems.

JOY Are they making progress?

TOM I think so. He didn't come home a couple of nights ago. I think that is a good sign.

JOY Unless he found a new woman.

TOM My Uncle Clint is not like that. Greyhorses are one woman men. If he doesn't get his wife back, he will probably become an old bachelor.

JOY Does he drink?

TOM No and neither does she.

JOY Weren't you once a drinker?

TOM From fifteen to about 20, but I stopped.

JOY That's very rare. How did you do it?

TOM I'm not sure. I think I just got busy ranching and didn't have time to nurse a hangover. My grandfather also told me the story over and over of my uncle's car wreck that killed him and his girlfriend, the grandmother to you and Wolf.

JOY And both of Tychee's parents.

TOM Yes. They were four good friends. I carry the guilt for my family and want to earn those friendships back.

JOY You have, even Wolf. Each of us somehow found a way to avoid drinking too.

TOM Ranching, crafts, cooking, and writing are probably all addictions too, but those can build a life rather than destroy one.

JOY Yes. I seem to feel a need to fill every moment with something. I'm trying to fill more moments with a walk or sipping a cup of coffee instead of just burying myself in office work.

TOM I've often said boredom causes drinking not poverty. Our people need a purpose: jobs, projects, crafts, small businesses—something to do besides drink or gamble or fight.

JOY I agree. *(hesitating)* Maybe I have an idea for Wolf's Indian school.

TOM I'm listening.

Joy reaches into her purse and pulls out an article to show him.

JOY This is about a magazine that was popular in rural areas in the 1980s. Teenagers interviewed elders, and then wrote and published the stories. My writing skills are more like editing skills right now, so a project like that sounds like something I have the courage to do. Our young people and I could learn to write together.

Tom looks over the article and likes it. Joy gets more excited, talking faster.

TOM This is a great idea!

JOY *(smiling)* We have lost so many of our good stories, but we could preserve what's left, dig out old scrapbooks and boxes of pictures. The kids could photograph relics and treasures.

TOM Grandfather has an old smoke-tanned leather pouch that belonged to his great-grandfather. I have no idea what is in it, why he keeps it, or the story behind it. He has often said we need stories about our people that aren't about wars and warriors and our numerous falls from grace. Your idea is perfect.

JOY We could start small, maybe just a tribal newsletter or post it as a blog to see if anyone is interested.

TOM Or . . . maybe you should start <u>professional</u> and produce a slick magazine so the kids and the tribe have something to be proud of?

JOY Really? You like it that much?

TOM I do. It sounds very exciting, Joy. I'm sure Wolf and Tychee will love it too. It might even be something the bank would sponsor as outreach. Do you want me to ask the directors?

JOY Wow! Yes! We could dig up old recipes. My mother has some from her aunts. Even though they were alcoholics, they could cook. Rules for games, fishing tips, hunting stories, how places got their names . . . the more I think about it, the more important it seems.

TOM Were those teenagers also excited about their magazine?

JOY Oh, yes. And ours would be too, especially if people they already admire get involved. Instead of Elvis, they need to know you and your grandfather, Wolf and Tychee . . .

TOM *(interrupting)* And you!

JOY Thank you. I'm actually beginning to believe that. You have given me so much courage. *(looking at her watch)* Oh, my gosh! I'm going to be late!

EXT. CROW FAIR, DAY

Montage of scenes from Crow Fair: fancy dancing, close ups of shells, elk teeth, feathers, etc. on costumes, reenactment of

Custer's Last Stand, teepees, parade, kids, pretty girls, grandmas horseback, rodeo, horses, horses, horses, etc.

Close ups of Tychee in an elk-tooth woman's costume dancing in one of the women's dances and Wolf riding as a warrior in the reenactment.

EXT. CROW FAIR MIDWAY, LATER

Tychee is still dressed in costume, Wolf still in war paint and warrior costume. They walk and talk among the festivities, occasionally stopping to purchase food or play a game.

TYCHEE Perhaps there is a place in the world of fashion for Native designers. Many of the tourists watching us are wearing *(makes air quotes)* "Indian Jewelry" and clothes with an "Indian vibe."

WOLF Yes. People who have no culture always seem to be looking for a way to belong to something. Maybe a costume helps?

TYCHEE The city look, the cowboy, the military look, the athlete.

WOLF *(sarcastically)* Fashion has found inspiration in Africa, China, Hawaii, France *(pause)* so why not here.

TYCHEE I sense some reservation in your thoughts? Do you think fashion would exploit our heritage?

WOLF Yes, but it seems that we can't make a living or feed our people without exploiting something. All life depends on sacrifice of something.

EXT. CROW FAIR, DAY

At another part of the fair, Tom and grandfather both dressed like cowboys, are not participating, but watching, leaning on the fence. As they talk, we watch.

GRANDFATHER *(pointing with his chin)* Looks like Uncle Clint and his wife are getting along today.

TOM They both love to watch their kids dance.

We see kids fancy dancing and Uncle Clint and his wife watching proudly. Clint has his arm around his wife.

GRANDFATHER Every time they fight and make up, they get along better. Maybe this time they will stay together.

TOM Maybe. I am surprised Eagle did not want to come along. He stays away from Wolf's school too, although I can tell he'd like to mingle with other kids.

We see some of the teenaged dancers performing.

GRANDFATHER He is still hiding something.

TOM I suppose he will explain when he's ready. I am impressed with the way he learns. I don't think he's ever asked me a question. He just watches . . .

GRANDFATHER *(interrupting)* . . . like an Eagle. He's almost as good at tracking now as you are. If he decides to leave us, I might not be able to find him.

TOM *(laughs)* So, what do you think of the fair, Grandfather?

GRANDFATHER It's good to see our people get together for a good time. Our history is good. Pride is good. The fair provides jobs, has revived old skills into small businesses. It keeps our children physically active, horseback, and dancing.

TOM I sense a "but" coming?

GRANDFATHER But . . . I would like to see us put more energy into a purpose other than entertainment. Entertainment keeps us frozen in the past, as though the only thing we have to be proud of is that we were once warriors. I come to this battlefield and watch a historic battle between Indians and cavalry soldiers. I go home and watch battles between Indian and Indian.

TOM Yes. Sadly, I get along better with white ranchers than our own. The white ranchers understand the rules and ethics of ranching. Some of my Indian neighbors have only been involved in ranching a few years, and it's harder to deal with them. It's almost impossible to deal with non-ranching Cheyenne.

GRANDFATHER This reenactment also makes our people long for a world that not only will never come again but never was. We never lived without sin in a Garden of Eden where our food fell in our laps. We had to produce. If you couldn't train a horse for hunting, you and the people who depended on you went hungry. Some of us made arrowheads or teepee poles to trade hunters for meat. It's the same today. There is no free lunch.

TOM Except when the US government or the casinos get involved. So is there another "but" coming?

GRANDFATHER But . . . I have no better answers. The fair is good for now. Although Wolf's school and Joy's magazine are giving me hope.

EXT. SCHOOL BOOTH AT FAIR, DAY

A montage from the "Beauty from Junk" booth at Crow Fair:

Some kids dressed like cowboys, hold restored bridles and items made from braided horsehair and rawhide: riatas, belts, hatbands, bracelets. Old leather has been cleaned and repaired and adorned with silver made from silverware (saddle and bridle conchos, bit hangers)plus hatbands and scarf slides. Other kids sell honey and candles. Several kids sit at a table selling Indian-look jewelry: an Aztec style necklace from a computer motherboard, wire patterns embedded in a clear plastic cuff bracelet, rings made from old keys, silver forks bent into bracelets, silverware handles as drop earrings, tiny gears from a watch or clock made into a pendant, and a concho belt made from silver spoons. Some stand beside stuff made from used horseshoes welded together (tables, coat racks, crosses, endless ideas). Some stand with a restored old car for sale and items made from old car parts: a glass-topped table made from tire treads, a barbeque cooker made from tire rims, a couch made from a rear end of a car, a bench made from old FORD pickup tailgate. A close up of hands trading money and grabbing copies of Joy's magazine from a stack quickly disappearing and being restocked. The name of the magazine is "Beauty from Junk" and on the cover is Grandfather Greyhorse at the grave with the cross made of horseshoes.

EXT. SCENIC OVERLOOK OF VALLEY, SUNSET

Around sunset the camera drifts over the reservation, across trees and pastures and creeks to a bluff overlooking a view of the mountains. We zoom in on a small campfire with Joy and Tom on a date, cooking over the fire and talking. They share a log, obviously placed there for admiring the view.

TOM Our booth was really a hit at the fair, especially your magazine.

JOY The kids were so happy. I have never had so much fun and all so gratifying. The magazine sold out the first day, and we have already begun brainstorming for next year. Thank you for persuading the bank to loan the kids the money and to let them create it on bank computers. I don't know if they were more proud of the magazine or of paying off their first bank loan. Thank you so much for giving me the courage.

TOM You didn't need my help with courage. Nobody has more courage than a single mom.

JOY There is something more I should probably tell you about that. *(hesitates)* You know I have a son. *(hesitates)* Or I should say, <u>had</u> a son. He ran away three years ago. I don't know why.

TOM Yes, I knew. That must have been very hard on you. Still is, I'm sure.

JOY I looked for him everywhere, tribal police, sheriff, game wardens, hospitals, everywhere. He had always been an "A" student, but he disappeared from school too. I never knew why, where he went, or even if he is still alive. He would be 17 now. Not a day goes by that I don't pray for him to come home.

As she chokes back tears, Tom reaches over and squeezes her hand, then holds it.

TOM Maybe as he started to become a man, he thought you would be happier without him interfering with your social life?

JOY That's almost the same thing Tychee always says. He was never a burden. He was my son. I would never trade him for a social life. It broke my heart.

TOM What was his name?

JOY Will. William Begay. His father was Navajo, so I named him after my Navajo grandfather.

While she talks, Tom's expression begins to change from conversation to realization.

JOY He always said he wanted to be a cowboy like his great-grandfather, but of course I had no way to help him learn those skills. I can only hope that somewhere a ranch took him in.

TOM That could easily have happened. Was he a hard-worker?

JOY Oh, yes. He always helped me, even as a toddler. He was so dependable, so earnest. I miss him terribly. He got a job at the garage so he could learn to take care of my car.

Joy begins to cry softly. Tom carefully puts his arm around her.

TOM I'm sure he is OK somewhere. He was probably just at the age when he needed to find a father.

JOY Thank you. I hope so. Tychee says that too. Once again, you give me hope.

As Joy tries to recover her composure, she changes the subject.

JOY So, why are you single?

TOM Me?

He jumps and nervously takes his arm away from her shoulder.

TOM I don't know. I guess Grandfather kept me too busy, and I was never handsome.

JOY That's silly! You are <u>very</u> handsome.

She is suddenly embarrassed at what she just said and looks away. Tom gently turns her head back toward him.

TOM You really think so?

They lock eyes. Eventually she nods yes, and they kiss.

INT. CASINO, DAY

Tom walks in and finds Tychee.

TOM Hey, can you go for a walk?

He looks up and around as though searching for hidden cameras and microphones.

TYCHEE *(warily)* I suppose.

They walk and talk around the casino grounds. When they approach a door, Tychee points out the camera and makes a motion to "shhh". Once past the security devices, they resume their conversation.

TOM What do you know about Joy Begay's missing son, Will?

She looks at him very seriously and takes a deep breath.

TYCHEE Security found him asleep in a corner one winter night three years ago. It was snowing hard, so no one could follow his tracks. I've been known to hide abused kids at the casino. But I know Joy and knew Will hadn't been abused. He told me he ran away to give his mother a better chance to find love and not be held back by an out-of-wedlock son. I'm sure he overheard something that damn Tart Wilson said to her.

TOM Tart Wilson doesn't bother her any more.

TYCHEE Thanks to you. Anyway, Will said he had a good job at a mechanic shop but he couldn't go back there or back to school because his mother would find him. He said he would run farther away if I betrayed his whereabouts.

TOM It must have been difficult for you to keep his secret and watch Joy grieve.

TYCHEE You have no idea.

TOM So you gave him a job?

TYCHEE Yes, washing dishes in exchange for a place to sleep, food, and a small salary. Eventually, he saved enough money for a used bike so he could keep an eye on his mother.

TOM Was he a good worker?

TYCHEE Very. Never asked questions, just watched and learned almost immediately. I paid for on-line classes,

and he quickly earned a GED. I offered to send him to college, but he wanted to stay near his mother. He was hiding close by the night you stopped Tart in the bank parking lot. Will said he was about to step in when you did.

TOM He sounds like a good son.

TYCHEE I wish he was mine and if I ever have one, I hope he turns out half as good.

TOM Anything else?

TYCHEE He kept an eye on Joy's car. Once a year he disabled it so she would have to call a tow-truck and a mechanic would find and fix any problems. Once, he told me her tires were dangerously worn, so he let the air out of one, hoping someone would change it and tell her it was time to buy new tires.

TOM *(smiles)* Is he still around?

TYCHEE When he didn't want to go to college, I asked what he wanted to do. He said cowboy. I knew he'd need to learn to ride a horse. Wolf had helped me hide abused kids before, so I arranged it. Joy and Wolf were not close, so Will changed his name to Eagle and Wolf did not recognize his own nephew.

TOM But the boy didn't want to live with Wolf because it was too far away to keep an eye on his mother?

TYCHEE Right. He kept working and living here. When Wolf needed help, he picked Will up horseback and brought him back horseback.

TOM Wolf is a great horseman, better than I am. You made a wise choice.

TYCHEE Thank you. Then one day Will disappeared and never came back. Wolf said he never came back to help him either. We thought maybe one of the kitchen staff warned him that he'd been spotted. We hoped he found a ranch job somewhere.

TOM I will ask Grandfather to watch for any sign of him. I think Grandfather knows where every stray cat sleeps.

They look at each other for a beat, each wondering how much the other really knows.

EXT. TOM'S RANCH CORRALS, EVENING

Eagle is out in the corrals, working with a young horse. Tom walks up behind him.

TOM Will?

Eagle jumps as though poked, stiffens, but catches himself and doesn't turn.

TOM Eagle?

EAGLE *(now turning, but warily)* What did you call me?

Their eyes meet for a beat, they both sort of know.

TOM Sorry. I didn't mean to startle you. I started to ask if you <u>will</u> help grandfather buy groceries tomorrow.

Their eyes meet again. Eagle nods yes. Tom walks over and puts his hand affectionately on Eagle's shoulder and nods toward the house.

TOM Your young horse has had enough for one day. Time to quit. Let's go see what Grandfather has cooked for supper.

Tom turns toward the house. He closes his eyes as though praying that Eagle does not disappear. In a few steps, Eagle catches up and bumps into him affectionately. Then Eagle sprints ahead and they race to the door, where they play-wrestle to be the first one inside, like a father and son.

EXT. AT THE GRAVE, SUNDOWN

Tom stands holding his horse at the same grave as in the opening scenes. Grandfather rides up.

TOM Eagle is Joy's missing son, Will. You knew that all along, didn't you?

Their eyes meet but Grandfather doesn't answer.

TOM You didn't tell me because you knew I would have to either betray him or her. I feel just like I did when I had to choose between staying here with you or moving to California with mother and her new husband.

Grandfather still doesn't speak.

TOM I chose you and never saw my mother again. Now I must choose between a boy and his mother. If I choose Joy, the boy who feels like my son will disappear. If I choose Eagle, I must give up the woman I love.

GRANDFATHER Someday, I will join my two sons here. Someday, our Eagle will fly to find his own mate. Love is like the wind.

TOM Are you saying I can't hold on to either of them?

GRANDFATHER I'm saying nothing about love is guaranteed or impossible.

EXT. WOLF'S TEEPEE, NIGHT

Wolf and Tychee are cuddled up like a loving couple, sitting by a small fire, sharing one blanket.

TYCHEE Do you live like this in winter?

WOLF *(laughs)* No. The Yellowtails built a comfortable ranch house beyond that hill and miraculously the big fire missed it because my horses had been grazing around it. *(teasing)* It even has running water. I like to spend spring, summer, and fall here, but once serious winter weather sets in, I hibernate in my burrow. Why?

TYCHEE Just curious. *(they kiss)*

WOLF You seem to love being here and teaching kids. Do you still enjoy your work at the casino?

TYCHEE I did. The casino helps me do so many good things like finance this or help abused kids, but there is also a dark side. How many lives do we ruin with gambling and all the evil that follows it in order to build a school? We could just as easily teach under a tree, maybe better. Is the good the casino does worth the cost?

WOLF I agree with the Greyhorses that handouts from the casino cause co-dependency just like all handouts. I'm happy we will soon no longer need casino money.

TYCHEE Alcohol, drugs, free money, gambling—we just trade one addiction for another and enablers hover around the reservations like buzzards, picking our eyes and hearts out.

WOLF If you are disillusioned, why don't you quit and come live with me?

He kisses her hair.

TYCHEE I'm in too deep. These are very dangerous people.

WOLF They said the same about General Custer.

Wolf gives Tychee a Cheyenne warrior look. Her eyes well up in tears. Wolf pulls her closer, holding her very protectively.

INT. INSIDE JOY'S CAR, DAY

On her way to work, just after breakfast, Joy passes the casino. She sees Tom embrace Tychee and hold his pickup door open for her to get in. Joy imagines the worst. Insert a black and white, sepia, clip from "Stay Away, Joe" of Joe womanizing with lyrics from the last stanza of the song.

INT. JOY'S DESK, DAY

A few minutes later, Tom and Tychee enter the bank together. Tychee goes to a teller window. Tom stops by Joy's desk.

TOM Let's cook supper again tonight on a fire.

JOY *(aloof)* I'm sorry, I have other plans.

TOM *(confused)* Is something wrong?

JOY Not at all. I'm just busy.

Joy shuffles some papers unconvincingly.

TOM Ok. *(hesitating)* I have a meeting that will probably last all morning. I will stop by on my way out.

JOY That won't be necessary.

TOM Joy . . .

JOY Goodbye, Mr. Greyhorse.

More stricken, Tom walks away.

INT. JOY'S DESK, CONTINUING

When Tychee finishes her business with the teller, she plops down happily in a chair in front of Joy's desk.

TYCHEE I wanted you to be the first to hear my good news. . . well, second, actually.

JOY I assume you took your own advice and picked a good man?

TYCHEE I did. And he picked me back!

JOY *(fighting tears)* I'm happy for you. You are a beautiful woman. I'm sure you could have any man you want.

TYCHEE I am moving to his ranch in a few days.

JOY That happened fast.

TYCHEE Not really. We have actually been spending a lot of time together, working cattle, getting our school up and running. I guess it just happened.

JOY I see.

TYCHEE He makes me feel so safe and brave that I quit my casino job this morning.

JOY I don't know what to say *(the tears are winning)*. Tom is a good man. You are a very lucky lady.

TYCHEE Tom? Oh, no, not Tom! I'm in love with your half-brother Wolf!

Joy's emotions are whirling, then she looks panic stricken.

JOY Wolf!? Oh that is wonderful! . . . But what have I done?

TYCHEE What do you mean?

JOY I saw you and Tom embracing outside the casino as I passed this morning on my way to work, you got into his pickup, and then you walked into the bank together.

TYCHEE We hugged when I told him about me and Wolf and quitting the casino. It was a hug of congratulations. He gave me a ride here because the car I drive belongs to the casino and I will need to buy one. Oh, my! Everyone knows you and Tom are a couple. Did you think I would . . .

JOY *(interrupting)* I was so stupid. A few minutes ago I basically told him to go away and leave me alone.

TYCHEE Fix it.

JOY But now he will think I don't trust him. And how can he ever trust me if I will break us up over nothing.

TYCHEE Tom has pride, not an ego. He will understand. Sometimes trust is built on sand and sometimes great love causes painful secrets that can destroy it.

JOY *(confused)* Now you are talking in circles?

TYCHEE Tom has fallen in love with you. You know that. Explain your mistake. You need to be honest, learn to trust and forgive each other. You're both walking on egg shells right now because this is all so new.

INT. BANK LOBBY, HOURS LATER

Joy's boss comes out of the meeting first and stops at her desk.

BANKER The directors and I are all headed to a long lunch. I won't be back until about 2:00.

Joy sees Tom coming. He's walking slowly, head down, the last in the line of directors. He doesn't look at her.

JOY *(nervously)* Tom?

TOM *(relieved and hopeful)* Yes?

JOY I'm so sorry. I saw you and Tychee embracing as I drove by the casino and then you walked in the bank together. I misunderstood. She told me her news and that you were simply congratulating her.

TOM *(smiling broadly)* You were jealous?!

Joy feels trapped and embarrassed, looks around the bank to see who might be listening.

JOY Ah, no . . . I . . .

TOM That's great! That tells me something I've been trying to figure out for weeks, something I had to know before I . . . *(stops himself)*

JOY Before what?

TOM Before I decide . . . *(pause)* . . . whether or not to continue to bother you.

JOY *(laughs)* You're not bothering me. I want you to bother me. If the offer still stands for a cook-out tonight . . .

TOM Even more so! Pick you up at 6:00?

JOY I'll make a salad.

He hurries to catch up with the other directors, but looks back twice, walking backward a few steps, grinning. Joy closes her eyes in embarrassment mixed with happiness.

EXT. SCENIC BLUFF, EARLY EVENING

At the same overlook, another cook out. They stand close, Tom with his arm around Joy, both looking out across the scenery. A small campfire burns behind them. They haven't begun cooking yet. <u>Three</u> steaks sit ready to cook.

JOY Now that you and Wolf are partners, are you going to persuade him to cut his hair?

TOM *(laughs)* No. I'm thinking about letting mine grow. Would you like that?

JOY I like you just the way you are.

They kiss.

TOM You helped me with my courage today.

JOY That makes me very happy. I have had my eye on you ever since my boss regretted so badly not being able to loan you money.

TOM What seemed like a tragedy at first brought you into my life, created friendships and partnerships with Wolf and Tychee, and landed me a seat on the bank board.

JOY You have already built up so much good will between the bank and our Native customers. It might take time to get everything you want, but you are already making a difference and the directors know it.

TOM I hope so. *(they kiss)* Lately I have been feeling so successful that I've been trying to gain the courage to tell you that I have deep feelings for you.

JOY So . . . *(shyly, mischeviously)* . . . how many horses do you own?

TOM *(looks puzzled)* Ten. *(pause)* Why?

JOY Oh, darn, that's not nearly enough.

She smiles fake-sadly and he begins to understand. He straightens proudly and over-dramatically motions with his arm, sweeping expansively across the mountains.

TOM But . . . I own a thousand cows . . . *(more humbly)* well, me and Wolf and the bank.

JOY *(laughs)* OK. That'll do.

BIG KISS!

TOM Does this mean you will marry me?

JOY Yes.

Another BIG KISS!

TOM Since that is settled, I have someone I want you to meet . . .

Tom whistles like a common poor will.

TOM . . . the young cowboy who has been working for me. His name is Eagle. He is like a son to me now. Grandfather has been teaching him to read sign, Uncle Clint has been teaching him how to get along with women, and I've been teaching him to cowboy.

As Tom talks, Eagle emerges horseback from the trees in full buckaroo/cowboy regalia (nice Navajo-creased black hat with an Eagle feather, wild rag with a buckaroo silver slide, pin striped vest, chinks, tiny bells on his cinch hobble and bridle throat latch, jingle-bobs on silver mounted spurs), and on a new saddle with 24-inch eagle-beak tapaderos. His hair is cut short like Tom's. Joy does not recognize him.

JOY *(laughs)* Well, at least, he's got two out of three expert teachers, and he certainly looks the part.

TOM Yeah, kids. He wants legally to become a Greyhorse. So I'm hoping you will agree to that.

Eagle steps off his horse, removes his hat, and smiles.

Joy almost collapses when she recognizes Eagle as her missing son, Will, but Tom holds her up. She covers her mouth with both hands. Happy tears!

EAGLE I'm sorry I've made you cry so much, Mother. I left so you could find a man to love, and so I could find someone to teach me to cowboy. Somehow, we picked the same man.

Eagle steps up to embrace his mother and they all three wrap their arms around each other. Eagle's horse nudges him. Tom and Eagle break apart to let the horse into the hug circle.

THE END

War on Sugar

Inspiration for War on Sugar

"The true soldier fights not because he hates what is in front of him, but because he loves what is behind him."
—G. K. Chesterton

Using false advertising to find a mate, gain respect, sell a product, or gain power all seem to cause wars of various levels of seriousness. As a cowboy photographer, I sold some of my photographs for advertising purposes and usually felt guilty. I sold one slide of a cowboy's boot in an oxbow stirrup to a cigarette company for more money than I was making at the time in six months. Did I want to use my skills to convince people to smoke? Another lucrative job was selling photographs to a boot company, but none of the cowboys in my photographs wore that brand of boots. Did I want to help persuade people to buy boots that I knew wouldn't hold up in working conditions? I have also watched helplessly as miles and miles of wind turbines and acres and acres of solar panels have destroyed some of the most beautiful ranch country in the world in the name of "green" energy. So my theme for the following script is truth and honesty in advertising.

Although I'm sure Hallmark movie producers see themselves as family-oriented and wholesome, their Christmas movies bombard audiences with free "advertisements" for sugar and seem somewhat oblivious to the harm some of their happy images can cause. As someone who has struggled with weight my entire life and am now fighting the early stages of Type II diabetes, watching those sweet movies is especially painful. Hallmark viewers probably form strong subconscious links between sugar/alcohol and love/happiness. Elaborate and expensive restaurant meals equal love, baking together equals love, glass after glass of wine, and cup after cup of hot cocoa equals love, over-the-top consumerism and decorations equal love. Hallmark is interested in helping viewers feel good and find love, but maybe they should help us make better food and drink choices along the way?

I doubt a single war has ever been fought when the two enemies didn't both believe strongly that their side was "helping" the human race, while the other side was "harming" it. On one side, food is spiritual, on the other it is "just business." Through advertising, those who raise various crops such as fruit and vegetable growers, cattle raisers, and wheat farmers compete by emphasizing the "health" benefits of their own crops. Unfortunately, too many customers take advertising very seriously and advertisers have learned to play deceptive games. Food choices have almost become an excuse for war. This is nothing new because even in *The Bible*, sheep eaters, pork eaters, and those who ate the fatted calves or worshipped golden ones didn't get along, and often still don't. So food is sort of a natural metaphor for thinking about wars and consequences. Advertising for a mate is even more sinister.

I come from a long line of war veterans. Family genealogy indicates that my ancestors probably fought in every war ever fought on and for our soil, beginning with Mayflower pilgrim William Bradford who fought beside the Wampanoag against mutual enemies. Later ancestors fought against Indians. Several served in the Revolutionary War and those that followed. I had ancestors fighting on both sides of the Civil War and in World War I. My dad and both his brothers fought in World War II: Dad as an Army Airforce airplane mechanic on a ship in the South Pacific, one uncle as a Navy sailor, and one as a Marine. The Marine uncle survived Iwo Jima and Okinawa, also serving in the Korean War, and was eventually killed in the line of duty while serving in the Iowa Highway Patrol. My brother served in the private-sector defense industry his entire life.

My classmates served in Vietnam as did many cowboy friends. For twenty years, I was married to a Bronze Star decorated cowboy Vietnam recon veteran. Many of my students were veterans of our more recent conflicts. Although I never served personally, deep respect for veterans is in my blood. In life, letters, and my dad's war journal, I listened to their complicated feelings toward war and service. Heirs to the o6 Ranch were also descendants of veterans, one member a Gold Star Mother. The ranch participated in a program to host troubled vets, using cowboy work as therapy. So I have strong feelings about "stolen valor," and those who dress like soldiers but never served. Still another way to practice stolen valor is to dress like cowboys or lumberjacks to look as though they do real work but don't. So my character, the salesman, combines several forms of stolen valor as a way to "fool" his farmer customers into trusting him. I couldn't think of worse traits to give a villain.

I also come from a long line of farmers who raised crops and cattle. I grew up on an Iowa farm that belonged to my widowed grandmother, and learned to love hard work at an early age. I'm quite proud of my cousins, Mark Miller and wife Mel, who are still active American farmers. I hope their children will farm. My farming ancestry also includes a bit of Amish (Pennsylvania Dutch), and I inherited some of those values. I happen to know that the reason the Amish don't use machinery, drive cars, or own TV's and phones is NOT because they are broke. I've heard many stories about farmers who lost their farms because they were too easily convinced by salesmen that more and bigger tractors and machines were the secret to success. Instead, those who bought the machines often struggled with debt and spent precious time trying to keep the machines running while their crops over-ripened or rained out. The heavy tractors also compacted the soil, sometimes forming a hardpan that prevented drainage or root penetration. For those who loved horses, the machines also took some of the joy out of farming. My ancestors worked with horses until the 1940s when they switched to tractors. My mom and grandma could both drive teams. My mom drove tractors but I never saw her drive a car. So I'm often called a Luddite, which I consider a compliment. Many traits shared by my characters Daniel and Elizabeth were inspired by this heritage.

One good friend, Rod Flournoy, a northern California rancher, still hooks up teams of workhorses for winter feeding. He says it's because he lives in the mountains where winters are cold. Vehicles with motors often don't start, but his horses always do. He says it's also cheaper, but I'm sure the main reason is that he just likes to work with quiet horses instead of noisy machines. Both people and horses need real jobs in order to be happy. Rod is also quirky about health and food, doesn't smoke or drink. His father, enjoying an evening cocktail while discussing food choices with his son, once said, "Well, Son, if you don't live to be 100, at least it will seem like it." So I borrowed that line. Today under Rod's management, the ranch produces "uncertified organic" beef for another family business on his mother's side: RichardsGrassfedBeef.com. The ranch has never used pesticides and the last application of chemical fertilizer was prior to 1997. His cattle graze freely on grass. Winter feed consists of grass hay, raised and baled on his large mountain-stream irrigated valley. From birth to table, Flournoy/Richards beef is probably some of the purest food on the planet. This friendship inspired my characters' desire to produce healthy food.

The inspiration for Daniel going to work for some rancher as a kid and later inheriting that ranch comes from a two-part interview I did with Bob Eidson (Cowboy Cowman Part I: "Cross HE and Shoe Bar Ranches" and Part II: "Those Circle Horses," *Western Horseman*, 1984). After serving in World War II, Bob needed a job and did what nobody else wanted to do for 30 years. When the owner died, he passed the ranch down to his only son. Nine years later, that unmarried son died with no heirs, so when the will was read, the hard-working cowboy veteran found himself suddenly owning 130-square-miles of ranchland dotted with oil wells. The government gave him six months to figure out taxes, accounting, royalties, and capital gains—things he only vaguely knew existed the day before. Most ranchers consider their cattle business a responsibility rather than wealth, so they sometimes will it to someone they know will take care of the land, animals, and employees. I also quoted Bob saying what almost every rancher explains as the philosophy behind how we raise our children: "You can't buy the kind of quality you can raise."

Raising a daughter in the cowboy world and watching my grandchildren grow up the same way, inspired scenes and character traits for the little grizzlies. Years ago my daughter and I co-wrote a cowboy poem, "My Big Buddy Ty" that tells the story about one particular gruff cowboy. When I saw the movie, "The Bear" the relationship between a cub and a big Kodiak reminded me of their friendship and inspired our poem. Ty inspired Daniel's speech about having the backs of our little grizzlies. An old man now, Ty still helps my daughter and her husband work cattle on their leases and is usually a guest at their Thanksgiving table. I can't think of a safer place for a kid than with any cowboy I've ever known. Cowboys might not always be the most upstanding citizens, but the ones I knew would defend a kid with their life . . . while at the same time ruthlessly teaching self-sufficiency, self-governance, and self-respect—also valued in military training. Rural kids learn to work hard very young and become not only useful to, but respected by, adults. Farm and ranch kids are involved in almost every job. The fencing crew scenes were inspired by some of the kids I watched grow up and helped raise. When my daughter was in high school, the 06 Ranch hired several of her buddies to build a set of pipe corrals at headquarters. The huge job took all summer.

The scene where Daniel changes a flat for Elizabeth in pouring rain was inspired by a "secret code" between my daughter and I about men. Once when we were bringing a herd of cattle from what we call on top down to headquarters for fall shipping, my daughter wanted to help. She was about 9 at the time and riding her own horse "Little Red." About half-way through the drive, it started pouring rain so everyone donned slickers, all except my daughter. We live in desert country so Little Red had not yet been slicker broke, and he was not a horse just any kid could ride. Not knowing how her horse would react, my daughter refused all offers to borrow a slicker and just rode stoically in the rain. By the time we trapped the herd at headquarters, she was absolutely soaked and chilled to the bone. Because she never complained, the cowboys were proud of her. I took her to the bunk-house, built a fire in the woodstove and wrapped her in a blanket until she stopped shivering and we dried her clothes. From that day on when some boy acted interested in her, if he wasn't "our type," one of us would whisper, "I don't think he's ever been wet." My daughter eventually married a cowboy, who would happily ride naked in the rain if it would only rain. So when Daniel says, "I've been wet before," it's not nothing. Being rained on would mean the same to a Marine or a farmer, but I imagine Elizabeth's salesman boyfriend would carry an umbrella.

My mother told me once that her mother "hated birds." I didn't argue but remember being shocked because I remembered my grand-mother loving birds. Every year Gram insisted we string popcorn and cranberries for our Christmas tree, not as decoration but as a gift to birds. After Christmas we packed away ornaments and took the tree with its popcorn and cranberry garlands outside. Gram would also cut suet (animal fat) into chunks and tie those on the branches. She said our tree would now help the birds who didn't migrate get through winter (I still feed suet to birds in winter). Gram's favorite song, which she sang regularly, was "Mockin' Bird Hill." And many of her favorite possessions had cardinals or robins on them. The only birds I remember my grandmother complaining about were those who swooped in when the fruit on her cherry trees ripened. Birds often damaged the fruit and garden vegetables she raised in her huge garden, but not to the extent they damaged cherries. When I conjure childhood memories of picking fresh cherries, I don't remember a single one without bird bites. My grandmother was famous for her apple pies because I don't think the birds ever left her enough cherries. Although I haven't made one in years, I could make a fantastic lattice-topped cherry pie—but from grocery store cherries. My personal favorite Christmas drink is cherry juice or cherry cider made by the Apache farmers around Hatch, NM (also the home of the best green chilis, and some great green chili wine). I stop at their fruit stands whenever I pass through their valley.

I was an ag major in college until my senior year when I switched to English, and then specialized in the way agriculture has been represented in American literature. When it came time to get a PhD if I wanted to keep my job as a college professor, I chose the University of Nevada, Reno. UNR seemed to be ground zero for the environmental movement that was bent on eradicating cattle grazing from public land. As the chair of my dissertation committee, I chose a vegetarian. I planned to either sink or swim. Another chosen member was the reining Edward Abbey scholar. At the time, Abbey's books were often quoted as support for environmental causes, but he once worked as a cowboy in southern Arizona. I did a lot of serious research analyzing Edward Abbey's work. Yes, he cursed beef eaters as part of his curmudgeon persona, but he ate a lot of steaks. He also made fun of vegetarians eating "pussy food," their screaming sentient veggies, and Indians wiping out native animals because they were hungry. Abbey wrote literature using environmental and food issues as metaphors and symbols, not as facts and role models. (For more see my published dissertation: *The Wild and The Domestic: Animal Representation, Ecocriticism, and Western American Literature*. U of Nevada Press 2000).

Another master of agricultural metaphor was Robert Frost. One of his most famous poems is "Mending Wall," about two farmers as they work to repair an old rock fence between them. One raises apple trees and the other raises pines for lumber. The apple raiser seems to think the fence is unnecessary, but his neighbor keeps repeating "Good fences make good neighbors." Curious, I did some research on the situation and it forever changed the poem's meaning for me. Without a barrier, pinecones will roll, sprout their seeds among the apple trees, and eventually choke out an apple orchard. The apple farmer says, "Before I built a wall I'd ask to know/ What I was walling in or walling out." He thinks neighbors only need walls when there are cows and compares his pine-raising neighbor to "an old-stone savage armed" who "moves in darkness." But they rebuild the wall anyway. The pine-raising farmer was protecting his neighbor's apple orchard. So my character Daniel rebuilds a fence to protect his neighbor's orchard from cattle he knows will only do it good.

Eating flowers recalls a writer's retreat I attended in 1998 in Missoula, Montana with nature writer Gary Paul Nabhan as instructor. He asked us to take a walk and spot something that "spoke to us" and then try to describe it in very fine detail, using all five senses if possible. Nothing was "speaking" to me until I spotted a sprig of common clover in bloom which reminded me of my childhood on our Iowa farm. After several minutes of note taking, I was not too impressed with what I had written, so eventually I popped the clover blossom into my mouth and chewed it. When I ate clover as a kid, it seemed very sweet, but I could hardly detect any sweetness at all as an adult. I had probably developed a weak palate for sweetness after a life of consuming sugar. So I wrote about eating clover.

Another literary influence was Voltaire's "Candide," which I taught in my world literature classes. After stumbling around the world from one terrible misadventure to the next, fighting wars, barely escaping death, repeatedly finding and losing the love of his life, the naïve and optimistic young Candide finally concludes that this is NOT a perfect world. In the end he decides the best we can do is to cultivate our own gardens. My farmer grandmother raised almost all the food our family ate. I raised a huge garden during my early marriage, and my daughter still gardens. The line "scare you to death" came from an old government wolf trapper listening to coffee shop vultures complain about the government and wishing "they'd just tell us the truth." It seemed like a line Voltaire would agree with, and probably Marines, cowboys, and gardeners.

As to details, I've watched lots of kids playing in the dirt. I like the line about stirrups and legs and use it often. I've been unable to change a few flat tires because the lugs had been tightened with impact wrenches. Anyone who lives on a remote rocky road or around desert thorns, doesn't trust those modern donut spares. New black felt cowboy hats "bleed" for a while until rain, dirt, and sweat finally stop that nonsense. I once witnessed a deer that had been hit by a car, crawling on its two broken front legs, trying to graze. I called the local game warden to come and put it out of its misery. That sight still haunts me. Although there are probably a thousand "recipes" for cooking a steak, my character prefers cowboy style over wood coals, just like steak has been cooked since we lived in caves. Daniel's recipe is my recipe.

I've tried to "fix up" lots of cowboys with women who might fit their lifestyle. One of the biggest mistakes I believe most people make when looking for a job or looking for a mate is advertising themselves as what they think the employer or prospective mate wants instead of who they really are. I always tried to convince my family and students not to do that. I said they might land a job or mate that way, but they wouldn't be able to keep it and even if they did, they'd be very unhappy trying to be someone they weren't. On the surface Elizabeth and Daniel seem like opposites, but as they get to know each other, they turn out to be very much alike, their food differences actually turn out to be minor.

We attach baggage and assumptions to choices we make about food, dress, religion, dancing or not and sometimes start wars over trivia. Then we turn people into enemies and monsters in order to justify war. My suggestion, through my character Daniel, is to honor FREEDOM through honesty and choice. That kind of freedom is worth fighting for.

War on Sugar

T. ORCHARD MONTAGE. DAY

In a dream, Elizabeth, in a gossamer dress walks through a peaceful orchard, picks an apple, and bites into it as we see a snake slither away from the tree. After biting the apple, she is bombarded by Santa, elves, children, grandmas, all tempting her with alcohol and sugar (cookies, hot cocoa, wine, cocktails, yule logs, gingerbread houses, chocolates, etc.).

INT. JUICE BAR. DAY

Returning to reality, Elizabeth, average pretty, not much make-up, simple hair, and dressed like a hipster, has dozed off behind her juice bar counter while waiting for customers. As the bells on her door jingle, she jumps awake. It's her boyfriend, Bob. Bob wears jeans, wellington boots, a black t-shirt with a military-style camo jacket and a Cabela's cap.

LIZ Oh, it's you.

BOB That's not a very friendly way to greet your boyfriend.

He leans across the counter and they quickly peck/kiss.

LIZ Sorry, Bob. I was having a bad dream. Business has been so slow.

BOB Maybe your customers have already started baking Christmas cookies?

LIZ That's exactly what I was dreaming about. How have the worst possible food and drink choices become so entwined with Christmas? It's become a homage to sugar and a war against health.

BOB Have you thought anymore about purchasing my company's cold press juicer?

Elizabeth pinches the top of her nose as though getting a headache. Her expression says, "Not this again."

LIZ I can't even pay my electric bill, Bob. I've asked a few regulars why they are coming in less often and they say Christmas has gotten so expensive that they can't afford juice this time of year.

BOB Well, they don't seem to have a problem spending cash on alcohol and candy.

LIZ Exactly. Everyone seems to associate juice with summer and Christmas with sugar and alcohol. So I've been trying to dream up ways to advertise healthier choices for Christmas.

BOB Any ideas?

LIZ Mostly I've been dreaming about losing the battle. The nightmare I was having when you woke me was about being attacked by Christmas movie characters force feeding me cookies.

"

BOB *(laughs)* Well, Lizzie, Christmas is big business and so is health food.

LIZ Not to me. Christmas and food should be about love. I show love by feeding the people I love healthy food and show love to myself by putting healthy food into my body.

BOB Sounds great in theory, but your juice contains sugar too. And how do your numbers add up?

LIZ *(getting irritated)* We better change the subject.

BOB *(looks at his watch)* I need to get going anyway. I have a meeting with another customer in a few minutes.

LIZ So am I just a customer?

Bob leans in for a good-bye peck/kiss. Liz obliges reluctantly.

BOB Aww, Babe, you know I didn't mean it that way. Now, come on, chin up. I'll show my little Lizzie some love with an expensive dinner Saturday night. Meanwhile, I'll dream up an advertising campaign for you.

She smiles weakly.

EXT. RANCH HOUSE PORCH. LATE EVENING

Two adults, Dad (mid-thirties, dressed like a cowboy, physically fit, wearing a hat) and Mom (mid-thirties, a little over-weight, dressed in jeans, t-shirt, and tennis shoes, long hair in a ponytail, no hat) sit in a porch swing. A third adult, Daniel (mid-thirties, military fit, dressed like a cowboy, wearing a hat), sits on a straight-backed chair that he has tipped back against the

side of the bunkhouse. Two children, Andy and Clint (dressed like miniature cowboys both wearing hats, Andy is seven-ish, Clint 9-ish) sit cross-legged in the grass just off the porch, pulling up weeds, tossing little rocks, drawing in the dirt with a stick.

ANDY Uncle Dan, are you a bachelor?

DAN I guess.

MOM And he'll stay one if all he does is work.

CLINT How come girls always want everybody to be married?

DAD *(laughs)* Yeah, Mom, how come?

MOM If I remember right, you were the one chasing me, not the other way around.

DAD Guilty.

DAN Well, Andy, I don't run into many women out here, except you guys. You're a bit young for me and your mama seems to be taken. So any suggestions?

ANDY You need to advertise.

DAN Like put a sign in my pickup window "Used Man For Sale Cheap"?

ANDY No. Like the boys at school do.

DAN And just how do the boys at school advertise?

ANDY Show off. Hit girls in the arm. Accidently bump into us. Tease. – You know, just act really, really stupid.

DAN *(laughing)* That sounds like great advice.

DAD When I was advertising for your mama, I guess I did some stupid stuff, maybe even accidently bumped into her, but I didn't hit her in the arm. Clint, how do you advertise?

CLINT I don't. I'm gonna stay a bachelor.

MOM Give him a couple more years.

ANDY It ain't rocket science, Uncle Dan. Just find a girl you like and act stupid. She'll figure it out.

DAN *(laughing)* Well, I'm pretty good at acting stupid. Where do you suggest I find girls?

ANDY Walk around where girls hang out and pick one.

DAN I've sort of tried that, but I'm not buying what most girls seem to be advertising.

DAD Yup. All that make-up, short skirts, high heels . . . girls would have more luck if they advertised who they really are instead of what they think men want. It's no wonder men get confused.

ANDY What are men confused about?

Daniel, Mom and Dad all look at each other.

DAN *(attempting to explain)* Most girls don't want to live like we do. They want fancy houses, fancy cars, meals in fancy restaurants, sidewalks and paved streets—places where they can wear high heels.

ANDY Well, just don't pick one of those. This ain't rocket science.

CLINT *(to Andy)* So when did you get to be an expert on rocket science?

DAD *(to Daniel)* There's a few good ones left. I found one. Put your old Marine recon skills to work.

Dan looks thoughtful, like maybe this isn't just a crazy idea.

ANDY The hard part will be figuring out if she likes you. Girls are smarter than guys. We don't act stupid.

MOM *(stifling a laugh and changing the subject)* Uncle Dan, do you want to come over for supper? I'm cooking spaghetti.

DAN Sounds good, thanks, but you guys are spoiling me. I gotta cook a little or I'll forget how. Besides, I gotta figure out what I'm gonna wear tomorrow to go advertise for girls *(winks at Andy)*.

INT. JUICE BAR. AFTERNOON

Daniel is walking down the street in town, looking at girls walking by and those inside stores. It is 5:00pm, about "Happy Hour." The girls are advertising (high heels, short skirts, tight zebra striped pants, etc.) His expression says he's not buying. Then he glances at one window and the camera zooms in on the word "bar." As his eyes refocus beyond the glass, he sees a girl behind a counter dusting bottles of fruit juice. He walks in acting like a cowboy entering a real bar. Once inside, he looks around like he might have screwed up but doesn't want to admit to making a mistake. The "bartender" (Elizabeth) is smiling at him. He steps up to order, turns away from her, leans on the counter with one elbow and faces the door as though it really is a cowboy bar.

DAN *(over his shoulder to her)* I'll take a beer, whatever you got on tap.

LIZ *(amused)* Are you an actor?

DAN What?

LIZ Well, dressed like that you're either some Hollywood actor or you're very lost.

DAN *(frowning)* I'm no actor and I ain't ever been lost.

LIZ Well, I don't serve beer here.

DAN So then why does your sign say "bar" if this ain't a bar?

LIZ My sign says "JUICE bar".

DAN Well The Gallopin' Goose Bar doesn't serve goose. You need to sell what you're advertising.

LIZ I do. I sell juice. Do you want to order one or not?

Dan looks dubiously around at the colorful display of juices.

DAN Do you serve anything that ain't pink?

LIZ *(sarcastically)* How about green?

DAN Maybe. I like green pastures and olive drab.

LIZ Well I have a green juice called "Clover." Would you like to try it—on the house? It's obvious that you're a bit out of your comfort zone.

DAN Clover, huh?

LIZ Yes.

DAN OK. I used to pick those purple clover flowers and eat them when I was a kid. But I don't eat flowers anymore.

LIZ I believe that.

She hands him a bottle of green juice. He looks at it with suspicion.

DAN Is this stuff sweet?

LIZ No added sugars.

DAN That didn't really answer my question. I don't eat sweets. I lost my sweet tooth when my adult teeth grew in.

LIZ Beer has sugar in it.

DAN What?

LIZ Not only that, but alcohol of any kind contains sugar and disrupts your body's ability to process it.

DAN You sure about that?

She points to a diploma for a degree in nutrition science from Arizona State hanging on the wall.

LIZ I have a degree in nutrition. Alcohol also disrupts the body's blood sugar balance and sets you up to crave sugar later.

DAN So sugar is the enemy, huh? Just as I thought.

LIZ Well, not all sugar. During digestion, our bodies change almost everything we eat into sugars, which we call calories and use for energy.

DAN Hummingbirds need a lot of energy, but they need real sugar. They'll die if we feed them honey.

LIZ Right. But we're not hummingbirds. We get plenty of calories from healthy food. Extra sugar is our enemy.

DAN Well, ain't you just a fountain of knowledge? *(sips)* Hey, this ain't bad.

LIZ It isn't bad.

DAN *(fakes confusion)* Ain't that what I just said?

She rolls her eyes. He grins, obviously pulling her leg. As he drinks, they lock eyes for a beat.

DAN So what's in this stuff?

LIZ Clover, kale, cucumber, celery, spinach, pear, cilantro, mint, and lime.

DAN Wow. That's quite a list. I can even spell most of those words, except cilan . . . ah . . . whatever.

LIZ *(amused)* Everything is locally grown organically from soil to bottle. No chemicals, no big words.

DAN So what's this magic potion supposed to do for me?

LIZ Boost immunity, reduce inflammation, promote digestion, increase energy.

Dan looks at her skeptically. She looks a little guilty, but the moment passes. He points to her sign on the wall and the camera zooms in. The sign says "The greatest fine art of the future will be the making of a comfortable living from a small piece of land. —Abraham Lincoln."

DAN I like your sign, only instead of a small piece of land, I'd change that to a big ol' ranch.

She points to the clock, it says six-thirty.

LIZ I close at six.

DAN Great. Let's go grab a burger? *(she frowns)* Never mind. I'll take that as a NO. Thanks for the clover. *(leaves)*

INT. FANCY RESTAURANT. NIGHT

Bob is dressed for dinner (white shirt, no tie, sport coat) and looking over the menu. Elizabeth is dressed in a non-sexy cocktail dress looking around the room at the elaborate decorations. Bob will order a much more expensive meal for himself.

LIZ Christmas is so commercialized.

BOB You sound like my grandma, Babe. You want to string popcorn and cranberries and decorate outdoor trees with suet cakes for the birds?

LIZ You can be so cynical.

BOB Just realistic. Christmas is big business.

Waiter comes to take their order.

BOB The lady will have your vegetarian special and water. I'll have a New York strip, medium rare, loaded baked potato, three sprigs of asparagus, and a glass of your house merlot.

LIZ Do you even know what the vegetarian special is tonight?

BOB No, but you don't have too many choices with your eating fad.

LIZ It's not a fad, and healthy doesn't have to be boring.

BOB No, but it has to signal deprivation, correct ethics, and high morals. It's all about identity.

LIZ What?

BOB Health food is a business, Lizzie, a big business. Just like Christmas.

LIZ What are you saying?

BOB Business is all about advertising and advertising is all about psychology: pride, love, friendship, loneliness. Christmas plays on nostalgia and guilt. People feel guilty about ignoring their parents and not spending enough time with their kids. So advertisers prey on that guilt.

LIZ And health food?

BOB Not to step on your toes, Babe, but health food doesn't really have much to do with health.

LIZ It does to me. I want to farm healthier and for everyone to eat healthier. If advertising causes customers to buy something they don't need or doesn't deliver what's promised, eventually customers stop trusting you.

BOB But only certain kinds of people come in your store, right? So who comes in? Mostly young, hipster, semi-wealthy singles, right? When was the last time a family or a blue collar worker darkened your door?

LIZ *(defensively)* Just today some cowboy came in. I thought he was an actor, but he seems to be a real cowboy.

BOB *(sensing a rival)* Oh? And what do you suppose he's after? Health?

LIZ Don't be silly. He's just a customer.

BOB And I'll bet your regular customers glared at him, right?

LIZ Well, there were no other customers at the time, but yes, they probably would have.

BOB Your customers and people like him don't mix. They're like oil and water. Health food and juice is about group identity, about being in fashion and signaling which political party you support.

LIZ Everyone is welcome in my store. I don't want to politicize health.

BOB Look, Babe, you can't be that naïve. Everything is politicized. Politicians are master advertisers and advertising is all about convincing people to buy whatever you're selling.

LIZ Advertising needs to tell the truth, if not, then you might be winning battles but losing the war. I don't want to sell a fantasy.

BOB Everyday someone says, "If it seems too good to be true, it probably is," but people still prefer the fantasy.

LIZ People also get angry once they've been fooled. Fool me once and you're a fool. Fool me twice and I'm a fool.

BOB Honesty is not comforting. Why do you think beer commercials always show a guy surrounded by beautiful women instead of sitting at a bar alone? Drink this brand of beer and women will fall all over you. Want to sell to women? Then connect to love. Wear this brand of mascara, and handsome men will drop down on one knee, opening a box with a diamond in it. Want to appeal to professional women? Wear these shoes and you'll get promoted. If you want to sit at the popular kids' table, then eat and drink the right foods.

LIZ That's ridiculous.

BOB Is it? What about the wonderful new "meat" made from plants? It's not aimed at real vegetarians like you who just don't eat meat, and it's certainly not more "healthy." The advertisers are targeting people like me who like to eat meat, like the taste and texture of meat, but who still want to be in fashion and avoid irritating their girlfriends. What do you think would happen to your business if you aimed your advertising at cowboys?

LIZ People are not that easy to fool.

BOB No? Then how did covering miles of desert with solar panels or miles and miles of wind towers become "green" energy? Once advertisers create an enemy, then anything else can be green.

LIZ So what do you advertise?

BOB Service.

LIZ Service?

BOB Yes. I am at your service to make your business more profitable and erase your problems with labor, insects, and processing . . . an endless list. I wear military camo so farmers subliminally assume I'm a veteran and trust me immediately. They even thank me for my service.

LIZ You're not a veteran?

BOB *(laughs)* Lord, no! I wear a Cabela's cap but I don't hunt or fish either.

Elizabeth frowns and sips her water staring at him.

LIZ So how should I advertise to attract customers during Christmas?

BOB Figure out who you want to attract and then what their weaknesses are.

LIZ I want to attract everyone, but not through manipulation. I'd rather try to figure out what I honestly have to offer and that my customers can't find anywhere else.

BOB *(he takes her hand and strokes it)* That's easy, Babe: Your beauty. Convince women they will look like you and men that they will attract women like you if they become regular customers.

Elizabeth is not pleased. She pulls her hand from under his. The server arrives with their food. On Elizabeth's plate is an edible flower. She picks it up, stares at it for a beat and pops it into her mouth.

EXT. SMALL CITY STREET. DAY

Elizabeth is strolling down the street, window shopping, analyzing how other businesses are attracting customers. Windows showcase products as suggested Christmas gifts and use Christmas colors to catch her eye.

INT. JUICE BAR. DAY

The juice bar front window has been miraculously transformed. It is tastefully decorated for Christmas with red and green juices. A green "tree" has been built using different shades of green juice and entwined with white twinkle lights. At its base sit two 4-packs with red and green juices, one tied up with a big red bow and the other with a big green bow. Across the top of the window is a sign "Wishing You a Healthy Christmas!" Dangling below the sign from strips of red ribbon is a row of small round bottles filled with red or green juice. On one side of the "tree" also hangs a vegetable wreath and sitting on the other side is a crystal punch bowl filled with red juice. Daniel walks in again and notices one customer working on a computer. Customer sees cowboy, frowns, gets up and leaves. Daniel looks sad but brightens when he looks at the decorated store. More wreaths hang on the walls, some made of fruits, some of veggies, some of aromatic herbs and some mixed. Juice is offered in various colorful packs done up with ribbon as gifts: green juices with gold ribbon, blue with silver, yellows and oranges with patterned ribbon. Single bottles are bound with a vial of water (like a bud vase) containing a single white rose and tied with various colors of ribbon. Gifts appeal to everyone: kids, lovers, athletes, nostalgia. Rustic "country" juice packs come in brown paper bags with burlap or bandana bows.

DAN Wow! This place looks real Christmas-ey, but how come there's never any customers in here?

LIZ There was one.

She points with her chin to the door just closing behind the laptop guy.

DAN Yeah, I guess I ran him off. Sorry. Somehow I always seem to look like the enemy. But you also need more than one customer, right?

LIZ I do. This place is packed in the summer with people standing in line, but the closer to the holidays it gets, the shorter the lines. Thanks to you, I'm working on that.

DAN *(genuinely shocked)* Me?!

LIZ Yes, remember a few days ago when you came in and made fun of pink? Well, I started thinking of ways I might be able to use color to advertise my products for Christmas.

DAN Like the green juice Christmas tree in the window?

LIZ Yes. I'm also trying to make everyone feel welcome, like these blueberry juice packs tied with silver bows for Hanukah and these gifts for children.

DAN And the wreaths?

LIZ I've been selling those like hotcakes: Fruit wreaths, vegetable wreaths, and aromatic herb wreaths.

DAN And I caused all this?

LIZ Yes! Well . . . I helped you a little. But you planted the seed. Plus I can use color to advertise for almost any holiday: Cinco de Mayo, Valentine's Day, Fourth of July . . . endless. Holidays all seem to have their own colors. I can even use pink at Easter. So whatever you want to drink is on the house again.

DAN Wow. My whole life I've been trying to convince women I'm not as dumb as I look and you're saying all I needed to do was make fun of pink?

LIZ Yes. *(laughs)* So what's your choice?

DAN Coffee, black.

LIZ *(rolls her eyes)* I don't serve coffee or anything with caffeine.

DAN Jeeze. You really are a health nut.

LIZ Yes, I am.

DAN Well, with all this stoic deprivation, you may not live to be a hundred, but it will sure seem like it.

LIZ *(sarcastically)* Haha.

DAN You know, a few years ago doctors were claiming that coffee would kill you. Then they decided coffee would save you. I don't know where that debate is today, do you?

LIZ Here try this.

She hands him a dark brown juice. He holds it up and looks at it dubiously.

DAN Well, it sort of looks like coffee except for being cold. *(smells it)* But it don't smell like coffee. *(takes a sip)* And it sure don't taste like coffee. *(takes another sip)* Not too bad though.

LIZ It's past closing time again. Why do you always seem to come in when I'm ready to close?

DAN I work all day.

LIZ So do I. And I have a mechanic coming any minute to fix one of my refrigerators.

DAN OK. Thanks for the cold coffee.

EXT. DESERTED ROAD. NIGHT

A dark and stormy night (scary music), Elizabeth is parked at the side of the road with a flat tire. It is raining hard. She is on the phone texting Bob and doesn't notice a vehicle cut its lights and pull up behind her.

LIZ *(text to Bob)* Come get me? Flat tire. Mile from home. Need a ride.

BOB *(text to Elizabeth)* Sorry. Dining with customers.

Elizabeth sits there for a beat, looks worried, deciding what to do. Suddenly she hears a sound like popping metal (hubcap being removed). Terror crosses her face. But she reaches for a rain jacket in the back seat, puts it on, puts the hood over her hair, grabs a flashlight, and opens her car door. Some man is bent down loosening the lugs. We can't see too well because of dark and rain. He's wearing an olive-green t-shirt and black cowboy hat. When he hears her open the car door, he stands and turns around. She shines the flashlight in his eyes, blinding him. The black die from his hat is running down his face giving him a sinister look. But we finally recognize Daniel. Has he been following her, stalking her? Elizabeth tries to act and sound brave.

LIZ What are you doing?

DAN Well, this tire looked flat.

LIZ I can change a tire.

DAN You can?

He hands her his four-way tire tool. She hesitates. Should she hit him with it or change the tire? She steps to the tire and tries to loosen a lug. She can't budge it. Jumps on the tire tool, still can't.

DAN You probably get your tire work done at a shop where they use power tools.

LIZ I guess.

DAN Well, those tools always tighten lugs too tight for most people to loosen.

LIZ Except you?

DAN *(laughs)* Well, I ain't Superman, but I do use my hands and back for more than pushing computer keys.

LIZ Are you stalking me?

DAN *(holds up his hands in surrender)* Whoa . . . I'm just driving home with some groceries. Saw a car with a flat and stopped to help. I had no idea it was you. What are you doing way out here?

LIZ Also headed home with groceries.

DAN Where do you live?

LIZ *(eyes him suspiciously)* I don't tell strangers where I live.

DAN Good idea. But if I was the boogie man, this looks like a great opportunity.

She stands there in the rain, holding the tire tool sort of in a defense position. However, she gets distracted by the muscles showing through his wet t-shirt.

DAN So are you gonna knock me in the head with that, or can I have it back?

She hesitates, but hands him the tool and he returns to loosening lugs. She now holds her flashlight on the tire so he can see.

LIZ Aren't you cold?

DAN I've been cold before.

LIZ But it's December and you're soaked?

DAN I've been soaked before.

LIZ Well, so have I, but not if I have a choice.

DAN You probably never had as much to prove as I did.

LIZ *(laughs)* Probably not.

She pops the trunk, grabs the spare donut, and carries it to him.

DAN *(sarcastically)* Oh, what a cute little toy tire! That should get you home safely. Car manufacturers—anything to save a buck.

They both look dubiously at the donut. He finishes changing it and stands facing her. Still pouring rain. She is mostly dry in her rain gear, but he's totally soaked.

LIZ You have black stuff dripping down your face.

DAN Yeah? Damn black hats always do that when new. That's why I took my shirt and jacket off. Does it make me look scary?

LIZ Not anymore. Thanks for helping.

DAN Thank you for deciding not to hit me with the four-way.

LIZ *(laughs)* You're funny.

DAN Want me to follow you home? That cute tire might leave you stranded again.

LIZ *(nervous)* I'll be fine.

DAN *(shrugs)* Your choice. *(turns to leave)*

LIZ *(looks at the donut)* Wait! OK. You can follow me home.

She starts to pick up the flat to put it in her trunk. He reaches to take it from her.

DAN Here . . . I have a tire shop at the ranch. It's not far. How about if I take your flat home, fix it, and put it back on early tomorrow morning so you can get to work safely? You won't even know I've been there.

LIZ *(bites her lip)* OK. Thanks. I'm braver in daylight.

DAN *(laughs, carries the flat to his pickup)* Me too.

EXT. LIZ'S HOUSE. LATER.

When they reach her house, Daniel waits until she turns on a light, honks and waves, she waves back, he drives off.

EXT. LIZ'S HOUSE. MORNING·

The next morning when she gets to her car, ready to head to work, she glances at the tire. It's fixed and has an olive-drab band-aid stuck to it. She smiles.

INT. JUICE BAR. ALMOST NOON

Elizabeth is sitting behind her counter with a bowl of cherries and pitting them one at a time with a chopstick and an empty small water bottle. Two customers are sitting at a table, talking and also pitting cherries. Bob enters wearing camo jacket and Cabela cap.

BOB Your decorations look great, Babe! You are finally starting to get the hang of advertising for Christmas. Still not too many customers, but like I always say, build it and they will come.

LIZ Thank you and I hope so.

BOB But what are you doing?

LIZ Pitting some of last year's frozen cherries.

BOB With a chop stick? They make machines for that you know, and I happen to sell them.

LIZ I know, for a mere twenty thousand dollars. I can barely afford chopsticks. Besides I need to keep my hands busy so I don't fall asleep.

BOB You will have a lot bigger crop of cherries this year because your trees have matured and we've been having perfect weather. You will have way too many cherries to pit by hand.

LIZ Maybe, but a few customers—like those two—also seem to enjoy doing something with their hands. It helps conversations flow more smoothly. I'm thinking about advertising cherry pitting as an activity—inside here during winter, maybe outside at the farm in summer. People need to stop staring at screens.

BOB There's a hat for every head. But it sure doesn't look like much fun to me.

LIZ A family of five came in earlier and they all sat around a table pitting cherries for two hours while drinking cherry juice. I offered them a discount for each pound of cherries they pitted. The parents seemed to use it as a teachable moment.

BOB Teachable for what? To prepare their children for assembly line job skills? Taking jobs from illegals?

LIZ More like teaching them where their food comes from and how much easier it is to talk when families work together. It also made my juices a little more affordable for them, especially when they consider their time here as a ticket-free family activity.

BOB If it wasn't winter, I'd think you've been out in the sun too long.

LIZ So, I guess that means you won't be coming in to pit cherries with me?

BOB *(laughs)* No, Babe, that won't happen. But I did come by to take you to lunch.

LIZ I brought my lunch today. I'm going to stay open and see if I'm missing customers who might come in at noon.

BOB Everyone leaves the office, goes to lunch at noon, and you don't serve lunch.

LIZ This may come as a surprise to you, but there are actually a few people left in this world who don't work in an office.

He pecks her on the cheek and walks to the door.

BOB Suit yourself.

LIZ And they don't all wear suits.

INT. JUICE BAR. LATE AFTERNOON

Daniel walks in with two cowboy kids.

LIZ Well, what have we here?

DAN This is my crew. They got thirsty after working all day, so I told their mama that I'd take them to town and we'd go to the bar.

LIZ *(very friendly toward the kids)* Well, you've come to the right bar.

DAN So you like cowboy kids, just not after they grow up?

LIZ They're so cute when they're little.

Kids frown.

DAN They don't like to be called little.

LIZ So what are your names?

DAN This is Andy *(girl)* and this is Clint *(boy)*. Andy and Clint this is . . .

Daniel waits for Elizabeth to say her name.

LIZ Oh, I see what you're doing.

DAN I'm just trying to introduce you to the kids.

LIZ Hello Andy *(Andy sticks out her hand to shake, they do)*. Hello Clint *(they also shake)*. My name is Elizabeth but my friends call me Lizzie.

DAN So, Elizabeth, can you recommend some juices for them?

LIZ Does that mean we are not friends?

DAN Right. Besides Lizzie sounds like a reptile.

Elizabeth is somewhat taken aback but recommends juices for each, describing the tastes and purposes. They each select one of the juices she recommends but not the one she recommended for that person.

LIZ Andy, I think you'll like my cherry juice. It is a mix between two different kinds of cherries. Sweet cherries are too sweet and sour cherries are too sour, so mixing them is just right.

Daniel chooses the cherry juice, but not Andy.

LIZ *(turning to Daniel)* The drinks are on the house again—for helping me with my flat tire.

DAN No. That was just neighboring. We live on the same road. You need customers, and I want to pay this time.

LIZ OK, that'll be thirty dollars.

DAN Whoa . . . *(holding up and looking at his small juice bottle)* is this stuff made of gold?

LIZ Have you priced a steak lately?

DAN Touché. *(hands her money)* But . . . I can work all day on a steak. I couldn't do much on one of these—except maybe yoga *(looking at one customer on a computer)* or type.

They take stools nearest to the cash register where Daniel can talk to Elizabeth. Andy climbs up and mounts her stool like it's a horse. Daniel reaches over to steady the stool but otherwise lets her struggle.

LIZ And what's wrong with yoga? It's great exercise.

DAN Well, people who work all day don't need exercise. Besides we'd rather get paid to exercise than pay somebody to let us ride around on their machines in stretchy pants, right crew?

Kids glare at Elizabeth and sip their juice like cowboys sipping beer. All three sort of slouch on the stools, leaning on the counter.

LIZ Just curious . . . do you people ever sit up straight?

DAN We sit and stand up damn straight all day long. So when we relax, we relax. Right crew?

The kids continue to glare at Elizabeth and sip their drinks. By this time the single other customer on the computer is looking over at the three ducks out of water and smirking.

ANDY Whater you smirkin' at, Mister?

CLINT How come you ain't wearin' no socks?

LIZ We teach our children to be polite to strangers at a young age.

DAN We teach our children to let strangers know they're dealing with young grizzly bears at a young age. If they get respect, they'll give it. Right crew?

The kids have finished their drinks. When Daniel rises, the kids slide off their stools. All three in one motion turn to walk out. Daniel turns back at the door, standing very straight, like at attention.

DAN You never asked, but my name is Daniel—after Daniel Joseph Daly, a Marine who won two medals of honor, should have been three.

Liz is not sure what his point is but knows his mood has changed.

LIZ So . . . ah. . . what do your friends call you?

DAN *(stiffly)* Daly's friends called him Dan. He never married. Some say because the corps never issued him a wife.

LIZ *(maybe a little scared of him again)* OK. Daniel it is.

Daniel turns crisply and walks out, following the kids.

INT. KITCHEN TABLE AT RANCH. SUPPERTIME

Ranch family of four (Andy and Clint, Mom and Dad) seated around square kitchen table.

MOM So, did you enjoy hanging out at the bar with Uncle Dan today?

ANDY Not really.

DAD Why not?

CLINT First off, it wasn't a real a bar, just a juice bar.

ANDY And Uncle Dan told us not to say a word while we were in there, just to sip our juice and give the lady bartender our cowboy stares.

CLINT So he could make googly eyes.

MOM Googly eyes?

ANDY Yeah. He just wanted to introduce us so he could find out her name. She knew it was a trick, but said her name anyway.

DAD Was she pretty?

ANDY *(dismissively)* She's a city girl.

CLINT One of them yuppies or hippies or whatever those people who don't wear socks are called.

ANDY Those people who look like the wind will blow them over.

MOM *(holding back a laugh)* Well, we can't allow Uncle Dan to make googly eyes at some city girl.

DAD *(smiling)* Yeah. We better nip this in the bud.

Mom stops smiling, suddenly becomes serious.

MOM *(to dad)* But we also better make sure we aren't raising children who think people who don't wear socks are their enemies.

DAD *(also stops smiling)* Right.

Both look at the kids.

INT. FEED STORE. SATURDAY MORNING

A female with her back to the door (and camera) is dressed like a farmer in rubber farm boots, jeans, plaid shirt, gimmie cap and is signing a ticket at the counter. Daniel walks in and patiently waits behind her. When she turns, he recognizes Elizabeth. Another customer stands behind them waiting, but they stare at each other for a beat and then stand there talking, totally unaware of anyone else.

DAN *(shocked)* Whoa . . . Elizabeth, what are you doing here?

LIZ Does that question mean I don't belong here?

DAN I'm sorry. I was just being protective of the kids the other day. They liked the juices and want to come back. So do I.

LIZ OK then, I'm sorry too. You were becoming a customer and I need customers.

FEED STORE SALESMAN *(interrupting)* Excuse me, but I need customers too.

DAN *(finally noticing the customer waiting)* Oh, yeah, sorry.

He takes Elizabeth's elbow and gently but firmly steers her away from the counter where they continue to talk.

LIZ As I was saying, I need customers, but I have also been sort of enjoying our . . . ah . . . arguments.

DAN *(laughs)* Yeah. Me too. I live alone and usually work alone or with kids, so I don't get much adult conversation.

LIZ Your children don't have a mother?

DAN Oh, they're not mine. I'm not married. Did you think I was trying to cheat on a wife?

LIZ *(embarrassed)* No . . . I . . . .

DAN Those kids belong to one of the married cowboys. They call me Uncle Dan, but I'm not their uncle either. It takes a village to raise our little grizzly bears, so we all pitch in.

LIZ Did their mother think you were taking them to a real bar where alcohol is served?

DAN Maybe, but she'd also figure it would be a cowboy bar. We cowboys might be sort of hard on each other sometimes, but most of us would lay down our lives for any kid, and their mamas know that. Did you ever see a movie back in the eighties called "The Bear"?

LIZ No.

DAN Well as usual Hollywood made it goofy—about a big male Kodiak who befriends an orphaned cub. In real life male bears eat cubs, even their own. But I liked it anyway because the movie sort of captured the bond between cowboys and kids.

LIZ For example?

DAN I don't remember it too well, but just when the bad guys are about to capture the cub to sell to a zoo or something, the little guy bravely stands up to fight and the old male Kodiak stands up right behind him. The bad guys run off and the cub thinks he scared them away all by himself.

LIZ And your point is?

DAN My point is that we give our little cubs lots of freedom, but we've always got their backs. There's almost always an adult grizzly standing right behind them.

LIZ I never thought about raising kids that way.

DAN The world is a dangerous place. We don't want our kids to grow up to be victims. But back to what you are doing here . . . and lookin' like that?

LIZ I'm buying winter feed for my sheep.

DAN But I thought you were a city girl?

LIZ I never said that. See, you jump to conclusions too. I'm actually a farmer. I raise all the fruits and vegetables for my juices. My parents both died young of cancer and my grandparents raised me on their farm.

DAN I'm sorry.

LIZ Long time ago, but I naturally became interested in health. When I was about to graduate college, my grandparents also passed within days of each other from strokes.

DAN Wow. That's a lot.

LIZ It's OK. I miss them all terribly, but my parents were in such pain and my grandparents' quality of life would have never been the same again. It was truly all a blessing—not so much for me—but for them. Anyway, as an only child and only grandchild, I inherited the farm. It was sort of a perfect storm and I put my degree to work while trying to live a healthier life.

DAN That's a healthy way to look at it.

LIZ As farmers they had all over-used chemicals—maybe even causing the cancer—so I am taking the farm in a totally organic direction. I want everyone to live healthier lives, me included.

DAN That's admirable, but most people can't afford to drink your juices very often.

LIZ I know, and I'm working on that, but between the soil and the bottled product, there are a hundred costs: mostly machines. I eliminate some distribution costs with my store, but I just spent this month's profit buying winter feed for the sheep that mow my orchards.

DAN I hear ya. The same is true in the cattle business. Beef customers want smaller, leaner, less expensive portions, but the middlemen who run the feedlots and packing houses won't listen. So we've also gone organic, butchering and marketing our beef as grass-fed and cutting out middlemen.

LIZ So have you been able to lower your prices?

DAN Some. If we sell local.

INT. FANCY RESTAURANT. EVENING

Bob and Elizabeth are on another fancy dinner date.

BOB You've been worrying about cutting expenses, so I've got a Christmas deal for you.

LIZ *(deep sigh, dreading his "deal")* I'm listening.

BOB How about free fertilizer for your cherry trees for Christmas? It is time to apply it to guarantee the biggest cherries.

LIZ I've been thinking about that. I can't advertise my cherries as organic if I use chemical fertilizer.

BOB Babe, you are taking this organic stuff way too seriously. Nobody else does.

LIZ What do you mean?

BOB People don't read the fine print. It's all about advertising, remember?

LIZ But organic means no chemicals.

BOB Depends on who you're talking to. Stuff labeled "All Natural" for example can include just about anything because every chemical, every heavy metal, even rat poisons, are made from "natural" ingredients found right here on earth. There's no other place to get ingredients. Advertise your juices as "raised with no herbicides and no fungicides," just don't mention fertilizer.

LIZ So, you want me to lie?

BOB Just think of it as smart advertising.

LIZ But one reason I want to farm organically is because my parents died of cancer. Organic is not about business to me, it's about life.

BOB Why can't it be both?

EXT. JUICE BAR.
MID-MORNING

Bob is just leaving when Daniel walks up to the door. They both eye each other disdainfully. Daniel tips his hat respectfully, Bob just brushes past him.

INT. JUICE BAR.
IMMEDIATELY AFTER

Daniel walks in.

LIZ Daniel! I'm so glad to see you! *(he looks surprised, shocked, pleased)* The machine and operator came this morning to fertilize my cherry trees but couldn't because some stray cattle were in there grazing. Can you help me get them out?

DAN *(amused)* Doesn't your boyfriend *(he waves his hand toward the door)* sell a machine that can remove stray cattle? Is he a veteran?

LIZ No. And no.

DAN Well, maybe some of your customers could use their laptops to remove the cattle?

LIZ HaHa *(fakes being irritated)* Can you help me or are you really just an actor?

DAN What you see is what you get. I just want to hear you admit that when you need a cowboy, you need a cowboy, and nothing else will do.

LIZ OK. You win. I need a cowboy . . . but just today.

DAN *(teasing)* That's a start. So, how much do you usually pay to get these trees fertilized?

LIZ What's that got to do with stray cattle?

DAN *(amused)* Nothing. I'm happy to help, but if trees are involved, we might need two cowboys. Do you have a horse?

LIZ No.

DAN Can you ride?

LIZ I had a pony when I was a kid, so maybe—if it's a gentle horse.

DAN I've got one of those. I'll be back to pick you up before noon. Can you close for an hour or two?

LIZ Yes. Not many customers come in around lunch. I will put a sign on the door.

DAN I'll be back as soon as I can.

LIZ But don't you want something to drink first?

DAN When there's cattle to chase, I'm not thirsty anymore.

EXT. LIZ'S HOUSE/ORCHARD.
NOON·

While Daniel waits for her to change clothes, he looks around curiously while unloading and bridling two already saddled horses from the trailer. She comes out looking sort of like a cowgirl: boots, jeans, winter jacket, wild rag, even a fairly decent hat (but sort of farmer looking).

LIZ So how do I look?

DAN Like a farm girl pretending to be a cowboy.

She frowns. He mounts, guides his horse to stand close in case she needs help, but she's able to get on smoothly.

DAN Stirrups ok?

LIZ Perfect. You evidently know just how long my legs are.

He shrugs sheepishly. They ride into her orchard, riding and talking. When they find the first heifer, he points to the brand (a C) and camera zooms in on it.

DAN I think I've solved your mystery. Looks like we're neighbors. See that C brand? These heifers belong to me. Well, to the ranch . . . and the bank. Anyway, evidently your farm joins our heifer pasture. Yearling heifers are bad about finding or making holes in a fence. I checked it before we put them in here but it's old and patched too many times. I'll get a crew out here to start a new fence this week-end. But are you sure you want them out?

LIZ What do you mean?

DAN Well, you are trying to think of ways to save money and eliminate chemicals and machines, right?

LIZ Right.

DAN You can't get much more organic or greener than Mother Nature's original fertilizer. Instead of paying for bags of who-knows-what and some machine to come and spread it around, why not just put these heifers to work? I'm sure the ranch owner will even be happy to pay you a little for the grazing. Once the weather turns hot again, these heifers will love all this shade too.

LIZ Will they chew on tree bark? Cherry trees have thin bark that's easy to damage.

DAN *(laughs)* Nope. Can't. Cows don't have any top teeth. They graze by wrapping their tongues around grass. They could lick it, but not chew on it.

LIZ Sheep do a great job mowing the rest of my orchard, but I can't use them for cherry trees.

DAN Yup. Sheep have both top and bottom teeth and make better mowers. I never saw a sheep chew on tree bark, but I ain't been around many sheep. Probably, like deer though, they'll nibble on soft, thin bark.

LIZ They do, I've watched them.

DAN But cattle won't, and with smooth bark, I doubt cattle will even rub on it to scratch an itch. Anyway, we will be wasting our time moving these heifers until I can fix the fence. So how about watching them for a few days and see how they do? I'll put a gate in the new fence to get them out.

LIZ I think that sounds OK.

DAN If you notice any damage, I can be here in an hour or less to move them.

LIZ OK.

DAN The heifers will also need water.

LIZ You probably saw those old pens close to my house? The sheep use one pen that has a water trough, but there are two pens. I will just need to open a gate.

DAN Sounds perfect. Cattle don't like to drink where sheep drink. I guess they share a few of our worst human characteristics, like being judgmental and clannish.

They return to Daniel's pickup and horse trailer, dismount, and Daniel replaces the two horses' bridles with halters in order to load them.

LIZ Free mowing, free fertilizer, free application of fertilizer, no bark damage, and I'll even get paid for letting them mow my grass. This is starting to sound too good to be true. Will they interfere with harvest next summer?

DAN I guess that depends on the size and noise of the machinery. Big machines might run them through a fence. If you use people, they'll just quietly move out of the way, and maybe out of curiosity watch from a distance.

LIZ I will be using a human picking crew and a pickup or two, probably about mid-June.

DAN Then they should get along fine. Plus, by the time your fruit is ripe, we'll also be throwing these heifers into the cow herd to meet the bulls. We won't have any nervous, yearling heifers like these again until almost Christmas next year, long after your fruit harvest. But anytime you want them gone, just give me an hour.

LIZ Hmmm. Who knew? How much do I owe you for helping me today?

DAN I don't know what a cowboy earns per hour, but it can't be much. But since the trespassers are mine, you actually helped me, so I should pay you.

LIZ Well, then I might give you another free juice again sometime.

DAN *(laughs)* Sounds like a trade. My stomach says it's time to eat. Want to stop for a burger before I drop you off at your store?

LIZ I'm already late—and besides *(warily)*, I don't eat meat.

DAN *(does a double-take)* What? Why not?

LIZ *(tentatively)* Animals are sentient beings who feel pain.

DAN *(laughs)* I'm sure your fruits and vegetables scream too when you stuff them through your juice machines. You need to read some Edward Abbey.

LIZ What does Edward Abbey have to do with it?

DAN *(amused with himself)* He just ate a lot of steaks for an environmentalist. Oh, and when I drop you off don't let me forget to grab four of your juice packs for Christmas presents. They'll be about twice as expensive, but healthier, than four bottles of Jack Daniels. I'm not much of a shopper.

EXT. JUICE BAR. AFTER LUCH·

Daniel and Elizabeth pull up at her juice bar in his pickup with trailer attached, hauling two horses. She is still wearing her cowboy clothes, but does remove her hat and carries it. Bob is waiting in his BMW for her to return and watches her unlock the door, both enter. Daniel leaves a few minutes later carrying juice packs.

INT. JUICE BAR. MOMENTS LATER.

Bob enters like he has just arrived.

BOB *(hiding anger)* Where have you been?

LIZ Oh, I had a little emergency with some stray cattle at the farm. I had to get some help.

BOB I saw that. Was that the same cowboy *(he pronounces the word as though it is distasteful)* who has been hanging around?

LIZ I just asked for his help with the cattle, that's all. I told you, he's a customer.

BOB So do you dress up in costume for all of your customers?

LIZ *(looking down at her outfit)* You mean like you do when you're pretending to be a veteran and an outdoorsman?

BOB I'm gaining customer trust, not advertising for a date.

LIZ Stop it. I asked him to help, and I needed to ride a horse too. Besides I'm dressed more like who I really am and what I really do.

BOB What will your regular customers think if they see you looking like some redneck?

LIZ I told you everyone is welcome in my store. I don't politicize health. I also want to cancel your fertilizer gift and the machine to apply it. I've decided to use cattle instead.

BOB Did the cowboy convince you to do that?

LIZ I make my own decisions. The cattle not only provide free fertilizer, they'll spread it around, and I'll even get paid a little for letting them graze and mow weeds. So, as you are always telling me, it pencils out, and I don't have to lie about raising organic cherries. But maybe I have another idea for some business for you.

BOB Great. I'm at your service. What can I do to help?

LIZ Do you sell netting . . . the kind to protect fruit trees from birds?

BOB No I don't. Netting is old school. But I do sell some great bird repellant.

LIZ I don't want bird repellant. I've told you a hundred times I don't want chemicals.

INT. JUICE BAR. DAY

Daniel comes in again. Elizabeth is dressed like a farm girl now and she will dress like this to the end of the movie (looser fitting jeans, white t-shirt, long-sleeved shirt worn over it like a jacket, sleeves rolled up, sometimes a long-sleeved t-shirt, sometimes a jean jacket). The place is packed with customers, some standing in line. He takes off his hat immediately, smiles at the other customers. Customers are more mixed this time and a few smile back. When he finally reaches the head of the line, he speaks quickly to Elizabeth who is scrambling.

DAN It sure smells good in here, and look at all these paying customers!

LIZ Thanks to you, again!

DAN Me?!

LIZ Yes. Thanks for complaining that your *(she makes air quotes)* "coffee" was cold. That was really a break through. Now I'm advertising and selling lots of hot juices, the most popular is cherry cider, even though it's my most expensive. People are even buying it by the gallon to serve hot as a red Christmas punch. Try it, on the house.

She hands him a paper cup with lid.

DAN Well, you look really busy, and I don't want to scare off any customers. Thanks for the cider.

LIZ You're welcome. And thank you . . . again.

She looks after him with a little affection, then waits on the next customer.

INT. FEED STORE. EARLY MORNING

Elizabeth is buying more sheep feed.

FEED STORE SALESMAN Will that be all today, Miss Elizabeth?

LIZ Do you sell netting to cover and protect cherry trees from birds when the fruit starts to ripen?

FEED STORE SALESMAN We sure do.

He taps a second on his computer, shows her the netting and price, she nods yes.

FEED STORE SALESMAN I should probably place the order for you in a couple of months to make sure they arrive by the time you'll need them.

LIZ OK. Put me on your calendar and order enough for 20 trees. I'll also need four of those long bamboo placement poles. Can you deliver it all to my cherry orchard?

FEED STORE SALESMAN You bet. I'll make a note.

Dan enters the store just as she is turning to leave.

DAN Well, hello. We seem to be on the same schedule for buying feed.

LIZ Yes, we do.

He walks her out the door.

DAN Are you busy Sunday?

LIZ No. I'm closed. Why?

DAN How about I pick you up and you can meet my fencing crew since they'll be working in your orchard.

LIZ OK. About eight AM?

DAN Perfect, see you then.

Dan turns around and re-enters the feed store.

EXT. RANCH FENCE LINE. MORNING·

Daniel drives up to the fence line with Elizabeth. Several teens of all colors, ages, genders, tattooed, purple hair, etc. are working on the fence (digging holes, setting posts, mixing cement in a bucket, welding corner posts and making a gate, stringing wire, screwing in stays, clipping wires to the posts, laughing and talking. Clint and Andy are helping too. Daniel and Elizabeth sit on his pickup tailgate watching the kids work.

DAN Neighbors are supposed to share the expense of a new fence, but since this is a short piece and you don't have livestock on the other side, I'll take responsibility.

LIZ You are being a very considerate neighbor.

DAN Good fences make good neighbors. How do you like my crew?

LIZ I'm surprised!

DAN You shouldn't be.

LIZ They just don't look like people I would expect you to hang out with.

DAN These are military kids from the base. At least one parent is actively deployed. Since I was raised in a military family, I know how hard it is to make friends, how boring life without friends can get, and how badly kids want something useful to do. I supervise and do all the wire stretching—the only part that can be dangerous. The younger kids fetch and carry. It makes me feel like Christmas to hang out with them.

LIZ Are your parents still alive?

DAN Yes, both active duty Marines, lifers. I only see them once every few years, almost never at Christmas.

LIZ So why do these kids make you feel like Christmas?

DAN I always spent it with other military brats. We were never really part of any other community. Christmas was a time to miss at least one member of our family and concentrate on duty.

LIZ So you connect Christmas with love?

DAN I never thought about it that way, but I suppose so. I never connect Christmas to gifts, food, or lights.

LIZ So what else do you connect love with?

DAN I guess the same things I think about at Christmas: my military family, community, forgiveness, and duty. I don't connect love to roses, chocolates, teddy bears, and candlelight.

LIZ So how do you show someone you love them?

DAN Service and forgiveness, I guess.

LIZ Forgiveness?

DAN So we can avoid wars.

LIZ Are you a veteran too?

DAN Yes, ma'am. Marine recon. Falluja. Operation Phantom Fury.

She looks at him very seriously, then like she's thinking back over their acquaintance.

LIZ Once a Marine always a Marine? Son of a Marine, even named after a hero Marine?

DAN Yup. Semper fi.

LIZ So what or who have you forgiven?

DAN You ask tough questions. *(breathes deep)* This country isn't perfect, but neither am I. That's why the world needed forgiveness so badly, which is what the original Christmas was all about.

LIZ We seem to have forgotten the forgiveness part.

DAN I have an ancestor who died at Shiloh during the Civil War, fighting in a grey uniform for his family and his community. Maybe he was on the wrong side, but I'm still proud of him. Proud of his sacrifice. Proud of his service. I believe our so-called leaders make lots of mistakes. But I love this country *(looks around with an expression like he's not sure what he means by that)* So I forgive them too.

LIZ Do you think soldiers are ever told the truth about what our wars are really about?

DAN Maybe not. I once heard a very wise old government wolf trapper say, "If they told you the truth, it would scare you to death."

LIZ Do Marines love people?

DAN *(laughs)* Fiercely.

LIZ Why do Marines always claim to be Marines for life?

DAN I consider fighting for my country like love, even when I think our side might be wrong. When you love deep enough, you accept the difficult jobs, serve, never give up, and never expect gratitude.

LIZ Why recon?

DAN Recon used my cowboy skills of lookin' for trouble and tryin' to fix it. When I came back, I could fit right back in.

LIZ Have you ever had PTSD?

DAN What is this, a job interview? *(sigh)* I don't think so. But I do struggle with survivors' guilt. Why was I spared? Why was I never injured? Those guys who came back without arms or legs or faces—those are the real heroes, especially the ones who figure out a way to keep serving. One guy, we call him Wheelie, sometimes drives a bus for these kids.

He's confined to a wheelchair, but he wears that wheelchair like it's a chest full of medals.

Daniel starts to choke up but swallows it. Elizabeth watches the emotion on his face intently, waiting patiently until he can go on.

DAN I'm not sure there is anything Wheelie can't do once he decides it needs doing. He's a master mechanic, machinist, engineer, welder—anything. He designed and built his own chair lift to get him in and out of the bus. He's a great role model for the kids because there's not much they want to whine about when he's around.

LIZ How was he injured?

DAN No idea. It's never come up. We've always been too busy on the next project to rehash the past. He even got married a few months ago. Instead of one best man, he had thirty-five standing beside him.

LIZ So why aren't you married?

DAN No idea. Time to stretch some wire.

He gets up and leaves her sitting. She watches him walk to the fence line.

INT. PICKUP CAB. EVENING.

Daniel is driving Elizabeth home. She is too quiet and he is concerned.

DAN You haven't said a word all the way home. Something wrong?

LIZ Marine recon. That means reconnaissance, right, like spying?

DAN *(laughs)* Well, more like research, like gathering information to figure out who is friend and who is enemy, what the problems are.

LIZ *(accusatory)* You have been reconning me, haven't you?

DAN *(surprised, then resigned)* People don't usually advertise themselves truthfully. How else would I get to know you or even find you?

LIZ So none of this has been an accident: the flat tire, coming to the juice bar, running into you at the feed store?

DAN Running into you at the feed store the first time and the flat tire were both accidents. But I did capitalize on the situations.

LIZ You put the *(uses air quotes)* "strays" in my orchard?

DAN Yes.

LIZ So this has all been one big lie?

DAN How is it a lie? I've just been trying to get to know you, and find ways to let you get to know me. Figure out ways I might be of service while making you stronger. I never asked for or expected anything in return, not even gratitude.

LIZ This is not the way to build trust.

DAN Evidently. I guess expensive dinners and bouquets of roses are better. That's not me, sorry.

They pull up to her house. She gets out and stares at him for a beat.

LIZ Stop following me.

She slams the pickup door and walks away. Daniel looks after her sadly and drives away.

EXT. ORCHARD MONTAGE. SIX MONTHS LATER.

Elizabeth is dreaming again. She's back walking the orchard in a gossamer dress with cherry trees in bloom. This time paradise turns into being chased by machines (tractors, juicers, pitters, stemmers, mixers, grinders, etc.) A leaf blower is blowing dollar bills and a vacuum cleaner is sucking them up.

INT. JUICE BAR. JUST BEFORE LUNCH

Elizabeth is asleep again. A book is open across her heart. She's been reading "The Machine in the Garden." Again, the jingle of the door bells wakes her.

BOB Asleep again? I thought June was the start of your busy season?

LIZ I just dozed off for a second. There's a rush from breakfast to mid-morning, and again mid-afternoon. But just before, during, and after lunch it slows down to nothing.

BOB Were you dreaming about sugar again?

LIZ No. This time I was being chased by stainless steel machines and a vacuum cleaner was sucking up dollar bills.

BOB Oh. I see where you're going with that. I also see you are reading "The Machine in the Garden" *(picks up the book)*. Karl Marx wrote that. Are you becoming a communist?

LIZ No, Leo Marx wrote it and he has some interesting thoughts about machines replacing humans and horses.

BOB Look, Babe, you can't run a business on nostalgia. If farmers and orchardists resist progress, they'll end up like cowboys—seen only in movies. History and commerce will leave you behind.

LIZ Every time I turn around, there's another machine to buy.

BOB You're investing in your future, Babe. You're reducing labor costs. It seems like a lot today, but it will all pay off.

LIZ But people need jobs too. Machines don't raise children, pay taxes, or become paying customers.

BOB *(ignoring her)* It had to be scary for pioneer farmers when they bought that first tractor. Do you think farmers should never have bought tractors?

LIZ The Amish didn't.

BOB *(laughs)* And they're all broke. They can't even afford a car. I bet they don't even have phones.

LIZ Thirty thousand dollars for a machine is a lot of money.

BOB And I—Bob Fielder—say thirty gallons of juice per minute is a lot of juice. You have a bumper crop of cherries on your trees and will need that juicer.

LIZ I need to think about it. Besides the hands-on part is what I like most about farming and even about this juice bar. I like making juice in small batches. I like pitting cherries.

BOB But you also want to bring your prices down, right?

LIZ Right, but I can't do that if I keep spending money on machines.

She looks at her sign on the wall and the camera zooms in: "The greatest fine art of the future will be the making of a comfortable living from a small piece of land —Abraham Lincoln."

BOB *(follows her gaze)* I don't like that sign. You need to replace it with one that says "The greatest fine art of the future will be the smart use of machines.—Bob Fielder."

LIZ You and your machines are taking all the enjoyment out of farming for me. Something is either broke down, needs sanitizing, oiling, upgrading, or replacing.

BOB You can't run a profitable business without machines, Babe. Labor costs are skyrocketing and pickers are impossible to find, not to mention undependable. Machines that shake cherry trees will soon replace the last pickers. Tree shakers are getting better every day.

LIZ I've read about them. We farmers are already being advised to plant trees whose shape will be more compatible with shakers. My trees have just reached maturity and this will be my first big crop. I refuse to start over.

BOB Write this down, Babe: Today I, Bob Fielder, recommended that you start planting new trees to be ready for the shakers. I'm trying my best to help you.

LIZ But half the cherries on my trees will always ripen early and the other half two weeks later. A machine can't tell the difference between a ripe and unripe cherry. I will waste half my crop by shaking the trees either too early or too late.

BOB Well, lucky for you, I still run a cherry picking crew on the side. I've got you covered for now. Besides cherry harvest is still a month away. So stop worrying. Let's go to lunch?

LIZ I brought my lunch.

Bob shrugs with irritation and leaves.

INT. FEED STORE. DAY

Elizabeth comes in with an envelope in her hand.

FEED STORE SALESMAN Hello, Lizzie, what can I do for you today?

LIZ Can I just leave this note for Daniel? Will you give it to him next time he comes in? I haven't seen him in a while, and I need his help. I don't have his phone number, don't know where he lives, and don't know how else to contact him.

FEED STORE SALESMAN Sure. He should be in later today.

LIZ Perfect. Thanks.

INT. JUICE BAR. DAY.

Daniel walks in just before closing time, but not smiling.

LIZ Daniel, you got my note. I need help again, but this time it's not a cowboy job. I hoped maybe some of your fencing crew might be interested.

DAN I'm listening.

LIZ My cherries are getting close to ripe so the fruit-eating birds are starting to show up. I ordered netting and bamboo poles from the feed store. The nets are very light weight, but it is still a two-person job to lift them up and over the tops of the trees with the poles. I could do it with one other person, but three extra would be even better. Two teams could finish more quickly.

DAN I'll ask the kids. If not, then at least I'll help you. I'm not too proud to get off my horse.

LIZ I'm sorry. *(rambling, not wanting to discuss their fight)* My . . . ah . . . a salesperson wanted to sell me some bird repellant, but I don't want chemicals. Also, I only need to repel the worst birds. I don't mind sharing with a few robins and orioles. I even tolerate woodpeckers because they are also after insects. But those starlings and blackbirds travel in huge flocks. They can strip an entire orchard in one day.

DAN Sounds like at least you are starting to figure out the difference between your bird friends and enemies.

LIZ *(realizing they are not just talking about birds)* A repellant would keep all birds away all year, and I don't want that. Netting is more selective.

DAN When do you want us or me?

LIZ How about 5:30 AM tomorrow?

EXT. ORCHARD. LATE AFTERNOON

Daniel pulls up with the two Apache boys in the cab of his pickup. They all get out and Elizabeth walks up to meet them.

DAN Elizabeth, this is Sam and Vic. They come from a long line of fruit growers in New Mexico.

LIZ *(to the boys)* Have you netted cherry trees before?

SAM Yes.

VIC On the Rez.

SAM Mescalero Apache.

VIC Our grandparents' orchards.

LIZ Great. I've never netted cherry trees before, so you can teach me.

DAN Sam you work with Elizabeth, and Vic you'll be my partner.

The boys nod and spot the netting and poles. They lay two poles on the ground beside each of the first two trees, along with a net for each. Then they start to load the rest of the netting into Daniel's pickup. Daniel and Elizabeth both follow their lead and help load. Once all nets are loaded, the boys hop in the back on top of the netting.

VIC Slow and steady.

Dan gets in the driver's seat and Elizabeth takes shot-gun. Dan watches the boys throw down nets via his mirrors.

LIZ They don't talk much.

DAN Nope.

LIZ I'm sorry about the other day.

DAN *(reserved)* No problem. We're here.

LIZ But I didn't just ask you to come because I needed help.

DAN You could have asked your boyfriend or customers?

LIZ I could, but none of them actually work.

DAN So it's not stalking if you need me?

LIZ I'm sorry. I've thought about it a lot. You were right. How else do people ever get to know each other?

DAN Andy says they advertise.

LIZ Advertise?

DAN Yes. She says the boys at school act stupid when they are advertising.

LIZ *(laughs)*. Andy! So what about the girls? How do they advertise?

DAN Andy didn't say, but the ones I've seen around town wear lots of make-up, fancy hairdos, short skirts, high heels . . . whatever they're advertising, I'm not buying.

LIZ I've never been very good at advertising.

DAN I like that better.

LIZ *(warily, not sure they've made up or what)* I don't know what to say.

DAN Since you weren't advertising, I had to figure out a way to find out more about you. I did it the only way I know—which evidently was my way of acting stupid.

LIZ It wasn't stupid.

DAN Well it didn't work.

LIZ I sent you a note, didn't I? Isn't that what the girls at school would do?

Both laugh and lock eyes for a beat.

DAN I never got a note before.

LIZ I never wrote one before.

INT. INSIDE DAN'S PICKUP. DAY·

After all the trees are netted, Daniel and the Apache boys are in his pickup cab. Elizabeth stands near Dan's window and hands Dan cash. He divides it evenly between the two boys, keeping none for himself.

DAN I'll take the boys home and be back. While I'm gone think about coming to the ranch so I can show you where I live and cook you a nice, lean, grass-fed steak. If you decide to come, you can make a salad to go with the steaks.

LIZ *(obviously wants to accept)* But I don't eat meat.

DAN Then make a good salad. You don't ever have to eat anything you don't want to. I'll be back. We need to talk.

LIZ Yes, we do.

INT. DANIEL'S PICKUP. LATER

Back in Daniel's pickup, Elizabeth holds a covered salad bowl on her lap.

DAN I know food means more to you than fuel. To me it's just fuel. You can eat or not eat whatever you want without judgment from me. All I ask is that you give me the same freedom.

LIZ But meat is unhealthy.

Daniel's face says he doesn't like this, but he's trying to make up. He decides to get it over with. Deep sigh.

DAN Who's healthier a wolf or an elephant? Vultures or rabbits? Even Whole Foods sells meat: Animal Welfare Certified, local, organic, grass-fed, dry-aged beef. The ranch sells it to them.

LIZ What does Animal Welfare Certified mean?

DAN No antibiotics, no hormones, free-range, humane processing.

LIZ But animals are sentient beings.

DAN Plants are alive too.

LIZ But they don't feel pain.

DAN How do you know? Do you speak plant?

LIZ Do you speak cow?

DAN Yup.

They both laugh. Daniel pauses for a moment and their eyes lock for a beat, then his face turns dark.

DAN Have you ever seen an animal starve to death?

LIZ No.

DAN Well, I have. Most wild animals die that way. I once watched a young healthy deer, hit by a car, crawling on its broken legs, still trying to graze because it was so hungry. I shot it and ate it. Have you ever seen an animal die of thirst?

LIZ No.

DAN Neither have I. I take that part of my job very seriously. I can't feed them all but I can water them all—from yellowjackets to wolves.

LIZ But killing animals is cruel, especially to eat them.

DAN Are owls cruel? Are spiders that eat hummingbirds? Male bears that eat their own cubs? Mother Nature's *(air quotes)* "natural" death is the cruelest death of all. When a wild animal's teeth wear out, they begin a slow painful descent into starvation.

LIZ Predators eat them.

DAN Predators don't want them. Once an animal is no longer strong enough to catch or walk between their food and water, they have to make a choice. They often die near water where I find them. If old animals could talk, they'd beg for a bullet. Nobody is crueler than Mother Nature herself . . . or Himself, whatever.

LIZ But murdering animals just for food when we can easily eat something else . . .

DAN So you consider harvesting livestock as murder? What about killing other people just because they disagree with our religion or our politicians? Is that murder? Are soldiers murderers? Am I a murderer?

LIZ This is becoming a very uncomfortable discussion.

DAN Yes it is. But if it is gonna be a problem, we might as well get it over with.

LIZ I need time to think. I just want everyone I care about to be healthy.

DAN Are you saying you care about me?

LIZ I'm saying that I want you to be healthy.

DAN And I'm saying that to me health involves more than food choices. There's mental health, physical health, economic health, societal health . . . all kinds of health. I even consider our food supply to be a matter of national defense health. Once we are dependent on foreign food, foreign-made harvesting and processing equipment, foreign labor, even foreign-owned land . . . then all our weapons of mass destruction will be worthless. Once our enemies have the power to empty our grocery store shelves, they'll have us on our knees.

LIZ I need time to think about this.

DAN OK. But, seriously, you don't have to eat any meat. I believe in freedom of choice . . . very deeply, both for you and for me.

LIZ *(trying to lighten the tone)* I don't have to eat even a bite?

DAN *(laughs)* No. But I will. I just want your company while I cook.

LIZ *(obviously wants to get along)* OK. I'd like to watch you cook.

EXT. YARD IN FRONT OF BUNKHOUSE. LATE EVENING˙

Evening at the ranch, bunkhouse in the background. Daniel and Elizabeth sit on each side of a handmade picnic table, staring into the campfire and up at the stars. A lantern sits in the middle of the table giving a soft light. A covered salad bowl sits at one end of the table along with two metal plates and two metal cups, two forks and one steak knife (for her, he will use his pocket knife). A galvanized bucket with a ladle handle sticking out sits at one end of the table. A small grate leans against one table leg ready for Daniel to place it on top of four rocks. The rocks frame the fire that has burned down to coals. The steaks sit out of Elizabeth's sight already seasoned on the other end of the picnic table bench that Daniel sits on.

LIZ This is nice. What a beautiful evening. So peaceful.

DAN *(dips the ladle and pours water into each cup).* All I've got to offer you to drink is water with no ice.

LIZ No beer or wine?

DAN I don't drink.

LIZ But you ordered a beer the first time you came in my juice bar?

DAN I was being stupid, remember. I saw you through the window, thought you were pretty, wanted to meet you, and figure out if you were single.

LIZ So when did you figure that out?

DAN As soon as I asked you to join me for a burger. If you were married or even had a serious boyfriend, you'd have said so right then, but you didn't.

LIZ If I remember correctly, I didn't say anything.

DAN Right. I knew you were single but just didn't trust me. I thought maybe I could fix that.

She smiles and shakes her head at his reasoning. He levels the coals, balances the grate on the rocks, and carefully lays two steaks on the grate.

DAN I do drink coffee, but seldom eat town food. I prefer to cook.

LIZ Then why did you keep inviting me out for burgers?

DAN I wanted to know if you ate meat. I suspected that you didn't.

LIZ You are one strange bird.

DAN I hope so.

A quiet pause as we listen to the fire crackle, a cricket chirping, maybe an owl hoots.

LIZ I hate to say this, but that smells so good. What's your recipe?

DAN Let steaks warm to room temperature; dust both sides with garlic salt and a little coarse-ground black pepper and while that soaks in, wait for the fire to burn down enough for coals. Then I let the coals work their magic. It's caveman cooking, well except for the pepper. Technology hasn't improved it and never will.

LIZ How did you end up here?

DAN I got tired of all the moving around, following my military parents. So I went to work for an old rancher when I started high school. My folks got to know him, liked him. When he offered this bunkhouse so I could finish high school in one place, they let me stay. I'm still here.

LIZ *(surprised, looks around)* So, you've been living right here, as my neighbor, since high school?

DAN Yup, except for a tour of duty. Uncle Sam paid for my degree in ag-business from the local college, and I kept right on working and living here.

LIZ And we never met?

DAN Nope. *(he turns the steaks)*

LIZ You never wanted to see the world?

DAN *(laughs)* I've been on every continent and across every ocean. I think seeing the world is way overrated. Finding home is much more difficult.

LIZ I feel at home on my grandparents' farm.

DAN And ten years from now?

LIZ Everything hopefully the same, but selling juices and produce that everyone can afford.

DAN Husband? Kids? *(looks at her sideways)*

LIZ I don't know. *(looks at him sideways)* So far I like the sound of helping to raise village kids.

DAN Yup. Lots of kids out there need a village. But they need the kind of help that makes them stronger, not the kind that makes them weaker. Steaks are done!

She opens the salad bowl and piles some on one plate and hands it to him. He places a steak on it and sits it where he had been sitting. She piles salad on her own plate and hands it to him. He takes her plate and looks at her.

DAN You don't even have to look at it. I'll eat it tomorrow.

LIZ Put it on my plate. I will just smell it.

He places the other steak on her plate and hands it to her. She looks at the steak dubiously. Smells it. Reluctantly she cuts a tiny bite, closes her eyes, and just as she is about to place it in her mouth, Dan speaks.

DAN The pretty little teenaged Hereford heifer that steak came from had big brown eyes and long white eyelashes.

She grimaces and puts the piece of meat back on her plate.

LIZ Why did you say that?

DAN *(laughs)* That's part of the way our village raises kids and horses. When we find something they don't understand or are afraid of, we poke at it, but they always have a choice. Eventually they ain't scared of nuthin'. Works every time. You didn't really want to eat that bite. You just wanted to please me. You don't have to do that. Just be yourself.

EXT. FARM HOUSE. NIGHT

They pull up to her farm house. Her side of the pickup is almost next to the porch. She gets out.

DAN *(quickly)* I'll walk you to the door.

She waits for him to catch up. He takes her hand to assist with the step up onto the porch. They face each other and he takes hold of her other hand.

LIZ I really had a good time today, both netting trees and watching you cook. Thank you.

DAN I enjoyed your company.

LIZ I'm sorry that I didn't eat any steak after all your trouble to cook it.

DAN I love to cook with fire. I said it was your choice to eat meat or not and I mean it. Food choice is not a contest, not my identity. This is a free country. I want you to feel free to make your own choices without pressure or manipulation. Freedom is not a game to me. It's non-negotiable.

LIZ I believe you.

Both lean in for a kiss. Dan stops and kisses one of her hands tenderly instead.

DAN I probably better go. I think you still have some unfinished choices to make.

LIZ See you soon?

DAN *(crooked smile)* See you soon.

They both keep a hold of the one hand until both their arms are stretched to the limit before letting go.

INT. JUICE BAR. DAY.

Bob walks in and Elizabeth looks up with determination.

LIZ Bob, we need to talk.

BOB Yes, we do. I don't like that cowboy.

LIZ Well, I do.

BOB *(ignores her)* It seems like every time I invite you to lunch or on a date lately, you're too "busy."

LIZ And when we are together all we do is argue about what I need to buy.

BOB I am just trying to help you to make wise decisions.

LIZ Look, you are a really nice guy . . .

BOB That's not usually the start of a conversation that ends well.

LIZ It's time we admit that a romance between us is just not working. We see the world too differently.

BOB So, you're breaking up with me?

LIZ I'm sorry.

BOB Anything I can say or do to change your mind?

LIZ No.

BOB *(big sigh)* OK. I can't say I'm surprised. I knew that cowboy would cause trouble.

LIZ This is not about him. It's about us.

BOB Can we still be friends? Still do business together?

LIZ Of course.

They hug. Bob kisses her cheek. Dan has pulled up with Andy and Clint at just the worst moment. When they are about to enter through the glass door, they see the embrace. Daniel stiffens, turns on his heel and strides back to his pickup, the kids hurry to catch up. He slams his pickup door, grips the steering wheel in frustration, and as soon as the kids are settled, drives away. Kids remain totally quiet and motionless.

INT. RANCH HOUSE KITCHEN TABLE. NIGHT

Andy and Clint are sitting on a bench on one side of the family's square table. Daniel sits across from them, with empty chairs at each end. Mom and Dad are putting the last serving bowls on the table, after they sit, everyone bows their heads to say their own brief silent prayers and almost in unison say "amen." They pass the food and talk.

MOM So how's it going with the pretty vegetarian farmer?

DAN It's not.

ANDY He saw her hugging some guy today.

Daniel glares at Andy who glares back.

DAD *(to Dan)* You fell for her didn't you?

DAN No.

He keeps his head down and continues eating.

MOM *(to husband)* Why did you say that?

DAD Because he's a guy and I'm a guy and you women never know what's going on until after we walk away.

MOM Well you didn't walk away?

DAD I never saw you hugging some other guy either.

DAN She also accused me of stalking her.

ANDY And they call you people grown-ups.

CLINT It's best to just stay away from girls.

ANDY Yeah. Because we're gonna break your little sissy hearts.

MOM *(glaring at Andy, then her husband)* Where does she get this stuff?

CLINT She pulls it out of her . . .

DAD Clint!

CLINT Yes, sir.

MOM Where did you hear language like that young man?

She looks accusingly back and forth between her husband and Daniel.

DAD Clint, answer your mother.

Clint looks at both men, crosses his fingers behind his back on both hands before answering.

CLINT At school.

Andy quickly opens her mouth to point out that Clint had his fingers crossed, both men quickly glare at her, and instead of speaking, she stuffs a forkful of food in it. Mom is not fooled and stifles a smile.

MOM *(teasing)* So, Dan, did you fall for her?

DAN Of course not. She was obviously in love with some salesman. I rescued her from him a dozen times—she called it stalking. I tried but she kept going back. She made her choice. It's a free country.

CLINT But you always told me a Marine never gives up?

DAN *(looks at Clint, big sigh)* Where does he get this stuff?

ANDY From a guy who used to be a Marine.

DAD Andy!

ANDY Yes, sir. But . . .

MOM Anne Marie!

ANDY Yes, ma'am.

Daniel looks at both kids with affection and smiles.

DAN The trouble all began when we started letting them sit at the adult's table.

Andy and Clint high five.

DAD So if you like her, fight for her. All is fair in love and war.

DAN Right. And love and war are real similar. In war you can make someone surrender, but you can't make them love you. Nobody has learned that lesson better than the United States Marines. You can make someone respect you. You can save them from the bad guys a hundred times, but you can't make them trust you. Love is always a choice and she made hers. I believe in freedom.

Andy and Clint look at each other.

DAD Does she know you own this ranch and live in the bunkhouse so we can live here in the big house?

DAN No. I wanted her to choose me, not what I own. She chose him. End of story.

ANDY You really have given up?

DAN Well, not technically, I still plan to find a woman someday who will love me as much as your mama loves your dad. But it just won't be this woman.

DAD So, what's your next move?

DAN *(big sigh)* Recon, I guess—as always—for the next mission.

Mom and Dad solemnly nod and resume eating. Andy and Clint look at each other. They haven't given up.

INT. FEED STORE. DAY.

Daniel is inside the store but off to one side. Elizabeth rushes to the counter, holding back tears. Daniel silently fades into the shadows.

LIZ Please tell me you know of someone I can call to pick my cherries?

FEED STORE SALESMAN I'm sorry Lizzie, the only person I know who still runs a picking crew is Bob Fielder. I thought you guys were dating?

LIZ Not anymore. That's the problem, I guess. *(She tries to shake off tears, but they well up)* I broke it off with Bob several weeks ago, but now that my cherries are ripe, he just informed me that he had been offered a bigger and better paying job for his pickers. He says my organic farm is small and doesn't pay as well as commercial operations.

FEED STORE SALESMAN You didn't have a contract?

LIZ No. He was my boyfriend. I never dreamed he would do something like this. He said it was nothing personal, just business. I'm sure that's true. Everything was always just business to him.

FEED STORE SALESMAN It's none of my business but I think he furnishes pickers just so he can leave farmers in the lurch when they need him the most. That tactic helps him to convince them that laborers are undependable and to buy one of his machines. He's good riddance if you ask me.

LIZ I totally agree. I just wish I had figured him out sooner. If you hear of anyone, please call me. I'm really desperate. *(she hurries out)*

DAN *(approaching the counter)* What was that all about?

FEED STORE SALESMAN Big Business Bob left her high and dry with a crop of ripe cherries and no picking crew. Said he got a better offer for his pickers from a bigger farm.

DAN What about their contract?

FEED STORE SALESMAN Didn't have one. Love is not only blind, it's also stupid.

DAN It sure is.

FEED STORE SALESMAN She'll never be able to find a crew of cherry pickers this late in the game. She might as well take that netting off and let the birds feast.

EXT. ELIZABETH'S ORCHARD. EARLY MORNING.

Elizabeth is in the orchard, exhausted, picking cherries, dirty, sweaty, a mess. A military bus pulls in with the military kids from the fencing crew who start piling out and lining up, waiting. The last three off the bus are Clint, Andy, and Daniel.

DAN I wasn't spying. I was already in the feed store when you came in upset. I told the kids you lost your cherry pickin' crew and might need them. So, here we are.

LIZ *(at first speechless)* Are these all Marine kids?

DAN Affirmative.

LIZ But isn't this illegal?

DAN That's Wheelie's job . . .

Dan points to the bus driver in a wheelchair who is lowering himself from the bus with a lift. Wheelie looks like a homeless man, but he has a laptop on his lap and heads in their direction.

DAN He looks a little scruffy right now because he's working as an undercover cop, but he's been accepted to law school, so his appearance should improve soon.

WHEELIE I have all the laws right here, Miss Elizabeth *(pats laptop)*. No school attendance problem because it's summer. *(reaches into briefcase attached to side of his WC.)* These are signed parental permissions and affidavits swearing to the kids' ages. Actual pickers must all be over 16.

LIZ But some of these kids are too little to be 16. *(she looks at Andy)*

ANDY We told you once, we don't like to be called little. Besides, some of us ain't pickers, we're water boys . .

CLINT . . . And water girls

ANDY . . . errand runners, sun screen providers. Stuff like that.

MK *(MK stands for any one of the Marine Corps kids)* If we wanna share some of our wages with them for sharing their water and sunscreen with us, whose business is that?

DAN You'll just write one check to me as the contractor. I'll pay my crew. If anyone gets in trouble, it'll be me. I've been in trouble before.

Elizabeth looks at him with relief, gratitude, and maybe more.

MK We believe in what you're trying to do. We believe in healthy bodies. We are all in great physical shape and we want to serve.

MK Why is it OK for us to play basketball all day out in the sun, bouncing our heads and knees on concrete slabs, but not OK to be paid to pick cherries to stay in shape?

MK Basketball gets boring. We want to do something real.

CLINT We want to work. We like to work.

LIZ But I can't hire kids to do dangerous work.

MK Ma'am. No offense, but our parents are Marines.

MK If cherry picking is so dangerous, how come it's OK for families with kids of all ages, even toddlers, to pick their own cherries for fun?

MK The only difference between work and fun is wages.

LIZ But you will need to climb ladders.

MK You mean those dangerous things attached to slides that we've been climbing since we were two?

ANDY I've been climbing ladders on slides since one and a half.

MK *(tallest kid)* I'll pick the tree tops. I like heights. *(he or she starts putting on an olive drab safety harness)* This safety harness has never been used to pick fruit, but it'll work. I've used it to prune storm damaged trees and climb electric and telephone poles.

Elizabeth looks to Daniel. He shrugs as though saying, "your choice." But doesn't speak, lets the kids do all the talking.

SAM Rule-makers don't have jurisdiction on the Rez.

VIC Apaches make New Mexico's famous cherry cider.

SAM Boredom causes alcohol and drugs.

MK We're here to fight for jobs for kids.

MK My father enlisted in the Marines when he was 18. This country was willing to let him take a bullet before they would let him vote or drink a beer.

VIC Machine salesmen and illegal picking crews want child labor laws.

SAM American kids need jobs.

MK Why is it OK for machines to replace kids who want to work and earn money, but not the other way around?

LIZ *(to Wheelie)* So how much do I need to pay?

WHEELIE Minimum wage is fifteen dollars in this state. They can only work eight hours per day, with a lunch hour and two fifteen minute breaks—which, depending on how long it takes, should be about one-third of what adult pickers would cost you.

MK And don't worry, Lady, our parents are Marines. . .

Andy elbows him in the ribs (she ain't scared of no Marine kid twice her size), he frowns at her, she frowns back, he backs down and corrects himself.

MK . . . and cowboys. *(Andy smiles)* We ain't a bunch of lollygaggers. We ain't gonna pick slow to earn more money.

LIZ You aren't a bunch of lollygaggers.

MK *(looks confused)* Ain't that what I just said?

He looks at Daniel who shrugs and stifles a smile. Liz closes her eyes in frustrated surrender, again looks to Wheelie.

LIZ Are you sure this is legal?

WHEELIE Yes ma'am.

ANDY And if it ain't, it should be.

LIZ *(looking affectionately at Andy)* Spoken like a true cowboy.

ANDY *(quickly gives a cowboy nod with her hat brim)* Yes, ma'am, I am.

Elizabeth starts handing out picking bags, older kids start grabbing and carrying ladders, and the two Apache brothers start un-netting the first tree.

EXT. ORCHARD. EVENING

Fast forward to an old tractor pulling a trailer piled high with boxes of cherries, tree nets all back in place. Kids sitting in a circle, laughing, talking, and drinking water. Elizabeth hands a check to Daniel.

LIZ *(to the crew)* You were right, this was much cheaper than the adult picking crew would have been, not to mention so much more fun and rewarding. You did a great job of picking just the ripe cherries and leaving the unripe. A machine can't do that. In a few days, I hope maybe you will all come back when the rest of the cherries ripen.

Kids all eagerly nod yes.

DAN They won't let you down.

LIZ Thank you all so much. I will look for more jobs that can be done better and cheaper by hand. You kids give me hope that maybe this country will be OK.

Marine kids all salute. Andy and Clint touch the brims of their hats.

DAN You can't buy the kind of quality you can raise.

LIZ Thanks for letting me join your village.

DAN You'll need to find your own village. This is just business. And to be completely honest, I own the ranch where I work. The old man left it to me when he died.

He looks standoffish, she looks hurt. He turns to follow the kids.

LIZ Daniel, wait . . . What have I done?

Daniel gets on the bus.

SCENE INT. JUICE BAR. AFTERNOON

Andy and Clint come in the juice bar with their parents and all four choose juices from the refrigerator. Elizabeth is waiting on a customer. When the family steps up to the counter, Elizabeth looks glad/surprised to see them and relieved.

LIZ Andy! Clint! It's so good to see you. *(kids don't smile, reunion turns awkward)* These must be your parents? Hi, I'm Elizabeth . . . um, a friend of Daniel's.

She offers to shake hands but the family doesn't respond.

DAD Nice to meet you. The kids wanted some juice. How much do we owe you?

LIZ *(taken aback)* It's . . . it's . . . on the house. Daniel and your hard-working children have done so much for me.

MOM We know that, but you paid them, and we can afford to pay for our drinks. You're a businesswoman and we are customers.

LIZ *(stricken)* OK. Forty dollars.

Mom and Dad look at each other quickly. It is more money than they expected. They don't have that much cash.

MOM Will you take a check?

Liz is even more ashamed of her prices.

LIZ Of course.

Mom writes a check, hands it to Liz, and they all turn to walk out.

LIZ Thank you, and please tell Daniel I said hello.

ANDY *(spins around angrily)* No! You were his girlfriend but you picked a bozo.

Liz and Andy try to communicate while the family tries to shush Andy, all talking over one another.

DAD Andy!

LIZ I didn't pick anyone else. What do you mean?

MOM Anne Denise!

ANDY We saw you hug him.

DAD Andy! That's enough, come on. *(He grabs Andy's arm and walks her out)*

LIZ No! That was a goodbye-forever hug. I had just broken up with him. I picked Daniel!

Clint is the last one out and the only one who hears her final sentence. Just as the door is about to close behind him, he sticks his head back in.

CLINT He likes pie—especially cherry.

DAD Clint!

Clint hurries to join his family.

EXT. BUNKHOUSE PORCH. EARLY EVENING

Elizabeth steps up on Daniel's bunkhouse porch cradling a perfect lattice-topped cherry pie in her hands. Before she can knock, Daniel opens the door and sees the pie. His eyes bug out. She starts talking fast, stumbling over her words.

LIZ Ah . . . I know you don't eat sweets . . .ah . . . but . . .

DAN *(grabs the pie)* Except for cherry pie!

Daniel smells it, closes his eyes in ecstasy, turns and walks into the bunkhouse carrying the pie like it's fragile and precious, and sets it on his small table. Behind him on the wall we can see a decorated Marine recon paddle. We don't need an explanation;

it just needs to be there for any Marines watching. Daniel grabs a fork and starts eating the pie out of the pan. Meanwhile Elizabeth follows him inside and keeps stumbling over words.

LIZ *(rattling)* I know it's full of sugar, and you have adult teeth, but it's all made from scratch . . . I picked every cherry myself . . . although I did buy the other ingredients. Oh, and I did bake it in an electric oven which, I guess is a machine, . . . and I know I shouldn't confuse love with food . . .

He freezes, stops stuffing his mouth, puts his fork down and swallows hard . . . staring at her.

LIZ . . . but the kids said . . .

DAN The kids?

LIZ Andy and Clint. They came in with their parents and Andy said . . . you saw me hug Bob but it was just a breakup hug . . . and Clint said you liked pie.

DAN Especially cherry pie?

LIZ Yes. Wait . . . I've been trying so hard to disconnect love and emotions from food and here I am . . . still trying to use food to say . . .

DAN *(gently taking hold of her by the shoulders)* Did you say love, twice?

LIZ *(hesitates)* Yes.

He finally kisses her.

DAN Believe me, I know the difference between food and love *(kisses her again)* and the difference between health and love *(another kiss)* and between saving the world and love *(another kiss).*

LIZ Your kisses taste like cherries.

They share another lingering kiss as the camera pulls away. We see Andy and Clint watching them through a window. They high five.

THE END

A Brand for Two

Inspiration for
A Brand for Two

"Give a girl the right pair of shoes and she can conquer the world."
—Marilyn Monroe

My theme for this script is "that danged ol' cowboy pride" made famous by Canadian singer/songwriter Ian Tyson. Pride, like most human characteristics, can be both an asset and a handicap. So it seemed a natural subject for creating tension. As an asset pride inspires a good work ethic, craftsmanship, even art. It can inspire honesty, fairness, responsibility. But as a handicap, pride tends to get in the way of love and compatibility. Pride can inspire jealousy, blaming, scapegoating, irrational competition, stubbornness, and lying. It can cause skilled craftsmen to make claims and promises they can't deliver and to hide their mistakes. Cowboys of both genders seem to have an overabundance of both kinds of pride.

I've never seen a cowboy movie based on horseshoeing even though it is a very important part of everyday ranch life. Shoeing is a complicated skill that non-horse owners and even horse owners often know little about. Horses living in deep dirt country or horses kept in stalls may not need shoeing, but they still need regular trimming as hoof walls grow like fingernails. Horror stories abound about those buying their first horse or adopting a government mustang and failing to maintain the horse's feet. Sometimes neglected horses are found unable to walk because their hooves have never been trimmed and have grown until they curl up like elf shoes. So part of my goal with "A Brand for Two" is to educate owners and save horses from misery.

In rocky country, horses can sometimes go barefooted when not being ridden, but if they walk some distance to graze or to water, their feet can wear off painfully short. If ridden, they usually need shoes, their feet trimmed and new shoes tacked on about once a month. Anywhere horses are shod, worn-out used shoes pile up, often lining the top rail of a corral. Always needing an extra buck, small-town entrepreneurs learn to use those worn-out shoes for everything from practical fence repairs to art. I own many of the items described in "Sam's Stuff" including a horseshoe wine rack (with nails to resemble prickly pear cactus), rasp bookends, and that strange ram's head hoof pick.

My first serious boyfriend, the only guy who ever gave me a diamond engagement ring, was a horseshoer for the mule concessions at Grand Canyon National Park where I worked two summers. My second-summer Grand Canyon boyfriend was also a shoer. I spent many hours in the shoeing barn watching them and their boss shoe the mules that took tourists up and down the trails or carried supplies and hauled trash to and from Phantom Ranch in the canyon's depths. The mules there were "hot shoed," meaning the shoes were heated in a forge, shaped and then while still hot, burned a little into the hoof wall to help prevent losing a shoe on the long trails. Some mules were sweethearts that I could easily distract on the end of a halter rope, but some were terrorists—not because of pain, but because of too much restraint. Some fought so hard they broke out of the stout swinging stocks they were pinned between as we humans scattered for our lives. They pulled down hundreds of wooden shelves and cubbies holding tools, shoes, nails, and calks. I also spent many hours waiting and visiting with the guides and packers on a rickety bench near the shoeing shop, a popular hangout. I've cleaned dirt and debris from horses' hooves with hoof picks but never trimmed a foot or tacked on a shoe myself. However, I've long ago lost count of how many hundreds, probably thousands of horses and mules I've seen shod and helped to distract.

Eventually, I wound up at Sul Ross State University (SRSU), first as a student, then ag department secretary, and finally English professor. While a student, I published my first magazine article in *Western Horseman* entitled "Goin' to College on an Anvil" (Jan. 1971). For it I interviewed a fellow non-traditional student, Karl Rogers, who was doing just that. Karl had shod horses on the Mescalero Apache Indian Reservation for a while and said, "When I left the reservation, I figured there wasn't a horse I couldn't shoe, but I soon found out that some of these horses that little girls ride will eat a man's lunch." His words, plus years of personal experience inspired the problems with spoiled, pet horses in this script.

For many years, my university had, in my opinion, the best farrier school in the world. To prevent crippling horses, students learned and practiced on cadaver legs shipped in from meat packing plants. Due to well-meaning but misguided horse lovers, US plants that processed horses for pet food or meat (shipped overseas) were shut down. This has caused undue suffering for old or crippled horses because now they must stand on those painful feet waiting to die of natural causes, sometimes for years. Children who want ponies grow up but someone must continue to feed and water those forgotten pets and absorb all the costs associated with feeding, mucking, veterinarian and hoof care. Closing the packing plants has caused desperate owners to abandon unwanted horses on the side of a road and leave them to starve like unwanted kittens. Shoeing schools can still import cadaver legs from other countries, but that doesn't help suffering horses in the USA.

Most inspiration for my characters comes from cowboys, students, and professors who taught in our shoeing and farrier school. Our first farrier professor with a PhD was Doug Butler, who has since become quite famous and owns and operates his own shoeing school today. At the time he had recently published a textbook, *Principles of Horseshoeing*, which was being used by nearly all similar shoeing schools and still is. After Butler left, through the years we hired many other highly skilled farriers to teach in the program, and I usually published at least one magazine article about each to help students find us, mostly in *Western Horseman*.

My female character Sam is very loosely based on a personal friend and female shoeing and farrier professor, Joy Scott ("Shoeing the Rodeo Horse" 1981). Joy was single at the time and a few of Sam's lines in the script come straight from our interview like "I guess I catch more flack from old-timers than anyone else. The ranching tradition doesn't quite go hand-in-hand with a lady shoeing horses. Since it is such hard work, I guess the challenge motivated me to try to learn." Even at the time, I disagreed with her interpretation that patriarchy motivated negative feelings toward a female horse shoer. Instead I blame chivalry. Joy also said, "Ideally the nails are placed on that portion of the hoof that will grow out and be trimmed off the next time the horse is shod." And she quoted the old shoer's motto: "Always remember the old saying, 'No foot, no horse.'" She was an excellent shoer and quickly gained customers in West Texas.

Almost every shoer I knew or interviewed from PhD farrier to first-year cowboy rookie said some version of "No foot, no horse." Nothing ever struck more fear in my own heart than starting to hear the clink, clink, clink of a loose horseshoe hitting rocks when I was still miles from home. I knew if that shoe came off I'd be facing a long walk, leading my horse. I think somewhere in my mind horseshoeing became a metaphor for human relationships. The saying "No foot, no horse" became "no foundation, nothing to build love on." My characters Rod and Sam share a good foundation: lifestyle and values. I've seen too many movies where some New York City businesswoman comes to the small town to "save the day" or some urban dude quickly learns to ride a horse and wins the heart of the female ranch owner. Prince (or princess) and pauper or superhero and commoner are just silly, unrealistic fairytales. Maybe it makes sense for movie stars to marry royalty because both have to deal with the constant spotlight, but not Cinderella. I think we need movies about reality: how to find a match that might actually have a chance of working, like the shared values, lifestyle, and work ethic that my characters Sam and Rod share.

Some of Sam's blacksmithing skills and words were also inspired by Lee Reeves in "Knives from the Anvil" (1983). Also a SRSU farrier professor, Lee mastered the art of making skinning knives on the small student forges in our shoeing barn lab. He said, "Back in the Middle Ages, knifesmiths fostered the idea that they used the elements: fire, iron, and air and did something magical to the iron to make it steel. They kept their techniques secret and claimed supernatural powers for their knives. That aura still persists." Lee liked to use native rangeland wood for knife handles (scales) and said customers often brought him wood from certain canyons or even a certain tree that held special meaning. I own one of Lee's beautiful skinning knives with a yellow algarita wood handle as described in the script. The algarita had been growing near a water well I once owned. I also did several articles about making, repairing, and changing the styles of spurs or bits using skills often learned in our blacksmithing and metallurgy classes.

One student, who was later hired to teach in our shoeing school, came to us with 21 years of experience shoeing race horses. Max Williams did his SRSU master's research on the race track tradition of lowering the heels of the foot to lengthen a horse's stride. He and his wife Judy had also trained and raced their own running quarter horses prior to returning to college and believed those lowered heels were causing injuries (bowed tendons, splints, and ringbone). When Max's research suggested that lowering the heels actually shortened the stride of his study horses by over 7, 10, and 14 inches, I published an article ("On Length of Stride" 1982). Another photo-illustrated article I wrote about Max was "The No-Fuss, First-Time Shoeing Session: A Step-By-Step Approach for Preparing Your Foal for the Farrier" (*Equus*, 1986).

The SRSU program often produced important news for the horse world and even the art world. One student, Rodney Rex Barrick, combined blacksmithing with his sculpting talents. Along with using a forge and anvil, he designed jigs and tools to create huge sculptures from half-inch round steel. He made small models in wire and then crushed them to determine the strongest possible designs. One sculpture of a 14-foot rearing horse ("Horse Sculpture" *Western Horseman* 1982) and another of three wolf heads still grace the Sul Ross campus. Because shoeing/farrier work is both a science and an art, there are lots of different techniques, tools, and ways of making do, so I've incorporated a range of tools like shoer's knee vs. hoof stand or expensive anvil vs. railroad rail. I've even known cowboys who used a cement step or rock as an anvil when shaping shoes. I've tried to emphasize the problem solving aspect of their different choices.

Methods of restraint were partly inspired by an interview with Mickey Dart, our registered Animal Technician, who taught in our two-year Animal Health Technician Program that trained and certified veterinarian assistants ("Restraining Horses" 1980). Mickey demonstrated and described several safe techniques and said, "When restraining a horse, the least amount of restraint is the best" and "remember that you are not trying to incapacitate the horse; you are merely distracting him enough to make him think about what you are doing rather than what the vet is doing." When my male character is trying to make sure the female shoer doesn't get hurt, he over does restraint until she reminds him to just distract the horse, not confine him. Mickey also described the Scotch hobble as "An old restraint that you don't see much anymore . . . . Here, you put a bowline knot around the horse's neck and draw up a hind leg. It is a very effective means of restraint, but be sure you use a soft rope or put a cinch around the hind leg and draw the rope through the rings, or he might burn himself." Since that was the type of restraint I'd seen cowboys most often use, that's the one my characters use to shoe poorly trained horses.

The 06 Ranch, where I lived for thirteen years, allowed trained SRSU shoeing classes, to practice on their sometimes 100-head horse remuda before spring branding and fall shipping. The student shoers were carefully supervised by their professors, the ranch cowboys, and the ranch manager/owner. By the time they graduated, I'm sure many of them felt there wasn't a horse they couldn't shoe. Horseshoeing is a science and an art and takes years of practice before anyone is worth paying or trusting.

I also held horses for, watched, paid, photographed, and interviewed numerous cowboy shoers who had taught themselves through trial and error. One of the best of those was Wally Wines, the official horseshoer for Yellowstone National Park at the time (Fall 1992 cover story for *Cowboy Magazine*, "Wally Wines: A Man of Tradition"). Wally said, "My dad started me shoeing when I was 12—his philosophy: if you're gonna ride 'em, you're gonna shoe 'em. Hunger taught me the rest." Inspiration for my ranch manager's character—cranky personality protecting a heart of gold—comes from Wally.

I also followed master horseman, Ray Hunt, around for years and wrote/published eleven articles about his horse handling methods in various magazines. Ray was sort of a cowboy Buddha to some of us and inspired other personality quirks and techniques in the script.. Like Ray, my characters are perfectionists not because of ego, but because horses and cowboys form a partnership that involves life/death situations for both every day (as are my characters when shoeing together, raising cattle, and maybe even marriage). My ranch manager takes those situations very seriously, like training his horses to stop when they feel a tug on a stirrup before the first ride. Many cowboys don't think about that until their foot is stuck and they're being drug through the rocks by a frightened horse. Ray Hunt spent time in each clinic demonstrating how to teach horses to react calmly instead of being frightened. The best cowboys think of every possible situation, thus the lines: "you don't miss much" and "that's my job." After I met Ray Hunt, everything I wrote or did was influenced by his methods and philosophy or by people who had learned from him.

One of those was "Ronnie Scott: New Mexico Horse Trainer" (*Cowboy Magazine* 1990). I photographed Ronnie demonstrating one of my favorite methods for relaxing a horse—sticking a finger in its mouth. Although traditionally cowboys don't talk much, they often "mansplained" their tricks to those they thought might get hurt trying it, which I use as motivation for my character's chattering. Restraint or training techniques have also always been a good source of jokes between the genders due to the belief that they don't "work" on people, especially women. So after my female shoer tries to use this old cowboy trick on Rod to help him relax, it "doesn't work" because her goal was a kiss. The reason for using a method is as important, maybe more so, than the technique. When the reason is manipulation or fulfilling a personal desire, it often doesn't work. Or as Ronnie explained, "Horses are not only a tool that I use in my work, they're good friends that I really respect."

The horse Zipper was inspired by a real horse named Zipper that was bred and raised on the o6 Ranch, named by the cowboy who started him, and for the same reason. Although a horse's registered name is usually recorded by its breeder, the cowboy who starts a colt to ride traditionally bestows the nick name that will follow it through its working career. The little girl's pot-bellied, white Welsh pony named Snowflake was inspired by my daughter's first horse with the same name and that looked and acted just as bad. Once when Snowflake's stubbornness made my little girl cry while they were competing at a kid's playday, I kicked the ornery little mare in her white-pot belly in front of the other kids and parents. Not my finest moment.

Most cowboys and horse shoers, both male and female, often suffer from work-related chronic injuries, especially back trouble. Although cowboys seldom own or use safety equipment, hammered metal is notorious for sending tiny slivers into eyes and skin, and welding hot metal results in sparks that burn holes into clothing or pop into shirt collars and slide down. Finger rings are considered dangerous for any job around tools, sharp objects, animals, and hot metal. Although sports medicine has made tremendous advances for athletes, the advice doctors give to those who work manual labor jobs is too often useless, if not insulting.

The quote about being careful what you put your brand on comes from the founder of the o6 Ranch, Herbert Kokernot, Sr. His son, Herbert Junior, a baseball fan, began sponsoring a semi-pro team in the 1940s and building a baseball field in Alpine, Texas. When his dad came to visit, unimpressed with the cheaply built field carrying the o6 brand, Herbert Senior said, "Son, if you're going to put the o6 brand on something, do that thing right." The final version of Kokernot Field was called "The Best Little Ball Park in Texas" by *Sports Illustrated* and the "Yankee Stadium of Texas" by *Texas Monthly*. A brand should have meaning, instill pride, and be easily recognizable but difficult to alter. I've seen several cowboys brand their leather chaps with either their own or a ranch's brand, and the o6 was one brand often burned proudly onto chaps or chuckbox, embroidered on shirts or caps, and engraved, overlaid, or inlaid on spurs.

Rod's story about the running iron comes from Albany, Texas when I was living on the 7W Camp of the Jim Nail Ranch about 1973. The town puts on a historical pageant every year called The Fandangle, and I liked to participate. One year I also volunteered to decorate one of the downtown store windows with family antiques. Mr. Nail offered to let me display the runnin' iron he claimed one of his ancestors carried when the Nail Ranch was getting its start. Truthful or not, the town loved his story. The oxbow brand, which represents both the stirrup that my character rides (as did his father) and a favorite spot on the river, also holds meaning for me. The most lucrative photograph I ever sold was a 2x2-inch slide of an oxbow stirrup.

Through the years, living and working on various ranches, I've also been permitted to run a few cows of my own. If a ranch allows this, it is a good idea to run a different breed than the owner, so there's no doubt about honesty or possible mix-ups. There is always a limit to the owner's generosity too. So the employee is faced with either selling to keep numbers under the limit or finding lease country. Many modern ranchers got their start like this, gradually building up their herd as they found more grazing land. After divorcing, I found my own leases, ran my own small herd, designed and registered my own "running N" brand (sort of an S on its side), and still have my branding iron, which was handmade by a blacksmith. Eventually I built my herd up to 50 head before I sold them to help finance my PhD. I've branded lots of calves, taught others to brand and learned to do every job I describe in the branding scene: heeling calves, flanking, vaccinating, ear marking, dehorning, and castrating. I've also used and photographed several ways to heat branding irons from wood fires to propane pots. Every crew has their own system and some do more "doctoring" (insecticide ear tags, drenching), depending on the country and prevalent diseases or insects. I've also included a few preferences, like when my character side-passes his horse to open a gate. In my opinion, gates that can be opened from horseback are a sign of good management.

Small details—like that real cowboy foreheads should be paler than the rest of the face, talking to barn cats, not counting change or reading contracts, thinking modern women are too skinny, calling feminists femi-nazis—all come from experience. Except for a year or two here and there, I've lived in or on the fringes of small towns, sometimes a couple of miles out, sometimes 20 miles out. So I've searched for jobs and ways to make a living in those places. Even while living within the Phoenix metroplex, the jobs I landed with my small-town skills were tractor parts girl and secretary. I also know my way around feed stores and tiny post offices. I once found a water leak under a large cement water tank like Charlie describes and had to find help to figure out how to fix it. Most of us are used to drinking warm water and "rodeo cool" beer because, even if we bothered with an ice chest, by the time the work is over the ice has probably long ago melted. Rod's line "Yeah? Well, I'll have had a great life" was inspired by a young rodeo cowboy I quoted in my book *Voices and Visions of the American West* (Texas Monthly Press 1986) who said, "People are always telling me, 'Dang you won't even be able to walk when you get older.' And I tell them, 'Yeah, but I'll have a whole lot more to talk about than you will.'" Rod's line about being happy to take Sam to the dance but not wanting her to shoe his horses, was inspired by one of my own memorable run-ins with patriarchy when the boss assigned me to partner with a feedlot cowboy to ride pens and look for sick animals. The cowboy said, "I'll be happy to go to bed with her, but I'm not riding with no woman."

I'm not sure where the expression "wall-eyed fit" comes from. My best guess is fishing. Walleyes have a reputation for being weak fighters. I grew up fishing with my dad and grandpa and we often caught walleyes on the Mississippi River in the colder water up near the rollers on Lock and Dam #12 at Bellevue, Iowa. I remember those walleyes as scrappers. So maybe, since all fishermen at one time also handled horses, the habit of a horse to show white around its eyes when scared might have come from the fish. In any event, both walleyes and horses seem to be sensible and calm except when spooked or feeling their oats in cool weather.

The barn and Miss Lane's ranch cook house were inspired by those owned by a long-time, letter-writing pal, Rodney Flournoy, a Mr. Darcy-type bachelor. Rod the character shares a few of the real Rodney's traits. Rod Flournoy not only owned his ranch (in Northern California) but also managed it and did many of the more "menial" chores like feed the chickens and irrigate. We have been friends for almost 50 years. I've eaten in his cook house several times and cooked for him and his crew one Christmas while his regular cook took a holiday. When between cooks or during their vacations, Rod himself often took over that chore too. He just in general did anything he asked of his employees, and often did chores he would never ask them to do. He never married—or at least not yet (now in his late 70s), but he did "raise" quite a few good cowboys, cattle, irrigators, cooks, and a lot of horses.

Through the years, I've also interviewed and watched as ranches were passed from generation to generation. On most large ranches, if managers are not also owners, they are usually trusted with a ranch checkbook to pay bills and sign paychecks. Some find out when the will is read that they now own the ranch and responsibilities.

My own parents, and the way I related to them and imagined they related to each other, inspired the scene where my characters talk about their parents. In Rod's mind, he loved his mother, but didn't respect her. He didn't think his father respected her either, only loved her. Rod thought his mother respected his father, but didn't love him, and showered her son with love that seemed more like manipulation. Rod wants and needs both respect and love. He loves and respects Miss Lane and vice versa, but not in a romantic way. He actually hopes to love a woman romantically someday but wants to respect her too. Sparks start to fly between Rod and Sam <u>because</u> she commands respect, not just "good manners" from him. Once attracted to her, it scares him. He's storming around (like an unbroken horse) because he knows he might have just "met his match" and his future may depend on the outcome. He's nervous, concentrating, and being very careful. Just like a good cowboy would be when handling a sensitive horse. Rod is a sensitive horse himself, like Zipper, who in the wrong hands would have been an outlaw, but in the right hands could be a sweetheart. A lot of their banter is "sacking out" or getting each other used to and working together the way cowboys treat horses: scare them little by little so they gradually start to trust the human. A good cowboy never hurts the horse, but makes life better for both of them. Sam sees through Rod's male chauvinism quite quickly (he hopes she's as smart as a horse). She is not the kind of girl to be fooled by a sweet talker, nor would she be a good match for a man who couldn't stand his own ground. Instead of a partner, she'd take advantage the way timid riders create spoiled horses. She knows just how to insult his ego: says he talks too much, points out his mistakes, and when he gets mad says his word and handshake are no good.

Rod probably "fell in love" with Sam the first time he saw her and vice versa, but the rest of the script is them testing each other and exposing their own hearts to more risk. Both horse and dog "training" run through the whole script. By antagonizing Sam's puppy, for instance, Rod is helping her train it. He doesn't want the puppy to trust even him until it is old enough to tell one human from another. Once it can, Rod becomes its trusted friend, just like he was to her older dog that died and like he hopes to be to Sam.

Sam is good at standing her ground and demanding respect, but she's not testing him, so he's doing it for her by shoeing together, partnering on cattle. Both of those activities would expose deal breakers like work ethic, honesty, trust, boundaries, etc. Inviting her to brand his calves is almost a marriage proposal in the cowboy world and he doesn't insult or question her knowledge of hot metal by telling her how to keep the branding iron at just the right temperature (he does <u>remind</u> her that she already knows). Once they both start to realize their friendship has the potential for the real thing, the flying monkeys arrive and they both start to make mistakes: playing games, lying, jealousy, pride, temper.

Sam's mothering clock is also ticking. She likes Rod but doesn't want to miss her chance for children. So she tries to hurry things along. This is a common mistake but often necessary too. When a cowboy is training a horse for some big event (maybe the cutting horse futurity) he often pushes for that last inch of improvement and loses ground instead. Timing is everything. But horses and people also tend to "suck their thumbs" and sometimes need a push. Sam's timing with Rod has been perfect until "crunch time." So Miss Lane and Charlie step in to save the day. Charlie is always in the right place at the right time, but never center stage. Rod was <u>scared</u> to take that last step until Charlie made Rod realize he might lose her. Rod finally becomes more scared of losing Sam than of risking his own broken heart.

Sometimes when a horse is scared, the answer is to let him get himself all tangled up in a soft rope. The more he fights it, the more tangled up he gets. A good cowboy teaches a horse to untangle himself. The result is usually that the horse finally KNOWS the human is there to help him, not to hurt or make his life worse. This tactic needs a skilled horseman to prevent injury. Rod is making his own life worse until Charlie's soliloquy begins to make sense and Rod remembers how to untangle himself. Charlie is the puppet master. He recognized that Sam and Rod would make a good pair before they even meet and then sets it up. He's sort of always hovering around to fix whatever needs fixing, unloading, restraining, lifting, and in the end is exactly the "horse whisperer" (deus ex machina or kick in the pants) that Rod needs.

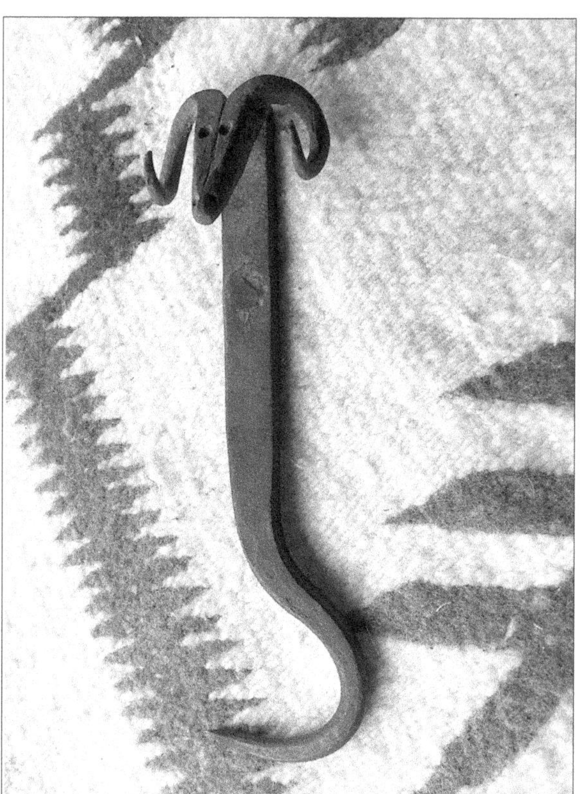

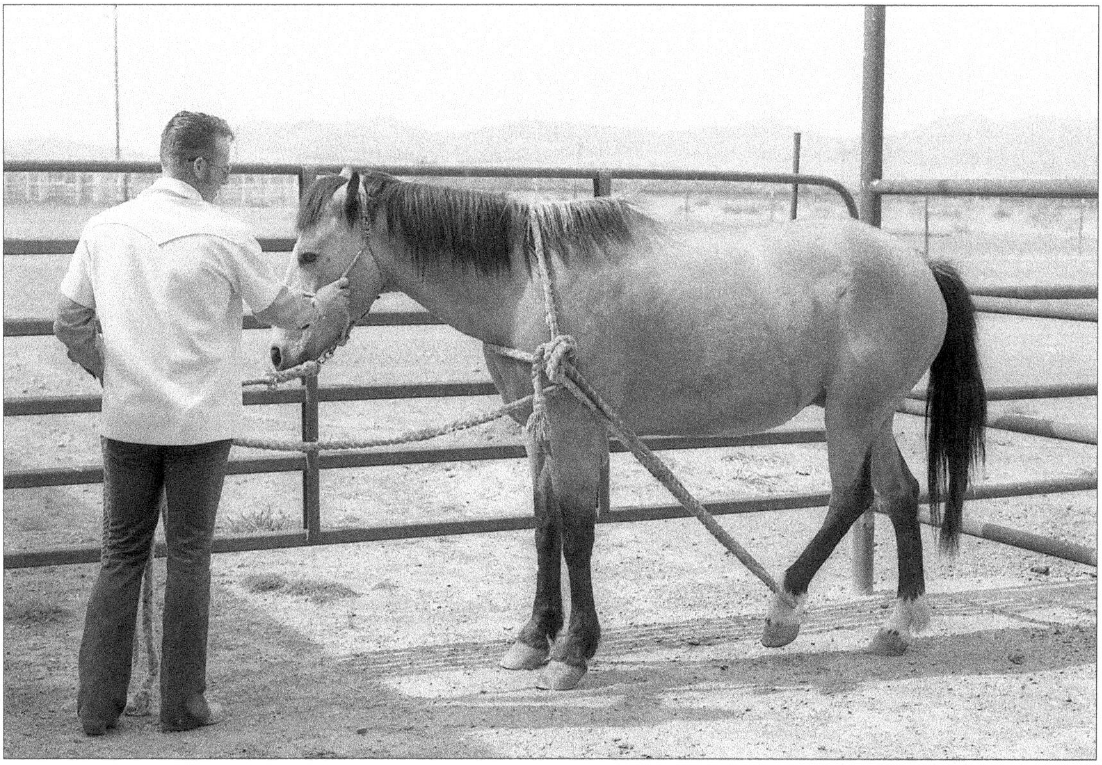

WATTS ARENA

   Inspiration for A Brand for Two

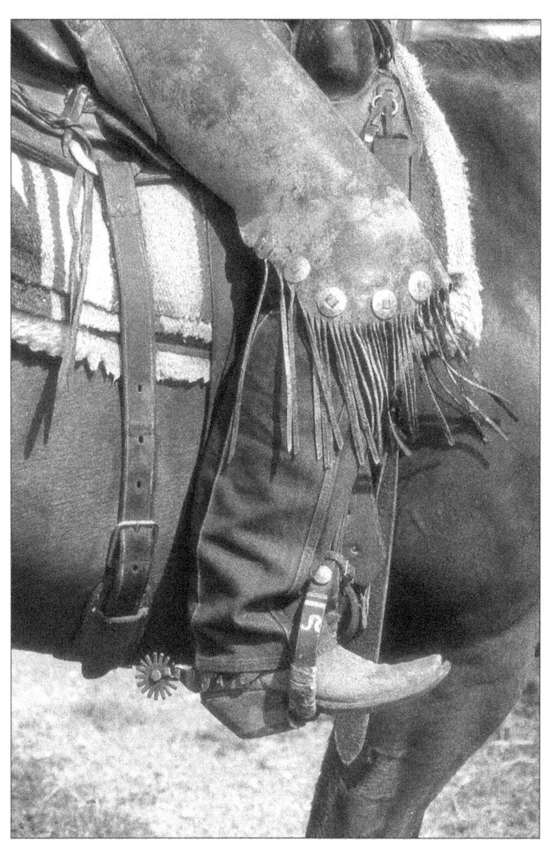

A Brand for Two

EXT. AREA AND SMALL TOWN—DAWN

Springtime in a rural landscape dotted with cattle ranches and a small town. Patches of snow on the ground.

EXT. RED BARN—MORNING

A nice anvil attached to a peeled tree stump sits just to the right of a sliding barn door. On the other side of the door is an old rickety bench. Rod (30ish cowboy) is shoeing a horse, wearing cowboy boots, well-worn chink-style leggins, loose Levi 501 jeans, and a long-sleeved light blue shirt with a tiny pattern. Sweat marks show on his shirt. His black cowboy hat sits upside down on the ground nearby. Indentions from his hat are visible around his hair. His forehead is whiter than his tanned face. His shoeing box sits near his feet. Attached to or near the barn is a corral. The horse stands near the anvil with its halter rope hanging to the ground, not tied. Rod has one of the horse's hooves resting on his own knee, rasping a groove under the nails that are sticking out of the hoof wall, and getting ready to clamp them tight with his clamping tool. Charlie (20ish cowboy, dressed similar to Rod) drives up in a pickup, gets out and walks over.

CHARLIE Hey, Boss, I found a water leak in the Twenty-Five Pasture. I'm gonna need your help because the leak is somewhere under that big cement water tank. Whoever built it that way shoulda stayed in town.

ROD OK. Let me finish this horse.

Charlie watches intently as Rod grabs his clamping tool and bends the nails into the grooves one at a time. When Rod finishes that foot, he drops it back to the ground, and rises slowly, arching his back as though in pain.

CHARLIE Is your back hurtin'?

ROD Yeah. Shoeing really bothers me lately. Guess I'm gonna have to go see about it.

CHARLIE As bad as you hate doctors, it must be hurtin' bad.

ROD I don't hate doctors, just what they prescribe. I already know what he'll say: stop lifting and rest.

Rod picks up another hoof to rasp . . .

CHARLIE If you'd teach me how to shoe a horse, I could help. You taught me everything else about handling horses.

ROD A horse can protect itself against an unskilled handler or rider, but not an unskilled shoer. Just one nail driven crooked or cutting a quarter inch too much off a hoof can cripple a horse, sometimes for life. If you want to learn, go to shoeing school.

Rod finishes and drops the second hoof, showing pain when he stands up for a moment and moves on to the third hoof. Charlie mimics Rod's voice and repeats what Rod "always" says.

CHARLIE I know, I know. "Go practice on dead feet. Don't practice on live horses that have to work for a living."

ROD Yup. No hoof, no horse.

CHARLIE On Saturday afternoons, when I'm off work here, I sometimes go help other shoers handle spoiled horses, but they all tell me the same thing.

ROD I could show you how to shape a shoe to fit a horse's foot, but that wouldn't help much because that doesn't hurt my back.

CHARLIE Did you go to shoeing school?

ROD Nope.

Rod drops the foot he's been working on and stands up slowly, again showing back pain.

CHARLIE Then how did you learn?

ROD By making mistakes and crippling good horses.

EXT. SAM'S PROPERTY AND SHOP—AFTERNOON

We fly slowly over snow-patched country, empty gravel roads, to the edge of a small town and an aging and small ranch house. Nearby stands an unattached metal building, set up as a blacksmith shop, with a garage style door and a regular side door on the west wall. On the east wall, on the

afternoon shady side of the building, is a bench for resting. Two almost matching well-worn Carhartt tan jackets have been tossed on the bench. We see a close-up of a horseshoer's calloused and beat up hands as they are finishing a shoe, clamping the nails, just as Rod did. Instead of the hoof resting on the shoer's knee, the hoof rests on a home- made hoof stand. As the camera pulls back, we see that this horseshoer is a girl! Her hair is held back in a messy braided ponytail. She wears tennis shoes, loose Levi 501 jeans, and long- sleeved t-shirt. Charlie has been helping her restrain a pot- bellied white Welsh pony. Sam and Charlie have slight sweat marks on their shirts, shirt tails half out. Sam is just finishing the last hoof. She places her shoeing hammer into a well-used shoeing box that is sitting near her feet, then she picks up and moves the shoeing box from the ground onto the open tailgate of her nearby old white pickup with a homemade "Tonneau" style cover over the pickup's bed. The cover is open. Tools, a few horseshoes and a piece of railroad rail (her anvil) sit on the tailgate. Inside the bed we see a few cardboard boxes. The pony stands calmly, wearing a halter, new shoes on all four feet, and tied to the hitching rail just outside the shed. The pony is relaxed, almost asleep, tail hanging limp. Charlie unties knots in the soft, limp rope he has been using to restrain the pony (with a Scotch hobble) while Sam shod it. Once the rope is off, Charlie coils it and hangs it over one of his shoulders. He has one shirt-tail hanging out and quickly re-tucks it back into his jeans.

SAM Thanks, Charlie, for giving up a Saturday afternoon to help me restrain that little sweetheart.

She hands Charlie some money, he puts it in his shirt pocket. Neither of them counts the money.

SAM I'd be in the emergency room without your help. I can usually handle fear, like a 10-year-old mustang straight off the desert that's never seen a human, but these back-yard horses that little girls ride can eat my lunch. Until I get to know them, it's so hard to tell if one is scared, spoiled, sulled up, asleep or what. The first time I shoe one I ask the customer to just drop off the horse and leave—just in case it acts like this one did.

Sam wipes her forehead with her long-sleeved shirt.

SAM If they see what I have to do to get their little darlin' shod or even just trim its feet, they think I'm killing it.

Sam reaches out and tousles the pony's forelock affectionately.

CHARLIE *(laughs)* Yup. Sometimes us horse whisperers hafta holler before we can whisper.

He grabs his jacket from the bench and heads toward his pickup parked near Sam's.

CHARLIE Wish I could be more help, Sam. My boss is a master with horses and taught me how to handle anything, but he's never let me shoe one. He always says, "No foot, no horse." He shoes all our working ranch horses himself. He says if I want to learn, I should go to shoeing school and practice on horses that don't have to work for a living.

SAM He sounds like someone I'd like to meet.

Charlie's expression changes to pleased, showing surprise that Sam wants to meet his boss. He is already plotting how to make that happen.

SAM Need some coffee?

CHARLIE I got a date.

SAM OK. Thanks again, Charlie. I really appreciate it.

CHARLIE Anytime. None of our horses act like this, and I'd get rusty if I don't practice. See ya.

Charlie gets into his pickup and drives away. Sam disappears into her shop and returns with coffee in a tin cup, sits on the bench and puts her jacket back on. Soon a mom drives up with her little girl. Sam unties the halter rope from the hitching rail and hands it to the little girl who throws her arms around the pony and kisses it. The mom hands Sam a check and loads the pony into a small one-horse trailer. Sam smiles sort of longingly at the little girl and tousles her hair just like she did the pony.

SAM You take good care of Snowflake, now, you hear. She's a sweetheart.

LITTLE GIRL *(big smile)* Yes ma'am, I will.

INT. DOCTOR'S OFFICE—DAY

Sam, sitting on an exam table, wears similar but clean clothes. The doctor holds her right wrist.

DOC It's just tired muscles right now, Samantha, but if you don't give this wrist a rest, the continued strain of over work will develop into something more serious: tendonitis, nerve damage, arthritis . . .*(pause)* . . . I know you shoe horses for a living, but you need to stop using a hammer as much as possible for at least a few months, maybe a year.

INT. DOCTOR'S OFFICE—
MOMENTS LATER

Rod is sitting on exam table, buttoning his shirt. His cowboy hat rests upside down on a nearby chair.

DOC It's just strained muscles right now, Rod, but if you don't give your back a rest, those strained muscles could pull your bones out of alignment and become a more permanent problem, leading to nerve damage, a slipped disc, or worse . . .*(pause)* . . . I know you're a cowboy, but for about a year you need to delegate anything that will strain your back. No horseshoeing, especially.

EXT. SAM'S SHOP—DAY

Sam's shop door is open. Sam and Charlie, both looking tired, have just finished shoeing a large feather-hocked, broncy-looking horse that stands tied to the hitching rail. It is wearing new shoes and Charlie's Scotch Hobble rope is piled on the rickety bench, along with their jackets.

SAM Need some coffee?

CHARLIE Sure. I got nothing to do until supper time.

Sam disappears into her shop, returning with two cups of coffee in tin cups, handing one to Charlie. They sit on the bench to rest and talk.

CHARLIE So, why did you decide to shoe horses? Sure seems like a hard job for a girl.

SAM It's a hard job for anybody. I guess I just like hard work and a challenge. I also thought I'd like the look on those old guy's faces when Sam shows up to shoe their horses and Sam is a female. But I'm getting kind of sick of that look.

Both sip their coffee and both stop to put their jackets on.

SAM Mostly, I knew the time was coming when I'd inherit this place from my grandma. I knew I wouldn't be able to afford to stock it and land can't help me make a living without any livestock. I didn't want to have to sell it, so I needed a small-town income.

Sam gets up and starts putting her shoeing tools back in the pickup bed. Charlie picks up her shoeing box to help. Sam continues to talk as they work.

SAM Job choices in this tiny town are limited: Post office? Feed store?

CHARLIE Yeah, people keep those jobs for life.

SAM Waitress? Dude Wrangler? I'm not that keen on people . . .*(pause)* . . . Nothing sounded as interesting as shoeing horses. Plus I like to be my own boss. So I went to shoeing school where I learned blacksmithing too. Now I'm officially a farrier, meaning I can do it all.

CHARLIE Yeah, my boss keeps encouraging me to go to shoeing school but it's expensive, and he needs me, and I need a job.

SAM Being a farrier is sort of like being a horseshoeing PhD. I learned all the bones and ligaments, metals and heat details, but it still took practice on a hundred horses before I was worth paying.

CHARLIE Yeah. I figured I'd need some kind of backup plan for a while.

Once her tools are put away, they return to the bench.

SAM I make pretty good money in the summer when the tourists are around playing cowboy, but all that dries up in the winter. Only crazy cowboys and an occasional little girl ride in the winter and usually the cowboys shoe their own horses. So, I do blacksmithing and welding in the winter.

CHARLIE This is probably a really dumb question, especially from somebody who claims to draw a check as a cowboy, but what's the difference? I thought all horseshoers were blacksmiths and all blacksmiths were horseshoers?

SAM Oh, not always, Charlie, maybe not even usually. And there are no dumb questions, just dumb answers. The short and dumbed down answer is that today cowboy horseshoers mostly do cold shoeing instead of blacksmithing and seldom ever heat up any metal.

Sam stands up from the bench, walks over to her pickup, Charlie follows. She pulls several sizes of new manufactured horseshoes from the boxes in her pickup bed and holds them up for Charlie to see.

SAM Blacksmiths used to have to make every horseshoe from scratch in a forge: punch the nail holes and cut the grooves, but like food, shoes come ready made in a box today, from pony size to draft horse.

Charlie inspects the shoes she is holding and peers in the boxes.

SAM After I trim, shape and level, I grab one of these factory shoes and whack it with this shaping hammer on my sorry home-made anvil.

CHARLIE Looks like it's made out of a piece of railroad track?

SAM Yup. Made it myself. Lots of cowboys make anvils out of rail. It's good steel.

Sam holds a shoe sideways on the anvil and strikes it with her shaping hammer. She winces from pain.

SAM I hammer until it matches the shape of each foot on each horse. Horse's feet are sort of like fingerprints, no two exactly alike *(pause)* Then I lay the shoe flat on top of the anvil, like this . . .

Sam lays the shoe on the anvil.

SAM . . .and whack it again until it is level so it will fit tight against the leveled hoof. Then I tack it on with factory made horse shoe nails and my shoeing hammer.

She holds up a nail from the top of her shoeing box and her shoeing hammer. As she talks, she grabs a box of nails from inside the pickup bed and shows him the box.

SAM Blacksmiths used to have to make each nail too, now nails also come in a box, razor sharp, and easy to drive . . . Oh, and I'm sure your boss has explained that we don't really drive the nails into the hoof or the horse would be crippled forever.

CHARLIE About 400 times.

SAM *(laughs)* We drive the nails at an angle so they curve and poke out of the hoof wall about an inch above the shoe. I want to be able to trim all the nail holes off at the next shoeing so the hoof doesn't start cracking. Then I twist the sharp ends of the nails off that are poking through the hoof wall, clamp the ends over *(holds up her clamping tool)*, and then hammer the bent nails down tight. Maybe 10 minutes of actual hammering, total. Easy peasy, although after several years, holding up those feet can be hard on a person's back, so I also use a hoof stand. There's lots more to it, but that's the short answer. Sorry I'm rambling.

CHARLIE Not at all. I'm interested. I try not to ask my boss too many questions because he prefers that I learn by paying attention. He doesn't talk much and is way better at showing than explaining. So what about blacksmithing?

SAM I'll show you. Come on.

Sam walks into her blacksmith shop and Charlie follows. They both sit their coffee cups down next to the coffee pot inside her shop. She walks over to her work bench and picks up a finished hand-forged skinning knife, pulls it out of the scabbard, and holds it up proudly for inspection.

SAM This is blacksmithing and it's a whole different ball game.

She picks up a railroad spike off the bench and holds it up next to the knife blade.

SAM This skinning knife started as a railroad spike like this.

The camera zooms in on a close-up of the knife and railroad spike. Then Sam walks toward her forge, lights it, and Charlie follows to watch.

SAM I begin by heating the spike. Blacksmithing is all done with heat.

As Sam explains, she waits until the forge is hot and then places the railroad spike in it. While the spike heats, Sam walks back to her tailgate and carries her anvil from the

pickup to a home-made metal table close to the forge. Charlie does not offer to help.

CHARLIE Propane?

SAM Yes. Someday I'd like a bigger forge but this one can handle small projects like a skinning knife.

Sam grabs ear and eye protection off her bench, puts them on, places the glowing spike on her anvil, and starts pounding the hot metal, wincing with each hammer strike. Charlie plugs his ears with his fingers until she stops pounding and returns the spike to the forge.

SAM Once the spike is white or red hot, I hammer it over and over, compacting and flattening, then reheating it, and hammering over and over until I get the shape I want. One knife takes hours of hammering, especially on my sorry anvil. It works OK for cold shoeing, but nor for blacksmithing.

CHARLIE So why not buy a better anvil?

SAM Ever priced one? A good one costs about fifteen shod horses or ten knives. If I sell a bunch of winter welding and blacksmithing stuff at the Fourth of July fair and save every penny I make during summer shoeing season, I stay just about one customer ahead of having to sell this place. Of course if I stopped eating, I could probably buy an anvil. And believe me, I've considered that.

Sam pounds on the spike again, this time laying it aside when it cools and turns off her forge. She moves her wrist around in a circle in the air, showing pain.

SAM I did a lot of hammering last winter, so now my wrist hurts, even just shaping shoes. Doc says it needs rest.

Sam rubs her wrist.

CHARLIE Well, you're a smart lady. Why don't you find an easier job that pays better?

SAM Well, you're a smart guy, kind of. So why don't you find an easier job that pays better than cowboying?

CHARLIE Gotcha.

He grins and turns to leave.

SAM Hey, thanks again.

CHARLIE Anytime. Just holler.

He leaves through the open shop door, climbs into his pickup and drives off.

EXT. RED BARN—MORNING

Rod and Charlie are sitting on the bench, resting.

ROD Our local sawbones doesn't want me to shoe horses for a while to rest my back. He says anyone can shoe a horse, which just proves that doctors don't know everything. I'm more particular about who shoes these horses than who rides them. I've never had to hire a shoer before, don't even know one. Do you? I mean a good one. I mean a real good one.

CHARLIE As a matter of fact I do, a real farrier, graduated from shoeing school, name's Sam Walker.

ROD Really good?

CHARLIE The best, ask anybody.

ROD OK, tell him to be here Thursday about sunrise.

CHARLIE *(smiling to himself)* You got it.

Charlie gets up and walks away, leaving Rod sitting.

EXT. POST OFFICE—LATER THAT AFTERNOON

The flag waves over the post office for a small town, small shops nearby, a few pedestrians, a few cars pulling up to park. Rod exits the post office through the front door. He notices Sam approaching and holds the door open for her, touching the brim of his hat for a lady.

ROD Mornin' ma'am.

SAM *(slightly irritated at the chivalry)* Thanks, but you don't have to do that. This isn't 1890.

ROD Is to me. Have a good day.

Sam passes into the post office, but doesn't look at him. As he walks away toward his pickup, he looks back.

EXT. FEED STORE— MOMENTS LATER

Sam and Rod run into each other again, at the feed store. One pickup attached to a horse trailer pulls out just as Rod arrives, so he pulls into the same spot. Sam's pickup is already parked in front of the feed store, tailgate open. Rod walks to the door just as Sam is exiting, struggling to carry a heavy box of horseshoes. He holds the door again and with a big smile offers to take the box.

ROD Here, let me help you with that.

SAM Thanks, but I got it.

ROD I can see that, but I want to got it.

Rod attempts to wrestle the box out of Sam's hands.

ROD I insist.

Their hands touch, they lock eyes. Sam gives him a mean look. Rod jerks his hands away and raises them in surrender.

ROD OK. Whatever.

Sam, carries the heavy box to her open tailgate only a few steps away. She slides the box of horseshoes under the bed cover and slams the tailgate shut. Rod remains standing nearby.

ROD You new around here?

Sam ignores him as she circles back to her driver's door.

SAM Not really. You must not come to town very often.

ROD You got me there.

Rod touches his hat brim as Sam drives away. She watches him enter the store in her side mirror. Rod doesn't look back at her.

INT. FEED STORE—MOMENTS LATER

Rod walks up to the counter to place his feed order with the male feed store clerk who is standing behind the counter. A cash register sits on one end of the short counter with an intercom beside it. On the walls, shelves and hooks hold other ranch and cowboy necessities: new nylon catch ropes, gloves, neatsfoot oil, saddle soap, etc. Seeing Rod, the clerk grabs an old-fashioned 2-copy order pad with paired white/yellow copies for store/customer, and a pen.

ROD I'm gonna need six quail blocks, and six sacks of chicken feed that your helpers can load in my pickup, and a ton of grass hay bales delivered Wednesday afternoon and stacked in the red barn, all charged to Lane Ranch.

The clerk jots the order down, tears off both the white and yellow copies, hands Rod the yellow, pushes an intercom button and reads the order to unseen employees in the back. He sticks his white copy on a long nail sticking up from a piece of board sitting on the counter that already contains three other orders.

FEED STORE CLERK You can pick up the quail blocks and chicken feed around back, as usual.

Rod wanders around the store for a moment, while ranting about women.

ROD What is the deal with women today? How come they don't want to be treated like a lady? My mama worked hard teaching me to act like a gentleman and now women consider good manners some kind of insult.

FEED STORE CLERK Yup. Seems like they'll regret that someday.

ROD They have no idea what they want. This year they want beards; last year they wanted us clean shaven. They want long hair, then shaved heads. Last year they wanted cowboys, now it's firemen. First they want bodice rippers and now they want us to ask permission to smile at them.

Rod picks up a bar of saddle soap and a bottle of Neat's-foot oil, places them on the counter, fishes out some folded bills from his shirt pocket and pays the Clerk while continuing his rant.

ROD Skinny jeans, suit coats two sizes too small, earrings, sissy slippers without socks, shirt tails hanging out? *(Pause)* A man just can't please a woman, and if he tries, he looks ridiculous. Does it improve if you marry one?

As the clerk takes Rod's money, we see a gold wedding band on his finger. The clerk deposits Rod's money in the cash register and hands back some bills and coins. Neither of them counts the change.

FEED STORE CLERK Nope.

ROD Well, I feel sorry for ya then.

This is obviously not the first time the clerk has heard Rod rant about females. He grins, shakes his head and rolls his eyes.

FEED STORE CLERK You been working for a female ranch owner for 10 years.

ROD Yeah, well that's different.

EXT. RED BARN — EARLY MORNING

As the sun rises, Miss Lane (late 60's, wearing stretchy mom jeans, leather tie shoes, and an expensive, colorful, embroidered tunic-length t-shirt, hair in a long white pony tail) is out watering plants in front of her house, which is just across the graveled parking area in front of the barn. With a push broom, Rod is sweeping loose hay chaff out the red barn's sliding door. He is expecting a male horse shoer, so he is unshaven, dirty from sweeping, with sweat stains on his wrinkled shirt. Sam's white pickup enters with an Ian Tyson song playing loudly on her pickup radio. She pulls up to the barn and backs her pickup close to a horse tied to the fence close to the barn door. Rod, holding his broom, looks up in shock as Sam steps

out. Sam is also shocked, mouth open . . . stammers.

SAM Oh no, it's YOU! *(long Pause)* ah, good mornin'.

She smiles nervously as she gets herself and her tools ready to shoe the horse. Embarrassed with his appearance and looking like a janitor, Rod quickly ditches the broom. He fishes a red bandana from his back pocket to wipe the sweat and dirt from his face and forehead and around the inside of his hat band. He watches Sam as she buckles on her shoeing chaps.

ROD Yeah, it's me. I don't look it right now, but I'm the boss. What are YOU doing here? And what do you think you are gonna do?

SAM Charlie said you needed some horses shod.

She opens her tailgate and grabs her shoeing box.

ROD *(confused)* I told him to hire a guy named Sam?

SAM Well, he did. That's me. But I'm not a guy.

ROD I can see that.

SAM Name's Sam. Short for Samantha. Nice to meet ya.

Sam extends her hand for a handshake. Rod ignores her offered handshake. Sam simply turns around and goes back to preparing her tools.

ROD Look, I'd be happy to take you to the Christmas dance, but no pretty lady is going to shoe a horse on this ranch as long as I'm in charge.

SAM (*frustrated*) Oh come on. I'm so sick of this routine. I've never had a single complaint. I know what I'm doing. You won't be disappointed. I've been shoeing horses for 10 years. Here, look at my hands.

Rod looks at her hands, then at her.

ROD I'm not questioning your ability. But men shoe horses for ladies, not vice versa.

SAM Oh for Pete's sake, just give me a chance. This is not 1890.

ROD It is around here.

He touches the brim of his hat to her, smiling big, and steps defiantly between her and the horse, folding his arms across his chest. Sam slams everything back into her pickup, throws her shoeing chaps in after, slams the tailgate, then trips as she climbs in, slams the door, and drives off in a cloud of dust.

INT. SAM'S PICKUP, MOMENTS LATER

Sam bangs her hand on the steering wheel once, winces from pain, and then turns up the country music, looking back at Rod in her side-view mirror as she drives away.

SAM Men can be so stupid.

EXT. RED BARN, MOMENTS LATER

Rod watches the pickup speed off as Charlie rides in on horseback. Rod turns to him angrily.

ROD What in the hell were you thinking? A female horse shoer?

CHARLIE You said you wanted the best. She's the best. She also needs the money.

A look of guilt drops over Rod's face and he takes a deep breath as he starts to drag his own showing box from under the tarp. Miss Lane is approaching.

MISS LANE Oh, no you don't, Mister. You touch one hoof and you're fired. I don't need a stove up manager. No more shoeing until Doc says so.

ROD (*humoring her*) Yes ma'am.

MISS LANE That's an order!

Rod looks at his boss with obvious affection but blows steam in frustration.

ROD Whatever you say, Miss Lane. It's your ranch, your horses.

MISS LANE Yes, it is. Yes, they are.

EXT. RED BARN—EARLY NEXT MORNING

As the sun rises, Miss Lane is out sweeping her sidewalk, obviously to keep an eye on Rod. Rod is sitting on the bench, waiting for Sam. This time he is clean shaven, wearing a clean and ironed shirt (like he is expecting a girl this time). Even the horse at the hitching rail is bathed and brushed. Rod is holding a barn cat in his lap.

ROD Well, cat, how do you do so little for so long and stay happy? Oh, so you're not happy, just pretending? I understand. (*Cat jumps off his lap.*) Enjoyed our talk. I feel better now.

Sam's white pickup enters the ranch, with the radio blaring. She pulls up to the barn and backs her pickup close to a horse tied to the nearby fence, and gets out. Rod watches

Sam as she exits her pickup and walks toward him. She has a big "I won" smile on her face.

SAM Mornin'.

Resigned, Rod stands up to properly greet a lady.

ROD Let's start over.

He extends his hand for a handshake.

SAM OK. Name's Sam. Short for Samantha.

They shake hands.

ROD Name's Rod. I'm the manager here, feed the chickens too.

SAM Nice to meet ya.

Sam walks back to her pickup and opens the tailgate and cover. She grabs her shoeing chaps, buckles them on, and starts getting her tools out.

ROD I need some help but just for a little while. I've always shod these horses. But the owner, Miss Lane, has ordered me to stop until the Doc gives me a green light. Doc says I gotta give my back a rest before I end up with a permanent problem. Doc says anyone can shoe a horse. We know that's not true. Right?

With an understanding nod, Sam smiles at Rod's compliment about her occupation.

SAM Right.

ROD I've got a good cowboy who's been working for me since he was a pup, name's Charlie, but I guess you already

met him. He recommended you. He says you're the best.

While talking, Rod walks to the horse and stands nearby.

ROD Charlie can do anything with a horse, but I never taught him to shoe because I didn't want him laming up our hard-working horses. So, this situation isn't easy for me.

SAM I figured that out the first time I was here.

ROD I thought we were gonna start over.

SAM Sorry.

She sets her shoeing box on the ground near the first foot she will work on.

ROD Never say you're sorry unless you mean it.

Sam shakes her head in frustration and approaches the horse, eyeing it admiringly. She runs her hand down the side of the horse's neck, under his stomach, across his back, butt, and down his hind leg. The horse stands perfectly, Sam is genuinely impressed.

SAM Nice. He's a real gentleman. This will be a pleasure.

ROD So you like gentlemen horses, just not gentlemen men?

SAM You can be very annoying.

ROD So now I'm not gentleman enough? Maybe you need to make up your mind what you want.

SAM Do you want me to shoe this horse or not?

*Rod hesitates, glances toward Miss Lane
who is still "innocently" sweeping her
sidewalk.*

ROD Yes.

*Sam reaches to pick up the horse's front foot
but the horse steps away from her. Rod is
embarrassed by the horse's behavior.*

ROD He always stands perfectly to be
shod.

SAM He's just not used to me. I
probably smell different.

ROD Right. He's used to smelling sweat.

SAM Oh. Don't worry, I sweat. I just
don't smell like a twelve-year-old billy
goat when I do.

*Frowning, Rod takes a quick whiff of his
shirt. Sam rubs the horse again then reaches
for a hoof once more, but the horse moves
away again.*

SAM What's his name?

ROD Zipper. The guy who started him
said he threw a wall-eyed fit every time he
heard the sound of a zipper.

*Sam lets Zipper smell her hand, inviting
the horse to get acquainted as Rod watches
her every move intently.*

ROD I figured he and I would get along
just fine because I don't wear anything
with zippers.

SAM Did you have a bad experience
with zippers as a kid?

*Rod is embarrassed again and ignores the
teasing.*

ROD I had to borrow a pair of Miss Lane's
jeans to get him over it *(hesitates)* . . . Just
for the Zipper sound. I mean . . . I didn't
wear them.

*Rod is obviously flustered and getting his
words tangled up. Sam laughs.*

SAM Do you usually tie him when you
shoe him?

ROD No.

*Sam unties the halter rope from the fence
and hands it to Rod.*

SAM Maybe he'll relax if you just hold
the rope.

*Now Sam easily picks up a foot. But, being
too protective of "the girl," Rod shortens his
grip on the lead rope and takes hold of the
side of the halter, confining Zip more than
usual again, and making the horse nervous.
When Sam starts to pull the shoe, Zip pulls
back and she has to drop his foot.*

ROD *(embarrassed again)* Sorry.

SAM Don't say sorry unless you mean
it. Look, I don't need your protection. I
know how to keep myself out of trouble.
This is not my first rodeo and this is not
even a rodeo. Zip's almost perfect, just a
little sensitive, which is good.

*Rod gives Zip more freedom. Sam rubs Zip's
back and the leg she wants to pick up.*

SAM My slightly unfamiliar moves make
him nervous. So don't confine him, just
distract him until he gets used to me.
Tickle his nose or tug on his forelock or
something.

Rod sticks his finger in the side of Zip's mouth and the horse reacts by sliding his tongue in and out, totally relaxing.

ROD How's that?

Sam feels Zip relax and easily picks up his foot and pulls the shoe.

SAM Perfect. What did you do?

ROD I stuck my finger in his mouth. Works every time.

Rod begins "man-splainin'".

ROD But you need to be careful that you know just where to stick your finger so he won't bite it off.

Sam ignores him, finishes that foot and moves on to the next one. Rod moves to keep her in sight and keeps talking.

ROD Your finger needs to slide into that empty space between his front teeth and molars.

Sam continues moving around Zip's feet, pulling shoes and trying to reassure Rod that she recognizes that the horse is perfectly trained and knows what she is doing.

SAM You do have a really nice touch, *(pause)* with horses.

Rod, pleased with the compliment, ignores her jab. As he holds the halter rope, he keeps moving to keep Sam in his line of sight. As he talks, he tries to impress her with his knowledge because he feels defensive over the way Zip has been acting. He is rattlin', man-splainin' again.

ROD There is a right way and wrong way to stick a finger in a horse's mouth. You need to watch for signs that he's

accepting you and seems more curious than afraid . . . a lot of little mental signs to look for . . . and watch for the slightest change in attitude, and . . .

Sam is back on the first foot now, rasping it level, she interrupts Rod's jabbering.

SAM Zip's leaning on me.

Rod is embarrassed again since a well-trained horse should never lean on a shoer. He reacts defensively with sarcasm.

ROD You're the horse shoer. Rap him in the belly with your rasp. Isn't that what you horse shoers do?

SAM How about if you stop watching me, take one step left, and square him up so he can keep his balance . . . *(pause)* Charlie said you didn't talk much, boy did he get that wrong.

Rod grimaces as though poked, embarrassed that Sam caught him talking too much, may have interpreted his quality control as interest in her, and she pinpointed exactly what was causing his horse to lean on her. Rod takes a step to the left, squares up his horse and himself, stops watching her, and stops talking. Sam drops Zip's foot, stands up, arches her back to stretch and rest it (but shows no back pain), and smiles.

SAM Much better. You're a fast learner.

ROD *(with a 'dammit' look)* Yes. I am.

Sam takes four shoes out of a box in her pickup bed, hangs them on her shoeing box, and then picks up Zip's left front foot and lays one horseshoe on the hoof, comparing the shape of the foot to the shoe in order to start shaping the shoe to fit. She steps to her "anvil" on the tailgate of her pickup, places the shoe on the anvil, picks up her shaping hammer, and starts to beat the shoe into a shape that will fit the shape of the hoof. Twice Sam moves back and forth between horse and anvil, picking up the foot, comparing the shape of Zip's hoof to the shoe and returning to her anvil to change the shape, trying to achieve a perfect fit. Each time she strikes the shoe with the hammer, she winces a little from the pain in her wrist. Rod notices her pain and frowns.

ROD What's up with your wrist?

SAM You don't miss much, do you?

ROD That's my job.

SAM Well, Doc says I need to rest it, but obviously that's not possible.

ROD Maybe you just need a better anvil.

SAM What's wrong with my anvil? It works just fine.

ROD Well, maybe for a cowboy, but it's not good enough for a real farrier who shoes a lot of horses.

Sam smiles at this compliment.

SAM Well, I could stop eating and buy an anvil, I suppose.

ROD You're already too skinny.

Sam smiles again.

SAM Thank you.

ROD That wasn't a compliment. You are too skinny. How about letting me shape Zip's shoes?

SAM *(insulted, feeling mistrusted)* Don't worry, his shoes will fit perfectly when I'm done.

ROD I'm sure they will, but it might be dark by then.

Sam frowns, turns away from Rod and heads back toward her anvil.

ROD *(softening his tone)* Hey, I told you this is not easy for me. Let me help you.

Rod drops the lead rope he's been holding and Zip stands perfectly in place.

ROD Let me keep a little of my chivalry intact. My back hurts, but my wrists are fine, and besides, I own a decent anvil.

Sam stops walking and turns back to face him. Rod takes a couple of steps toward the barn so he can reach and grab the corner of the tarp covering his anvil. Dramatically, and with a slight smile, he pulls the tarp off, revealing his beautiful anvil, attached to a stump, with his own shoeing box sitting at the base.

ROD *(proudly)* This doesn't belong to the ranch, it's mine.

Immediately, Sam walks over to admire and inspect the anvil. She holds the half-adjusted horseshoe and her hammer in one hand and pets the anvil with her free hand.

SAM Wow. That's a beauty. OK. You got a deal but only because I want to see this baby in action.

Sam offers Rod the half-shaped shoe. Rod inspects it briefly, grabs his own shaping hammer from his shoeing box, and steps up to his anvil without even looking at Zip's foot. He hooks one end of the shoe around the horn of the anvil, strikes it once with his hammer, then quickly lays it flat on top of the anvil and strikes it once to flatten it. He hands the shoe back to Sam.

ROD Here ya go. You almost had it.

Sam picks up Zip's foot and lays the shoe on his hoof. She is genuinely surprised and impressed that it fits perfectly. Rod steps back to Zip to pick up the halter rope.

SAM Perfect. How did you do that?

ROD Well, I've been shoeing 'ole Zip once a month or so for about five years. Even a dumb cowboy like me should be able to remember how his feet are shaped by now. He's got tricky-shaped feet, that's why I picked him to test you.

SAM I should have guessed. Can I keep his old shoes? I make Christmas wreaths and wine racks out of used shoes.

Sam quickly reaches for her shoeing hammer in the shoeing box, puts a handful of nails in her mouth, and tacks the shoe on Zip's hoof.

ROD Sure. I've got a whole fence rail with used shoes lined up along it down at the corral. You can have 'em all, probably 10 years' worth.

Time passes until Sam is finished with that shoe. Then Rod steps around her to inspect, but doesn't speak.

SAM Well?

ROD *(with a shrug and smile)* Looks OK, for a girl.

Sam smiles and shakes her head in mock frustration as she hands Rod another shoe. Instead of taking the shoe, Rod feels around Sam's wrist tenderly like a doctor would— and like a horseshoer would when searching for lameness injuries or disease in a horse's bones. The silence continues as Sam allows

Rod to "examine" her wrist, without pulling away.

SAM So, what do you think? Feel any navicular? Is my wrist still sound?

ROD Sound as a dollar. Just needs a little rest, and a better anvil.

INT. MISS LANE'S HOUSE— AT THE SAME TIME

Miss Lane, who has been watching the two from her window, smiles to herself, an idea seems to be brewing in her head.

EXT. SAM'S SHOP—A FEW DAYS LATER

Rod, driving a fairly new Ford F250 flatbed, drives up with his anvil attached to the big stump, secured to the cab of his pickup and backs up to the door to Sam's shop. Charlie and Cody (another young, clean-cut cowboy) drive up in an older pickup and park nearby. The three men exit their pickups, Charlie and Cody climb onto Rod's pickup bed to untie the anvil.

INT. SAM'S SHOP—AT THE SAME TIME

Sam, wearing ear protectors, has her back to the door. She is sharpening a skinning knife on a grinding wheel, sparks are flying. The grinder is attached to a bench with tools organized neatly above the bench, some hanging on the wall, some sitting on a shelf, some attached by leather strips with loops for individual tools. Busy working, Sam doesn't hear the three men arrive, but notices her dog get up and go to the door. Seeing this, Sam turns around just in time to see the men unloading the anvil. Sam rushes to the door and stands there speechless as Rod directs Charlie and Cody where to place the anvil—just inside the shop door, within both easy reach of her forge for blacksmithing and within easy reach for use when shoeing horses tied outside at her hitching rail. Sam's dog sniffs Rod who reaches down to scratch an ear.

ROD What's his name?

SAM *(in shock, wide-eyed)* Thor. What are you doing?

ROD Miss Lane heard about your wrist and your sorry anvil.

SAM Miss Lane knows about my wrist?

ROD Small town. Everybody around here will know if you've got holes in your underwear. Miss Lane doesn't miss a thing. She says that if my anvil is sitting out there by the barn, I'll be tempted to use it and she doesn't have time to keep an eye on me all the time. She suggested I loan it to you before she has to fire me or I permanently cripple my back. I agreed that maybe you could use it while I can't.

Sam steps to the anvil, speechless, but looks concerned.

SAM I can't accept this.

ROD It's just a loan. Don't go getting all femi-nazi on me. I will haul our ranch horses over here until Doc and Miss Lane release me from prison. We'll see if it helps your wrist. You're not much shorter than I am, so it should fit you or you can always stand on a box.

Rod stops momentarily, sizing up the placement of the anvil.

ROD Is this about where you'd want it?

Charlie and Cody wait for further orders from Rod if Sam decides she wants the anvil

moved. Sam runs her hand over the anvil admiringly.

SAM That's the perfect spot, but I can't believe you'd trust me with this.

ROD I figure a real farrier knows how to treat an anvil. Besides, Zip checked you out. He told me you're a real good shoer too, maybe better than me.

Hearing this, Charlie and Cody look at each other very surprised. Rod indicates with a slight nod of his head that they are free to leave. They walk back to their pickup and drive off as Rod continues to talk, walking deeper into Sam's shop.

ROD Zip said you just needed a better anvil.

He reaches down to scratch Thor again.

ROD Thor, huh? Why Thor?

SAM In mythology, he's the god of thunder, slings a hammer.

Curious and nosey, Rod begins to walk around snooping, picking up things and laying them back in place, as Sam watches amused.

ROD This is quite a set-up. You must be doing some blacksmithing too. Your forge is sort of small, so your projects can't be very big.

SAM Right. *(heading toward it)* I'm limited a little but I make anything that will fit into it from twisted fireplace pokers to horseshoe-nail jewelry. I also do a lot of welding, mostly sticking used horseshoes together.

Sam walks back to her bench where she had been sharpening the knife and picks it up.

SAM My specialty is making skinning knives to sell to hunters, or more often to their wives. They make good gifts.

Sam carefully turns the handle of the sharp knife toward Rod so he can grasp it safely and passes it to him to inspect. Rod looks impressed. He holds the knife up in front of his eyes, looking down the top edge, checking for straightness, and inspecting and testing the sharpened edge with his thumb for defects, finding none.

ROD Very nice. I'll take one.

SAM Don't you want to know what I charge first?

ROD Judging by your anvil, I'm sure whatever it is, it's not enough. If you can make a knife like this on that piece of junk, I'm willing to pay up just to see what you can do on a decent anvil. So promise you'll make my knife on my anvil?

SAM *(grinning)* Promise.

Rod continues poking around Sam's shop.

ROD Why are you doing all this forge work if your wrist is bothering you? You have to do 100 times more pounding than it would take to shoe a horse. That's probably what's causing your wrist pain.

SAM Well, except for old cowboys like you, nobody around here rides horses in the winter.

ROD I'm not old.

SAM Right, I didn't mean old as in age, I meant old as in old-fashioned, traditional.

ROD Well then say what you mean.

SAM *(ignoring his sharpness)* I get plenty of summer shoeing business when tourists are here playing cowboy, but that dries up in the winter. I have to do whatever it takes to keep the taxes paid on this place and groceries on the table *(pause)* But back to your knife order. What kind of wood do you want for the handle?

ROD What do you recommend?

Sam pulls out a piece of algarita root.

SAM I like to experiment with different kinds of wood. Right now I have this nice piece of Algarita from West Texas. It's just a scrubby desert bush, but the roots sometimes get big enough for a knife handle.

She hands the root to Rod who looks it over.

SAM Because of dry weather stress, the wood is real dense, like a South American hardwood. Beneath the grey bark, the wood is sort of bright buckskin yellow with sage-green veining running through it. Makes a beautiful knife handle. Or I have some oak, madrone, mesquite . . .

ROD *(interrupting)* That dense Algarita wood sounds perfect since you think I'm kind of dense. I'll be back Monday morning with two more horses to shoe.

Rod walks out of the shop, Sam watches him go.

INT. SAM'S SHOP—MORNING

Sam, again wearing ear and eye protection plus a brace on her wrist, has her forge fired up and has heated a railroad spike to red hot, takes it to the new anvil and begins to hammer it flat to begin a knife. She sees her dog move and looks up to see Rod

ROD What's this?

SAM Oh, that's my brand.

*Sam's Brand is shaped like a "C", or an
open sided circle, like a horse's hoof. Rod
looks at Sam, stiffly, sort of angry.*

SAM I inherited this place from my
grandma, but I'm struggling to hang on
to it. Someday, when and if I can ever
afford some cows maybe this land will
provide a little income instead of just
expenses. Anyway, that's the brand I plan
to use. I call it a horseshoe.

*Rod looks intently at Sam, as if expecting
trouble.*

ROD Well, I hate to tell you, but that
brand is already taken. It's registered
in this county and the three counties
surrounding us.

*Rod notices that the forge is still burning
so he carries the branding iron over to the
forge and sticks the brand end into the forge
while he continues to talk. Sam watches
him with a puzzled look, not sure what he
is going to do.*

ROD This is <u>my</u> brand. I call it an oxbow,
after the kind of stirrups I ride and a nice
bend in the river not far from here, also

called an oxbow. The shape makes a good
clean brand, doesn't blotch.

*Rod carefully watches the branding iron
heating up in the forge, waiting for it to
get just the right color to indicate it is hot
enough to leave a mark, but not too hot
to damage the metal. After a few seconds,
Rod pulls the branding iron from the forge
and walks to his anvil. He carefully places
the "C" so it appears more like a U, sticks
the brand against the stump and burns
his oxbow brand into the wood while he
continues to talk.*

ROD This iron holds heat good.

*He placed his brand so it can be easily
seen by anyone bringing a horse to be
shod or stepping inside Sam's shop door.
Symbolically, Rod is "marking" his
possession and maybe claiming some
territory here at Sam's, like a male dog
peeing on a tree.*

ROD Nice iron. But you can't just design
a brand and start using it. It has to be
approved and registered at the local
courthouse. It needs to be something
nobody else is using and totally unlike
any neighbors' brands.

*Rod starts to cool off the branding iron
by twisting the hot end in some loose dirt
and then leans it up against the door
frame opposite his anvil so it can continue
cooling. Sam looks at Rod with surprise and
concern.*

SAM Sorry. I didn't know. Maybe I can
add an "S" inside the horseshoe?

ROD Nope. You can't do that either. For
example, Miss Lane's brand is a rafter, sort
of like a wide open and upside down V.
It's been registered in this state since 1890.

Rod bends down and draws Miss Lane's brand in the dirt with his finger. Sam leans over his shoulder to see.

ROD Nobody else can register a rafter by adding any combination of letters, numbers, or other marks.

He draws a letter under the rafter and brushes it out, draws a number beside the rafter and bushes it out.

ROD The rules are to prevent anyone from adding to her brand in order to rustle her cattle. Plus an "S" inside a horseshoe would just blotch and look like a tennis ball.

He draws the horseshoe/oxbow brand with an "S" inside the curve and then scratches it all into a circle to show the "blotch."

EXT. SAM'S SHOP—MOMENTS LATER

Arriving back at his horse trailer, Rod unloads the two horses, tying the first one to the trailer and leading the second one over to the hitching rail and tying it there. Sam continues their conversation while she buckles on her shoeing chaps and gets her equipment ready.

SAM They don't teach us about brands in shoeing school, and neither did my grandma. I will design something else, get your approval first, and register it before I make myself another branding iron.

ROD A brand isn't just a clever design. It represents who you are, your reputation. What you put your brand on represents what kind of person you are, what you can do, what's at stake, what you're willing to fight for. It stands for your life, what you care about. A wise old man once told me that if I was gonna put my brand on

something, that "something" needed to be the best . . . like that anvil.

Rod unties the horse from the hitching rail and holds it. While they talk, Sam works around the horse: pulling shoes, trimming, rasping, and leveling the hoof.

ROD A horseshoe would be the perfect brand for you, though, so maybe you could have my oxbow brand someday and call it a horseshoe.

SAM Why would you say that?

Sam is ready for Rod to start shaping the shoes for her, so Rod ties the horse to the hitching rail again. They continue to talk while he shapes a shoe. Once she approves the shape and before she begins to nail it on, he again unties and holds the horse.

ROD Well, a brand has to be re-registered every few years or someone else can claim it. I don't own the ranch where my cows get their groceries. Miss Lane lets me run 20 cows and one bull for free, maybe as sort of a retirement fund or maybe to keep me around. Anyway, right now 20 cows, their calves, and a bull are wearing my brand and eating Miss Lane's grass. If anything happens to her, the next owner might not let me run any cows of my own on the ranch.

Once in a while, Sam rejects a shoe that doesn't fit the hoof to her satisfaction. When she does, Rod steps to the horse, and looks over her shoulder while she lets him see the fit. Then he makes an adjustment on the shoe and she approves the fit the next time he hands it to her.

ROD Or we might get into a drouth and Miss Lane might need the grass my cows are eating. Or she might just change her mind. I've never been sure how long

I might own anything to put a brand on. So, I've never owned a branding iron. Right now I only need to brand at most 20 calves every year in order to send them through the sale barn in the fall because I can't keep them. So I just use a running iron.

SAM A what?

ROD Running iron. I thought any blacksmith would know what a running iron is?

SAM Not this one.

ROD A runnin' iron is just kinda the handle to a brandin' iron that's bent into a slight curve at the end instead of having an actual brand attached. Hold on. I've got one in my pickup.

He walks out to his pickup (also giving her a chance to rest without making a big deal of it) and pulls a running iron from behind the seat, bringing it back to show her.

ROD I just use the curved end like a pencil. Heat it up and draw my oxbow.

He draws his oxbow brand in the dirt with the running iron while Sam watches.

ROD The curved metal slides through the calf's hair real easy, burning on the brand just about as fast as a regular branding iron would.

Rod and Sam continue to work while Rod talks. When Sam finishes shoeing the first horse, Rod inspects the shoes, nods yes, and Sam smiles.

ROD You need a rest?

SAM Yes.

He picks up his running iron and leads the shod horse to the trailer. Sam goes to her pickup's tailgate and holds up a bottle of water from a case of warm water sitting near her tools.

SAM Need water?

Rod shakes his head no. Sam takes a long drink from the bottled water, sits on the tailgate and watches Rod switch horses before joining him back at her hitching rail to shoe the second horse. They resume their conversation.

ROD Back in the old days, and maybe still today, cowboys carried small, hinged runnin' irons on their saddles. They could step off, build a little fire, and brand a calf as soon as it was born. *(pause)* Some say, only cattle rustlers carried running irons. I heard of an old Texan who owned a big ranch with oil wells all over it, 100 sections . . .

Rod notices Sam's confused expression.

ROD A section is a mile square. There are 640 acres in a section so that means his ranch was 64-thousand acres. Texans usually talk in sections, meaning in square miles, instead of acres. Anyway, he always bragged that his ancestors got their start using a running iron. Nobody knew if he was telling the truth or joking. He did let the nearby town display what he claimed was his grandfather's old running iron in a store window one year during some celebration.

Sam frowns, Rod laughs.

ROD Don't worry, I'm no thief. Being a cattle rustler today doesn't carry the same kind of romance it once did, at least not around here. We prefer honesty.

SAM Why can't you keep your calves?

ROD I told you. Miss Lane lets me run 20 head. I can't exceed that number. No matter how perfect my heifer calves might be, or how much I might want to keep them as future cows, I have to sell them. I'm not complaining. I feel real lucky to run a few of my own cows. Very few cowboys have that privilege. It's not my ranch. Someday I hope to own a little place of my own, or at least that's my dream.

SAM So what's your plan?

ROD I don't have a plan, just a dream. You sure do ask a lot of questions.

SAM Well, you need a plan or someday you'll be just another old stove up cowboy with 20 toothless cows between him and starvation.

ROD Yeah? Well, I'll have had a great life.

As they finish the final shoe, Rod unties the second horse and inspects the shoeing job. He leads the horse back to the trailer where he loads it and then unties the first horse from the trailer and loads it too, then gets into his pickup. Sam grabs her now cooled branding iron that has been leaning against the door frame and walks to Rod's pickup just as he is about to drive off and sticks the branding iron, handle first, in his open window.

SAM Here, take this. Call it rent on the anvil, or in case I dent it.

Rod looks at the branding iron, and then at Sam.

ROD I can't accept this.

SAM Sure you can. I just gave it to you.

ROD Then let me buy it. What do I owe you?

SAM Nuthin. You already explained why I can't use it, but you can.

Rod looks at Sam, then the branding iron, and tries to hand it back.

ROD Can't.

SAM Come on. Compared to the use of a beautiful anvil, it's nothing.

ROD It is not nothing to a man who's never owned a branding iron before.

SAM Oh, here we go again. You are loaning me probably the most expensive anvil I've ever even seen, and I'm just giving you a piece of beat-up bent iron. It's got nothing to do with your manhood . . .

Realizing what she just said, Sam blushes and quickly covers her mouth with one hand.

SAM Did I actually say that out loud?

Rod laughs at her embarrassment.

ROD Now that we cleared that up, thank you.

He places the branding iron on the seat next to him, pats it, touches the brim of his hat to her, starts the pickup, and drives off still laughing. Sam watches him drive away, still embarrassed.

EXT. LANE RANCH CORRALS—MORNING

One hundred Angus cows with their black calves mill in the corral as we witness spring branding. Charlie is riding in among the herd, heeling one calf at a time with his rope and dragging it to the fire. Two other cowboys, Cody and Gabe (a young, handsome, brash, jovial Hispanic with a black moustache) are flanking. Miss Lane is branding, Rod follows her doing the knife work of ear marking and castrating, and Sam follows Rod vaccinating. Miss Lane stands at the branding fire (can be either a wood fire or a propane pot), waiting, her hand resting on the handle of one of two Rafter branding irons. Rod and Sam stand together. Rod is pointing things out and explaining to Sam who looks eager but nervous. They are almost done with this pen full. Charlie finally signals that there are no more unbranded calves by making a "throat cutting" motion with his hand. Miss Lane swaps out the Rafter branding irons for Rod's Oxbow that has been leaning against the fence. She twists her hot irons in the dirt to clean and start them cooling and leans their handles against the fence, out of the way behind the fire. Meanwhile, Cody opens a gate and Charlie pushes all the cows and calves out of the branding pen. As Rod opens a gate on the other side of the corral, Gabe bridles his horse, removes the hobbles, and brings in 20 head of Horned Hereford cows with their calves that have been waiting in another pen. Meanwhile, Charlie hobbles his horse outside the pen where it can graze, removes the bridle and hangs it on his saddle horn, and steps up to take his turn flanking with Cody. Gabe settles the cattle by riding through them and gets ready to rope. Miss Lane walks over to Sam, holding her hand out to take the vaccine gun from Sam.

MISS LANE Here, let me have that vaccine gun. Rod wants you to do the honor of branding his calves with his new branding iron.

SAM Me?

MISS LANE *(laughing)* Yes, you.

SAM But I don't know how.

MISS LANE You've been helping us for three days and watching me. Rod will help you. Don't worry. He's a perfectionist, so he'll make sure you do a good job.

Sam looks nervous, but walks over to the branding fire and stands where Miss Lane had been standing, resting her hand on the Oxbow branding iron that is now hot and ready to go. Gabe is already on his way toward her dragging a roped calf by two heels. Cody grabs the rope and Charlie grabs the tail to bring it down.

ROD Ready?

Sam looks worried but shakes her head yes.

ROD OK, just wait until the flankers have the calf on the ground before you run to it with the iron. They should have it secured and the rope off by the time you get there. You don't want to be too early and let your iron get cold, but you don't want to be late and make your flankers hold the calf any longer than necessary or they'll get cranky.

GABE *Heifer!*

Once Charlie and Cody have the calf down, Rod and Sam run to the calf, Cody holds the calf's heels. Rod reaches around Sam, his arms around her, and holds the branding iron with her.

ROD You want to line up the top of the branding iron with the calf's spine because he's stretched out of shape a little. I don't want that brand crooked when he stands up. Now plant the iron firmly right here *(pause)* and hold it until the hair stops smoking. Now lift it. *(pause)* See that even tan color?

Sam nods.

ROD That's what you want, that's perfect. OK, go put the iron back in the fire.

Sam is beaming and does a little happy dance. Everyone laughs at her. Rod quickly digs out his pocket knife and quickly ear marks the heifer calf. No need to castrate or dehorn. Simultaneously, Miss Lane is right there and injects the vaccine. Cody and Charlie release the calf and stand up to await the next one. Charlie, who was holding the heels, grabs the tail and lets the calf pull him to his feet. Rod and Miss Lane go back to stand beside Sam at the fire and wait for the next calf. Rod is still smiling at Sam's happiness, explains more.

ROD On a black calf you want that branded skin to look grey not pink. On a Hereford calf, tan. Pink is too much and you might have to doctor a wound for a few days. Grey or tan is just right. You don't want a deep burn, just singe off the hair and stress the skin enough to make it peel and leave a scar. When you lift the iron, you can place it back on again if you don't see even color, but be careful to place it in exactly the same spot. If you leave it on too long, there's not much you can do. You'll get a feel for it after a few calves.

GABE Bull!

Gabe brings in another calf, so the system starts over: branding, vaccination, and this time it's a bull so Rod earmarks, castrates, and also dehorns it with some dehorning spoons. As the process continues, Rod watches over Sam's shoulder but lets her hold the branding iron alone. When she

picks up the iron to look at the color, she looks at Rod and he smiles.

ROD Pretty good for a girl.

Sam is happy and makes only a slight a face at him, and they stand together back at the fire again, waiting for another calf.

ROD And don't let your iron get too hot or too cold *(pause)* but I don't need to explain that to a farrier.

Sam grins and quickly adjusts the iron in the fire to either move it closer to the heat source or away.

INT. SAM'S SHOP—MORNING

Rod walks into Sam's blacksmith shop. Thor comes up and sniffs him. Rod scratches his ear, and walks toward Sam, who has her back to him, welding. As Rod approaches Sam, he reaches out and touches her arm. Sam jumps out of her skin.

SAM Aaaa! How did you get past Thor?

ROD *(laughing)* Whoa. Easy there. He knows I'm one of the good guys.

Rod points at his cowboy hat.

ROD Black hat.

SAM I thought bad guys wear black hats and good guys wear white.

ROD Only in Hollywood.

SAM So what can I do for you today?

ROD It's what can I do for you. It's supposed to rain all day, so Miss Lane sent me to hammer since you vaccinated her calves.

SAM What?

ROD Your wrist hurts, mine's fine. I'm sure you've got a bunch of blacksmithing to finish before the Fourth of July fair, so I'll do the work, you give the orders, just the way you women like it.

SAM You know, I'm starting to get used to the stoooopid way you talk about women. It just isn't bothering me anymore. I'm not sure if that's good or bad.

ROD It's good. I was hoping you were at least as smart as the average horse.

INT/EXT. COLLAGE—PASSING OF TIME

Sam and Rod doing things together: Rod removing nails from old horseshoes and hammering them flat. Sam welding the shoes together or painting them. On a picnic. Riding around in a pickup laughing. Fixing a flat together. Watching it rain. Sitting on the bench and pointing out stars in the night sky. Rod sneaking up past Sam's dog and touching her on the arm, scaring her to death, and laughing. Drinking coffee or bottled water on the bench, resting. Sam driving up to the ranch with her dead dog, crying, Rod comforting her in his arms. Rod and Charlie burying Thor. Rod and Sam driving to Thor's gravesite for a picnic. Sam marks Thor's gravesite with a welded sign saying "Thor" made of horseshoes on a metal stake. Meanwhile, Rod picks wildflowers, hands them to Sam, and she places them on Thor's grave. Rod comforts Sam in his arms while she cries.

EXT. SAM'S SHOP—EVENING

Rod pulls up to Sam's Shop. She is sitting on her bench, resting and enjoying the evening with a cup of coffee. Out of his pickup window Rod holds a new German Shephard puppy with a red bow around its neck. Sam runs out to the pickup and grabs it. As it snuggles up to her, it turns back to bark at Rod.

ROD *(with mock anger)* What the hell?

SAM *(laughing)* Maybe your days of sneaking up and scaring me are over! *(snuggling the puppy)*. Good Boy!

EXT. 4TH OF JULY FAIR— AFTERNOON

Small town booths set up in the park to sell food, games, etc. Sam's booth is two boards laid across two tall saw-horses to form a counter. Two pieces of pegboard hinged for transportation stand up behind the counter. Hanging from the pegboard and made from used horseshoes are wreaths, wall hooks, coat racks, picture frames, crosses, a towel holder, linked hearts, inspirational words (courage, try, faith), and a gun rack. Displayed on the counter are a wine rack, paper towel holder, book ends (one set made from old rasps), and hoof picks. A homemade sign that says "SAM'S STUFF" hangs from the front of the counter with letters made from used horseshoes. Standing in front and to each side of the sign are yard art flowers, small animals, a boot scraper—all made of used horseshoes.

ROD Wow. We made a lot of stuff. This is looking pretty good.

SAM Thanks. And thanks so much for helping. I wouldn't have half this much to sell without your help and it wouldn't look so good without your help setting up this booth. Just a few more details, and I'll be set to open at one, on schedule.

ROD How come you just brought one knife and want it hanging here in a plastic box?

He hangs a clear plastic box displaying a knife behind her on the pegboard.

SAM I don't want anyone picking up one of my sharp knives, pulling it out of the scabbard, and cutting off a thumb. And there'll be lots of kids around.

ROD Good thinking.

SAM Plus, the kind of people who really need a knife like I make, usually want to design their own. I can show them a sample and then explain the different choices. One is enough to show my skills.

ROD That reminds me, I'm still waiting for my skinning knife with the algarita handle.

SAM I know. I've started it a couple times but haven't been satisfied yet. I want it to be my best work.

ROD Now I'm getting nervous that maybe I should have asked the price.

SAM *(laughing)* Yup. You should have. You might be out of the cow business once I shake you down.

ROD Seriously, I've never seen better made knives anywhere and I've sharpened a lot of knives.

SAM Thanks.

ROD All this stuff made from old worn out horseshoes is amazing, although I don't personally have much use for a wine rack or a hoof pick with a bighorn ram's head for a handle.

He picks up the hoof pick and makes a face like he doesn't think this one is very practical.

SAM *(laughing)* Agreed. Some things are for collectors or people who want a "rustic" look. As long as they hand me money, I don't care what they do with it.

Rod traces his finger affectionately around one horseshoe in the wine rack.

ROD This shoe looks like one of Zip's.

SAM It probably is. I've even had a few old cowboys bring me the shoes when one of their pet horses died, wanting me to make them a coat rack or something. They'll tell me to be careful not to change the shape of the shoes because they want to remember that particular horse.

ROD Maybe I'll have you make me something from Zip's shoes when his time comes.

They both pause for a beat. Sam reaches up and affectionately, briefly, rubs one of Rod's shoulders as though to cheer him up from the future sadness of losing his favorite horse.

ROD If you're still around.

Rod looks at Sam hopefully.

SAM I'll be here.

They lock eyes for a beat, then Sam pulls her hand away quickly.

ROD Well, I better go so I don't run off your customers. I'm gonna go watch the team roping slack while you scoop up money. I'll come back to help you pack up.

SAM Thanks. See ya later.

EXT. SAM BOOTH AT FAIR— EVENING

As Rod walks back up to the almost empty booth, Sam's puppy barks at him. Rod stomps his foot at it to scare it more. Sam laughs.

ROD Wow. Looks like you almost sold out! Good for you.

SAM *(grinning)* Yup. Just one little box left of stuff that didn't sell. Got my taxes paid for another year, maybe with enough left over for a decent anvil. Which reminds me, how is your back?

ROD *(avoiding the question, changes the subject)* Guess you didn't have any hoof pick collectors stop by?

He picks up the bighorn pick from the box.

SAM *(laughing)* Yeah. Maybe that one wasn't such a great idea. Doesn't look too handy to clean a horse's hoof with, does it?

ROD It would look good hanging on a wall though.

SAM *(laughs)* The book-ends sold out fastest. I need to make more of those next year, even the pair I made out of worn out rasps sold. Guess everybody in this small town owns a lot of books.

ROD Hungry?

SAM Starving. I missed lunch.

ROD OK, let's go get a burger. That's about the only place still open. I will send Cody and Gabe to pick up this lumber early tomorrow morning.

Sam grabs the small cardboard box with the items that didn't sell, and they head off camera together, puppy following on Sam's heels.

EXT. SAM'S SHOP— SUNDOWN

The sun is just about to set. Rod's ranch pickup and trailer are parked just outside the shop door. Sam and Rod load four horses into the trailer, then sit on the bench next to the garage. Sam arches and stretches her back but shows no pain.

SAM Long afternoon.

ROD Yup. Four horses. We make a pretty good team.

SAM *(looks away, then back at Rod)* So, why are you still a crabby old bachelor?

ROD What? Where did that come from?

SAM Well, you are not totally awful as I first thought. So, it seems like someone would have gotten you hobbled by now.

ROD And you think that is any of your business because . . .?

SAM Because I'm your friend, or at least I think I am. Am I?

ROD Maybe. Why do you want to know?

SAM I'm writing a book.

ROD Gonna be a very boring book if it's about my love life.

SAM Well if it's that boring, it shouldn't be difficult to talk about.

ROD OK. For starters, I don't believe in love. I believe in respect.

SAM Why am I not surprised?

ROD I loved my mother, but I didn't respect her. It seemed like my father felt the same way toward her. I never liked that. I respected my father but I didn't love him and I think that's how my mother felt toward him. I didn't like that either.

SAM Interesting.

ROD And you?

SAM I think I respected both of my parents, but I'm not sure I loved either of them. Both were very strict and neither were very loving. But maybe love and respect are just words.

ROD I might agree with that.

SAM Maybe love is more about who I want to be with, how often, when I want to be with them, and how they make me feel about myself. I'm grateful for my raising and still want to see my parents occasionally, but not for long *(pause)* at least not since I became a teenager. Right now, I mostly love my job.

ROD I'm grateful for all my dad taught me. He was the best cowboy I ever met. But unless forced, I didn't want to be with him because I could never please him, never measured up to his desire for perfection. I guess I inherited his worst fault.

SAM I can see that.

Rod frowns, Sam smiles.

ROD When I was young, I did like to be with my mother, because she was very affectionate, kissing my skinned knees and hugging me when I was sad. But as I grew up, she made me feel smothered, like she used her affection for control or guilt trips.

Sam looks at Rod with understanding.

SAM I fear those things too. When I start to feel controlled, or like I don't measure up, I stop wanting to be with that person. I think what I might call love is wanting to be with someone who gives me freedom, encouragement, and lets me fly. Someone who helps me realize what I'm capable of and lets me be a better me. Someone I can trust completely. *(pause)* Maybe more like a partner.

ROD *(deep in thought)* Yeah.

SAM Seems like even spoiled horses make better partners than people.

ROD Amen to that.

Their eyes lock. They both look away quickly, then back at each other once again. They both stand up and face each other, a full moon lights up the otherwise dark sky.

SAM *(maybe anticipating a kiss?)* Well, goodnight.

ROD Goodnight.

Rod's jaw is locked and he swallows hard. This has been a deep and scary conversation for him. Sam slowly reaches up and tries to stick her finger in the corner of Rod's mouth. Rod grabs her hand, laughs, and then relaxes immediately.

ROD What are you doing?

SAM *(coyly)* Just seeing if I could stick my finger in your mouth without getting bit *(pause)* you know *(pause)* like you did to relax Zip that first day I shod him.

Rod looks suspicious but remains relaxed and with renewed confidence. He hasn't released Sam's hand, so he turns it over into a gentleman's grip on her fingers and kisses her hand like she's a lady.

ROD Those old cowboy tricks don't work on people, believe me I've tried.

They look at each other for a beat, Rod fakes being romantic with googly eyes.

ROD Besides, your finger tastes like an old thrushy horse's hoof.

Sam reacts in a mock rage. She beats playfully on Rod's chest with both fists, while Rod playfully tries to protect himself. The puppy dashes up to protect Sam and starts barking at Rod.

SAM *Rodney James Williams you're impossible!*

ROD *Did you say possible?*

SAM *IMMM—possible! Sick'em!*

ROD *(laughing and backing up) OK. OK. I'm leaving. I'm leaving.*

Sam reaches down to the ground and finds a tiny rock, picks it up, and throws it at Rod's foot.

SAM Git!

Laughing even harder, Rod turns around and heads to his pickup, stops and turns back, still laughing. Sam throws out both arms as if to booger a horse and stamps her foot.

SAM I said git!

INT. ROD'S PICKUP— MOMENTS LATER

Puppy still barking, Rod still laughing and then smiling. He shakes his head and climbs inside his pickup cab. As he drives away, he watches Sam in the side mirror as she puts the back of her hand up to her mouth and nose.

ROD *(under his breath)* Ha. She's smelling her hand!

As he drives further, the look on his face changes from mirth to shock.

ROD Orrr, is she kissing it?

As Rod drives off into the darkness, in his side mirror he sees the glowing porch lights of Sam's house dissolve into the night sky.

INT. SAM'S SHOP—DAY

Sam is at work with her shop door open, ear and eye protectors on. Rod pulls up with horses to shoe and tries to enter stealthily but the puppy barks. Rod tries to shush him so he can scare Sam. Sam turns around catching Rod, laughs, and pets her puppy.

SAM Good boy, Heppy! Protect your Mama from that evil, mean man. Good boy Heppy!

ROD Heppy?

SAM After Hephaestus, Greek god of blacksmiths.

Rod fakes a jump at Heppy and makes him bark more.

ROD You noisy little shit.

SAM *(laughing)* Don't you call my good watch dog mean names!

EXT. SAM'S SHOP—LATER

Sam is under a horse, tacking on shoes. Rod is leaning on his anvil.

SAM I had an idea.

ROD When a female has an idea, a man is about to get in big trouble.

SAM Stop it. I'm serious. What about *(pause)* if, instead of selling your calves next week, you keep your heifers and lease my grass? It's been growing for several years but I can't afford to buy any cattle to eat it and it's becoming a fire hazard. You said you raised some heifer calves that you'd like to keep but can't. I need to figure out a way for this place to help pay its own way. So you could lease pasture from me, keep your heifers, help me get through winter, and add to your retirement fund. What do you say?

A silence drops over Sam's shop as the two work, although every time Rod steps back inside the shop door and up to his anvil after handing or retrieving a shoe to or from Sam, the puppy barks at him.

ROD Scary, but maybe not a bad idea *(long pause as they both think)* I don't know. You get mad at me at least once every hour for something, so I'd just get my heifers unloaded and you'd change your mind. I'd have to load them back up, and take them to the sale, maybe on a day when the price was down.

SAM Well, it's even scarier for me because you are way more likely than I am to get in a big huff, and pull out right after I spend all the lease money.

She drops the horse's foot and sticks out her hand.

SAM Come on, let's give it a whirl?

ROD Whoa. Not so fast. We need to sign a contract, not just shake hands. I don't trust women.

SAM *(rolling her eyes)* Good idea. I don't trust men either, especially you. Even my dog doesn't trust you.

ROD Yeah. The ungrateful little fur ball. *(to the dog)* You forget who brung ya here in the first place.

Heppy barks at Rod, Sam laughs.

SAM *(pause, then serious)* We'll sign a contract. There's only one lawyer in town. He helped me with all my inheritance paperwork, so he already knows this place. I'll have him draw one up.

ROD Let me think about it.

SAM No. If you think about it, you'll talk yourself out of it. You need pasture and I need money. Let's just do it.

ROD You sure have gotten bossy since you started using a decent anvil.

SAM Deal?

Sam sticks her hand out again, Rod still doesn't shake it.

ROD How many head can you run?

SAM I'm not sure.

ROD What? That's the craziest thing I ever heard. How can we make a deal if you don't even know how many head your country can support?

SAM You make everything so complicated.

ROD That's my job.

SAM OK, so where do we start?

ROD First, you find a copy of your deed. Go to the courthouse if you have to.

SAM Can't I just tell you how many acres I own?

ROD Size don't tell me how much can be grazed. I've seen country where a thousand acres wouldn't support a jackrabbit. I need to see the deed so I can draw a rough shirt-pocket-sized map. Then we need to get horseback and go see what you've actually got: fences, corners, gates, water. *(pause)* Can you ride a horse?

SAM I feel more comfortable under a horse than on one, but I'd ride one of yours, yes.

INT. FEED STORE—MORNING

The clerk is behind the counter and Rod is standing in front of him trying to place an order.

FEED STORE CLERK Heard you're leasing some grass from Sam?

ROD Ahh. She only just mentioned it yesterday. How does word get around this town so fast?

FEED STORE CLERK *(shrugs)* Hey, it's just because we all love you *(pause)* well, mostly Sam.

ROD Right. Don't worry. We plan to sign a very legal and binding contract so I can't take advantage of her. *(pause)* Any more questions or do you still sell feed here? If so, I need ten sacks of oats.

EXT. RED BARN—LATER, AFTERNOON

Charlie is sitting on the bench, waiting to help unload. Miss Lane walks over when Rod pulls up with the 10 sacks of oats. Rod tries to grab a sack, but Charlie elbows him out of the way. Seeing this, Miss Lane smiles. Charlie unloads and carries the sacks into the barn while Rod resigns himself and looks coyly at Miss Lane.

MISS LANE *(a look of what's going on?)* Heard you are leasing some grass from Sam?

ROD Don't give me that look. Nothing is going on. She's got extra grass but no cows, I've got a few good heifers that I hate to sell. So we're trying to make a deal. That's all.

MISS LANE Uh, huh. How much country does she want to lease?

ROD I'm sure she'd like to lease all of it. She needs the money. But she has no idea how many head it will run. I'm trying to help her figure that out.

MISS LANE Well, if it's more than you can handle right now and you need a third partner for a while, I'm in.

ROD Thanks. That might be a great idea. I think you and she might even share a fence line down along the river.

MISS LANE I also heard that you've been shaping the shoes for our horses while she's doing the shoeing.

ROD Well, even though Doc thinks anyone can shoe horses, this ranch of yours rests smack on top of those horses' feet. I'm following your orders, but I want their shoes to fit perfectly *(pause)* And shaping shoes doesn't hurt my back.

MISS LANE Uh, huh.

Rod arches his back and stretches his arms upward toward the sky.

ROD Besides, my back is almost well. I'm pretty sure Doc will give me a green light next week.

MISS LANE So, if he does, what are you gonna do? If you start shoeing our horses again, you'll need to bring your anvil back here, and you won't have a reason to go see Sam.

ROD I hadn't thought that far ahead.

MISS LANE Uh, huh. Well maybe you should. Maybe you better get that lease *(pause)*, so she can afford her own anvil, of course.

Rod frowns at her like she's obviously meddling in his business. Miss Lane smirks at him. She knows exactly what is going on.

EXT. SMALL TOWN— MORNING

As the camera floats over scenic pastures and the small town, we hear the church bells ring. Then we see Rod riding one horse and leading another to Sam's shop.

EXT. SAM'S SHOP—AT THE SAME TIME

Meanwhile, Sam has pulled the garage door shut and locks it, bends down to pet Heppy (no longer a pup) and motions for him to stay, leaving him to guard the shop, his water and food nearby. Then she walks out to meet Rod. He arrives at Sam's shop

horseback and leading a saddled horse. He steps off, wearing worn and similar but newer chink leggins than the ones he shoes in, and hands his lead line to Sam. Turning to the horse he's been leading he starts to replace the halter with a snaffle-bit bridle and McCarty. Sam steps up to Rod's horse, pets its neck, then takes a hold of his oxbow stirrup.

SAM So, is this an oxbow stirrup like your brand?

Rod continues to get her horse ready, tightening the cinch, adjusting the stirrups.

ROD Yup. Those belonged to my dad.

SAM I always heard that oxbows were dangerous, that if you bucked off it was easy to get your foot hung and drug to death.

ROD Well, the first thing I teach a bronc is to stop when he feels a drag on a stirrup. I also try not to aggravate my horse to the point where he thinks he needs to buck me off to get relief.

The two horses are saddled with well-used, cowboy-style saddles, clean and well-oiled. Rod hands Sam the reins to her horse and takes back his get down line, tightens his own cinch and mounts. Sam looks at the horse she's about to ride.

SAM So what's his name?

ROD *(reassuring smile)* Gentleman Jim.

Sam smiles and nods at the name. She starts gathering up the reins to mount.

ROD I started him. I named him. Miss Lane has ridden him some. That's her saddle too. She said you are welcome to borrow it anytime.

SAM So do you call him Gent or Jim?

ROD Gent

SAM *(stepping on without hesitation)* OK, Gent, I'm ready when you are.

ROD Do the stirrups feel like they are about the right length?

SAM Perfect. Obviously you know just how long my legs are.

Rod grins sheepishly as the two ride out across the country.

EXT. LANDSCAPE— MOMENTS LATER

Rod and Sam ride across her property, investigating it.

EXT. GATE—LATER

Rod side-passes his horse up to a gate to open it from horseback.

ROD I thought we'd find a gate here. Now we're leaving your property and heading into Miss Lane's river pasture. We can use this gate to just drive the cattle back and forth to brand or ship. And that pretty river oxbow I told you about is just over that hill.

EXT. RIVER OXBOW—LATER

As Sam and Rod ride up to a beautiful oxbow bend in the river, we see a grassy spot, shade trees, and a handy rock for sitting. Rod steps off his horse and stands close to Sam and her horse as she dismounts, ready to help her if necessary. Sam dismounts cleanly, on her own. Rod hobbles both horses and removes bridles, hanging them on the respective saddle horns.

ROD This is a good spot to stretch your legs for a few minutes since you're not used to riding.

Sam steps up to stand close to Rod, admiring the scene.

SAM You were right, this is a beautiful spot. I see why you like it.

ROD Yup. If Miss Lane ever sells this place, and if the ranch has to be split up to make that happen, I hope I'll have enough saved up to buy this pasture . . . *(pause)*. In reality, though, this spot is prime real estate. It would fetch the highest price and be the first piece to sell as a scenic location for some movie star's mansion. *(pause)* I'd need a million bucks.

Sam notices Rod's sad mood and changes the subject.

SAM So, how many head do you think my property can run?

ROD Well, your grandma took good care of it. Your fences look pretty good, . . . *(pause)* gates can all be opened horseback, *(pause)* good live water running through it with enough fast water to stay open during winter *(pause)* lots of grass from being rested, although that might be more of a fire hazard than an asset. Old dried out grass looks pretty waving in the breeze, but it's not very strong. You'd just produce skinny cows that that look like they're trying to live on kale.

He looks Sam over as though accusing her of trying to live on kale. She gives him a mind-your-own-business look.

ROD Still, I say it will run at least 100 head. My eleven heifer calves won't make a dent. I will find out what other leases around here are bringing and pay the same amount per head. I could keep my nine steers too and Miss Lane said she'd throw in enough to fill it up and mow your grass. So I can put together 100 head for you.

Sam doesn't speak, just listens. Rod walks over to sit on the rock. Sam follows. They admire the scenery for a pause.

ROD So, what would you think of weighing the steers before we put them in here. Then weigh them again when we sell them and share the profit 50/50 on the pounds they gain? I can pay for my heifers now, but you'd have to wait until next November for both steer checks.

SAM I can wait for the steer money, thanks to you. I've made more money this year than usual and already have my taxes in the bank. I'm anxious to buy a new anvil, but maybe that can wait. Doc doesn't seem to be too anxious to let you go back to shoeing horses.

ROD *(changing the subject)* You have nice easy country, sheltered, and well-watered, so the steers should pack on quite a few pounds. Miss Lane lets me make these kinds of decisions, so she will agree to whatever we suggest. It'll be just as easy to babysit 100 calves as 20, probably easier, but you have to help me babysit.

SAM Of course. Sounds perfect. It's a deal.

Sam offers to shakes Rod's hand again, this time he does.

ROD As soon as you're rested, we can ride from here to the Lane Ranch red barn, put up the horses, and I'll give you a ride home.

EXT. LANDSCAPE — MOMENTS LATER

Rod and Sam head up the river in the opposite direction from where they began, camera floating overhead.

EXT. SMALL TOWN — DAY

We float over the small town, eventually zooming in on the law office. Rod and Miss Lane pull up in one vehicle, Sam in another. They park.

EXT. CLOSE-UP LAW OFFICES — SAME TIME

The name painted on the door reads, "FRED COOPER, LAWYER." As they enter, Rod removes his hat and holds the door for Miss Lane and Sam.

INT. LAW OFFICE — MOMENTS LATER

The secretary/receptionist escorts them into Mr. Cooper's office, exits, and closes the door behind her. Fred Cooper (white shirt and tie, no jacket) rises as they enter. He and Rod shake hands. Only two chairs sit in front of his desk. Once Miss Lane and Sam each take a seat, the lawyer sits in his chair behind the desk. Rod remains standing, holding his hat. Fred pulls a clipboard with paperwork from atop his desk, handing it and a pen to Sam first.

FRED Here is the contract we have been discussing. Each of you needs to sign every copy of this original.

They all sign without reading it, Sam first, then Miss Lane, Rod last.

FRED Here's a copy of what you just signed *(hands one to each)*. I'll officially file the original with the Clerk's Office. Once filed, it will be legally binding until next November, a year from now, when you will need to renegotiate.

SAM *(smiling proudly)* Wow. I'm not just a stinky, sooty farrier anymore, now I'm a real rancher!

ROD *(teasing)* Well, more like a stinky, sooty farrier who owns some land that she's leasing to a real rancher and a stinky cowboy—but it's a start!

Everybody laughs.

MISS LANE Come on you two, and you too Fred, let's go eat lunch. Rod's buying *(pause)* with my checkbook of course!

More laughter.

EXT. RED BARN—MID-DAY

We drift over the Lane Ranch, across patches of property, past the barn and on through the kitchen window of Miss Lane's house.

INT. MISS LANE'S HOUSE— AT THE SAME TIME

Inside the very large rectangular kitchen/ dining room combination, a front door near the dining room table faces the barn. A back door near the kitchen sink faces east. Rod, Sam, Charlie, Gabe and Cody sit waiting comfortably at a large dining table adjacent to the kitchen. Everyone is dressed in clean clothes but nothing fancy. They laugh and talk but we can't fully hear them yet. Carrying a platter with a large Thanksgiving Day Turkey, Miss Lane walks carefully past her chair at the kitchen end of the table to the other end where she sets it down in front of Rod. The rest of the fixings are scattered around the table in serving

bowls, ready to pass. Rod stands and prepares to carve the bird. Sam is seated next to him and Charlie next to her. Cody and Gabe sit on the other long side of the table. Cody rises to hold Miss Lane's chair until she is seated. The large room is sparsely decorated with a traditional ranch cook-shack feel. A few old simply-framed black and white photos hang on the wall, along with some deer antlers that are tacked to boards and hung widely-spaced. Four hats hang on four different antlers. As the scene comes to full volume, we hear the loud chatter and laughter with everybody talking at once, having a good time. Rod carves and serves turkey as plates and food are passed around.

MISS LANE Here's a toast: Happy Thanksgiving to the best crew an old lady could ever hope for! Thank you God and Mother Nature for all our many blessings.

The cups and glasses click/clang together in celebration. Toward the end of the meal, when everyone's mouth is full and the room quiet, Gabe speaks to Sam.

GABE So Sam, I don't see a ring. Are you single?

The room goes completely silent, forks suspended ominously in mid-air. Sam glances quickly at Rod. He doesn't look at her. He's poker faced, staring toward the kitchen over Miss Lane's head. Cody glances at Sam, who looks down at her plate, then Cody glances at Charlie, who looks at Miss Lane. Miss Lane also looks down at her plate. Too much time passes. Sam finally looks up, swallowing hard, and finally speaks.

SAM Yes, I'm single.

GABE Great! Wanna go for a ride this afternoon? I found a real pretty spot down by the river. It's kind of an oxbow.

Gabe turns toward Rod.

GABE Can I saddle up a horse for her, Boss?

ROD Sure. No problem.

Rod gets up from the table and picks up his plate, silverware, and glass.

ROD I've got some things to do. Thanks for the nice Thanksgiving meal Miss Lane.

Rod takes his utensils to the kitchen, scrapes his plate into a doggy bowl sitting on the counter, places his plate near the sink and his glass nearby, and his silverware into a bowl of bubbly dish-soap water already waiting in the sink. Sam quickly rises from the table to follow Rod.

SAM Thank you, Gabe, but I need to stay and help Miss Lane clean up.

She quickly picks up her plate, glass, and utensils and follows Rod to the kitchen, but he has already gone out the kitchen's back door. Gabe is confused and looks at the others who seem to be frozen in time.

GABE Did I say something wrong?

Cody points back and forth between Sam's empty chair and Rod's empty chair. Gabe's expression changes to understanding. He speaks softly so Sam can't hear.

GABE Ahhh. *(pause)* I see. I'm so sorry.

MISS LANE *(quietly)* You've only been with us a month. You didn't know. No harm done. It's just *(pause)* complicated. *(louder)* I'll get you boys some pie and coffee.

Miss Lane stands and heads to the kitchen where she and Sam wash dishes, but don't talk. The cowboys gossip quietly, so Sam and Miss Lane can't hear them.

CHARLIE *(to Gabe)* They're definitely a couple, but the boss don't know that yet.

CODY Or maybe he knows, but he ain't ready to admit it.

GABE Or maybe he's scared. Dang, I'm so sorry.

CHARLIE Don't worry, Gabe. It'll blow over by tomorrow, especially since she turned you down.

EXT. SAM'S PROPERTY—DECEMBER DAY

An overcast sky, snow drifts down and around Sam's shop. Rod walks up to the closed shop door and knocks. Heppy barks inside at the closed door.

INT. SAM'S BLACKSMTH SHOP—MOMENTS LATER

Sam is fully geared up for blacksmithing, her metal in the forge. When she notices Heppy barking, she opens the door. Rod holds out a check. Sam is glad to see him, but hesitant, not knowing where she stands.

ROD Miss Lane asked me to bring this shoeing check.

SAM Thanks. *(pause)* C'mon in. It's cold out there. It's good to see you. You haven't been around since Thanksgiving. I've been worried that something is wrong.

Rod steps in and closes the door, but remains standing close to the door, ready to leave. Sam turns off her forge and lays the hot metal aside.

ROD Nope. Nothing wrong. I'll send Gabe next weekend to help you hammer.

SAM *(irritated)* Gabe? I'm not interested in Gabe, if that's what you're implying. He's a nice guy and lots of fun, but I didn't go for a ride with him at Thanksgiving, and I'm sure you already know that. I feel terrible about the whole situation. I was just enjoying everyone's company, and must have given him the impression that I was flirting. I wasn't and hope that turning him down didn't embarrass him.

ROD He usually succeeds with women, so a little humility was probably good for him. I'll send Charlie then.

SAM No, Rod. I want to work with you, as always.

ROD *(as though he didn't hear)* I saw Charlie here helping you last Saturday. Looked like you guys had some horse in a Scotch hobble with one foot tied up. *(pause)* That doesn't seem like your style.

SAM Not all horses act like yours do. When I first moved here, I had to handle a lot of spoiled horses. *(pause)* I'd tried to schedule them late on Saturdays when Charlie was off work and could help. He's got a good way of tying up a foot that makes it real easy to loosen the knots when a horse stops fighting or I finish, whichever comes first. *(pause)* He's great help with spoiled horses. He's gentle but firm, not scared of nuthin', and on those rare occasions can lay one down to be shod without rubbing off a single hair with the ropes. *(pause)* Once he handles a horse a time or two, then that horse has learned better manners and I can handle it myself. Now it's really rare to find a spoiled horse around here.

Sam notices Rod frowning, realizes she is praising Charlie too much and tries to correct it.

SAM I knew someone had taught Charlie very well . . .

Sam glances sideways at Rod.

SAM He told me that someone was you and that you've been like a father to him.

ROD *(bristling)* Yeah. Well I'm not old enough to be his father.

Sam realizes she poked another sore spot in Rod's evidently very fragile ego. Again she tries to fix it but is starting to get irritated that she has to be so careful.

SAM I know that.

ROD I just needed to rest my back for a few months. I'm not riding a rocking chair yet.

SAM Never said you were. I was just trying to compliment you about how well you taught Charlie. *(pause)* It's like a vacation to shoe horses that you've touched in one way or another, or someone you taught. *(pause)* I've never met anyone as good with horses as you are.

Rod finally begins to relax.

SAM *(changing the subject)* Oh, and by the way, Miss Lane asked me to come by and take her to the Christmas dance. You told me once that you'd be honored to take me, but you probably don't remember. Anyway, I might *(pause)* maybe, dance with you if you asked me. *(pause)* If you come to the dance, that is.

INT. DANCE HALL—DOWNTOWN, EVENING

A country band is onstage, performing Ian Tyson's waltz, "Cowboy Pride." Couples are waltzing, cowboy-style, counter-clockwise around the floor. Sam is wearing a long cowgirl-style denim dress with nice boots and a Western Belt, a sparkly Christmas scarf, hair curled. She is sitting beside Miss Lane on folding metal chairs watching people dance and talking. Rod walks in wearing a white starched shirt and starched Levis, red wild rag tied cowboy-style around his neck, new black hat, his best town boots shined. Their eyes meet. Rod walks across the dance floor, right up to Sam.

ROD *(to Sam)* Have you two pretty ladies seen Sam?

SAM *(accepting the compliment)* You clean up pretty good yourself.

ROD You sound like Sam, but you don't look like Sam. What have you done with my ole buddy Sam?

SAM Do I need to tie up a foot to get a dance?

Rod extends his hand out to Sam, asking her to dance. When she stands, he puts his hat upside down on her chair seat to save her spot while they dance. Sam rises and puts her hand in Rod's. Rod brings her hand up to his face like he's going to kiss it, instead he smells it.

ROD You don't smell like Sam either.

Miss Lane laughs. Exasperated, Sam tries to break free of Rod's grip but he laughs, holds on tight, and whisks her out onto the dance floor.

SAM So, which Sam do you like better?

ROD That's not a fair question.

SAM Why not?

ROD It assumes only two possible answers, either good old Sam or this new pretty Samantha version. But there might be dozens of possible answers *(pause)* like that maybe "it depends", or maybe that "I don't like either one."

Sam starts to pull away again but Rod laughs and hangs on, pulling her closer.

ROD *(more seriously)* Or, maybe that I like both.

They dance, very close, until the music stops. He walks her back to the chair and retrieves his hat. Then, Rod is suddenly nervous, not knowing what to say.

ROD Want something to drink?

SAM *(smiling)* Water, with a twist of lime.

Rod heads to the drink table and pours two waters and squeezes lime juice into each as the dance music resumes. When he turns around, he sees Sam dancing and laughing with Charlie. Miss Lane is dancing with Gabe. Immediately, Rod sets the drinks down and walks out the door. Sam and Charlie both race to catch him, but once they get through the crowd, Rod is already driving away.

INT. SAM'S PICKUP—AFTER THE DANCE

Sam drives with Miss Lane in the passenger seat.

MISS LANE Thanks for the ride. I had a lovely evening. I so enjoy getting out and visiting with everybody, but I don't like to drive after dark.

SAM I'm glad you enjoyed it.

MISS LANE It seemed like you enjoyed only one dance.

SAM Was it that obvious?

MISS LANE Small town. We pay attention.

SAM He's hopeless. It's hopeless. He just seems to be one of those guys that a girl could spend 20 years of her life hoping and waiting for something to happen and never even get kissed. No matter how hard I try, I always do or say the wrong thing. I want a family, maybe a kid or two before it's too late. I'm sick of this. Charlie and I thought a little competition might move him off high center. But we hurt him instead. Now I've ruined everything, made things worse, and an even bigger mess. It's time to give up.

MISS LANE I can't help with your 20-year problem. You'll need to fix that on your own. But maybe I can at least help with the Charlie problem.

SAM *(worried)* You're not going to fire Charlie?

MISS LANE *(laughs)* No. The opposite. I'm gonna let Charlie know I've got his back in case Rod tries to fire him.

SAM Rod would do that?

MISS LANE No, but Charlie would expect him to. Charlie is pretty good with rank old stud horses, maybe he can talk some sense into Rod if I tell Charlie that I'll protect his job.

EXT. MISS LANE'S HOUSE— MOMENTS LATER

The lights of Sam's pickup light up the exterior of Miss Lane's house.

MISS LANE And just between us girls, I have named Rod my sole heir to this ranch in my will. Don't tell him or his stubborn pride will probably make him quit. I never married or had any children. Being an only child, I don't even have any nieces and nephews, either. I have a couple of cousins, but they're worthless. I'd have been out of business years ago without Rod's frugal management and sound advice.

Miss Lane places her hand gently on Sam's hand that's tightly gripping the steering wheel.

MISS LANE Rod has earned this place, but I don't want to leave it to an old bachelor. Ranching can be a very lonely life. He needs a partner. So, I've got as much at stake in your project as you do. Don't give up just yet. Let's see what Charlie can do.

They both exit Sam's pickup. Sam escorts Miss Lane to her front door, making sure she doesn't slip on the ice and snow.

EXT. SAM'S SHOP— AFTERNOON

Rod knocks on the closed shop door. Sam answers the door but does not invite him in. She is not smiling either.

ROD I just came by to let you know that I found another lease and I'll be picking up my heifers in a few days.

Sam's eyes look panicked and desperate, but her voice stays firm.

SAM Oh, no you won't.

Her anger surprises him.

SAM I should have known I couldn't trust you. When you get mad, neither your word nor your handshake is worth a damn.

ROD *(shocked)* What?

SAM Luckily, we signed a contract. You have to stay until next November, or I will sue you. And you're still responsible for Miss Lane's steers too. Now I know why even so-called friends need a binding legal contract.

ROD Wait a minute *(pause)* I didn't mean . . .

SAM *(interrupting)* But after November, you'll be totally free to do whatever the hell you want to because I have accepted a job teaching horseshoeing in Colorado, and I'll be selling this place to Miss Lane when our lease agreement is up.

Sam holds out her hand. In it is a leather belt sheath with the yellow handle of a skinning knife sticking out of it.

SAM Here's your knife. And you can pick up your anvil anytime.

Rod hesitates, then takes the knife. Sam holds out her hand for money.

SAM *(firmly)* Two hundred bucks!

Rod digs a money clip out of his front pants' pocket, peels off two evidently $100 bills and pays her. She turns back to her shop and closes the door, leaving him standing in the snow. Rod stands there for a while holding his hat, finally puts it on,

turns and walks toward his pickup. Looks forlorn.

EXT. RED BARN—THE NEXT DAY

Rod and Charlie load two horses into the ranch trailer, the barn in the background. Both are wearing coats.

ROD Take these horses over to Sam's.

CHARLIE Why? *(nervously)* You always take them.

Rod looks at him sharply, Charlie looks down, doesn't want to be disrespectful toward his boss.

CHARLIE Yes, sir.

Charlie haltingly struggles for courage.

CHARLIE But I thought you and Sam were *(pause)* ah . . .

ROD *(interrupting)* All we have is a business deal. I'm sure she'd rather see you.

CHARLIE *(getting braver)* Now, wait a dang minute!

Charlie starts walking around his boss, Rod has to turn to face him.

CHARLIE I'm not going to let you blame me for your own poor decisions. We thought . . .

ROD *(interrupting)* I saw you helping her with one those spoiled backyard horses she has to shoe. You're a good hand. She needs someone like you to help her with horses like that. Those kind of horses can hurt her.

CHARLIE She only asks me to help because she thinks something is wrong with your back . . .

Rod winces at the mention of his back. Charlie walks around Rod in the other direction getting braver.

CHARLIE . . . other than a yellow streak.

Rod winces again upon hearing this.

ROD Yeah, well you're young and good looking and have a real strong back. I'm sure she'd rather see you. I just want everybody to be happy.

Charlie continues to walk a circular pattern, so Rod has to keep turning.

CHARLIE Yeah? Well making her happy mostly depends on you. You're the only one she looks at like she might not need her own foot tied up.

ROD You're crazy. She barely tolerates me because she needs our business, an anvil, and now a lease.

CHARLIE I'm not crazy . . .

Charlie hesitates, pausing in his steps, watching Rod intently, and starts circular walking in the opposite direction.

CHARLIE . . .but you're crazy if you let her get away. I mean, look at her, she's cuter than an Aussie pup. Plus she can shoe horses and owns some grazing land. What more could a man ask for?

ROD Will you stand still? You're making me dizzy.

Seeing his tough talk is starting to get through Rod's stone wall, Charlie gets braver, talking faster.

CHARLIE While you've been pussy-footin' around acting like a mangy coyote, she's tried everything to get you to make a move. She doesn't know if you're scared or spoiled, teasing her or testing her, interested or uninterested. *(pause)* and I don't think you know either. *(pause)* Now she's even lying— she's not taking any teaching job in Colorado, she just told you that because she wanted you to admit you care. *(pause)* And you do care. You've been lying too and for the same reason—Doc said your back was fine three months ago but you don't want Sam to know so you can keep hanging out with her. *(pause)* You haven't found another lease. You haven't even looked. And now you two have even got me to lying because me and Sam thought maybe a little healthy competition and jealousy would force you to make a move. Sam's my friend. I want her to be happy but that all seems to depend on you. You are about to convince her to give up. It's just a matter of time before you blow it. And *(pause)* I'm not lying now—believe me, if you break her heart, for 300 miles in any direction, every unmarried cowboy—and a few married ones—will be standing in line for a chance to mend it. They'd be running at her now if that big anvil with your brand on the stump wasn't sitting right in her doorway.

Rod smiles as though pleased with himself.

CHARLIE If you break her heart, word will travel fast, might be traveling right now. A feller might even need a head start to get to the head of that line, so yeah, I'll be happy to take these horses to Sam's, you betcha I will!

Charlie stops circling around Rod, and struts off, heading toward the pickup, to take the horses to Sam's.

ROD *(in his definite boss's orders voice)*
Stop.

Charlie freezes in his tracks.

ROD Nothing is broken yet.

Rod walks calmly around Charlie and then stands defiantly between him and the pickup.

ROD I'll take these horses over there. You go take a cold shower.

CHARLIE Sorry, Boss.

ROD Don't be, I needed that, whatever it was. *(pause)* But I won't need it again, so don't make it a habit.

CHARLIE Yes, Sir. I mean, no, sir.

Rod hollers over Charlie's shoulder toward the nearby barn door.

ROD Are you happy now, Miss Lane?

MISS LANE *(sheepishly coming out of the barn)* How did you know I was here?

ROD Charlie would never talk to me like that if you hadn't put him up to it.

MISS LANE You don't miss much. *(pause)* Usually.

ROD Now if you two meddlers will excuse me, I need to go stop a train.

Rod turns and hurries to his pickup. As he drives off moments later, in his side view mirror, he watches Miss Lane and Charlie high five each other.

EXT. SAM'S SHOP—LATER

Rod pulls up at Sam's with the horses. Sam walks out with her shoeing chaps in hand, ready to shoe. She doesn't speak and has a forlorn, hopeless look on her face. Rod, parks and steps out, walks up to her and holds out his hand like asking her to dance. After hesitating, looking at him, and hesitating again, she gives him her hand reluctantly and confused.

ROD Let's talk.

Sam hangs her shoeing chaps on the horn of the anvil, Rod then leads her toward his pickup, gripping her hand tightly.

SAM Where are we going?

ROD I'm not sure yet, but how about we try some honesty first.

At his pickup, Rod turns to face Sam, still holding her hand.

SAM What do you mean?

ROD Have you really ordered a new anvil?

SAM *(hesitates)* Not yet, but I will today.

ROD Are you going to Colorado?

SAM *(searching Rod's face, not sure what to say)* No. This is my home. This is where my heart is.

ROD I haven't found another lease either. I like the one I've got and I gave my word.

SAM *(tentatively warming up to tell the truth)* I thought if I could make you feel jealous, it might prove to both of us that you cared about me.

ROD You did a good job of that.

SAM I never intended to hurt you.

ROD I'm not hurt just ashamed of acting so stupid.

SAM Charlie is like a brother . . .

Sam pauses to make sure Rod heard "brother" instead of "son."

SAM . . .to you and to me.

ROD Maybe you guys needed to wake me up. I'm awake now, and I'm sorry.

SAM A wise man told me to never say you're sorry unless you mean it.

ROD I am really sorry, and I really mean it.

SAM You don't have anything to be sorry for. I'm the one who should be, and am, very sorry.

ROD I should have trusted you both. Jealousy is for insecure 16-year olds.

SAM So are tricks and playing games. My wrist has been fine for months, but I was afraid you'd stop coming around if I told you.

ROD My back has been fine for months. I kept it a secret so I could keep coming around.

SAM *(laughing)* We make quite a pair.

ROD *(nervous, not laughing, talking fast)* Yes we do. And I am thinking that if I buy another bull and put him with my heifers next fall, pretty soon they'll be dropping calves and then pretty soon there'll be more heifers and then more cows and more calves. So I was wondering if maybe you'd want to just make our partnership more permanent, maybe my brand *(pause)* <u>our</u> brand could stand for both an oxbow and a horseshoe.

Rod reaches in his pickup bed and brings out his branding iron and starts walking Sam back to her shop, still holding her hand.

INT. SAM'S SHOP — MOMENTS LATER

As they walk into the shop together, the now grown up Heppy doesn't bark, just watches them, maybe sensing that something important has changed. Rod lights Sam's forge and as soon as ready, sticks the branding iron into the forge to heat it up.

ROD and, . . .

SAM *(confused, interrupting)* . . . and with a contract?

ROD *(dead serious, deep eye contact)* Of course—not that I would ever break my word, but to give us time to bring me, maybe us, to our senses—with a very legal and binding contract.

SAM For how long?

ROD *(nervously, with deep eye contact)* For life.

Sam, her eyes locked with Rod's, wells up with happy tears as she starts to realize what he is really asking.

SAM Are we still talking about cattle?

ROD No.

SAM Oh, Rod, yes! I'd love to be your partner for life! Yes! Yes! Yes!

At last, the two finally kiss.

ROD I love you, Sam. I'm sorry I took so long to say it.

SAM I love you, and love is not just a word to me anymore.

ROD I know.

SAM I'm so happy.

ROD Me too, partner.

Their next kiss is long and engaging.

ROD There's one more thing—

Rod grabs the hot branding iron, and heads toward the anvil, Sam follows. Now outside, Rod lifts her shoeing chaps off the anvil and lays them out on the ground.

ROD I know it's too dangerous for a farrier to wear a ring because a horseshoe nail or a chip of metal could get caught under it, so how about this?

Rod holds the now hot iron over one leg of her shoeing chaps, waiting for permission to brand. Sam smiles big and nods yes. Rod applies the brand to the bottom of one leg of her chaps. When it is burned in . . .

SAM Gimme that.

She takes the branding iron from him and applies it to the other leg of her chaps. When it is also burned in, she picks up her chaps and buckles them on, squares up toward Rod, looking very proud, big smile. Her hands on her hips, she wears no make-up, her hair is a total mess, cap on backwards, soot on her face, sweat stains and welding holes burned into her shirt.

SAM So, how do I look?

ROD Perfect.

They embrace once again with a long kiss and Heppy joins them, not barking. Rod reaches down to pet him as the camera drifts up and away.

THE END

Taming Biñon's Daughter

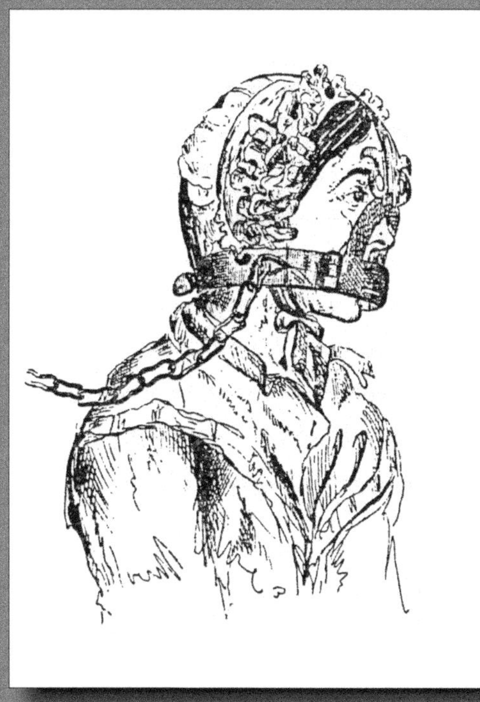

Inspiration for Taming Biñon's Daughter

"For how do I hold thee but by thy granting."
—Shakespeare, Sonnet 87

Cowboy philosopher Tommy Vaughn doesn't look much like a scholar, except for his Ben Franklin style glasses, but I will be forever grateful to him for bringing Shakespeare and horsemanship together for me. It changed my life.

During my senior year of college, I switched my major from agriculture to English when I finally admitted to myself that I'd have a better chance of finding a job in a rural area as a teacher than as a female cowboy. In 1970 a few jobs were available to single women in agriculture but mostly in some kind of office, usually government. I didn't want that. So, instead of the usual Bachelor of Arts, I graduated with a Bachelor of Science in English with a minor in agriculture. Along the way, I had of course studied and learned to love Shakespeare.

After graduating, I married a cowboy and for the next twenty years lived on remote ranch camps. I raised a feisty daughter who could hold her own on a cowboy crew of grown men by the time she was six. By the time she was twelve, she was bossing some of those men when gathering cattle in country that she knew but they didn't. About 1988, with my daughter in high school, I found myself back in college and working on a master's degree. I'd also been to the first cowboy poetry gathering in Elko, Nevada and had become quite active as a participant, publicist, and critic. My obsession with horsemanship reached a peak about the time the Elko gathering bosses asked me to do a photography presentation for the program.

The media had been making fun of cowboy poets as uneducated, so I wanted to challenge that stereotype. I had often read where reporters had been surprised to find a shelf containing *The Harvard Classics* in some remote cow camp. I'd seen that same collection, published in Spanish, deep in the heart of northern Mexico's ranching country. I didn't personally know anyone who read Louis L'Amour or Max Brand. I had always thought "westerns" were written and made into films by city people for city people, not for us. What we actually read was and is very eclectic. One cowboy friend read classic texts from Eastern religions, another read a lot of Tolstoy, one liked Dostoevsky, and another liked Dickens. One who lived in the shadow of El Capitan in the Guadalupe Mountains read a lot of John McPhee. Several were also fans of classical poetry.

I like to challenge stereotypes, so I decided to record some of the local cowboys and ranchers who preferred "classics" and who didn't participate in the cowboy poetry gatherings. I paired their voices with my photography to help the audience understand why they chose particular poems. Local windmiller and cowboy Don Coleman picked Longfellow's "From My Arm-Chair," which I paired with photos of saddles and old cowboys in rocking chairs. Rancher Roddy Schoenfeldt chose the prelude to Chaucer's "Canterbury Tales" which I illustrated with photos of him driving his wagon and team of big horses through spring wildflowers. One was obviously a mare with a loose colt by her side, sometimes nursing. Rancher Gage Holland had an extensive leather-bound collection of Rudyard Kipling that would put most university libraries to shame. He chose Kipling's "If" easily paired with images of ranch work. Ranch manager Randy Glover recited Lewis Carrol's "Jabberwocky," and I had fun pairing it with photos of cowboys being their version of humorous. Finally, Tommy Vaughn chose Shakespeare's Sonnet #87. He said he could read and understand Shakespeare because he'd been raised reading the King James Version of *The Bible*. He said the sonnet reminded him of Ray Hunt's style of horsemanship. I illustrated it with photos of cowboys interacting with horses, including several of Tommy riding in a Ray Hunt colt class. I called my slide show "Cowboys Do the Classics."

Tommy's choice stunned me. Suddenly I remembered lines and moments from Shakespeare's plays like Richard III's desperate plea "A horse! A horse! My kingdom for a horse!" From Bolingbroke to Hot Spur, Prince Hal to Falstaff, Othello to Macbeth, Shakespeare's plays revealed character or lack of it through horsemanship. As a cowboy journalist I had been writing about Ray Hunt every chance I got and had published over eleven articles about him. I had also returned to college for a master's degree and was searching for a thesis topic. Tommy handed me a perfect subject that combined horsemanship with classic literature. How could I have missed it? From Greek myth to Chaucer to Freud, control of the horse had been used metaphorically and symbolically to represent governing oneself, fitness to govern others, and relationships between men and women.

In spite of the fact that entire libraries have been written about Shakespeare, only a handful of scholars had even noticed his almost constant reference to the horse and horsemanship. Caroline Spurgeon, describes Shakespeare as "unique among the dramatists of his time, for he shows a sympathy with and an understanding of the animal's point of view and suffering which no one else in his age approaches. This is especially marked in the case of horses and birds, the two he loves best." Another scholar, R. E. Oakeshott, said mistakes and misconceptions about horses and horsemanship can be found throughout classical literature, "but not if Shakespeare wrote the play."

Just the word horse appears in his plays 247 times, not counting words like stallion, mare, spurs, bridles, and saddles; plus archaic horsemanship language like "yerk," "trammel," and "advance" --words unfamiliar to today's readers. One popular legend was that Shakespeare's first job in London was holding horses outside the theatres. Maybe young Shakespeare was able to correct some fidgety horse habits while their riders were watching a play. As the tale passed down through the ages, it expanded to include "facts" such as that Shakespeare became so good at holding horses he couldn't keep up with demand and supposedly trained young boys to help him. When gentlemen and ladies arrived to watch a play and asked for Shakespeare to tend their horses, one of his young protégés would step up and say, "I am Shakespeare's boy, Sir." For many years, even after Shakespeare's death, so the story goes, the boys who held horses at London theatres were called "Shakespeare's boys."

My own theory is that when he came of age, young Will rode to the big city to chase girls. As often happens when a country boy goes to town where everyone is a wannabe horseman, his horse and horsemanship can get him noticed. Soldiers needed courageous, dependable horses for the wars while noblemen and their ladies wanted horses that could dance and prance. Well-trained horses were needed for travel, for bearing burdens, pulling carts, coaches, and plows, or for racing, hunting, recreation, and simply exercise. Horses were also important to the monarchs for parades. Since the horse is no respecter of rank, princes had been encouraged to learn to ride since Plutarch (46-120 AD) because "the sons of kings could not properly learn anything except the art of horsemanship." Royals were flattered, humored, and agreed with; but a horse, since he does not know whether his rider is a nobleman or slave, rich or poor, queen or subject, treats all riders equally and honestly.

So aristocrats might hire a country boy to start colts and train horses for them. To me this is a much more plausible basis for Shakespeare's eventual friendship with royalty than their recognition of his ability with a pen, especially during a time when attending a play ranked right up there with cock fighting.

So for two years, I blinded myself reading horsemanship books on microfilm that had been published during Shakespeare's day: Thomas Blundeville (1560, 1565, 1580, 1594), Christopher Clifford (1585), T. Bedingfield (1584), John Astley (1584), Nicholas Morgan (1609), Michaell Baret (1618) and one published in 1610 by an author named simply Browne (probably Sir Anthony Browne, Master of the Horse to Phillip II of Spain). The horsemanship of Shakespeare's day astounded me in both its stupidity and cruelty. I thought that when people used horses every day, they would have been the most in tune with them. I expected horsemanship to have gotten progressively worse as people traded horses for automobiles and their understanding of a horse's mind for a motor. But that is not what I found.

Several of the first books ever printed or translated from French, Italian, and Spanish into English were horsemanship books. This foreign-inspired horse training, called collectively "The Manage," stressed elaborate costumes and refined, controlled movements. Because Manage trainers thought horses were basically stupid, they trammeled their legs with leather straps to "teach" them to walk. They dug deep trenches in the ground in order to "teach" maneuvers by riding around and around in those trenches. Some tried sugar lumps and carrots (bribery) or petting, but those timid approaches usually resulted in spoiled horses that often became dangerous and vicious, just like spoiled children.

Most "trainers" preferred cruelty. They embedded ground glass under the skin over a horse's ribs so that when spurred, a horse that was slow to obey supposedly improved. Sometimes a hedgehog was tied in their tail, so (no surprise) horses frequently ran away and couldn't be stopped. Runaway horses were hit in the face with cudgels or burning torches. Studs were taught to whoa by jerking on strings that had been tied around their scrotums. Bits were designed to cut a horse's tongue and teeth pulled in order to make a bit "fit" better.

An exceptionally cruel Spanish horse trainer named Prospero invented a popular hinged metal noseband with teeth. He crossed the reins to use it like a vise and carried a hammer to occasionally rap the teeth deeper into a horse's velvety, tender nose. After discovering this horse trainer, I could never read Shakespeare's play "The Tempest," with its seemingly "wise" father figure named Prospero quite the same way again. After approving my 165-page thesis, my professors told me that I had forever ruined Shakespeare for them: now all they saw were horses.

Just as there is rivalry today between various urban-based training styles and country cowboys, so there was in Shakespeare's day. Eventually I found Gervase Markham's books (1593, 1599, 1605, 1607, 1615, and more). I believe Markham influenced or was influenced by Shakespeare, and the Earl of Southampton was a patron to both. Markham wrote for the rural English hunter and found the cruelty as well as the dancing and prancing of The Manage quite silly. Markham's methods were based on a genuine affection and respect for the intelligence of the horse. He treated horses like fellow beings instead of pets or possessions. Because of this respect, Markham discouraged either cruelty or gentleness when training horses because horses were smart enough to learn manipulation too. While Manage riders tried to force or coax, Markham taught communication and mutual respect.

Markham, of course, reminded me of Ray Hunt. As I leaned on the fence or on my saddle horn and listened to Ray explain how to communicate with horses, I always had the strange feeling that he wasn't just talking about horses and riders but about relationships in general. (For more about this method see Tom Dorrance, *True Unity: Willing Communication between Horse and Human;* and Ray Hunt, *Think Harmony With Horses: An In-Depth Study of Horse/Man Relationship.*) During the Renaissance, people were also "trained" to be better children, soldiers, servants, and wives through similar cruel methods as those used on horses. Cranky women who talked too much were forced to wear a "shrew's bridle," a device that fit over her head and contained a bit with knives designed to cut if her tongue moved, very similar to the cruel bits used on horses. Husbands were amazed when this treatment did not produce a docile, loving wife but instead often resulted in their eventual cuckoldry.

At the time, I was also struggling in my own marriage and often interviewed other cowboy wives. The "happily-ever-after" ending of so many stories is a wedding. But that is just the beginning. A real marriage is never easy and takes constant work, practice, honest communication, and respect. Cowboy spouses, who imagine riding off into the sunset together on well-behaved horses, will be shocked the first time their horse dumps them on the ground and their spouse continues on with the cattle, not even looking back.

Females, especially those raised in the cowboy world, and who might even be better hands than the men they marry, will be devastated to hear an edict from the boss that "women can't ride on this outfit." One said it well when I interviewed her for "Fran Locke: Cowboy's Wife" (*Western Horseman* 1984). Fran said, "Mom used to pack us in a salt pannier when we were about a month old. I started riding when I was about three, and dad had us breaking colts when we were six. We all helped him ride and brand and break colts, and he taught us to rope when we were real young." Later she met a handsome cowboy but he "used to tell me when I helped him that he didn't approve of women riding. When we got married, I told him that I rode and that's all I knew because that's how I was raised. I figured if he didn't like it, he'd get used to it. I just ignored him and rode anyway."

She fought the situation for several years through moves from ranch to ranch, searching for answers. The frustration in her voice broke my heart: "I've asked a lot of people and they always say that's just the way it's always been. They've never really given me any reason why. A lot of people say women get in the way and I'm sure some women do. But I know a lot of men that get in the way, too." At the end of my article we thought maybe they had finally found an ideal job for both of them, but they have since divorced and both remarried several times. I also found after interviewing old timers that banning women wasn't "the way it's always been." Whether or not women are welcome on a crew seems to cycle through history. Every cowboy wife I knew struggled with some form of this situation and was often considered a "problem" because of it.

As a problem woman myself, my favorite play was Shakespeare's "The Taming of the Shrew." My favorite movie version was the Meryl Streep and Raul Julia version. It captured the chemistry between Kate and Petrucio and that in the end Petrucio does not tame Kate. But I still believe the play needs horsemanship for full understanding.

Shakespeare was famous for "stealing" ideas, then working his magic, and this play is no exception. Scholars are convinced he was inspired by a ballad written around 1580 and sold as "A Merry Jest of a Shrewde and Curste Wife Lapped in Morel's Skin For Her Good Behavyour." This violent tale describes how a henpecked husband killed his most faithful horse, Morel, and skinned him. He then wrapped his disobedient wife in the bloody, salted hide and waited for it to dry and shrink until his wife was squeezed into submission. Happy ending! In my version that follows, when I describe Kate as "a rodeo bronc wearing a female skin" it is a nod to this origin story.

This vicious original makes Shakespeare's version (c. 1593) look comparatively gentle as he follows Markham's horsemanship methods of respect and choice. Petrucio comes to town looking for a wife and finds Kate, who is anything but gentle. Instead of wrapping her in rawhide or putting her in a "shrew's bridle," he likes her spirit, finds her witty and fun to talk to. He concludes that "the world has talked amiss of her," and tells her that she has simply been treated poorly by her father and manipulative sister. He tells her that because of this poor treatment her behavior has been totally justified. Kate hears understanding for the first time in her life.

I was the "mean" older sister who was constantly in trouble for making my spoiled rotten, "sweet" little brother cry, even though he always deserved it. I raised a daughter who, now as a USDA/FSA County Executive Director, rides herd over ranchers in five rural West Texas counties (Brewster, Presidio, Pecos, Terrell, and Jeff Davis). She raised a daughter who gave up her college scholarships after a year to cowboy. As I write this, my granddaughter is living alone with three horses and two dogs on a remote ranch camp inside the Choctaw Reservation on the Oklahoma side of the Red River. In short, I know strong women.

In one chapter of my master's thesis, I went through this play line by line bringing out Shakespeare's constant references to horsemanship. Like a good horseman, Petrucio respects Kate's intelligence does not want to be her master nor her slave. At the play's end, Kate "meekly" offers her hand to help her husband mount his horse, but only because she knows he doesn't need or want that. They are both just fooling party guests into believing Kate has been "tamed" so they can win a bet. Kate was not aware of the bet, but by this time she trusts Petrucio enough to know that when he asks, there must be a reason. They are partners. I think the sense and meaning of this play is "confusing" because no one understands horses, horsemanship or women.

Shakespeare's suggestions for human relationships as well as Markham's horsemanship methods were quickly forgotten or ignored, maybe because they took too much time, thought, and effort. People preferred fear, punishment, and gadgets . . . and still do. It seems that horsemanship, like history, repeats itself and I thought it was time for a refresher.

As several of Shakespeare's most famous lines remind us, not everything is as it appears: "All the world's a stage," "All that glitters is not gold," and "Fair is foul, and foul is fair." Illusions run rampant through his work from disguises to lies, from "honest" Iago to a "dead" Juliet. His "nonsensical" line in Taming, "the oats have eaten the horses" is cut from the same cloth. "The Taming of the Shrew" is a good example of illusion. Academics often refer to it as one of Shakespeare's "problem" plays or an "early play" because it seems disjointed, sexist, and abusive . . . unless you see through the illusion with the eyes of a horseman. I also wanted to explain "horse whispering" (which I thought had been ruined by Hollywood) as <u>real</u> horsemanship, not magic.

So I searched for parallels in my cowboy world that were often misunderstood: like rodeo, bucking horses, and those who "break" horses. I needed an "untamed" setting, "untamed" horses, and an "untamed" girl. Eventually setting and characters started coming together. What better choices than Las Vegas, rodeo bucking stock, and the daughter of a rodeo stock contractor? I decided to set my version in Nevada, an often misunderstood "empty" place, beloved by horsemen for its wide open spaces. The line "one thousand miles of sage" comes from a cowboy poem about Nevada that I once heard Jerry Pardue recite. I'm not sure who wrote it, maybe Jerry.

Las Vegas is the current home of professional rodeo's national finals. Those who don't understand rodeo, think the bucking horses and bulls are either exceptionally mean animals or mistreated. In fact, they are athletes who lead pampered lives except for the eight seconds when they wear a "bucking strap" to let them know it is time to kick up their heels. Breeders desire a cranky attitude to get better performance. But much of the action is trained as the harder they learn to buck, the quicker their work-day of eight seconds is over. Rodeo cowboys don't dread the worst buckers, but revere them. When competing for prize money or titles, judges score both rider and animal. So the better the animal bucks, the better the cowboy can score. I try to make that clear in the first quick scene as the world champion cowboy congratulates the stock contractor who raised the world champion horse that just bucked him off.

I began by changing the names. Shakespeare's Italian names are easier to follow when watching the play performed, but for English-speaking readers, all the identity switching and name changing is almost impossible to follow on the page. So in my version, Kate stayed Kate, but Petrucio became Paul.

I loosely base Kate's father (Baptista renamed Buck Biñon) on a real Las Vegas casino owner, Benny Binion. Binion was a very controversial (some say mobster, some say saint) casino owner responsible for bringing the National Finals Rodeo to Vegas and famous for raising some of rodeo's best bucking stock. I read several books about Benny Binion that portrayed him as a cruel and dangerous Mafioso, but cowboys who knew him defended him fiercely. They said he often fed them, loaned them money when they were broke, or gave them jobs. Binion ran a high stakes, no-nonsense casino rather than noisy nickel slot machines. Shakespeare's opening scene with Sly (a casino drunk in my version) is often deleted because it doesn't seem to have anything to do with the story of Kate that follows. But to me, in true Shakespearian fashion, it completely sets the stage: Is Kate what people say and believe she is, herself included, or is she more? If a person, animal, or drunk is treated differently and could see themselves differently, would they behave differently? I use the situation to have Biñon, a concerned casino owner who does not drink (neither did the real Binion) introduce Tom (loosely based on Tom Dorrance and Ray Hunt and their horsemanship theories) to a modern psychologist. Biñon wonders if horsemanship could help his addicted friends too.

The real Benny Binion was complicated. He knew gambling could be an addiction. He knew rodeo could be deadly. He knew cowboys who hung out around him often became alcoholics. Yet, I knew rodeo cowboys who were willing to die on their sword defending Binion's character. Cowboys throughout the West also swore his horses made the best ranch horses they ever rode—once you gained their trust. One personal friend drove stage coaches for Binion down the streets of New York and pulled by Binion horses.

In "Breaking Colts with Donnie Slover" (*Western Horseman* 1982), I quoted John Birdwell, a Whiteface, Texas rancher who said Donnie was "an extraordinarily good hand. He broke a bunch of four- to six-year-old Binion horses for me and there were some mean horses in that bunch. Donnie's the only man I know who would have stayed with them. Yet he was easy with them, didn't abuse them, and treated each one like an individual." That band of about 30 Binion horses tried Donnie's skills pretty good but mostly because of their age. Other cowboys had also "rode at" them (meaning unsuccessfully), teaching them bad habits and mistrust along the way. Donnie began with the older horses and said when he got down to the three-year-olds that hadn't been touched, he felt like he was on vacation. J. J. Gipson, manager of the Four Sixes Ranch at Guthrie, Texas at the time called Donnie "one of the finest I know."

Most ranch cowboys value horses with "spirit." I also interviewed Bob Eidson, who explained the horses he preferred to raise:

> *Something I think people have cut too hard on is disposition. You get these horses too gentle and they get like everything else— they haven't got any 'want to' left in them. I know one outfit that had a lot of trouble getting their horses broke, so they went to hunting a stud with disposition. They worked on it and worked on it until it got to where they'd lope off two or three miles from the ranch and they were a-foot. A kid could ride any one of them, but they couldn't go anywhere, either. That's one thing about these Go Man Go, these Flashy Go, horses of ours. The first thing you got to do is get them gentle because every one of them will pitch if you let them. If one ever throws anybody off, watch out, because you've got something going. They get a little smarter every day. But if you get them gentle, they're just danged pets.*

Another of my name changes also has a rodeo connection. Since most men don't run around today with "servants," I changed those to employees. Originally I had Lucky (Lucentio) traveling with two employees, (following Shakespeare's version) and named them after two Lambert rodeo brothers: Chuck (Biondello) and Cody (Tranio). I had been sort of the unofficial "rodeo mom" at Sul Ross when the Lamberts and Tuff Hedeman were getting started. Cody was always the most famous of the Lambert brothers because he rode bucking stock, but his brother Chuck actually won more money roping. Their semi-friendly rivalry became kind of an inside joke, and I even wrote an article about Chuck once for a college rodeo magazine that I titled "Cody's Brother." So, in my script, Cody humorously gets to pretend to be his rich boss Lucky, while Chuck has to pretend to be Cody's employee. In the end though, I decided to just cut the Chuck character out, adding one more insult for poor Chuck Lambert. That is probably only hilariously funny to me, but I think most writers include a few "insider jokes" to entertain themselves.

Another humorous insider name change is Thomas for Paul's friend Hortensio. When Thomas disguises himself as a musician, he goes by the name of Riley. That switch is named after my real musician grandson whose first name is Thomas, middle name Riley, and goes by Riley.

Then, I printed Shakespeare's dialog in one column and side-by-side "translated" every word of the original into more modern language. I wanted to keep Shakespeare's brilliance but modernize the language and situations (travel, arranged marriages, servants). Shakespeare exposes several common romance mistakes. Men seem to fall for "sweet" women and are always surprised when that sweetness turns out to be manipulation. The poor want to marry for money, the rich want extreme beauty, and age desires youth. These weak reasons produce empty marriages. Paul's line to Thomas: that because Kate comes from a wealthy family, "she might be looking for something in a man other than money" hints at his hope that she might want to share his life on a remote ranch.

Horse trading is also often misunderstood. So I kept two scenes that are examples of good horse trading. As a horseman, when Paul hears Kate described as untamable and mean, he "hears" smart, spirited, and interesting. Throw in the detail that she's pretty to boot, and she sounds perfect! One man's trash is often another man's treasure—or a woman's. Buyers are usually looking for a bargain and sellers for the best price, so in horse trading illusion and trickery often rule. Both Biñon (seller) and Paul (buyer) are master horse traders. Paul admits to being the son of a famous horseman. I gave him the last name of Marble because the Marvels were famous Nevada horsemen and ranchers. Since Biñon knew the family, he would know that Paul would be a good horse trader. Paul knows he knows, so it would do no good to pretend disinterest, a common horse trader's trick. Instead, Paul "pretends" to misunderstand when Biñon denies Kate's suitability for marriage, and says, "I see you don't want to part with her," another horse trading trick. When Paul offers to risk his entire fortune on the match, Biñon is confused and even warns Paul against the deal.

The first meeting and sparring between Kate and Paul is also horse trading—this time Paul is trying to sell himself. Kate believes what her critics say about her and quickly exhibits the behavior that has kept men away. But Paul reinterprets each move in a positive way, constantly reassuring her that she has had good reasons for behaving as she has. When she stomps away from him, he says "Yes, let me watch you walk," then asks, "Why does the world claim that Kate limps?" Lameness is the one fault in a horse that would scare off a horse buyer.

And Kate knows she doesn't limp. A lot is happening between them in this "humorous" scene.

A few other things I drew on: I have written numerous magazine articles on horse diseases and injuries. I've interviewed horse traders, veterinarians, and those who train horses and dogs. I've been a teacher at a small border college specializing in at-risk students. I spent two years living in Reno, Nevada while acquiring a PhD and often ate in casinos, but didn't gamble or drink.

After I had been working on my script for a while, a friend who coaches high school one-act play performances expressed interest. The teacher in me wanted to help high school students understand Shakespeare, so I began to condense and clean up the play for students, softening or deleting Wild Bill's funny sexual innuendos. Although still a little long, my hope is that eventually it might be adopted for performance by rural high school kids who understand horsemanship and rodeo and who might already own all the "costumes" needed. I still have a full screenplay, but I'm including the shorter version here.

I cut a few characters and scenes, but kept the ones considered "problematic," especially those that in my opinion would have been important to Shakespeare. For example, I left out short "interrupting" scenes where the drunk reappears. In "Hamlet," when instructing the visiting troop for the play-within-a-play that will trap his uncle as the murderer of his father, Hamlet says:

Let those that play your clowns speak no more than is set down for them, for there be of them that will themselves laugh to set on some quantity of barren spectators to laugh too, though in the meantime some necessary question of the play be then to be considered. That's villainous, and shows a most pitiful ambition in the fool that uses it.

I've always interpreted Hamlet's instructions as Shakespeare's own thoughts on humor. He wrote for the riff raff of London and was sort of forced to keep them entertained with bawdy jokes, but his purpose was deeper. I think he would approve of cutting jokes. Frustration with interruptions to a good story is also an old cowboy tradition. Once a story begins, nobody interrupts.

When Paul arrives on their wedding day dressed in ridiculous clothes and riding a Biñon branded horse that is full of injuries and diseases caused by neglect, over-work, and abuse—he's now testing Kate.

Is she willing to marry him just to get out of her father's house, or can she see the good man hidden beneath the surface, as he did for her? Paul is again also sacrificing his own image to continue changing the attitude of her town and family toward her. Kate finds herself suddenly surrounded by sympathetic, concerned neighbors ready to defend her against this "monster." She feels sympathy for the first time. Instead of a monstrous shrew, she's now a fair damsel in need of rescuing from this "clown" and "cruel" horseman. Paul is also revealing to Kate that deep down her town and family actually do care about her wellbeing.

Paul handles his relationship with his future father-in-law masterfully too. From their first meeting, Biñon immediately began to wonder if Paul was just another naïve sucker or if Kate had been previously undervalued. Seeing his Biñon brand on such an abused horse would break his heart. Did Paul inflict those abuses or did he rescue this horse and bring it home? From his generous financial arrangement when asking for Kate's hand to now refusing to change clothes, Paul is insisting on trust and respect, even when he looks like a clown. Both Kate and her father would also <u>know</u> that in the rodeo world, nobody deserves more respect than a good rodeo clown. Although they provide comic relief for the audience, bull riders trust the "clowns" with their lives, and sometimes so did Shakespeare.

I also chose to keep the falconry scene even though it seems to inspire the cruelest treatment of Kate and seems unrelated to horsemanship. However, practitioners of Dorrance/Hunt horsemanship methods of making the right thing easy and the wrong thing difficult and always offering a choice often claim it works just as well on everything from insects to college students. Country horsemen of Shakespeare's day were usually excellent falconers too and the training methods sometimes overlapped. Markham wrote that using the haggard training technique of hunger and sleeplessness on a colt was too cruel, but on an older horse that had become "mad and desperate," he said, "in mine own knowledge and experience, will tame either man or beast." Markham also said that when a horse is "first coming into the stable, ... Let him take all his food out of your hands, so shall you make him gentle and tame." To modern audiences this treatment seems abusive, but Paul isn't <u>starving</u> Kate, she's just hungry, and he wants to satisfy her hunger personally. Providing hand-held food and drink is common practice for initial gentling of any wild animal, bird, or prospective mate.

Yes, "For how do I hold thee but by thy granting."

Although the knocking scene between Paul and Billy seems like slapstick humor, I (and I believe Shakespeare) use it as a communication game played between the two friends to keep them both on their toes. Misunderstanding and delusion is often the root of all trouble between both rider and horse and between humans. Paul is almost constantly using horse communication methods with Kate. Once they understand each other, he immediately moves on. He doesn't drill.

Paul totally respects Kate's intelligence, memory, and reasoning ability. He seems to hear her every inner thought. The ending is a classic example. He <u>knows</u> she does not want to go into another room with the other wives who obviously don't like her. So he <u>knows</u> she will more than willingly come running when he asks, although maybe stomping on her scarf was something they needed to practice the moon and sun trivia to achieve. Paul "sounds" like he's ordering her to obey, but he's actually setting her free. He <u>knows</u> she's been waiting her whole life to give her sister, and the other women who misjudged her, a good piece of her mind.

The final scene, to me, is like a haggard flying higher and higher in concentric circles and then dropping out of the sky right on target. As soon as Kate finds out there was a <u>reason</u> her husband called her and that she has won them a substantial bet, her trust in him soars. When she also realizes her behavior has now made her the fairest woman in the room, it soars even higher. Kate's final speech is what a haggard might say if a haggard could speak. In one fell swoop her speech gathers for her partner the respect of his father-in-law, the other husbands, and every man in Shakespeare's audience, then and forever. Like a haggard, Kate gets all their hearts. Her husband has helped her to put her intelligence to work for, instead of against herself, not at his expense, but with his blessing and encouragement. What woman wouldn't love a man like that? When horse and rider achieve that kind of partnership, they will risk their lives for each other.

Will it work on addiction? We don't know, and even Shakespeare doesn't say. I created an ending to tie the opening and ending together, but as usual, maybe the Bard is right. He always believed in the intelligence of his audience from kitchen maid to king.

   Inspiration for Taming Biñon's Daughter

Taming Biñon's Daughter

Cast

Often misunderstood or considered Shakespeare's problem play, the plot, culture and character names have been modernized. Now set about 1980 in Las Vegas, a widowed father of two marriage-aged daughters is greatly feared and respected by all—except his daughters. The sweet sister manipulates him through obedience while the terrible one fights back. Several suitors compete for the sweet sister's hand, but no one wants anything to do with Kate—until the right man comes to town looking for a wife. He agrees to marry Kate. His "taming" consists of showing her what her bad behavior looks and feels like, and when she wants to change, they practice together. In the end Kate wins a bet for them as well as the hearts of all men everywhere and for all time. The focus on horse and hawk training stays true to Shakespeare's original. Shakespeare was a master at understanding human nature and the problems people create for themselves. He learned a lot about that from horses. His plays hold a mirror up to society's foibles. This play humorously tackles conflicts between couples, parents and children, friends and rivals by using Shakespeare's favorite philosophy: "All the world's a stage." Things are not what they seem and the many disguises help expose various forms of misunderstanding and manipulation. Several minor cast members could play several parts.

POSSIBLE MUSIC: Chris LeDoux (Tougher than the Rest, Look at you Girl, He Rides the Wild Horses), Kenny Rogers (Gambler Broke Even), Madona (Gambler), Elvis (Viva Las Vegas), Ian Tyson (Summer Wages)

BIÑON: The father of two daughters, Buck Biñon, owns a Las Vegas casino, raises rodeo bucking horses and bulls, dresses and talks like a gangster

KATE: His "bronc" daughter, messy red hair, usually dressed like a buckaroo (jeans, long-sleeved tucked in shirt, hat)

BONNIE: Kate's "sweet" sister, blonde hair, usually dressed like a modern lady

PAUL MARBEL: Nevada horseman/ rancher, dresses like a conservative cowboy, marries Kate

BILLY: buckaroo who works for and dresses like Paul, but with a large wild-rag

COOK: works for Paul, should be an old stove-up cowboy in white bib apron

LUCKY LUCIANO: Son of a Chicago gangster, dresses like a rodeo cowboy with a big gold buckle that says "LUCKY"

and a huge diamond ring, pretends to be Professor Boris (Bore Us)

CODY: Luciano employee, pretends to be Lucky

DON AHORN: Old, rich casino owner, suitor to Bonnie, dresses over-the-top Vegas style with string tie

THOMAS: young and handsome, suitor to Bonnie, pretends to be Riley, a musician

DRUNK: buckaroo in first and last scene, dresses like Billy

TOM: wise elder horseman, white shirt, silver-belly hat

DOC: a psychologist, wears "professional" jacket

BARTENDER/DOLLY: fancy Vegas chorus girl

WIDOW: matronly

STAFF/EMPLOYEE: various uniformed Biñon employees

OFFICIANT: dressed like a Vegas "preacher"

RODEO ANNOUNCER: never seen, voice off-stage

COWBOY: rodeo cowboy dressed like a saddle bronc rider

GUESTS: voices off-stage

Taming Biñon's Daughter

DARK THEATRE WITH CURTAINS CLOSED

Rodeo music begins. A voice is heard off stage.

RODEO ANNOUNCER *(offstage)* This is the ride you've been waiting for, Folks. Coming out of Chute #1 is Shawn Davidson, World Champion Saddle Bronc Rider. He's on Kate's Choice, Bucking Horse of the Year, bred and raised by none other than Las Vegas's own Buck Biñon.

Sound of crowd cheering, then groaning, followed by buzzer.

RODEO ANNOUNCER *(offstage)* Kate's Choice wins again! But that cowboy made one heck of a ride on one heck of a horse, so let's give them both a big hand.

Sound of crowd cheering.

CURTAIN REMAINS CLOSED BUT LIGHTS COME UP ON IT

Cowboy wearing rodeo chaps, hat, and spurs with a braided bronc rope slung over one shoulder enters stage right. Biñon (Heavy-set man dressed like a Las Vegas gangster in rumpled white suit, black shirt, white tie, black boots, black hat?) enters stage left. When they meet, they shake hands.

COWBOY Thank you, Mr. Biñon for raising such a great buckin' horse.

BIÑON You bet, Shawn. If you can't ride him, nobody can.

COWBOY Well, maybe us rodeo cowboys can't, but I'll bet your wild daughter Kate can.

BIÑON Yup. She rides him now, but without the buckin' strap.

Shawn tips his hat to Biñon and both continue off stage in opposite directions. Before the curtain opens, Biñon hurries to take his seat at a table.

INT. HORSESHOE CASINO

Curtain opens. The stage is dimly lit like the inside of a Las Vegas casino. The stage should be set up with a round table and three chairs on stage left. A door is visible near the table. On stage right a bar sits on a riser. A sign over the bar says "Horseshoe Casino" with a string of rotating white Christmas lights around it. The sign and bar should be designed to quickly convert the area to a rodeo arena railing in front of box seating, and later to a porch. A spotlight illuminates a cowboy slouching on a stool and leaning on the bar. A fancy Vegas lady bartender stands behind the bar polishing a fancy glass before placing it on a serving tray that already contains two bottles of water and a cocktail.

The cowboy throws his beer glass off stage, sound of glass shattering.

BARTENDER OK. You've had enough, Pal. I'm cutting you off.

DRUNK *(slurred)* What choo talkin' about, I'm fine.

BARTENDER Break one more glass, and I'm calling the cops.

The drunk puts his head down on the bar and seems to sleep.

As the lights come up farther, the bartender brings the tray of drinks to the small round table where three people sit: Biñon, Doc, and Tom. They talk while she serves Doc the cocktail and hands Tom and Biñon each a bottled water, plus the fancy glass to Biñon. Tom and Biñon twist off the caps and Biñon pours water into his fancy glass.

DOC *(to Biñon)* You don't drink?

BIÑON Never have. I'm a high stakes gambler. Need every brain cell I got.

TOM *(raising his water bottle)* Me too.

DOC *(raising her cocktail)* I stop after one.

BIÑON *(raising his glass)* Here's to sobriety.

They toast.

BIÑON So, Tom, I hear yer horsemanship methods help cowboys break buckin' horses. You tryin' to put me out of business?

They all laugh.

TOM Nope. All horses need to make a living. Buckin' horses lead a pampered life for eight seconds of work once a week, so I approve.

They all laugh.

BIÑON Doc here is the best shrink in Nevada, and Tom's the best horseman anywhere. Thought you two otta meet and talk because I been wonderin', Tom, can your legendary horse whispering be applied to people?

DOC Tom, yes tell me about your magic.

TOM Well, first it's not whispering or magic. If humans genuinely believe their horses are intelligent, then those horses will be intelligent.

DOC So you are saying if we expect horses to be stubborn, they will be stubborn?

TOM Yes, because we will treat them differently . . . and vice-versa. If a horse believes a human will hurt him, that horse will be afraid and defensive. A horse is no less than what we say he is.

BIÑON Hmm. Is that why my friends always please me and my enemies don't?

TOM I don't know much about people.

DOC But, Tom, you're saying our expectations influence results in both horses and riders?

TOM Yes.

SPOTLIGHT RETURNS TO THE DRUNK

The drunk slowly slides off the barstool and lands with a thump on the floor, obviously passed out. The three quickly turn to look.

DOC Does he need help?

BIÑON Absolutely. But how? Every afternoon he drinks himself angry, then passes out.

DOC Yes, addiction is our biggest problem.

BIÑON That guy just gave me an idea. What if we scoop him up, haul him to my house, soak him clean, and dress him in my silk pajamas. When he wakes up, we treat him like he's me: rich and sober. Dolly here *(motions toward the bartender)* can pretend to be his wife. These girls all wanna go to Hollywood.

DOC That's probably not legal, but we <u>are</u> in Las Vegas. I'm curious now if he'd behave differently if treated differently.

BIÑON We can tell him he fell off a fence, hit his head, and musta been dreamin'. Tom, whadaya say?

TOM I know you're trying to help him, but I'm not tricking or lying to horses. This sounds more like manipulation and that usually doesn't work.

BIÑON We help horses and dogs lead happy lives, but with humans we stand around with our hands in our pockets. C'mon, Tom, let's try. You in?

TOM No, but I do remember a story about a man who once tried his horsemanship skills on a woman. A father had two daughters, one was very sweet, but the other was . . .

Lights go out.

EXT. LEFT WING UNDER THE "RODEO ARENA" SIGN

A spotlight illuminates an arrow-sign that points toward and says "Las Vegas Rodeo Arena." Lucky and Cody enter. Lucky is dressed in black with a white belt and big buckle that says "LUCKY." He wears a big diamond ring and a diamond hatband around his black hat. Cody is dressed in jeans with no belt, a red shirt, black hat, no hatband, no ring.*

LUCKY I feel like a kid in a candy store, Cody. I'm so glad Dad sent me to Vegas.

CODY Yeah, lucky for you, Lucky, but I'll be jobless and wearing cement boots if I don't keep you out of trouble.

LUCKY My father must have decided it was time to test my raisin' in a town he doesn't own.

CODY *(Sigh)* Right. Vegas ain't Chicago, *(pause)* but this ain't my first rodeo either.

Spot light goes out.

EXT. RODEO ARENA BOX SEATS

When the lights come up, the "bar" has become a box seating section at the rodeo with 4th of July bunting across the front of the bar, and a "fence" (the casino sign tipped over?) in front of six chairs, grouped as one, two, and three with three in the middle. All chairs are empty.

Enter Biñon, Kate, and Bonnie, taking seats in the three chairs. Thomas has followed them and stands behind the Biñons, flirting with Bonnie.

Lucky and Cody enter and make their way to the two chairs, talking as they walk.

LUCKY Hey, Cody, do you know those two pretty girls?

CODY No, but I'd say they are probably here to help welcome you—Lucky Luciano—to Las Vegas.

An older gentleman enters alone and dressed to the nines Vegas style, looks rich. He makes his way to the box with one chair and also begins to engage in conversation with Bonnie, competing for her attention with Thomas.

Kate scowls at both flirting men and at her smiling sister.

BIÑON I told you two clowns to leave Bonnie alone until her older sister, Kate here, is married. I ain't gonna tell you again. Are either of you interested in Kate?

KATE Dad! Am I a toothless old mare you're trying to sell for dogfood?

DON Sorry, Biñon, your Kate's too rough for me. But Thomas here is just looking for a wealthy wife.

KATE Is my own father trying to force me to accept one of these bozos as a mate?

THOMAS No mates for you, Kate. You will never find a husband unless you become as sweet as your sister, Bonnie.

KATE Don't worry, Junior, I'd comb your hair with a pitch fork, paint your face like a clown, and throw you in with our bucking bulls.

CODY Hey, Lucky, this is more fun to watch than the rodeo. That red-head has quite a temper.

LUCKY The blonde is perfect: mild mannered and beautiful. Those two other men are after her already, but that doesn't worry me.

BIÑON rises.

BIÑON Come on, Bonnie, I'm taking you home 'til Kate finds a husband. I'm not punishing either of you, I just want to find good husbands for both my daughters.

KATE *(shouting at Bonnie)* This is ridiculous and you know why. You are his spoiled pet, and we both know your sweetness is just an act.

BONNIE Sister, this is not my wish. But I must obey our father.

Bonnie rises and quickly exits.

THOMAS Mr. Biñon, with all due respect, this is so unfair.

DON You should have trained Kate's wicked tongue a long time ago. It's too late now. Kate is ruined and you should lock her up instead of Bonnie.

BIÑON My mind's made up. If either of you know of any tutors who can home-school Bonnie while she waits, I'll pay 'em well. Kate, you stay and watch the rodeo.

Exit Biñon.

KATE *(in a rage, rises)* I refuse to sit here with a sign around my neck: "HUSBAND WANTED." No one decides if I stay or go. That's my choice.

She exits.

DON Thomas, see what you've done. That wild cat will never find a husband, so we're doomed.

Thomas walks over to Don's chair.

THOMAS I have an idea, Don. We should work together to find a husband for Kate.

DON A husband? Impossible. We would need to look for an animal trainer if not the devil himself.

THOMAS I say husband.

DON I say devil. Because you are poor, you think any man would be willing to marry a rich man's daughter, but marriage to Kate would be like living in hell with golden furniture.

THOMAS There are plenty of fellows who would marry a wild cat . . . if she has money enough . . . And Kate does.

DON Since, unlike you, I don't need money, I wouldn't know.

THOMAS Wealthy women don't want an old rich guy like you, they want a handsome young husband, like me. Poor men who are not as handsome as I, have to settle for a flawed wife anyway. So a rich one would be a prize no matter her faults. Once we find Kate a husband, we can find out if Bonnie prefers handsome over wealth. What do you say?

DON OK. You find the man and I will pay him $10,000 to marry Kate. Meanwhile, I will find a tutor for Bonnie.

Exit Don and Thomas together.

LUCKY *(in sort of a daze)* Cody, I think I'm in love with that blonde. And since I am both rich and handsome, she will choose me. I must find a way to get to know her.

CODY Oh no! Once a Luciano's mind is made up, nothing can stop him. Were you so distracted that you didn't notice the problem?

LUCKY I saw only Bonnie's beauty.

CODY Then you better wake up. Bonnie's father has locked her in the family home until her sister from hell finds a husband.

LUCKY What a cruel father! But didn't he also say he would hire tutors for Bonnie.

CODY So . . . are we thinking the same thing?

LUCKY Tell me your idea first.

CODY You will pretend to be a tutor?

LUCKY Yes. With a fake goatee, an ill-fitting suit jacket, and gravy stained tie, I'll look just like a college professor.

CODY But what will you teach . . . machine gun handling?

LUCKY I'll teach Shakespeare.

CODY Can you understand that stuff?

LUCKY No, but nobody else does either, so I'll fake it while you pretend to be me. Nobody knows us yet. Here, wear my belt and buckle, my hat, and this big diamond ring.

They switch hats, and Cody puts on the belt and ring.

CODY Old man Biñon will kill us both.

LUCKY Not when he finds out who my father is. Biñon is no match for a Chicago Mafia family, and he knows that.

CODY If this goes sideways . . .

LUCKY Introduce me as Professor Boris to that old man so he will offer my services to Biñon. Then introduce yourself to Biñon as Lucky Luciano, son of Antonio, and make all the pre-wedding agreements.

CODY I'm gonna be killed.

LUCKY *(backhanding Cody in the chest)* I'm a Chicago Mafioso and you are a Luciano goon. You telling me you're afraid of a small-town Vegas wannabe gangster who's never played with the big boys?

The lights go dark.

DOOR IN FRONT OF THOMAS' HOUSE

A spotlight illuminates the door as Paul and Billy approach.

PAUL It's a long way from the ranch to Las Vegas in more ways than one. Our old friend Thomas lives here. We might need his help. So, knock, Billy.

BILLY Knock who Boss? Has someone already made you mad?

PAUL Idiot. Make a fist and knock.

Paul makes a fist and reinforces his instructions to Billy by knocking on his own temple.

BILLY Knock you in the head? Why on earth would you want me to do that?

PAUL *(irritated)* Knock right here, right now, or I'll knock you in the head.

BILLY Are you are trying to pick a fight? If I knock first, I know which of us will get the worst of it.

PAUL Billy, do you speak English? How can you possibly misunderstand? If you won't knock, then I'll ring.

Paul wrings Billy's ear.

BILLY Owww!

PAUL Then knock when I say knock!

Billy punches Paul softly in the arm, then Paul knocks Billy down. Hearing the commotion, Thomas comes out of the door.

THOMAS What's going on here? My good friends Billy and Paul! What are you two coyotes doing in Vegas? And why are you fighting?

Thomas helps Billy to his feet and steps between them.

BILLY I quit! He told me to knock him in the head and I refused. When he insisted, I hit him softly on the arm. I should have really wacked him the first time.

PAUL Thomas, I told this idiot to knock on your door and he refused.

BILLY *(to Paul)* Knock on the door? That's not what you said. You just said, "Knock." We are in Vegas! Everyone knows what knock means in this town. *(to Thomas)* When I asked who he wanted me to knock, he struck his own head *(Billy knocks on his own head)*. And now he claims to have simply asked me to knock on your door? I work for a crazy man.

THOMAS So you two are just playing one of your games?

Paul and Billy laugh and Paul gives Billy a friendly clap on the shoulder.

PAUL The <u>only</u> reason I keep Billy around is to keep me on my toes. If I don't explain myself absolutely clearly,

he will figure out a way to misunderstand and do the opposite of what I want.

Billy smiles proudly, strutting around. Then points at Paul.

BILLY He came to find a wife. So he needs to practice communicating.

THOMAS Ahhh. So that's the happy wind that blows you into Vegas from your sagebrush kingdom?

PAUL I wouldn't call it a kingdom, but my father has died, left me the ranch, and now I need to find a wife . . . if she's rich enough. Ranching is an expensive and lonely business.

THOMAS Unfortunately, Paul, I do know of a girl whose very rich father is anxious to see her married. She will someday inherit a huge fortune, but I wouldn't wish her on my worst enemy, and certainly not on an old friend.

BILLY Look, Thomas, Paul doesn't care if she's got as many diseases as 52 horses and not a tooth in her head. If she's got gold, he's your man.

THOMAS OK, Paul, but I personally would not wed her for all the gold in Fort Knox.

BILLY Just between us, Thomas, he's only using gold as an excuse so if he doesn't like her, he can say she doesn't have enough money.

THOMAS *(to Paul)* So you won't have to hurt her feelings?

PAUL If she's already rich, she might be looking for something in a man other than money?

THOMAS OK. But don't say I didn't warn you. She's young, beautiful, and well educated, but also the most abusive, bossiest, meanest, most violent and dangerous woman ever born. She's a rodeo bronc wrapped in a female's skin.

PAUL I can ride anything, no matter what bad habits they've been taught, even if they squeal as loud as thunder when the clouds of autumn crack.

BILLY He's never met a horse he couldn't tame. Although, he hasn't tried to tame any women yet.

PAUL Just tell me her father's name.

THOMAS Buck Biñon. As you know, he raises the rankest rodeo bucking stock. His eldest daughter's name is Kate, famous for her wicked tongue and so tough she rides her father's horses. That should tell you all you need to know.

PAUL It certainly does! She's the perfect match for me. I know her father's horses well and prefer them. Biñon was a friend of my deceased father. I will not sleep, Thomas, until I see her. I'm heading to Biñon's place right now.

Paul starts off, then stands by to hear what Billy says, and reacts with amusement.

BILLY Let him go while he's in the mood, Thomas. If she knew him as well as I do, she'd know temper tantrums won't work. He will blind her with his rope tricks until she has no more eyes to see with than a cat.

THOMAS Huh? That makes no sense, Billy, cats can see perfectly, even in the dark.

Billy shrugs. Paul laughs, starts again to leave but Thomas grabs his arm.

THOMAS Wait, Paul, I'll go with you. Biñon also holds the love of my life in prison. I'm competing for his younger daughter Bonnie against an old rich man. Biñon has forbidden us both from seeing Bonnie until Kate the witch is married.

BILLY Kate the witch! Of all the names for a girl, that is one of the worst.

THOMAS Perhaps through you, Paul, I can gain access to Bonnie. I can play any instrument. If I disguise myself as a music teacher, will you offer my services to old Biñon? He wants to hire tutors for Bonnie while she waits for Kate to find a mate. If I can spend time alone with Bonnie, I'm sure she will fall in love with me.

BILLY That sounds like a great plan! Young people should always work together to trick the old folks.

Enter Don, with Lucky disguised as a professor.

THOMAS *(loud whisper)* Shhh, Billy! That old man is my rival, but I don't know the other one. Paul, just wait here a minute.

BILLY *(to Paul)* A handsome young man with no money competes for a woman against an old rich guy. That seems like a fair fight.

DON Ok, Professor Boris, speak of love on my behalf, and I'll pay you well.

LUCKY/Boris I promise to use more beautiful words than Shakespeare himself.

DON What a wonderful stand in! He will easily win Bonnie's heart for me.

BILLY *(to Paul)* This old geezer is an idiot!

THOMAS Hello Don.

DON Oh, hello, Thomas. I'm headed to Biñon's with this tutor for Bonnie. He not only can read but understands Shakespeare.

THOMAS That's nothing. We have found a fine musician for my beautiful Bonnie.

DON She is _my_ Bonnie.

THOMAS This is no time to argue, Don. We're working together, remember? And I have even better news. I found a husband for Kate! My friend Paul here has agreed to marry her if she's rich enough.

DON Have you told him about her?

PAUL I've heard she is headstrong and brawling. If that is all, then I have no fear.

DON I can't believe our luck! Where did you come from?

PAUL Born and raised on a northern Nevada ranch. I must back up my inheritance with a larger fortune to survive drouths and low cattle prices, so I'm looking for a rich wife no matter her faults. It also gets lonely out there in the sage.

DON Such a life, with such a wife, sounds like hell to me! But you certainly have my blessing. Do you really plan to marry Kate Biñon?

PAUL Do you think a little screaming and complaining will scare me off? I've been riding Biñon horses all my life. Most cowboys go weak in the knees when they hear a horse comes from that bloodline. I smile. I've seen it all: kicking, pawing, biting, runaway, buck, rare up and flip over. Horses act like that for a reason, and I have the skills to calm them. You think I'm afraid of a scolding woman? Pffft! Might as well fear children holding frogs.

BILLY Believe me, Don, he's not afraid of anything.

THOMAS I also promised that you would pay him well to marry Kate.

DON My fortunes are at your service, provided he succeeds.

BILLY I wish I were as sure of a good dinner tonight as I am that he will finish what he begins.

Enter Cody pretending to be Lucky.

CODY/Lucky Can you fellows tell me the way to the Biñon house, the father with two beautiful daughters?

PAUL I hope you're not interested in the daughter who screams.

CODY/Lucky I love no screamers.

THOMAS Wait, are you then after the sweet daughter of old Biñon, yes or no?

CODY/Lucky And if I am, is that a problem?

DON Not if you go away.

CODY/Lucky Why? These streets are as free to me as to you.

DON But Bonnie is not. I have chosen her for my wife.

THOMAS I have chosen her for _my_ wife.

CODY/Lucky Gentlemen, gentlemen. In Greek legend, Leda's beautiful daughter had a thousand suitors, and one more shall sweet Bonnie have: me . . . Lucky Luciano. Biñon knows of my father, and just as in that Greek legend, I will succeed where the two of you fail.

THOMAS We all have our hearts set on Biñon's youngest daughter, but her father will not give his blessing until her older sister is married. My friend Paul here has accepted that challenge. Don has promised to pay Paul ten thousand dollars if he succeeds. Will you agree to match that?

CODY/Lucky You bet I will.

DON Paul, I will also throw in the best horse in Nevada.

Paul nods his acceptance of the deal. The spot light goes dark.

EXT. BIÑON RANCH PORCH

Lights come up on the porch (hanging plant, "Biñon Bucking Stock Ranch" sign?). Kate has one of Bonnie's arms twisted behind her back and is pulling her hair.

BONNIE Sister, please let me go. I will give you all my jewelry and my best dresses. Just stop hurting me.

KATE Say which man you want!

BONNIE Believe me, sister, I have never yet laid eyes on any man I could love.

Enter Biñon.

BIÑON Kate! Let poor Bonnie go! I'm so ashamed of yer devilish spirit. What's wrong with you?

Bonnie pulls away quickly and runs into the house through the door.

KATE *(raging at her father)* You always defend her, while you shame and blame me? I know she is your pet, your spoiled darling. She can choose a husband from many, while I will be forced to accept some ape from hell.

Exit Kate through the door, following Bonnie.

BIÑON I'm a dangerous man, not to be messed with, except where my daughters are concerned. With them, I've been weak and now cursed.

Enter Don, with Lucky disguised as a professor in ill-fitting jacket, stained tie, and goatee; Paul, with Thomas disguised as a Willie Nelson-style musician, braids hanging from a bandana, short white beard; and Cody pretending to be Lucky, carrying a guitar and a large book: The Complete Works of Shakespeare. Thomas somewhat hides behind Paul so Don doesn't recognize him.

BIÑON Is this a parade?

PAUL Good morning, sir! Do you have a wonderful daughter named Kate?

BIÑON *(cautiously)* Well . . . I have a daughter . . . named Kate.

PAUL Mr. Biñon, after hearing of her beauty and wit, bashful modesty, and other wondrous qualities, I have come to seek your permission to ask her to be my wife. As a gift to your house I present . . .

Presenting Thomas disguised.

PAUL . . . a friend, skilled in music, to tutor the guitar. His name is Riley, born in Texas.

BIÑON Yer welcome here, Paul, and so's Riley, but my daughter Kate does not fit your description, which causes me much grief.

PAUL I see you don't want to part with her.

BIÑON Oh, no. Don't misunderstand. I am simply telling the truth. Where do you come from? What is your name?

PAUL Paul is my name, the late John Marbel's son. My father was well known throughout Nevada.

BIÑON I knew him well, a fine man. I'm sorry to hear of his passing. He was one of the best horsemen I ever knew.

DON Neighbor Biñon, I am sure you are grateful for Paul's musician. I also want to present a tutor for fair Bonnie . . .

Presenting Lucky disguised as a college professor.

DON . . . This young man is a college professor from Reno. His name is Boris.

BIÑON Thank you, Don, and welcome Professor Boris. *(turning to CODY/Lucky)* And you are also a stranger. What are you doin' here?

CODY/Lucky My name is Lucky. Once you hear my father's name, I'm sure you will consider me the proper husband for Bonnie. I also bring gifts toward her education.

CODY/Lucky hands the book to LUCKY/ Boris and the guitar to RILEY/Thomas.

BIÑON Lucky huh? That's quite a name. But I don't believe in luck. Where do ya come from?

CODY/Lucky From Chicago, Sir; son of Antonio Luciano.

Biñon raises his eyebrows, impressed but a little afraid.

BIÑON A mighty family. Although I never met your father, I know of him. He's sorta like me, and we ain't exactly Sunday school teachers. You're welcome too. *(keeping one eye on CODY/Lucky, Biñon hollers over his shoulder for an employee)* James!

Enter a Biñon employee in uniform.

BIÑON . . . take the professor to Bonnie's room and the musician to Kate.

Exit employee with LUCKY/Boris, carrying the book and THOMAS/Riley, carrying the guitar.

BIÑON Now, let's take a walk in the orchard. You are all invited to stay for supper.

PAUL Wait, Mr. Biñon, I need to get back to my ranch and can't hang around town to dine or leisurely date your daughter.

BIÑON OK. The two of you go on. I will catch up.

Exit Don and CODY/Lucky.

PAUL As my father's only child, I am his sole heir and have increased my inheritance rather than spent it. What will your daughter bring to our marriage?

BIÑON As a wedding gift, I have promised each daughter a million bucks. When I die, they each get half of everything.

PAUL If Kate survives me as my widow, she will inherit everything. If we divorce, she will still get half of all I own.

BIÑON That's quite an opening bid. My late wife signed a pre-nup and woulda got nothing. I wanted to be worth more to her alive than dead. A feller can't be too careful.

PAUL I don't gamble for nickels, Mr. Biñon.

BIÑON Impressive. But first Kate must also agree.

PAUL That part will be easy. I ride nothing but Biñon horses and certainly do not treat them like babies. I know how to make your daughter happy.

BIÑON That sounds promising, but be prepared.

PAUL I'm as prepared as mountains are for winds.

Re-enter THOMAS/Riley, with a broken guitar around his neck.

BIÑON *(laughs)* So you can't break my daughter Kate to the git-tar?

THOMAS/Riley She broke the guitar to me! A machine gun may please her, but never a guitar. I think she'll make a better hit man.

PAUL Wow. I love her ten times more than I did before. I must see her!

BIÑON Riley, come with me. I have another guitar and Bonnie will treat ya better. Paul, I will take you to Kate, or do ya want me to send Kate to you?

PAUL Please send her here to the porch.

Paul paces nervously as he talks to himself.

PAUL I will show her how much I like her spirit. If she screams, I will tell her she sings as sweetly as a mockingbird defending its territory. If she sulls up and will not speak a word, I will compliment her careful conversation, and if she tries to send me packing, like Billy I will misunderstand and thank her for asking me to stay. If she rejects my proposal to marry, I'll name our wedding date. Here she comes, Paul, speak!

Enter Kate warily.

PAUL Good morning, Kate, I hear that's your name.

KATE I'm sure you heard much more. But yes, those who gossip about me do call me Kate.

PAUL Sometimes you are called Katherine and sometimes Kate the witch. I have heard your virtues praised around town and your beauty compared to others, but I see for myself the prettiest Kate in the entire world. I am moved to ask you to be my wife.

KATE Moved? Then remove yourself.

PAUL Not unless you come with me.

KATE I will scream.

Paul walks closer.

PAUL I will cover your scream with kisses.

KATE I will beat you with my fists.

PAUL Sounds like a good way to massage my tired muscles.

KATE I will refuse your every command.

PAUL I will grant your every wish.

KATE This silly sweet talk is not working. Try something else.

PAUL Ah, ha! You want me to keep trying! Look, Kate, I know I'm only one of many men competing for you, but I love horses. Not only that, I love Biñon horses.

KATE From the bleachers, I'm sure. As few men can ride them.

PAUL I ride nothing but Biñon horses, Kate.

KATE For how many seconds?

PAUL I'm no rodeo cowboy. I ride them for life.

KATE You don't look beat up and bruised enough.

PAUL So, you like my looks?

KATE Only when you look away.

PAUL But I can't take my eyes off you, Kate.

KATE Nor should you, if you value your life.

PAUL I value our life, Kate, together, with you by my side in work and pleasure.

KATE I will refuse to work and will give you no pleasure.

PAUL Only because no one has asked you to do what you already want to do.

KATE You are a smooth talker with a devil's tongue.

PAUL Yes, I am. Kate, come here.

KATE Do I look like some Vegas call girl?

PAUL I'm here with you, Kate, not in some casino with one of them. I am a gentleman.

KATE That I'll test.

Kate attempts to strike him but he dodges.

PAUL I know you are a proper lady, properly raised, and who will make a loving wife—but only for me. I was born to tame you. I am your soul mate.

KATE I don't believe in soul mates, and no man can tame me.

PAUL That is very true, but you will want to tame yourself now that you've found a man who will love you as you want to be loved.

KATE I don't want to be loved.

PAUL I have heard your father wants you to marry first, before your sister. I understand now why no man would consider your sister if he thought he had any chance with you.

KATE I don't want a husband.

PAUL Come on, Kate, of course you do.

KATE I certainly don't want you.

PAUL I hear your words, but your eyes betray your bluff.

He takes her hand gently.

KATE Let me go or I'll bite you.

But she doesn't bite or try to pull away.

PAUL I was told you were rough and sullen. But that was a lie. I find you fun and witty.

He releases her hand, she immediately stomps away.

PAUL Yes, let me watch you walk. Why does the world claim that Kate limps?

She spins back to face him.

PAUL You are not lame. Lameness is the only reason I would pass up a Biñon bred and raised horse—or woman.

KATE Go away!

PAUL If you reject me, tell me where I can find another like you?

KATE My younger sister.

PAUL Her phony sweetness is only manipulation. She is spoiled and boring. You are honest and interesting, just lonely.

KATE I am fine.

PAUL You are very fine, but not happy. I will make you happy. Today I love your beauty, intelligence, and your spirit. Your beauty will fade, but I will love your intelligence and spirit more every day.

KATE Where did you study all this wise and fancy talk?

PAUL So, you think I'm wise?

KATE Maybe wise enough to keep yourself warm.

PAUL I will keep us both warm, Kate. But enough sweet talk. Your father has given me his blessing. He offered a million dollars as a wedding gift and promises you half his estate upon his death. I promise you <u>all</u> of my estate upon my death and half if you divorce me. What have you got to lose, Kate? If you don't like me once we are married, you can always have me killed.

KATE That is not a joke.

PAUL Am I laughing? I know who I'm dealing with. I told your father I didn't gamble for nickels. Now I'm telling you that I am betting everything, including my life, on this marriage. If you want more, I can only promise hard but rewarding work, good horses to ride, sunrises, sunsets, and moonrises over a thousand miles of sage and a thousand miles of silence. If you prefer diamonds, neon lights and clanging slot machines, then walk away now.

Kate doesn't speak and doesn't walk away.

PAUL C'mon, Kate, marriage is a high stakes gamble, and as your father is fond of saying: there's no such thing as luck. Here he comes. Don't reject me, Kate.

Re-enter Biñon, Don, and CODY/Lucky.

BIÑON Well, Paul, how are you doing with my daughter?

PAUL How else but perfect, Sir? I never start anything I can't finish.

BIÑON What do you say, daughter?

KATE *(angrily)* You call me daughter? You have clearly shown your so-called tender fatherly regard.

PAUL Father, you and the entire world have been wrong about her. She has good reason to be angry and fights only for her own self-preservation. She's not vicious, but modest and lady like. Tomorrow will be our wedding-day.

KATE I'll see you hanged tomorrow first.

DON Paul, did you hear that?

CODY/Lucky Is this is your idea of success, Paul?

PAUL Be patient, gentlemen. I have chosen her and she has chosen me. It's incredible how much she loves me and how easily she won me over. I am headed to town for a ring and wedding clothes. Provide the party, Father, and invite the guests.

Kate appears frozen. Biñon looks from her to Paul to her.

BIÑON I don't know what to say. *(pause, looks at Kate again, she says nothing).* I guess we have a match!

DON Amen!

CODY/Lucky We are all witnesses!

PAUL Father, these two gentlemen have pledged ten thousand dollars each toward this marriage, please collect and hold those debts for me. Don here has also promised the best horse in Nevada. Kate, you pick the horse. Father, bride, and gentlemen, goodbye until tomorrow.

Exit Paul and Kate in opposite directions.

DON Was a match ever made so suddenly?

BIÑON Well, this _is_ Vegas.

DON So now, Biñon, Bonnie is free to marry me.

CODY/Lucky No! Bonnie is free to marry _me_!

DON Youngster, you can't provide for her as well as I.

CODY/Lucky Grandpa, I can produce a thousand times more than you can even imagine.

DON Women prefer older men.

CODY/Lucky Younger men.

BIÑON Shut up both of you. My daughter is high maintenance. She ain't gonna follow no empty wagon. So, Don, what's your offer?

DON My house is the envy of Las Vegas. My art collection is sought after by museums. I own three casinos. Yes, I am older, but this would be an advantage to her. I might die tomorrow and all would be her's. And if while I live, she remains only mine, all I own is hers.

CODY/Lucky Ha! You old fox. That *(he makes air quotes)* "only mine" is your intended escape because it will be highly unlikely that a young, beautiful woman, pursued by many, will remain faithful to a dried up old man. Listen to me, Mr. Biñon, I am my father's only son and only heir. You know I outbid this old man both in looks and in wealth.

BIÑON Yes. Your financial offer is the best, Lucky, but . . . Bonnie must also agree.

DON *(aside)* I have lost all hope to marry Bonnie. Instead, I will marry the first beautiful woman my money can buy.

Exit all. Stage goes dark.

EXT. BIÑON PORCH

When the light comes back up. THOMAS/ Riley and LUCKY/Boris stand toe to toe, fists clenched, about to fight. Bonnie is sitting demurely in one of the porch chairs.

LUCKY/Boris *(holding the book)* Back off, Guitar Picker!

THOMAS/Riley *(holding the guitar)* You back off, Bo-ring Professor.

BONNIE Gentlemen, please, there's no need to argue. I will take lessons only at my pleasure. First, Professor Boris will finish reading a sonnet, while Riley tunes his instrument.

Lucky sits next to Bonnie and opens the book.

THOMAS/Riley You'll stop when I am in tune?

LUCKY/Boris Go tune your guitar.

THOMAS/Riley walks off the porch but hides behind a bush to watch.

BONNIE Now, where did we leave off?

LUCKY/Boris Here, Miss Biñon, at the end of Shakespeare's Sonnet Number 87 *(reads dramatically)* "So thy great gift, upon misprision growing,/ Comes home again, on better judgment making./ Thus have I had thee as a dream doth flatter / In sleep a king, but waking no such matter."

BONNIE Now explain what that means.

LUCKY/Boris Things are not always as they seem . . .

He rises and looks to make sure THOMAS/ Riley is gone. Returns and places his arm around Bonnie.

LUCKY/Boris Now, as I was saying, I'm Lucky Luciano of Chicago, son of a very wealthy and powerful man. While we get to know each other, my employee, is pretending to be me and making arrangements with your father.

BONNIE I believe you have honorable intentions, but I don't quite trust you yet.

LUCKY/Boris Trust me, Bonnie. I can give you anything your heart desires.

THOMAS/Riley reenters.

THOMAS/Riley My instrument is now in tune.

BONNIE Professor Boris, it is Maestro Riley's turn now.

THOMAS/Riley Take a walk, Boris *(pronounces it Bore-us)*

Nobody talks to a Luciano like that. LUCKY/Boris bows up and stands his ground, ready to fight.

BONNIE Please, Professor, I'm too shy to practice music with an audience.

LUCKY/Boris reluctantly leaves the porch, but also hides behind the bush.

THOMAS/Riley Miss Biñon, let me show you where to place your fingers.

THOMAS/Riley hands Bonnie the guitar, steps behind her chair and wraps his arms around her, adjusting her fingers on the strings.

THOMAS/Riley Bonnie, it's me, Thomas, in disguise. I have come to be near you. I love you so much.

Bonnie escapes his embrace, jumps up, and turns on him angrily.

BONNIE You call this love? I call it trickery.

LUCKY/Boris dashes back onto the porch, again ready to fight, but at the same time a Biñon staff member enters through the door.

STAFF Bonnie, your father wants you to leave your studies to help get things ready for your sister's wedding.

Exit Bonnie with Staff. LUCKY/Boris turns on THOMAS/Riley ready to rumble. THOMAS/Riley backs up.

THOMAS/Riley *(to LUCKY/Boris)* If Bonnie is going to flirt with every new man who comes along, then you can have her. I don't want a cheating wife. I know a widow lady who will be faithful.

Exit THOMAS/Riley quickly. LUCKY/ Boris makes a "yes" movement with his arm and exits strutting in the opposite direction.

EXT. BIÑON PORCH— WEDDING DAY

When lights come up, major players in the wedding party assemble on the porch: Biñon (wearing boutonniere), Bonnie, Don beside fancy girl Dolly, Thomas arm in arm with an older woman, and CODY/Lucky and LUCKY/Boris. All are standing around as if waiting. Wedding-style music is playing softly.

BIÑON *(To CODY/Lucky)* Lucky, Kate is dressed and waiting. The wedding guests are all seated in the garden and waiting *(he motions off stage)*, but we have not heard from or seen the groom. What do you say, Lucky, about this shame of mine?

BONNIE The shame is Kate's, Father. I tried to tell her Paul was joking. He wants to play the great man and plan a wedding, yet he never intended to marry. The world will point at my sister and say, "Look there goes Old Maid Kate. Crazy Paul left her crying at the altar!"

THOMAS Be patient Mr. Biñon. Paul does enjoy a good joke, but he's honest. I swear his word is his life. If he's alive, he will be here.

Bonnie exits into the house.

BIÑON Such an insult would anger a saint, and it's far worse for someone with Kate's temper. Anybody who hurts one of my daughters might get hurt too and never know who did it.

Billy rushes in, out of breath, dressed as always but wearing a boutonniere.

BIÑON Is he coming?

BILLY Almost here, he's horseback.

A horse's hooves are heard clomping off stage. Everyone turns to look off-stage, gasps in unison, and begins whispering.

BIÑON His horse wears my brand but it is barely alive: lame and scarred from mistreatment, snot running out its nose, burs in its mane and tail.

THOMAS He's using a cheap, torn up bridle crudely repaired, attached to a rusty grazer bit with mismatched split reins. Why?

BILLY The saddle is even worse! It looks like an old worn out parade saddle that came from a Mexico City dump.

Paul enters dressed like a homeless rodeo bullfighter.

CODY/Lucky Paul, why on earth do you come here lookin' like that?

PAUL A horse and a man is more than one . . . but I am running late.

CODY/Lucky First we were afraid you had decided not to come and now . . .

BIÑON Please change clothes so you don't embarrass Kate and disrespect this solemn ceremony.

CODY/Lucky I have a suitcase full of nice clothes in my car. We are the same size.

PAUL No. I'm ready to marry.

BIÑON *(ominously)* Do ya plan to marry my daughter dressed like that?

PAUL *(defiantly)* I'm done talking. She is marrying me, not my clothes.

Kate enters, looking radiant in her wedding dress. Bonnie walks behind her as Maid of Honor. This is the first time Paul has seen Kate dressed like a woman with her hair combed.

PAUL *(truly awed)* Oh, my! What a beautiful Bride . . .

Kate slowly looks him over. Off-stage the wedding guests begin shouting. Kate looks toward the voices and appears to be waking from a dream. This is the first time she has ever heard anyone take her side. She looks at Paul. He smiles as though he carefully planned this moment for her, which he did, by willingly taking on the role of villain so she could be the beautiful heroine, and too good for such a man. She looks back at the sound of the voices.

A GUEST Don't do it Kate.

A GUEST He's not good enough for you.

A GUEST He was late.

A GUEST He's so disrespectful.

A GUEST He can't be trusted.

A GUEST Kate, you deserve better.

A GUEST He's a monster.

A GUEST He will hurt you.

DON Look at how he is dressed, Kate. He's a disgrace.

LUCKY/Boris Look at the horse he rode in on. It is almost dead from cruel mistreatment, over work, poor shoeing, rope burns, beatings, starvation and disease—Is that how you want to be treated, Kate?

BIÑON Daughter, you don't have to go through with this.

BONNIE Father, let me marry first. Then Kate can choose a better mate than this from those I reject.

Paul offers his hand to Kate and waits.

PAUL You comin' Kate? Or are you stayin'? Your choice.

GUESTS *(in unison)* Don't do it, Kate!

Kate hesitates, but takes Paul's hand and steps off the porch. They exit together toward the wedding guest voices. As the music changes to "Here Comes the Bride" the voices groan in unison.

CODY/Lucky hangs back to speak to the real Lucky.

CODY/Lucky I easily out bid old Don, and he's already married the Vegas queen you just saw on his arm. Thomas didn't like Bonnie flirting with you during her lessons, so he married the rich widow standing beside him.

LUCKY/Boris Now all we have left to do is expose my true identity.

CODY/Lucky Biñon has also demanded that Bonnie approve of her match with you.

LUCKY/Boris Don't worry. My charms have already won over fair Bonnie.

CODY/Lucky I hope you can charm her father too. I still believe he will kill us both.

Lights Fade out.

INT. PAUL'S RANCH KITCHEN DOOR.

A spotlight finds Billy standing at the door. The nearby round table is now covered by a red and white checkered table cloth.

BILLY Hey Cook, you in there?

Cook, wearing a white cook's apron enters through the door.

COOK Where else would I be except the ranch kitchen? How are Paul and his new wife getting along?

BILLY You'll soon see. She slept some in the pickup last night while Paul and I drove. When I came to give you his orders after midnight, they went to their bedroom. He said he preached, yelled and swore, threw the blankets here and the pillows there, saying nothing was good enough and he wanted everything perfect for her. She looked like she was waking up from a dream.

COOK Has he gone crazy?

BILLY Maybe. I think he is showing her what her behavior looks and feels like. Neither of them slept a wink.

COOK Sounds like he's killing her with kindness. That should put them both in a foul mood.

BILLY He ranted until too late for breakfast and explained that you did not feed anyone late to a meal, nor did you allow snacking between meals. He said that was your way of making sure everyone showed up on time.

COOK That's a good idea! I think I'll try it.

BILLY Maybe the rest of us will try nailing your wrinkled, moth-eaten hide to the side of the barn. Anyway, this morning we saddled up and made a big circle horseback so Paul could begin to show her around the ranch. A cold rain blew in and soaked us. But she seemed to love it.

COOK She must be nearly frozen and starving. I already have a fire built, as instructed.

BILLY Are the cobwebs swept? Have the cowboys shaved and showered? Is everything in order?

COOK All is ready, Mr. Trickster.

BILLY Except for a shared apple, neither of them has eaten since we stopped for a burger yesterday afternoon.

COOK That sounds like his falconry training? I thought he was gonna horse whisper her?

BILLY *(Billy shrugs)* Is the mutton cooked?

COOK Yes, but I will never get that smell out of the kitchen. The buckaroos and I have already eaten some good roast beef, and I have hidden a plate for you as instructed. Now, more stories!

BILLY Well, they already had a falling out.

COOK Oh, no! How?

BILLY She fell out of her saddle and into the mud, and thereby hangs a tale.

COOK So let's hear it!

BILLY Well, we were coming down a steep mountain trail. I was in the lead, then Kate, then the boss riding behind her.

COOK Both on one horse?

BILLY Of course not, you idiot. Now you've interrupted my story just to be funny and made me mad. If you hadn't interrupted, I'd have told you how her horse fell and she under it in a boggy place. I'd have told you how he did not help or give her suggestions, how she appreciated that and picked herself up; how he beat <u>me</u> because her horse stumbled; how he swore and I cried; and how she waded through the mud to pull him off me. I'd have told you how her bridle got busted, how I lost my rope, and how we all rode on . . . but now you won't get those details because you interrupted.

COOK Wow. Sounds like he has become the tyrant, and she the hero.

BILLY Yes, the oats have eaten the horses.

COOK That makes no sense.

BILLY *(shrugs)* I read it somewhere.

Lights fade out.

EXT. OUTSIDE ON RANCH

A spotlight comes up on the stage wing. A fake yucca indicates "outside." Billy and Paul enter. Paul has a hawk resting on his large glove.

BILLY As instructed, I told the buckaroos to keep Kate distracted until one of us returns. I guess you want them to see her in action with that new horse.

PAUL Yes. After she defended them against me, they like her, but I want them to respect her too. When they see how she can handle a horse, they'll be won over. I also needed time to think. I've been showing Kate what her behavior looks like and setting it up so she can make friends. I'm convinced she wants to change now, but bad habits are hard to break.

BILLY She also defended me from you and the cook from you. So we all like her. Your plans seem to be working.

PAUL They're working for all of <u>you</u>, but not for me. She seems to trust me less today than at our wedding. So, I've been thinking about falconry. Do you know the difference between an eyas *(pronounced eye-us)* and a haggard?

BILLY Of course, but you must want to talk about it.

PAUL An eyas is a chick, plucked from the nest, and hand-raised. They're fairly easy to bond with by withholding food and sleep, then hand feeding and hooding it for peaceful sleep. But an eyas usually turns out spoiled, lazy, and cowardly, preferring the handouts and hood to the hunt.

BILLY So Kate's sweet sister is sorta like an eyas?

PAUL A true falconer prefers a wild caught adult haggard that is already brave, self-sufficient, and deadly.

BILLY Like Kate.

PAUL The wilder and fiercer the bird's personality, the better hunter it will make. But a haggard knows it can already provide for itself. It doesn't need a partner.

BILLY So if a haggard knows it can provide for itself, why does it come back?

PAUL It might not. When set free to hunt for the first time, if a wild bird returns, it's for a reason deeper than meat.

BILLY And you want that kind of bond with Kate.

PAUL That bond is not based on fear or reward and it's even stronger than what we humans call love. Once formed, a haggard will also fly after larger, fiercer game than it would ever hunt alone.

BILLY Just like horses and riders when they rope some bull?

PAUL Yes. I can create a bond like that with a wild hawk, a horse, and a dog, but I'm not sure about a woman.

BILLY So what are you gonna do?

PAUL I don't know. I'm drinking from a fire hose here. Kate is searching too. If she doesn't decide to trust me soon, I am worried that this hawk/horse treatment will break her spirit, which is what I love about her most.

BILLY Maybe you should just be honest about what you are doing?

PAUL Maybe, but it's also important that she has confidence in herself and knows that I know she will figure it out without my help.

BILLY That's deep.

PAUL I'm not trying to boss her or change her. Everything is for her own benefit, so she can get what she wants and make her life better. Only if she believes that . . . will she want to be with me.

BILLY Like a haggard.

PAUL Yes. If Kate decides she wants out of this marriage, I'm a dead man walking.

BILLY How can I help, Boss?

PAUL Pick up my package at the post office and stall for time. Guard the kitchen while I wait for my hawk to bring a bird that I can cook for Kate.

Spotlight goes dark.

INT. TABLE AT PAUL'S RANCH

Kate is seated dejectedly at the round table with her head in her hands. Billy stands guard with a package at his feet. Paul enters through the door with a plate of food.

PAUL Sweetheart, why does my beautiful Kate look so sad?

KATE I am exhausted, starving, and so discouraged.

PAUL Look my love, my hawk and I have caught you some fresh meat, a dove, food fit for a queen. I have dressed it, cooked it, and now serve it myself.

He carefully places the plate of food in front of her. She grabs a piece and stuffs it in her mouth quickly.

PAUL *(frowning)* Surely, my service deserves a thank you? Yet not a word?

He takes the plate away and hands it toward Billy.

PAUL Here, Billy, give this to the dogs.

Billy reaches for the plate. Kate rises angrily to face Paul.

KATE This is abuse! You will not let me eat or sleep . . . why?

PAUL Horses can't talk but they're honest. It's much harder to be honest with a human and get honesty in return. Humans lie and play all sorts of tricks. So, to be honest, I worked hard to bring you this meal and even the poorest service deserves thanks.

KATE OK. I'm sorry, Paul, it's delicious. Thank you. Please, let me eat. I am so hungry.

PAUL That's better. Eat! Eat it all. It will help you sleep like a baby.

Kate notices a small round dark object on the plate (can be a dried cranberry). She stabs it with her fork and holds it up.

KATE What is this?

PAUL Do you know anything about falconry, Kate?

KATE A little. I know a human and a raptor hunt together for the benefit of both, sort of like a horse and rider.

PAUL Yes. But the hawk doesn't really need the human and the human doesn't really need the hawk. Yet they make each other's life more interesting and fun.

KATE Still like a horse and rider.

PAUL The human makes the hawk's life better by plucking and skinning the prey. They share in the feast, but the hawk always gets her favorite morsel, one that she previously had to dig for—the heart.

KATE So are you giving me the heart?

PAUL Mine yes. Always. But I need to give <u>that</u> one to my hawk.

Paul takes the tiny heart off Kate's fork and places it in his shirt pocket. Kate smiles as she forks another piece of dove and places it tenderly in Paul's mouth.

KATE Thank you, Paul. Thank you for everything you are doing for me. I see now what my behavior looked and felt like, but breaking my old habits is difficult.

PAUL You are doing great. By sticking up for my crew, they all like you, and after watching you start that new horse, they also respect you.

KATE I can tell you don't normally treat them like you have been or they wouldn't be so loyal.

PAUL Right. We are sacking you out, giving you chances to react, chances to make choices.

KATE As I have been doing to you.

PAUL I know. Have I passed inspection?

KATE So far. But I don't expect perfection. If a horse demanded perfection, we'd never be able to ride one. Instead they ignore our mistakes and give us chance after chance. Horses are incredibly patient, even with the stupidest of humans.

PAUL Except Biñon horses. They're a little less patient and demand more. They will fight back against stupidity. But once you gain their trust, as you know, no bloodline makes more dependable partners.

KATE Few people understand that.

PAUL Few people can ride them. But you can.

KATE Thank you. And so can you.

PAUL Thank you. Now we must learn to trust each other as we do our horses.

Let's see, it is now seven o'clock in the morning.

KATE Paul, look at the clock, it's already ten.

PAUL Oh, Kate, you are still crossing me. Before we return to Vegas, it shall be whatever time I say it is.

KATE *(temper rising)* Do you plan to make a puppet of me?

PAUL *(calmly)* Do you plan to make a puppet of me?

KATE Your betters have allowed me to speak my mind . . .

PAUL My betters?

KATE I'm sorry. I didn't mean that.

PAUL It's easy to get along with a horse when all you are doing is petting it. When you start asking for a dependable working partner, the trouble begins.

KATE A woman would be made a fool if she didn't have the spirit to resist. I must protect myself. I must speak my mind or my heart will break.

PAUL Men too, but are some things more important, some less?

KATE Are you saying we should battle only over important things?

PAUL We should never battle.

KATE But surely, I'm allowed an opinion.

PAUL Always, but we should practice on trivia so we can work together as a team. Practice, not drill. Then, when we must do battle it should be us against the world, not each other.

KATE I am not a child, who needs to practice trivia.

PAUL In a split second, when we ask a horse for every ounce of speed he's got, or to stop on a dime—he never hesitates. Never. He never asks why. That comes from practice. Is that abuse?

KATE I see.

Paul snaps his fingers. Billy scrambles forward with a shopping bag, pulling out a feminine white blouse, a mid-calf denim skirt, and a pink silk wild-rag.

KATE Can't I even choose my own clothes?

PAUL That's not what I ordered. Billy, send them back.

Kate grabs the clothes from Billy and holds them up to her body, swirling round. Billy attempts to grab them.

KATE No. I love them.

PAUL Well, I don't.

KATE Well, I do, and I need a party outfit.

PAUL OK. Then keep them. I wanted to be sure you liked them and weren't just trying to please me. Do you see the difference, Kate?

KATE Yes. Yes, I do.

PAUL Now, Kate, see how bright the moon shines!

KATE The moon? Paul, you know it is the sun. It's day light now. We both know it is the sun.

PAUL Kate, we need to practice so that when the stakes are high, we won't hesitate. We must trust each other completely. We must respond instantly even when one of us doesn't understand the purpose or the danger. So it shall be moon, or star, or whatever I say before we return to Vegas.

KATE OK, husband, let it be the moon, or sun, or whatever you please. If you want to call it a candle, then from now on, it will be a candle for me too.

PAUL I say it's the moon.

KATE I know it's the moon.

PAUL Then you are mistaken. It is obviously the sun.

KATE How foolish of me. Anyone can see it is the blessed sun. But it's not the sun, when you say it's not. The moon changes just like your mind. Whatever you call it, then that's what it is for Kate.

BILLY Ha! The game is won! Let's go to Vegas!

PAUL And now, I demand that you kiss me, Kate.

They all laugh, Kate and Paul lean in to kiss, and the lights go dark.

EXT. DOOR AT BIÑON RANCH

A spotlight lights up the door. Cody is waiting nearby in his normal clothes. Lucky (now wearing his own clothes) and Bonnie rush through the door.

LUCKY *(to Cody)* Great News, Cody! Bonnie and I are married!

As they all hug each other, Biñon appears in the doorway. Bonnie, Lucky, and Cody all break apart. Bonnie and Cody look at each other in fear. Lucky looks confident.

BONNIE *(to Biñon)* I'm so sorry, Father.

BIÑON Why? What have you done?

LUCKY Mr. Biñon, Bonnie and I are married. I'm the real Lucky Luciano, the real son of Chicago's Antonio Luciano.

BIÑON *(ominously to Cody)* You ain't no Luciano?

LUCKY No, Father, I am Lucky Luciano. Cody is my employee. What he did, I forced him to do.

BIÑON *(to Lucky)* And you ain't no professor?

BONNIE No, Father, Lucky pretended to be a professor so we could get to know each other, and we fell in love.

LUCKY *(to Biñon)* My love for Bonnie made me force Cody to trade identities with me. He said you agreed to my financial offer as long as Bonnie was willing, and she is. So we found a priest and are now happily married.

BIÑON *(threateningly)* So, you tricked me in order to marry my daughter? That may not be so lucky. I ain't never killed a man who didn't deserve it.

Exit Biñon.

LUCKY Don't look pale, Bonnie. My father is more ruthless than yours. My father will fix this.

Lucky takes his phone out of his pocket and punches in numbers.

LUCKY Hello, Father. *(pause)* Yes, we are married. *(pause)* Thank you, I'll tell her. But her father . . .

Spot light goes dark.

EXT. BIÑON PORCH

Lights return to porch area. Everyone has made up. A waiter serves drinks all around. Biñon, Paul and Kate, Lucky and Bonnie, Thomas and Widow, Don and Dolly all sit, stand, or lean on the porch.

LUCKY It's great to see everyone getting along! Father Biñon, sister Kate, brother Paul, Thomas with your loving widow, and Don with your beautiful bride.

BIÑON Dinner will soon be ready. I hope everyone is hungry. Meanwhile, here's to successfully getting rid of both my daughters!

Everyone laughs and toasts.

THOMAS Where's Billy?

DON And Cody?

PAUL They figured this would be a boring party, so they took the day off and went looking for excitement.

BONNIE Aren't you worried for their safety?

PAUL Ha! I'm more worried about what those two might do to Las Vegas.

DON Yes, Biñon, Vegas should have stuck to attracting retirees. You may regret inviting a bunch of cowboys to town.

BIÑON *(smiling broadly)* We'll see.

PAUL Vegas offers nothing but comfort and kindness.

THOMAS For both our sakes, I wish that was true.

PAUL It sounds like Thomas's widow is to be feared.

WIDOW *(to Paul)* Then don't tease me, if you're afraid of me.

PAUL *(to widow)* You misunderstood my meaning. I mean, that Thomas is afraid of you, I'm not.

WIDOW A man afraid of his own wife thinks everyone else fears their wife too.

PAUL *(laughs)* Good come back, Widow.

KATE *(irritated)* Widow, where did you get the idea that my husband fears me?

WIDOW I conceived of it through your husband's actions.

PAUL She has conceived by me! How does Thomas like that?

THOMAS My widow means that your problems with Kate gave you the idea that I would be afraid of my wife too.

PAUL Very well mended. Kiss him for that, good widow.

KATE *(still irritated)* What do you mean that Paul is afraid of his wife?

WIDOW Since your husband is afraid of you, he thinks my husband is afraid of me. And now you know my meaning.

KATE That is a very mean meaning.

Kate is trying desperately to control her temper. She looks to Paul for reassurance. He blows Kate a kiss.

WIDOW Right, and you are a very mean and angry woman.

KATE I may be an angry woman toward you, but not toward my husband.

PAUL Sic 'em, Kate!

THOMAS Sic 'em, widow!

DON Biñon, how do you like these quick-witted folks?

BIÑON There's more than one kind of education.

Bonnie rises.

BONNIE Come, Ladies, let's leave these foolish men to their jokes, teasing, bragging, and insults. We will retire to the living room for more civilized conversation.

The widow and Dolly quickly follow Bonnie. Kate hesitates. She does not want to go with these women who obviously don't like her. She wants to stay with Paul. He nods at her for reassurance. Reluctantly, Kate follows the women out of the room, looking back twice.

PAUL The women have found a way to dodge our friendly bullets. Here is a toast to all who have shot and missed.

THOMAS My wife did not miss. We all know your wife has you at bay.

BIÑON Ha, Paul! That bullet shoulda hurt.

THOMAS She hit the bullseye, right Paul?

PAUL Well aimed, I confess, but missed. Ten to one it hit the three of you in the heart.

BIÑON I'm sad to say, son Paul, but I think we all agree that you ended up with the worst wife.

PAUL Well, I say no, and intend to prove it. Let's see whose wife comes fastest when her husband calls. Shall we bet on it?

THOMAS Sure. What is the wager?

LUCKY One hundred dollars.

DON Let's make it five hundred.

PAUL Five hundred dollars? Pffft, I'd bet that much on my dog, but a thousand times more on my wife.

LUCKY OK, one thousand then.

THOMAS Agreed.

DON Agreed.

PAUL I don't gamble for nickles, gentlemen. A million dollars!

Biñon whoops and slaps his knee.

BIÑON Now we have a bet!

Thomas, Don, and Lucky eye each other. They know this bet will be easy to win from poor Paul, but they are not sure which of the three of them has the most obedient wife.

LUCKY Agreed.

DON Agreed.

THOMAS My widow has not made me as rich as the two of you, but I believe she will prove more obedient than your young wives. So, count me in.

Biñon nods to the waiter who pulls paper and pens from a pocket and hands each man a bit of paper and a pen. While talking, they each sign and hand the papers to Biñon and hand the pens back to the waiter.

PAUL *(to Biñon)* Father, hold our bets. We will send this waiter to fetch our wives one at a time.

THOMAS Who wants to go first?

LUCKY I will. Waiter, tell Bonnie to come to me.

Exit Waiter

BIÑON *(to Lucky)* Son, I'll cover half your bet that Bonnie comes the most quickly.

LUCKY Thanks, Father, but Lucianos always cover our own bets.

Re-enter Waiter alone.

LUCKY What? Where is my wife?

WAITER Your wife says she is visiting now and prefers not to come.

PAUL Ah, ha! Your bride prefers visiting to coming when you call! One down!

DON Yes, and the kindest one too. But, Paul, your wife will send a much worse message.

PAUL We'll see.

THOMAS I'll go next. Waiter, please ask my wife sweetly, with kind words, to come to me. Be sure to say please.

Exit Waiter.

PAUL O, ho! Begging! Surely with kind words and a well-spoken "please," the good widow will come.

THOMAS I'm merely being polite. No matter how much you might beg, your stubborn wife will refuse.

Re-enter Waiter alone.

THOMAS Oh, no! Where's my wife?

WAITER She says you men must be playing some silly trick. She asks that you to come to her.

PAUL Oh, my! Another wife refuses! How intolerable.

DON Waiter, go tell my lovely wife I have a nice gift for her.

Exit Waiter.

PAUL Ah, so you think if you bribe your young gold-digger with jewelry, that will surely work?

Waiter returns alone.

WAITER She says she will accept your gift later.

PAUL What intolerable wives! No husband should put up with such disobedience. Waiter, go tell my wife that I command her to come to me immediately.

Exit waiter.

THOMAS When she refuses, all bets will be off.

LUCKY Right. No one can win the bet.

BIÑON Look! Here comes Kate, almost on the run!

Kate dashes into the room out pacing the waiter who trails behind.

KATE What do you need, Paul?

PAUL Where are your sister and the other two wives?

KATE They sit gossiping by the fire.

PAUL Go fetch them here. If they refuse, force them to come to their husbands.

Exit Kate.

LUCKY This is frightening.

THOMAS Yes it is.

DON I wonder what comes next.

PAUL Next comes peace and love and a wonderful life—for me. But the trouble has just begun for all of you.

BIÑON Paul you win the bet hands down, and I'll add another million as another wedding gift for a new daughter. Katherine is so changed!

PAUL I will show you all even more evidence of Kate's virtues. Here she comes with the disobedient wives.

Re-enter Kate smiling, with Bonnie, gold-digger and widow all frowning but following Kate.

PAUL Kate, that scarf does not look good on you, throw it under foot.

Kate obeys immediately and stomps on the scarf.

WIDOW Lord, let me never be brought down to such silly action by my husband!

DOLLY Nor I!

BONNIE Sister, what foolishness makes you act like this?

LUCKY I wish you had been half as foolish fair Bonnie. Your pride and wisdom just cost me a million dollar bet.

BONNIE Don't blame me! You are a fool for making such a bet. I am not your puppet.

Widow and Dolly snap their heads accusingly toward their husbands. Don nods and Thomas shrugs in admission.

PAUL Kate, you just won us a million dollars from each of these husbands because of their disobedient wives. You also won us another million from your father because he was so pleased with your behavior. Now I order you to tell these women how wives should treat their husbands.

WIDOW You are mocking us. We will listen to no such speech.

PAUL Come on, Kate, I order you to tell them all off good and begin with her.

BONNIE She shall not.

PAUL I say she will.

Kate has been waiting her whole life for this moment and has written and rehearsed a speech like this in her mind for many years. She is more than ready! She blows a kiss to Paul, he blows a kiss back, and Kate begins.

KATE Ladies! Be quiet. Anger makes you ugly. My good husband laid the world at my feet on our wedding day by sacrificing his own reputation in order to convince all of you that he was the monster, not me. Never before that day did any of you or the other guests have one kind word to say to or about me. But quickly you all rose up against him in one voice to say that I deserved a better man. Well, there is no better man. He saw through your gossip, manipulation, and the reasons for my defensive behavior. All Paul has ever asked in return is my heart.

Love should never become a contest of wills. Marriage is like the partnership between bird and falconer or horse and rider. Each trusts the other that nothing will be asked without reason. Some men try to beat, bribe, or pet their horses and wives into submission, but Paul makes it a beautiful dance, anticipating my every desire. When my husband asks, I obey, not because I am afraid of him or no longer respect myself, but because I want to please him with all my heart, just as he pleases me. He makes the world see me as he does, and I want the world to see him as I do. Ladies, if you want to be treated like a queen, you must treat your husband like a king.

Kate kneels before Paul and bows her head. Paul rises, walks to Kate, reaches down, gently takes both her hands, and lifts her back to her feet.

PAUL *(to Kate)* What a perfect wife. *(to Lucky)* Your name is Lucky, but I am the lucky one. You lost and not only this bet, as did you Thomas, and you Don. I not only won the wager, but I picked the best wife.

KATE Father collect the bets. While my husband and I seek a place to kiss in private.

Kate walks off while Paul stands there beaming proudly, basking in the jealousy of the other men. Kate calls to Paul over her shoulder.

KATE You comin' Paul, or are you stayin'? Your choice.

Paul leaps to catch up and they exit arm in arm. The other couples look at their own mates warily.

LUCKY It's a miracle.

THOMAS I can't believe my own eyes and ears.

DON Paul has tamed the shrew.

BIÑON *(smiling)* Kate ain't tamed and she was never a shrew. She just found a mate who let her be what she always wanted to be. The rest of us were too blind to see it.

Lights fade out (could end here as Shakespeare does) or . . .

INT. HORSESHOE CASINO

Lights come back up on the casino table that began the play with Biñon, Tom and Doc seated with the same drinks.

BIÑON *(laughing)* Yeah, Tom, I remember that story well. I always get a kick out of it.

TOM You would never want to break a woman's spirt any more than a horse's

spirit. I don't think a drunk can or should be tricked or manipulated into sobriety. Someone, possibly himself, needs to recognize and convince him of his true worth. Then maybe he can set himself free.

THE END

It's Not About Sex

It's Not About Sex

The main inspiration for this chapter was my honest reaction to the June 2023 cover of *Glamour UK* magazine. It featured a topless and obviously transgender "man" staring at the camera, "his" very pregnant body painted to look like "he's" wearing an open suit coat and tie. If the magazine's goal was attention . . . they certainly got mine. I had recently published a memoir of my life as a freelance writer for livestock, horse, and ranching magazines. It wasn't selling as hoped, maybe because of my cover. So I immediately sat down and composed this defensive rant.

I call it a monologue but it's not about vaginas. The "Vagina Monologues" actually do mention horses but only in the way a twisted mind imagines the reason little girls love horses. Riding a horse has nothing to do with sex. If you are sitting a horse well enough to actually ride it, there is no physical connection that would "stimulate" anything except your heart and mind.

I've even read that a camera and pen are considered subconscious phallic symbols and when used by women indicate penis envy. There are more ways to silence women than a shrew's bridle.

I thought this rant might serve as a fitting close to a collection of scripts about cowboy romances. My goal with the scripts and in my own life was to inspire mutual respect and partnerships, not domination and submission, not sex. Sex is a part of life, of course, but focusing on a few seconds of pleasure seems like a sad way to live a life.

The monologue explains its inspiration, so I don't have much more to add except a few alternate book covers of me looking more female and wearing my first pair of boots, my daughter flanking calves and moving the remuda, and my granddaughter leading, watering, and then spinning three of her many horses. We are all girls, women, and ladies happily riding tired and fresh horses through the cowboy world. If I could have a do over, I'd pick one of these photos for the cover of *Making Circles*.

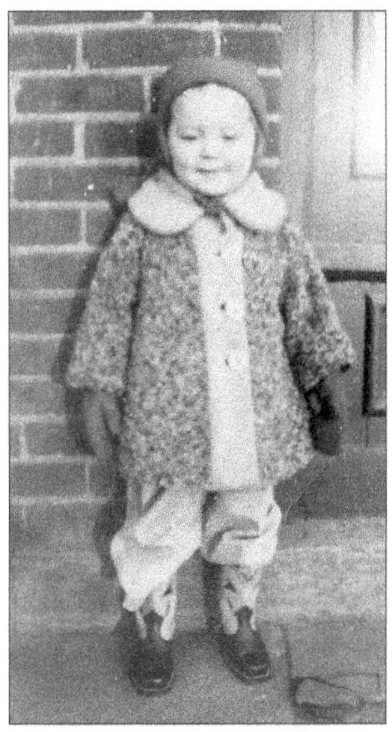

It's Not About Sex

INT. BARE STAGE. SPOTLIGHT

A lone female actor dressed similarly to the book cover of Making Circles: The Memoir of a Cowboy Journalist *sits on a stool in the middle of the stage. The stage is dark with a large projection of the book cover visible behind her. She holds the book and alternates a dramatic reading of selected passages with speaking her mind directly to the audience.*

I've been writing, photographing, and publishing books and articles about cowboys since 1971, but female voices like mine have only recently gained respect in the non-cowboy world. I am especially proud that my most recent book *Making Circles: The Memoir of a Cowboy Journalist* won an award from the Western Writers of America. But when I saw the pregnant "man" on the cover of the United Kingdom's *Glamor* magazine, I felt a surge of fear and wondered if sex was the reason my book wasn't selling.

My book's cover photograph, by one of my idols Jay Dusard, shows me at the peak of my prowess, dressed in full cowboy regalia, and staring at the camera with confidence. You would have to look close to realize I'm a female. Dusard's haunting large-format portraits of male and female cowboys from across the American West rank right up there with black and white portrait masters like Yousuf Karsh, Diane Arbus, Edward Curtis, and Dorthea Lange. I had always been proud of being one of Dusard's subjects, but does this photograph imply that this book by "Barney" Nelson is about a female pretending to be a man? Society's focus on sex is giving me a headache, and readers might be judging and rejecting my book by its cover.

As a kid growing up on an Iowa farm, I was a typical tomboy, which in those days had nothing to do with sexuality. It just meant that instead of the kitchen, I loved to hang out around the barn—thus "Barney." As the first-born kid of a first-born kid, my dad and grandpa took me farming, hunting and fishing while they waited for my little brother and male cousins to grow up. For years, my manly skills stayed a few steps ahead of the boys.

When my little brother and I began our "real" education, we attended a one-room country school with only eleven classmates. We country girls wore boys' jeans, not because of any mix up about our identity, but because dresses let in too much cold air while trudging to school through deep snow. Iowa winters don't mix well with bare legs. Our sensible saddle shoes were protected and warmed by manure-smeared four-buckle overshoes also worn for morning and evening chores. At recess we all played the same games—usually baseball—or roamed the surrounding timber learning to recognize poison ivy, poison oak, and poison sumac. No dolls. No fire engines. No teeter totters. I did, however, always wear bows on my long brown pigtails, and nearly always had an unrequited crush on some boy.

I also rode Shetland ponies. Horseback riding doesn't pair well with dresses either, although I can and did ride side-saddle in long skirts later, mostly in parades. My family moved to Arizona and then I moved on alone to Texas. Along the way, I learned to love horseback cowboy work, which doesn't lend itself to bare legs either. The desert's brush and thorns soon convinced me that leather chaps were a necessity for survival, as were a broad-brimmed hat, long-sleeved shirt, and sometimes a vest or jacket. We call the big scarf a "wild rag," but it's for temperature regulation, not wildness or fashion. Wound around my neck a couple of times, it can warm body temperature, or soaked in water will cool blood enough as it passes through my neck to prevent heat stroke. It can also double as a tourniquet or sling, but I mostly wore one to wipe dust from my camera lenses.

Even spurs are not some symbol of toxic masculinity, but when used properly, are just an extension of a rider's heels. Cues to the horse should be subtle so the rider doesn't adopt an awkward position when the need to hurry or get out of the way arises. Awkward positions can result in buck offs. When a horse and rider are communicating as a team, cues are imperceptible—like reading each other's mind. But spurs have an even more important role than sending subtle messages to horses. My book explains:

READING: *Part of the romance in riding out horseback before dawn with a good crew is the music. There's the percussion of* *steel-shod hooves striking rocks with horses grunting, farting, groaning, snorting, and blowing rollers as their bodies and attitudes adjust to carrying weight on their backs. Horses with crickets in their bits play ratchet music with their tongues. Cold leather creaks and groans as saddles warm up. There's the swish of fringe on fringe and the flag-like snap of wildrags in the wind. Surrounding it all is the tinkle of bells. If there are buckaroos on the crew, actual tiny brass or silver bells chime as they swing from bridle throat latches, the bottom of stirrups, and chinch-to-flank-strap hobbles. Mostly the sound of bells comes from the ching, ching, ching of spurs and jinglebobs ringing with every step the horses take. The sweeter the music, the classier the crew. When the rest of the world talks about class, they mean a ranking based on money. When cowboys talk about class, they mean earned pride.*

Spurs are sort of a metaphor for all that. Unfortunately, in today's sexualized society, no telling what a female dressed like a man and wearing spurs might represent.

In the cover photo, I'm also holding a whip in one hand. Uh. Oh. But it's not THAT kind of whip. It's an Australian-style stock whip. The only place where my book has approached any bestseller status is in the Pacific Islands where that whip would be recognized for what it is: a cowboy tool. Cracking it to make a threatening sound will start cattle moving across a canyon or a well-placed sting on the nose will turn around a cranky bull. Using a stock whip saves time, steps, yelling, and sometimes lives. Off to one side in the picture stands my cheap camera resting on a cheap tri-pod. It probably looks like porn equipment. I have one foot propped up on my bedroll, which may remind viewers of Columbia University's "mattress girl." Oh my.

My book does include a chapter on gender, but even that is still not about sex. Instead I give tips on how to handle peeing in a pasture full of men and how to get along:

READING: *Sometime in the late seventies or early eighties, my spouse and I bought a horse from Apache Adams. Apache had a reputation for being able to ride anything with hair on it. So if you bought one of his "gentle" horses, you might be taking a chance. We named our new horse Apache but called him Patch. If I remember right, he was a stout little sorrel with no markings and could do anything. When first saddled, though, he usually had to buck a few kinks out. Cowboys call that "cold backed." He bucked real straight and not real hard, and when he was done, he was done for the day. So even I could and did ride him. The first morning I was allowed to ride with a big outfit crew, we saddled up in a big pen and I stepped on Patch. He blew up in the middle of the fifteen or so cowboys and horses, but I didn't buck off. The boss's wife thought he was one of their horses and asked, "What horse was THAT?" So real fast it went from, "oh, hell, another damn female," to grins and slapping me on the back. So if you're a damn female and want to go along, I recommend riding a cold-backed horse the first morning. It's even better if you can also say, "He's mine—bought him from Apache Adams."*

Most cowboys accept women who can actually do the job. Granted, being a female in a mostly male world did have some downsides. However, history has forgotten that the first place women got the vote was in Wyoming, not Massachusetts. The entire West had granted women's suffrage before the East Coast even started seriously thinking about it. Rural men have always relied on their hardworking, responsible women. Still, I never considered myself a "feminist," just a good old girl who wanted to earn the privilege to work as a member of a good cowboy crew. Maybe instead of the subtitle "The Memoir of a Cowboy Journalist," I should have subtitled my book, "The Memoir of a Cowgirl Journalist"? But I am 77-years-old, long past the age when anyone would call me a girl.

Besides, words matter. I never liked being called a "cowgirl" even when young because to me that conjured up images of a movie star in fringed skirt, hat perched precariously on the back of her head framed in blonde curls—big smile—obviously a ditz who didn't know the difference between a spade bit and a snaffle. So, like female actors and female flight attendants, I preferred to be called a female cowboy because I could actually do the job. Nobody ever called me a write-ress, a photog-ress, or a professor-ess. Cowboy is a verb, not a noun—it's a job, not a costume. Once my grandmother passed the age of sixteen, she became a farmer, not a farm girl, and she earned that title:

READING: *When my hardworking Iowa grandmother's husband died in her lap of a massive heart attack, she thought her life was over. He left her with one final year of debt before their farm would be paid off and with a corn crop in the field that should have paid it. Then Mother Nature slapped Gram with an early frost, freezing that corn crop before it matured and ruining it for most uses. Immature and undented, it would also mold. Good neighbors harvested the damaged crop and dumped the unshucked ears in her corncrib. Her problem was what to do with it. Cattle can eat moldy corn without harm, so Gram decided to go deeper into debt, buying steers to feed over winter and trying to pack enough extra pounds on them to make that final farm payment come spring. Cattle can't survive on corn alone. They need roughage like hay to keep their rumens working. So Gram decided to chop the whole ears into mouth-friendly disks. This would allow her steers to eat the cobs and husks, good roughage, as well as the corn, moldy or not, and require less hay. I think, though, more than the money, she needed something challenging to do, something that would keep her almost constantly busy. So through her tears and that long Iowa winter – through rain, sleet, or snow, often in well-below zero temperatures, every day, pretty much all day—my grandmother sliced those ears of corn by hand with a machete, one ear at a time. Then she carried bucket after bucket of slices to her steers. In the spring she paid off the farm.*

No one ever accused Gram of wanting to be a man. But I still worry that maybe I should have added some earrings and lipstick to that photograph on my book cover, or at least showed my hair. My long hair is pulled back into a tight ponytail to keep it out of my eyes and mouth, to keep it from snagging on brush limbs, from going up in smoke around the branding or cooking fire, and from tangling in the camera strap around my neck. Rodeo queens might wear their hair in fluffy curls, but they are not doing the same work. If their hat blows off, some cute saddle bronc rider will pick it up for them. If my hat blew off, it would sail off and disappear into some canyon. I'd sunburn badly, especially my forehead, and my fellow laborers would tease me unmercifully.

The closest my book gets to politics is the chapter on cowboy school, which I compare to US Navy SEAL training: sifting out the weak for the safety of the team. I describe several of my human and animal teachers and give examples of lessons. The chapter begins:

READING: *I remember standing around a campfire one rainy morning while the o6 cowboy crew was cussing and discussing education. I complained that my writing students didn't come to class, didn't do their homework, and didn't listen. So one by one, the cowboys started telling stories about school. Most of them claimed they never went to class, never did their homework or listened to the teacher. I knew them. Some had more money than others, but they all led pretty good lives that didn't seem related to how many years they spent in school. Some had quit college after the second day, some lasted almost a year, some seemed to have spent half their lives in college. Some were better hands, some had happier marriages, maybe better kids, maybe better health. But again, it had nothing to do with school.*

READING: *If I remember correctly, two of us were doctors (one M.D. one Ph.D.), several hadn't finished high school, one had a forestry degree, two had law degrees, and one was called a preacher. Several had agriculture degrees, one a degree in dancing. Several were musicians or artists or owned their own business. Three of us spoke no English, at least three spoke no Spanish, and the one we all respected the most could neither read nor write nor speak correctly in any language. Two had ancestors on the Mayflower, two had ancestors who met the boat. Three were illegal immigrants, one of those from Canada. Two home-schooled their children, one sent them to a private school. Several didn't believe in children. One had everything he owned in a war bag that was sitting out there in the rain. One of us was probably worth several million dollars. One, we all agreed, was worth absolutely nothing.*

READING: *Our religions ranged from fundamentalist Christian to atheist to Taoist, Mormon, Ghost Dancer, and luck. We were married, divorced, single, co-habiting, one-night-standing, and abstaining, either by choice or not. Three of us were alcoholic, two went to meetings, one didn't. One smoked pot. We ranged in age from 70 to 10, our politics from red or blue radical to who-the-hell cares? We were one Sioux, Apache, African-American, Australian; four Hispanics, one British-Irish-German-Scottish-French, and God only knows what else. Four of us were female. We were almost all wearing hats or caps, boots, spurs, and slickers in various stages of wear and tear and cleanliness. Hunkered down in our slicker collars with rain dripping off hat brims, the only two points we all agreed on were that the rain was good and we didn't learn to do what we were doing in school.*

So, if my book is not about gender, kinky sex, formal education, or any kind of politics—what is it about? Mostly it's about freelance journalism and how I taught myself the trade by paying close attention, writing letters, newspaper columns, magazine articles, and teaching. My stories and examples immerse the reader in the REAL cowboy world, not the one from Hollywood, Nashville, or tv; not the world of "the last of a dying breed" as created by voyeuristic writers who come to visit us for a few days; not the cowboy as fashion, fantasy, loose cannon, New York City "cowboy," or even those from rodeo and horse shows. My world was working class cowboy and my subject choices emphasized practical problem solving and role models.

My purpose for writing the book was to convince modern journalists (and film producers) that they have a responsibility to find answers, not just expose evil. Focusing on evil, makes evil seem normal. You find what you look for. I wrote:

READING: *Cowboy and livestock magazines don't publish dirt, scandal, murder, porn, muckraking, activism, politics, soul-bearing confessions, or titillation; nor do they seek to expose the edgy, dark side of human nature. Consequently, I had to teach myself to write for magazines that wanted problems solved, ways to cope, trails to follow, new ideas, hope. I believe that when you look for evil, you will find it. If you look for answers, you might find them. You can't find what you don't look for. Today's journalists are masters at ferreting out freak shows and corruption. Mainstream writers and photographers often mine our "local color" for the odd, the violent, and the angry, and they present that as normal. To me the only time odd was interesting was when it solved a problem in a particular situation. Why give publicity to people with no answers? Why lionize the corrupt, the druggies, the dishonest, and the murderers and make them famous? Why give Pulitzer Prizes to bring down a president or destroy the reputation of our soldiers? To me, journalists have become wannabe detectives, prosecutors, judges, and traitors. Evil is not truth—not even a half-truth. But nobody seems to be teaching young journalists how to find and write about anything except evil. They can't seem to find answers or write about anything positive, unless it's sappy stuff about someone leaving a waitress a thousand-dollar tip. That stuff reads like fluff. Serious positive is the hardest to find and to write. Cowboy and livestock magazines don't publish stories about people who murder and steal horses or about corrupt horse owners. Nor do they publish stuff on petting horses and feeding them sugar lumps.*

I believe most of society's problems are caused by boredom, and I struggled with that too:

READING: *Probably the most difficult thing about living on a remote ranch camp is boredom. Boredom drove me crazy. So I tried lots of different things to entertain myself. I gardened and canned and cooked. I sewed and quilted and crocheted. I hunted and fished and butchered meat, inventing new recipes for wild game. I persuaded my husband to acquire a milk cow so I could make butter, ice cream, cottage cheese, and cheese. I decoupaged, oil painted, and threw a few clay pots on a wheel. I taught myself to tie a few fancy knots with strips of rawhide and to hitch horsehair. I joined a garden club and learned to arrange flowers, learned to ride sidesaddle, and using my grandma's recipe baked bread and beat all the little old ladies at the county fair. Mostly, though, I pushed a pen across paper.*

I always admired the idea of finding a Zen-like practice, or at least my understanding of it. Instead of bouncing around, I decided to focus on cowboy journalism as my humble practice: embracing solitude, avoiding boredom, accepting aging and death as part of life, and maybe fixing one tiny piece of the metaphoric broken mirror at a time. Too much modern writing is what I call "navel gazing" and it's even worse when the gaze focuses below the navel. There's a big world out there, People, for the sake of your sanity—look up! Find a practice. I recommend learning to do something— especially something hard that can't be mastered—like writing or cowboying— although anything can become a practice. The more you learn about serving tea or raking sand, the more particular you become and the more you realize there is to know. The Zen "trick" is sort of that no practice however humble can be mastered.

My book is also about how my practice gradually reached beyond the boundaries of modern magazines to explore agriculture's past and its role in literary classics and the environmental movement. I included ideas from my master's thesis investigating Shakespeare's use of horsemanship and from my Ph.D. dissertation, which exposed the way American nature writers had stereotyped wild and domestic animals. As a college professor, I taught research by investigating endangered species or the persecuted big cats and canines of the world. My book is about how urban areas have Orientalized the American West, how Thoreau described cows creating wild apples, about Edward Abbey mothering windmills and black female college presidents afraid to say "the C-word" when meeting a real cowboy. I also . . .

READING: *. . . exposed the imaginary differences between wilderness and home, between wild and tame, between native and nonnative, between agri-culture and hunter/gatherer-culture, between vegans and carnivores, and between grazing and overgrazing as simply ideological, romanticized, postmodern, postcolonial, dualistic power structures, blah, blah, blah—or in my own, much easier-to- understand language: bullshit.*

I don't regret the purpose of my book. I wouldn't change a single word or leave out a single story, and I certainly don't want to be considered a "victim" of gender and sexualized stereotypes. I considered myself the luckiest woman in the world as I hope can be read between the lines. To me even love is not about sex. But I do wish my book had a different cover. I worry that with all this fuss about sexual identity, parents and grandparents will stop taking little girls fishing and hunting. Farmers will stop

allowing their daughters to drive tractors.
Ranchers will once again bar women
and girls from the pastures and corrals as
"the way it's always been." We girls have
come so far, fought so hard, and risked
so much.

Did we tomboys and female cowboys
repeatedly bloody our noses against
barbed wire fences—only to be shamed
and cancelled today as "girls who
pretend to be men"? Will my cowboy
granddaughter's daughters have to go
back to wearing dresses and Mary Janes
no matter how deep the snow? Will they
take away our horses?

THE END

Acknowledgements

A special thanks to all the people whose words, stories, and images I use—both named and unnamed. Thank you for all the wonderful memories that are still giving me something to do in old age. I was the luckiest woman in the world to have shared this wonderful life with you. Thank you to the o6 Ranch for the opportunity to live there during the best years of all our lives. Thank you Ray Hunt and Tom Dorrance, you actually changed the world while I watched. Your influence was a rock dropped into still water—still making circles.

Thanks to Don and Linda Coleman, my oldest and dearest friends, who read every word of this manuscript several times. Thanks to all those who read most, one chapter, just bits and pieces or talked me through and answered questions: Betty Tanksley, Christi Dillard, Dick DeGear, Riley Spencer, Nelson Sager, Cheryll Glotfelty, Jim and Mel Miller, Emily Kitching, Ronnie Scott, Donnie Slover, Craig Carter, Leo Eaton, Robert Polanco, Rod DuVoll, Tommy Vaughn, Steve Titla, Wails Yellowtail, Butch Small, Margie Brooks, Sadie Dawley, Peter Scott, Wally Wines, Rodney Flournoy, and my daughter Carla Spencer.

I also want to thank all those named or unnamed in the introduction and inspirations.

Thank you Hartnett family, especially Donel and Duke Hartnett, grandson of Ramón Hartnett who cooked for the o6 Ranch during the time I lived there. A too-late thank you to Vincent J. "Vince" Lavallee, Jr., a U.S. Border Patrol Agent for 24 years in the Alpine, Marfa, and Presidio area from 1978 to 2002, retiring as a supervisor. He passed in 2023 at 77.

Special appreciation to Tish Wetterauer, a fine artist, who designed my words and photographs into a beautiful book that I'm very proud of and hope she is too. I also want to thank her for her patience with my endless corrections caused by paranoia as I tried to be my own editor and proofreader.

To all the others that I have forgotten to mention, please forgive me.

All of you gave helpful criticism and advice or simply encouragement. I needed both. Any remaining mistakes are my own.

Unfortunately one chapter, "A Brand for Two," represents my own initiation into and education about Hollywood. I had been approached by a "used car salesman" years earlier about selling the movie rights to one of the books I had written. We never agreed, and I never signed anything. After I wrote this script (my first), I dug out the used car salesman's phone number and asked if he wanted to read it. Of course he jumped at the chance and promised to "help" turn what he called my "story" into a movie script (although I had already written it as a screenplay). Naively, I paid this self-proclaimed producer-director, "Skilled in film, screen writing, music publishing, television, public relations, talent contracts and concert promotions" $2500 for his "help" and a signed a "Development, Deal Memo" that basically said I was paying for formatting, "pitch" materials, and contacting possible production/distribution companies, and that

> *. . . screen credits shall read, "Written by Barney Nelson," and/or "Story by Barney Nelson," and "Screenplay by Barney Nelson and [. . .]. The resulting screenplay shall be registered, owned and marketed by the parties herein and any compensation shall be shared in accordance with industry standards. All disputes arising under or in connection with this Agreement shall be resolved by binding arbitration in Los Angeles in accordance with the rules of the Independent Film and Television Alliance.*

Then for several months our "partnership" became a comedy of errors. My name began showing up on Internet searches as a co-producer with him. I told him we had not made that kind of agreement and asked him to remove my name. He knew nothing about the horse or farrier world and all of his suggestions were crazy—like to have the Welsh pony wag its tail to show relaxation. I finally got so disillusioned with his "help" that I stopped corresponding. Although I was dumb enough to send money and sign, I did save relevant emails and text messages. If this "story" ever actually becomes a movie, it will probably need arbitration. I caution any aspiring writers to be very careful of new friends who circle the fringes of Hollywood. Don't sign any contracts, especially until THEY pay YOU. Access is actually controlled by very strong unions and agents. So I would especially like to thank that used car salesman for making me less naïve. I also need to thank all the hundreds of actors, producers, and agents that I contacted but who wouldn't even acknowledge my emails.

I finally gave up on Hollywood and decided to do something more creative and unique. This novel in dialog is the result. None of my "stories" may ever be performed on stage or screen, but maybe they are worth reading.

About the Author

Barbara "Barney" Nelson, PhD is definitely a female. She has been a freelance female cowboy journalist since 1971 while making her living as a secretary and college professor at Sul Ross State University in Alpine, Texas. She is the author or editor of eight books and countless magazine and professional journal articles. Retired, she now carries water in a bucket to birds, mule deer, javelinas, grey foxes, and whatever other wildlife comes to her door for a drink. She also writes a weekly column for a tiny weekly newspaper, *The Jeff Davis County Mountain Dispatch*. A direct descendant of Mayflower Pilgrim, William Bradford, she likes to claim that even though she owns only a few acres today, her family has been in the agriculture business on this continent for fourteen generations, seventeen counting her grandchildren. She has published eight books including:

Making Circles: The Memoir of a Cowboy Journalist (2021)
Western Writers of America Spur Award Finalist for Best Western Contemporary Nonfiction

"It belongs in all collections of books about Western culture; it particularly belongs in all university libraries featuring studies of the West. It is a treasure trove of insight."   —Tom Bailey

The Wild and the Domestic (2000)

"Her informed and loving voice for our responsible use of land, our responsibility for other species, and responsible living provides a vital and seldom articulated perspective on ranching and the rancher's stewardship."   —Mary Clearman Blew

"Barney Nelson has written a stunning book . . . deserves to be ranked with the best writers of the century."   —Linda Hasselstrom

Voices and Visions of the American West (1986)

"As good as the photos are, and they cover everything . . . it is the words between the images that make this book so special . . . She has made this book wonderful by allowing the people who actually live the cowboy life to tell us what they are feeling, what they know, and why they do what they do."   —Darrell Arnold